Captain Adam

Captain Adam

DONALD BARR CHIDSEY

CROWN PUBLISHERS, INC.
NEW YORK

To a different Deborah,
daughter of Dean and Virginia Graves,
is dedicated this little lesson in
how-to-get-your-man

Captain Adam

PART ONE

———◆———

The Freedom Suit

1   He had a chip on his shoulder, a grudge against the world; yet as he dressed in the darkness, putting on his freedom suit again, Adam Long had to admit that here, this moment, he couldn't complain. He was right on the edge of glory. Nothing could stop him now.

The freedom suit was made of linsey-woolsey and he'd had it only a few weeks, though he was twenty-three. The added months of apprenticeship since his twenty-first birthday had been imposed as punishment for offenses that otherwise would have been long since forgotten—and Adam didn't give a hoot anyway, now. For he was free at last. What's more, he was master of a vessel. In a few hours he was going to get a chance to show the world, the big world outside of this town, what he could do.

But first he had to see Elnathan Evans. He knew Zeph would be away from home now. He was smiling as he strode over to the Evans house.

"I've come to say good-bye, Elnathan," he said as the woman opened the door, and drew him into the house.

"Oh, Adam, can't you stay awhile? He won't be back for a couple of hours. Our last time—"

"It's partly to see him I'm going. The owners. At Blake's."

"What time do you sail?"

"Sunup."

It was hard to keep from singing. But with the woman it was different; and when after a while she spoke again the catch in her voice startled Adam. Elnathan Evans was not a demonstrative female by day. Folks just didn't associate emotion with her. Yet here she quavered.

"Adam?"

"Yes?"

"How long will you be gone?"

"Can't say. Two-three months, maybe four."

"You'll be careful? You won't get killed?"

"Well—"

"They tell it's mighty tricksy down in those waters, Adam."

He grinned, and found one of her hands. He could scarcely see her. "I won't get killed," he promised. "And another thing I won't do—I won't forget who it was talked her husband into getting me the command. Seth Selden would've had it, wasn't for you."

He kissed her.

"And you'll be back, Adam."

"Oh, sure."

Chuckles clucked around inside his throat and chest. He reckoned he felt right sorry for Elnathan, in a way. She did seem cut up about his going, and he was touched by this, as any man might be. But he teemed with excitement; expectation yeasted within him; he could hardly wait for the time when he'd be ordering the hook up, to put out in the blithesomest boat ever built. Though he had made two voyages aboard of *Goodwill to Men*—the only ones the schooner had logged, one a coaster, the other to the sugar islands—and though his apprenticeship to Mr. Sedgewick had ended, formally, such a short time ago, Adam Long for some years now had not been taking many orders. On land as a carpenter, at sea first as a hand and then as mate, he had known his business, shining as one who was best left alone. But he had not been giving orders either, to speak of. And it seemed to him that he was born to give orders.

Wasn't he, in the opinion of some, if not of others, a son of the Earl of Tillinghast? *He* believed this anyway. The story hung about his life like a wispy fog, coiling away soundlessly whenever you tried to touch it, drifting back again in long languid ribbons; but he thought that it had been his mother—she died when he was five—who told him. There was no mention of it, of course, in the only paper she had left—a copy of her indenture contract. There was nothing here on this side of the Atlantic to prove the story or even point toward its proof. Some day he would prove it! He'd go right to England, to Tillinghast, the castle, and demand a settlement. But he wasn't going to do this hat-in-hand, wheedling, an unwanted bastard who sneaked in through the scullery. When Adam went to Tillinghast it would be with a sword at his side, gold in his purse.

He smiled as he touched lovingly the solid woodwork of the handsome house, and looked out the broad window facing the sea.

It was like being between two worlds. On his left was warmth, comfort, security, even luxury, he reckoned, though it could scarcely be thought luxurious in comparison with homes at Home, from what he had been told of them. On the other side was a prim garden, clipped grass, the street and trees all silent, a vague glow that was Blake's tavern, and the bay itself, bland, beautiful, silvered by the moon, peppered now with sloops that scarcely rocked; while beyond, out on Goat Island, half awash, yet still seemingly reluctant to be submerged, still struggling to stay out of the muck, swung the triced remains of Thomas Hart. Adam himself, together with hundreds of colonists, had watched the turning-off of this pirate two years ago, since which time, as required by law, the body had dangled *infra fluxum et refluxum maris*, between high tide and low. On a quiet night like this, when the changing waters turned it, you could sometimes hear the links squeal. But the stink was gone. Everything was gone except the gallows, which had lurched out of kilter in the shifting mud, and the chain, and the trussed white bones that the sea refused to take.

It doesn't pay to be a pirate, folks said. Maybe it doesn't pay to be a fornicator either? He was too happy to care.

From here, too, Adam could see the breastworks and redoubt they were building on the island; they planned to call it Fort Anne after the new monarch. He could see the guns there. For everything these days was war. It would come any day. The world waited for it, fascinated. Nobody could have told you *why* it was coming—something to do with who should be King of Spain—but coming, for whatever reason, it assuredly was.

He put his arms around Elnathan, held her close and kissed her a long while.

"Good-bye, good-bye," he said and was off down the street.

It was a comfortable down-sloping street which led direct to the bay, not such a street as they'd have at Home, from what Adam had heard, but a good street, or lane, lined with trees. It was cool now, for this was getting close to ten o'clock, and darkish, the ruts and dust all dappled with egg-shaped moon spots. There was no sort of pavement. On either side, though Adam couldn't see them well, were firm rectangular houses, shakes-roofed, clapboard-walled, some of them even painted, set near together and near the street, houses that respected themselves and expected to be respected. In the making of more than one of these the apprentice Adam Long had had a hand.

He drew a deep tremulous breath. He thrust his hands deep into his breeches pockets. He was about to start for the tavern—when he remembered that he had another appointment.

"Seems like it's my night for meeting women," he marveled.

Deborah Selden, who lived right across the way, was, however, no Elnathan. Nor was she by anybody's description saucy. It had startled Adam Long no little to receive a note from her this afternoon. The note had been noncommittal, only asking him to meet her at her house at nine that night and to treat this appointment as confidential. He assumed that it was something to do with the schooner, her father, Obadiah

Selden, being a quarter owner. It could be a message to somebody down in the islands or a request for some certain fruit or for dress goods. Women were always asking sea captains such favors. But why the secrecy? It was not like Deborah Selden, what he knew of her.

Admittedly he didn't know much of her. Nobody did. She had heaps of handsomeness and a bosom that was unsettling, yet already she was nineteen and not wed. That could have been her father's fault. A widower, Obadiah Selden guarded his only chick with an assiduity virtually fanatical. You could almost hear him cluck as he fussed around her. He forbade her to bundle, which in itself was enough to keep many of the lads away. You never did meet up with her at the raisings and huskings and bees, the weddings and funerals and christenings; and if she went to some distant place, like say the Providence fair, it was in the company of her father, who hated to let her out of sight and acted to be afraid she might fall down and get broken like a set of false teeth you couldn't replace. So nobody knew Deborah well.

The Selden house, which Adam faced now, was half in darkness, half alight. It was a one-story house, as firmly foundationed as Obadiah's own fortune. On the right, as Adam knew—though he had never been in the house—were the parlor and kitchen, and here tonight there was light, where no doubt Obadiah was poring over papers in preparation for the sailing. The left side contained two bedrooms. They were dark.

"Mister Long!"

It caused him to jump. He had never before been so addressed. True, he rated the "Mister" now; but he was not yet used to it.

The voice, a woman's, had come from the Selden house, the unlighted side. Squinting, peering, Adam stepped across a patch of grass.

"It's me, over here."

"Oh, it's you?"

Deborah stood in a nightrail, and she had her dark hair in two braids hanging down front, which made her look a whit like a Narragansett, only of course not anywhere near as dirty.

"Can't sleep?" he asked politely. "But there's no pinkletinks."

For this was April.

Her smile, though shy, disconcerted. She was looking directly at him. It wasn't right, her standing there in such a garb. He sure hoped that she was blushing. She ought to be.

"I—I just thought I'd say good-bye, Mr. Long. Or maybe I ought to call you 'Captain' now?"

"Aye."

"You're sailing tomorrow, isn't that right?"

"Aye. Sunup."

12

"For the islands?"

"Aye."

He could be chattier than this; but he was wary, alert. After all, this was Obadiah Selden's daughter; and it had been Obadiah, won over by his neighbor Zephary Evans, who in turn had been won over by Elnathan his wife, whose vote had given Adam the captaincy over Obadiah's own brother, Seth, incidentally himself a one-eighth owner of the schooner of which Adam Long owned but a sixteenth.

Adam did not aim to buss anybody's behind, but at the same time it never did any harm to have manners.

"You—you love that vessel, don't you, Captain?"

"Aye," soberly. And he added: "I helped build her."

"I know."

"Yes, I reckon I love her all right."

"Like she was a woman?"

"More."

Had she seen him come out of the Evans house? He smelled trouble. She kept smiling at him, but it was a small smile.

"No doubt you're wondering why I sent for you, Captain? Well, I'll tell you. I want to ask you a question. A very important question."

"Aye?"

She leaned close, her hands white on the sill, and her eyes, dark brown, all but black, were enormous in the darkness. She swallowed carefully, deliberately, then said:

"Will you marry me?"

2   Man is a vain animal. Adam Long's first feeling, aside from the shock itself, was one of joy. He was pleased, he tingled. This only for an instant. Immediately afterward anger flooded him, so that his temples throbbed and pounded, his eyeballs ached, the very hair of his head seemed to crickle; and he lowered his face to hide the tears of rage, the dark flush of fury.

So he came cheap, did he? If a husband had to be had, and that in a hurry, why not Adam Long, the son of an indentured servant long dead? How could he resist? What friends did he have, what patron, or property? Why, the fool owned nothing in this world save the clothes on his back— and a one sixteenth interest in the schooner *Goodwill*. Your own father owned a quarter of that schooner, and his friend Zephary Evans owned another quarter, while your uncle Seth, who had dearly wanted the captaincy, owned an eighth. The captain, then lucky to *be* a captain, was perforce a man who'd do as he was told.

It was plain to Adam too why she had written him on the very eve of the sailing. Oh, she was no fool! Just before he had the final meeting with the owners, a matter merely of hours before sailing time, he would be likelier to panic. A week earlier, even a few days earlier, and he might have been able to wriggle out of it, argue himself clear, or even uncover her true lover. But now, tonight, truly he was trapped. He could take her—she must have planned it this way—or he could lose his command.

Adam kept his head down. He must wait until he could speak clearly, without any chokiness.

He did not, of course, even consider this unexpected offer. Aside from the rage into which it threw him, the insult it constituted, there were plain hard realities to be considered. Adam was much too young to think of marrying. Marriage was marriage, something that once done you couldn't change; and when he took unto himself a bride it would be on his own terms. Deborah Selden, even though pregnant, could be esteemed the coziest catch in Newport, indeed anywhere in the colony; but the ambitions of Adam Long went a long way beyond Rhode Island. Colonials, even the very best of them, were not for him. He would rather be the second man in Rome, or the third or fourth or fifth, than the first man in a little Roman village.

Presently he heard a sob, and looked up.

"I'm dreadful sorry to hear you got in trouble."

She shook her head, added waves of color sweeping her face.

"Oh, no," she whispered. "It isn't *that!*" She patted her belly. "Not *this,* Captain!"

He thought it in bad taste. Wasn't it enough that she took him for a slavey? Did she have to pretend to take him for a fool as well? But he swallowed carefully, concentrating on the need for quiet, for manners.

There was too much at stake for him to let his temper snap.

Deborah was looking right at him, nothing furtive about her.

"No, Captain, it's unmaidenly, I grant you. A lady shouldn't speak up. But what else could I do? *You* can pick the girl you want to marry, and try to win her. *I'm* supposed to sit and wait. I can't even place myself in men's way. I've tried to attract your eye, Captain. I couldn't."

"You're thunderation pretty," Adam muttered.

To avoid her gaze he threw his glance to the left. Light slitted out of the Selden doorway only a few yards away, the other side of a clump of lilac, and spewed across the grass—Obadiah Selden in the front room, beyond question, going over his accounts. What a jolt he'd get if he could hear this!

"And now you're going away. So I spoke." She patted her belly again, quivering the nightrail. "But it's not this, Captain. No."

He did not reply, only stood there looking sideways at the slats of light on the lawn.

After a time he became conscious of her silence, and it occurred to him that she was waiting to hear his answer.

"I'm filled with delight," he said cautiously. "Never knew you was eying me. But—we sail at dawn."

"The sailing could be put off."

This was true. The law required that public notice of a marriage be posted fourteen days in advance, and the men had already been signed on the *Goodwill,* so this would mean fourteen days of victuals for them; but it was not a large crew and Adam could find things for them to do.

Adam wetted his lips.

"Even if I was in a position to wed, which I ain't—even if we had time—your father'd never consent."

"My father would never agree to my marrying any man at all."

"That's what I mean."

"But he would have to agree if I told him I was going to have a baby by you."

Now Adam Long was no prude. The son of the late Aramead Long, whom folks sometimes referred to as "The Duchess" because of the airs she'd put on, knew his Newport, waterfront and back country alike. He'd had as much schooling as any there, more than most. He had visited, on the coasting trip, New York and Philadelphia, and also Perth Amboy in the Jerseys. He had been down to the islands. Though not much of a meeting attender, he was a child of his environment; and Rhode Island and the Province Plantations at this time were a hodge-podge—or a hot bed, if you will—of queer and generally liberal sects. In addition to the members of his own church, Adam all his life had known Seventh Dayers, Anabaptists, Methodists, Sabbatarians, Huguenots, Congregationalists, Seekers, and the Lord only knew what else. Newport itself, notoriously, was cluttered with Quakers. Why, there were even a few Jews.

This was the frontier, after all, where men being busy called things what they were, neither they nor the women seeing much profit in concocting other names for them.

It was esteemed no sin, though indeed the preachers preached loudly against it, to be pregnant before marriage—the awkwardness entered only when the girl *stayed* single—and many a wife serenely boasted, afterward, that she had caught her husband by getting herself caught first.

But such a suggestion as that just voiced—saying they'd done it when they hadn't at all—Adam had never before heard. He was shocked.

"Maybe we shouldn't've started talking about this at all."

"That means your answer is—no?"

"Yes, ma'am. I reckon it does."

She turned away, and the darkness engulfed her, so that Adam was left facing a blank space, agape. But he remembered his manners, and gave a little bow.

"Good night, ma'am," he called softly.

He heard a sob, that was all.

3   Adam had not been permitted to enlist his own crew, as a proper captain should: they were assigned to him, for one reason or other, by the money men. But Resolved Forbes, the mate, Adam surely would have signed on anyway.

Forbes was twenty, smallish, abstemious, almost ostentatiously clean. He might have been taken for a Quaker—unless you'd seen him, as Adam had, in a fight.

"Young Rellison aboard?"

Forbes nodded.

"Bond? Mellish?"

"Aye."

"Drunk?"

"Well, they're sleeping now."

"Peterson? Waters?"

"Going to have trouble with those two," Forbes offered.

Adam nodded, and hoisted his jack. He took a deep gulp.

"Aye," he said.

A lubber was bad enough, a sea lawyer was bad; and a couple of lubberly lawyers at sea would be unbearable. However, he would reach an understanding with Waters and Peterson later—off soundings.

He looked around, squinching his eyes against the smoke.

Commercially this was the center of Newport, after dark the convergence of the counting houses. Call it the town's Rialto. There was nothing la-di-da about it. The walls were unpainted. The ceiling was low. There wasn't any floor: there was just dirt, packed as hard as rock. Two quartets of long pine boards laid on sawhorses were the tables. There was a serving bar at one end, and behind that the barrels and bottles—and Blake himself. A bench ran around the other three sides. There were a few joint-stools, but most of the customers who did not use the bench sat on empty kegs or else stood at the bar. No woman ever was allowed in the place, praise God. The prices were fair, the liquor generally good. It was an orderly ordinary: you seldom saw a fight there. Yet so poor was the light—Blake was parsimonious with his candles—and so crowded the benches, causing men to lean close to one another with lowered voices, so thick, too, was the tobacco smoke, and so low the ceiling, that Blake's to an uninstructed outsider might have looked a very den of conspirators and thieves.

Farthest from bar and door alike, no more really than an end of one of the long tables, was what was known as the Adventurers' Corner. This was not meant for common seamen (who only adventured their lives) but rather for men of affairs, who adventured their money. It was here that voyages were planned, profits counted. Nothing marked it off from the rest of the room, yet no man who was not an investor in the deal-at-hand would have the temerity to cross even a corner of that space, much less to sit there.

Adam Long, who had never before been there, now as a part-owner of the schooner rated a seat in the Adventurers' Corner.

Zephary Evans was there, a lank slabsided man with lugubrious eyes. Zeph was a shrewd business man, even though he did permit his wife to lead him around by his very large long nose. Every now and then he would swoop that nose down toward his pot, at the same time half raising the pot toward the nose, and he'd make timorous contact with his ale, acting as though he expected it to explode in his face. Then he'd put the pot down, and he'd straighten and stare in somber resentment at it.

Next to Evans was Seth Selden, a smallish man with a face as malicious as that of a monkey. They did say that Seth was sprightly off soundings; but for all Adam knew of him, the man, with his ramrod back, his holier-than-thou cold eyes, truly belonged in Boston, your proper port for disapprovers. Here in the ordinary tonight, disappointed as he was, outraged to have been passed by for a younger man, Seth sat straight, mouth drawn, chin high, while his nostrils seemed to twitch as though he found the odor of the place objectionable.

There were three others in the Adventurers' Corner, owners of small parts of the schooner. Indeed, they were all there excepting Adam Long and Obadiah Selden. Adam was in no hurry.

"Everything's ready, then?"

"All bung-up and bilge-free, sir," said Resolved Forbes.

"Good. Go back aboard. I'll be along soon."

When the mate went, Adam did not move. He sensed that he was being looked at—or if not looked at, thought about. He'd known the feeling before, sometimes even in church. Oh, he had some friends, though he had never sought friends! But in any given gathering here in town he could feel like a straining pile the weight of the dislike of him, the jealousy of him. Tonight it was worse than ever. Though no man glared at him, the air fairly crackled and spat, as with summer lightning. They said he was too big for his breeches. He didn't care. He'd be on the high seas soon.

Obadiah Selden came in.

Obe was a man of bulk—square, firm, solid. He walked as though wading through ankle-deep water, and his eyes, under busy brows, habitually were cast down. His lips were intwisted and tight, like those of a man who holds a mouthful of verjuice he doesn't dare either swallow or spit out.

Ignoring his associates, he came directly to Adam.

Adam rose to greet him. This was not merely because of respect for an older man. Obadiah Selden carried a heavy oak stick.

"Captain Long," in a very low voice, "may I see you outside?"

Adam said nothing, only went around the table and followed the man out, stepping aside to give him precedence at the doorway.

Every eye in the tavern was on them.

They went back to the place where Ben Blake had his well. There was a low wall around it. Even before they got there, before the older man spoke, Adam Long knew what Deborah had done; and in spite of himself, and his rage, his fear, too, he couldn't help admiring her.

Still Obadiah Selden did not look at him. After a moment Obadiah said in a low voice: "My daughter has told me about—about you."

Adam said nothing.

They couldn't see the bay from here, but they heard the querulous squeal of the chains by which Thomas Hart's body hung.

"The sailing must be postponed, so's you can get married. After that I'll pack you off fast enough! And keep you off! I'll send you here and there and everywhere— The child," added Obe Selden, dropping his voice again, "will be brought up to be a true God-fearing Christian. We can do that much anyway."

It was so easy. This merchant would move him, the sailing man, from place to place on the surface of the globe, as readily as though he were a wooden piece in a game of draughts. No hint of examination. No breath of doubt. What was the word of a propertyless bastard? Why even ask for it?

"We'll tell 'em in there"—Obe lifted his stick toward the tavern—"that the sailing must be postponed. You're the master. You can think of a reason."

"No," said Adam.

"Eh?"

It was the first time Obadiah had actually looked at him, and the look fairly frightened Adam. The man's face was extremely dark, almost purple. He seemed scarcely able to breathe.

"You haven't told me yet what your daughter said."

"God strike you, ye whelp! *You* know well enough!"

"Maybe if I was allowed to talk to your daughter alone—"

"*No*, damn your soul to hell! You'll not talk with her again till you marry her—and not after that, either!"

Adam said, very carefully, very quietly: "I didn't get her pregnant. I haven't had anything to do with her. And I won't marry her."

"*Why, you—*"

Adam could easily have avoided the blow. He was never to know why he hadn't. He saw Obadiah raise the stick; but he didn't stir.

He felt it touch the left side of his head like the swift sting of a beer, and slish off his left ear.

"*Will ye have more of that, ye misbegotten mongrel?*"

Adam made no answer.

Obadiah raised the stick again; but after a moment, quivering, he lowered it. He turned suddenly, and stalked back to the tavern.

Adam touched the side of his head, and his fingers came away wet. There wasn't enough moonlight for him to distinguish color; but he tasted it, and it was blood all right. So he fetched up the bucket from Ben Blake's well, and using a tip of the tail of his shirt he mopped the wound and cleaned it, and held the cloth there until the bleeding had stopped. Then he patted back his hair, straightened his coat and cravat, and went into the tavern to take his place, for the first time, in the Adventurers' Corner.

4   It was as good as town meeting for the customers, for although the men concerned with the *Goodwill* tried to keep their voices at a seemly pitch they sometimes let their feelings get the better of them. In any event, even when the very words themselves couldn't be distinguished, everybody at Blake's knew what was being said.

This was no organized association or committee, never had been. Obadiah Selden and Zephary Evans were the largest owners, and ordinarily Obadiah as the older would be looked upon as the chairman or moderator. Tonight Obadiah sat in silence, his chin on his chest.

Seth Selden was no longer there: he had been called away while Adam was out back with Obadiah.

Zeph Evans did most of the talking.

"No need to go over it all again," he told Adam. "Some were for you but most were against. 'Twas said you lacked experience."

Adam made no response. His principal supporter, as everyone knew, had been Zeph Evans, who had won over Obe Selden. Neither Zeph nor Obadiah was likely to entrust any mentionable part of his property to a man who lacked experience; and they all knew that, too.

"And then, you know how we feel about the charter—"

Adam nodded. He did know this. Of the colonies, Rhode Island and Connecticut alone operated under their own charters and were not subject to royal governors, excepting naturally in admiralty matters and matters directly pertaining to the throne, such as treason. There were those in London who did not think this a good thing. The other colonies were sassy enough as it was, these men believed, without having before them such examples of all but independent states. Especially there were Lord Cornberry, the royal governor of New York, who covetously eyed Connecticut, and Colonel Joseph Dudley, royal governor of Massachusetts and New Hampshire, and vice admiral of all New England, who sought to annex Rhode Island. The best way to bring this about—that is, a revocation of the two charters and thus a squashing of the spirit of independence—would be, these two politicians were agreed, to send Home evidence concerning the notorious disregard of the Navigation Acts in these colonies, and especially in Rhode Island, and particularly in Newport. Step on financial toes and the yelp that resulted could be heard a long way. The conviction of Thomas Hart, the pirate, had helped. But there should be more.

Yes, Adam Long knew this. Everybody knew it.

"It's been said around town that you couldn't possibly have made enough money to buy a share of the vessel just by bespoke work here and the wages you made while you was at sea. You *couldn't* have."

"I didn't," said Adam.

"'Tis said you must have done a bit of business now and then out at Contraband Cove."

"Why, sure. And so did you." Adam looked around. "And you and you and you and you," he added.

He leaned forward, hands on knees.

"There isn't a man-jack at this table ain't had his share of smuggling. Why make any bones about it?"

Nobody said anything. Nobody dared to.

"And as for that story that I ever had any dealings with Thomas Hart two years ago, whoever says that is a liar."

"Captain Hart himself wouldn't tell," Zeph Evans pointed out, "but *somebody* in this town was certainly his agent."

"Somebody certainly was," Adam agreed, "but it wasn't me."

"Do you know who it was?"

"No."

Zeph moved his hands as if seeking papers to shuffle.

"Well anyway, as I say, one of our members has asked for another vote on whether the captain should be you or Seth Selden, and that's what we're going to do now. Even though Seth himself's not here."

"You can't do that! You appointed me, two weeks ago!"

"It's our boat," Zeph Evans said coldly.

"Who was it suggested this?"

Zeph did not answer. He didn't have to.

Adam objected to the taking of the vote. He said that it was illegal. He said that it would destroy the confidence of possible future investors, not to mention that of sailors who might be signed on, if the owners got to juggling masters on the very eve of sailing.

He raised his voice, and they looked reproachfully at him.

He declared that while he did not have a written contract he did have what amounted to an unassailable verbal contract, each and every one of them having formally agreed to abide by the wishes of the majority in the matter of choosing a captain. That contract would stand up in any court of law, he averred; and unless he was permitted to sail tomorrow at dawn in full command of the schooner, without any further qualifications or modifications or interference, by God, sir, he'd sue.

This gave them some pause. But in a moment they came to realize, without even having conferred, that in fact he had no contract at all, and what the whole thing came to was his wishes against theirs.

They prepared to take a vote.

"You *can't* do this!" he cried. He told them how he loved that schooner. How he knew her every block and plank, every trunnel even. How he had helped to design and build her, arguing about her, fitting her, fashioning her. He reminded them that after her launch he had sailed with her before the mast, and then, on her second voyage, at the nomination of her original master, the late Captain Welsh, as mate. He pointed out that he had made all his local arrangements for the sailing as skipper, cutting off his connections, leaving himself not even a cot ashore to sleep on. He told them that less than an hour ago, right here in this room, he had made a final check with his mate. "Why, even my *chest's* aboard!"

"It can be taken off," said Obadiah Selden.

They would have listened longer. They would have listened all night, if Adam could think of enough things to say. He couldn't.

They took the vote.

It was done in a dignified manner. Each sixteenth was one vote. There were no ballots. There was no raising of hands, or even of voices.

With Seth Selden absent, the tally was: 13 for Seth, 1 (his own) for Adam.

After that, one by one, they went out. Excepting Obadiah, each stopped by the stool where Adam sat long enough to bid him good night. He never answered. He sat there, slumped, staring at a tankard half full of ale that had gone flat.

Others, too, left the ordinary. The tobacco smoke swirled, thinning. Ben Blake began to collect flagons and to snuff out candles.

Soon even the murmurous sound of talk from the street died.

There was only one candle left, and it guttered low.

Ben Blake came over to him.

"Sorry, Long." Not *Captain* Long or *Mister* Long, just Long now. "Sorry, but I'm closing up."

Adam rose. The left side of his head hurt, where Obadiah had hit him. He went out.

5   The moon was down. A land breeze had sprung up, setting the maples ashiver, slatching the surface of the bay: Adam Long's sailorman's cheek told him this the instant he stepped outside the tavern.

The door was closed behind him, and the last candle was put out. He had the town to himself.

There was no sense going to Mr. Sedgewick's. Mr. Sedgewick hadn't been conscious for two days, had not even recognized folks for more than a year. Adam had pulled out of there three days ago. All the same, his dragging feet led him in that direction—until, realizing where he was, he brought himself up short.

Was he quitting? Was he going to let them do this to him?

He stood, pondering. He had to do something. If he bowed to this decision, here is right where he'd stay—here in Newport—for the rest of his life. He knew that.

But—what fight could he make?

On his left, as now he noticed in the starshine, stood the town pillory. Not far from Mr. Sedgewick's house, it hadn't been used in years. Adam could remember a few times when somebody had been stood there, his neck held fast by the oaken beam; but even on those occasions the boys had never been given a chance to throw things at the head the man couldn't move, for there was always a bailiff stationed to guard the prisoner. Only once, in Adam's memory, had anyone been kept there for more than a few hours. This was a blasphemer and thief, a thoroughgoing reprobate named Sharpy Boardman, and not only had he been stood at the pillory all one day and all one night, but his ears, by order of the magistrate, had been nailed into place. Yes, a nail had been driven through the fleshy top of each ear and into the beam. It probably hadn't hurt Boardman much, he hadn't made a sound when they did it —Adam was there—but it meant that he could not even wriggle and roll his head as the others had done, which after a few hours must have been torture. Folks had felt bad about it, Adam knew. They had passed with averted heads, not wishing to seem to jeer. It had not been necessary to keep the boys from throwing things.

Nevertheless there Sharpy Boardman had stayed, all that day and all that night. In the night Adam Long could hear his groans. They were low groans, as if he didn't know he was making them; but they went on and on. Others must have heard them, but nobody else did anything. Adam, nine or ten at the time, couldn't sleep. At last he had sneaked down from the loft and filled a jack with water and carried it out to the man. He had held the jack up to the man's mouth. Adam was mighty scared! He'd have got whaled proper if he'd been caught! The man had drunk every bit of the water, Adam tipping the jack up for him: Adam had had to stand on his toes to do this.

"God bless ye, lad!"

"I couldn't get at the rum," Adam had said. "They put it where I can't reach it."

Next morning, early, they had worked the nails out and hoisted the beam. By the sentence Sharpy Boardman should have remained there all that day, but the feeling was that he'd had enough—and maybe too much. Folks were a mite ashamed of the whole business, and the magistrate had signed a special commutation order. The pillory was never used after that, though it was left here, just as Adam Long faced it now, in order to serve as a warning to those who might be planning wickedness.

They'd had cool milk and some spirits, too, and even some bread, when they loosed Sharpy Boardman; but he had paid no attention to these. He had not lingered to lave in his humiliation, but had run, staggered rather, down the hill to the harbor, where without hesitation he had taken the first berth that offered. They were needing men bad in those days, any kind of able-bodied man, and within three hours of the time he quit the pillory Sharpy Boardman was bound south for the islands. He had never been seen in Newport since.

Well, dad-blame it, that was right! The ruffian's instinct was sound! Get out! Go to some place where your scars won't show, and where, even if they are seen, you can invent a story to account for them.

Down the hill, then, to the edge of the bay.

Adam Long, too, ran it.

And presently he felt under his feet the blobby cobbles of the water-front, and he stared across at *Goodwill to Men*.

To any but a lover's eye this vessel might have seemed a monstrosity. It was longish and most astoundingly thin: it must have been four or five times as long as it was broad, this schooner. It scobberlotched in other respects. That there was no forward castle was not extraordinary —many vessels were built that way nowadays—but there was no after castle either! A man on the poop—or where the poop would have been if there had been a poop—was but little higher above the water than one in the waist, which wasn't, properly speaking, a waist at all. The bow-sprit was scarcely steeved but extended out at much the same angle as the deck itself, nearly parallel to the water. The tall sticks weren't sparred. The bows were not apple-cheeked, as bows should be, to push the water away, but sucked-in, giving the whole forward part of the hull a knifelike appearance. Come a good high sea, the old-timers around the yard used to predict while *Goodwill* was building, and that crazy craft would dive right plumb into it and never come up again.

Nineteen out of twenty saw the schooner this way, as a freak.

The twentieth saw it as an interesting if disconcerting experiment.

Adam Long saw her as a bride.

A bride for somebody else?

He wheeled around, hands clenched, scowling, as though at a shouted challenge from the town, which, however, slumbered on. He glared at it, as at a rival for the affections of his beloved.

He must get out of here! He had his fortune to make, and they weren't going to hold him up—not any longer!

The white Moses boat, the schooner's gig, was not paintered to the stringpiece, as it should have been, and to find another boat at this hour might be difficult or noisy—or both. Well, he didn't need a boat.

He took his shoes off and stuck them into the pockets of his coat.

The water was cold, and he swam swiftly, lungingly, weighted by his clothes, but dogged, making scarcely a ripple.

Resolved Forbes popped his eyes with an almost audible click when his captain pulled himself over the larboard gunwale.

"This'll hold through morning. Let's have the hook up."

"Aye, aye, sir."

Afraid of fresh air, as sailors so often are, the hands had closed the forecastle hatch. Resolved Forbes flung it open, shouted an order. He returned to Adam.

"Reason why the Moses wasn't there—"

"I was about to ask you that, Mister."

"Man named Seth Selden came aboard with her, little while ago. Said he's an owner. Said he'd decided to go along, as a passenger."

Adam nodded amiably.

"Drunk?"

"He was getting that way."

"Where is he now?"

"Asleep in your bunk, sir. Should I put him ashore?"

With a minimum of grumbling, all things considered, sleepy men walked the capstan. Jethro Gardner, the hard-bitten bosun, made for the halyards. Adam himself took the tiller. He shook his head.

"No." He doubted that there was anything in this part of the world could catch *Goodwill*, but he wasn't going to take any chances of Seth's raising the town. Wait till they'd left Brenton's Reef well astern. "We could use an extra hand. Let him asleep. I'll take care of him later."

You had to pay some way for all that speed. *Goodwill to Men* in any kind of sea was a roller. She was a pitcher, too, and would take over all sorts of green water, which fact, together with the sucked-in bows and quarters even more cramped than was customary, made the forecastle in dirty weather a miserable place. The officers' cabin, a tiny one reached by ladder through a slide-hatch on the after deck near the tiller, was scarcely more commodious, though it was less likely to be wet.

When Adam Long went below, dawn was graying the deck and the vessel was truly outside, standing about in a lively manner, but booming.

In the middle of the cabin was his own sea chest and on top of that Seth Selden's. Resolved Forbes' effects were neatly stowed away in the larboard locker and his chest was under the larboard bunk. On the starboard bunk, asleep, indeed snoring, was Seth Selden.

This was the captain's berth, to which Seth had not lingered to hear himself elected. Here was, in fact, though he didn't know it, the real skipper, the legal one.

In his two hands, upright, though the cork was out, was a bottle of rum, half empty. It was good rum, too, as Adam knew, who'd bought it —no dunder, nine pence a bottle. Adam corked it and put it away. He stood a moment, staring at the mean-faced man. He began to grin.

He drew back his right foot.

A portion of Seth Selden's backside hung over the edge of the bunk. It was not a large target; and Adam might have done better, too, with more room to swing in—nevertheless the kick was a hearty one and it slammed Seth against the bulkhead, so that he woke screeching.

Adam grabbed him by the front of his fearnought and yanked him off the bunk and to the foot of the ladder, not far. He drew back a fist as red and almost as large as a Westphalian ham.

"Stowaway, eh? Well, we'll keep you busy! You want to get along on this vessel, Mr. Stowaway, you'd better learn to listen to the captain!"

Seth looked at the fist. He wet his lips.

"Do I make myself clear?" asked Adam Long.

Seth nodded.

Then Adam seized him fore and aft—collar of fearnought, seat of breeches.

"You, up there! Stow these things in the forecastle!"

He heaved Seth to the deck. He heaved Seth's chest after him.

Adam took off and hung up his freedom suit. It was not a very good suit, the sort of thing Mr. Sedgewick would give him, having been legally obliged to. Adam would get better suits soon, much better ones; but he thought that he might always save this one.

It swung back and forth with the movement of the schooner.

Naked then as the day he was born, Adam Long knelt and said his prayers. Afterward he got into the starboard bunk and turned his face to the wall. There were tears in his eyes, he didn't know why. He must have been mighty wrought-up. It was some time before he fell asleep.

PART TWO

---◆---

Won't Anybody Buy My Eels

6 There is not much that's noble about a bowsprit, at least to a sailing man, who thinks of it primarily as a thing you sit over when you want to relieve yourself—the head of the vessel, dedicated to a practice not good for neatness when she's climbing into weather—but the *Goodwill* bowsprit was something special. To Adam Long it was a humbling post, an article to be gazed on as another might gaze on a skull, an hourglass, or some similar *memento mori*.

For Adam had opposed this bowsprit. He would have had it steeved at a much sharper angle. *Goodwill*, though more or less a community venture, represented the most advanced ideas in design. "The ship of the future," a few proudly averred. "A tarnation freak," said others. Throughout her building the yard had been visited by men who shook their heads, clucked their tongues.

"She won't even *float*, that hooker! She won't *float!*"

A lad of less than twenty then, a 'prentice who had never been to sea except as a baby when his mother brought him over, Adam nevertheless had insisted upon plenty to say about the construction of *Goodwill*; and in most matters, indeed in all but this one, he had been loud on the side of the ahead-lookers. But concerning the bowsprit he'd gone conservative. A straight-out sprit would weaken the hull. The elimination of the sprit-sail—there just wouldn't be room for a spritsail the way they were building *Goodwill*—would cost speed. It would put too great a strain on the sticks. It would make the whole vessel look silly.

Well, he'd been crashingly wrong; and this was his private scourge. He had vowed that whenever he felt himself waxing cocksure he would go forward and have a good long look at that bowsprit.

He did this the first morning out. The day was a dandy. *Goodwill* fairly leapt through the water, and all was atauto aloft and alow—in Jeth Gardner the bosun's phrase they had cracked on everything but the cook's shirt. The seas danced bright in the sun.

Peterson, a sullen man, lumpy, grumpy, strong but not willing, and Eb Waters, who hailed from Massachusetts and was otherwise objectionable, occupied the sprit this morning. Captain Long smiled at them.

"Prayers when you're finished," Adam called. "Eight bells."

Peterson hawked, spat.

"I aim to be here a long time," he said.

"So do I," said Eb Waters.

"Five minutes," conceded Adam.

It was perhaps a good thing, this early example. Adam gave them seven minutes, and then, when they all but refused to obey an order, he made things clear. It was necessary to knock Peterson down and to all but break Waters' arm; but it was worth the trouble.

The others, with a single exception, gave forth no squawk when they learned about prayers-every-morning. Most of them reckoned they'd only have to work during that time anyway, and they'd liefer pray than work, as who wouldn't? They were the more mollified when Adam announced that the Sabbath was to be respected aboard of this vessel. Most skippers, though they might be churchgoers ashore, stuck to the slogan "No Sundays off soundings"; but Adam Long had other ideas.

"Says in the Book we should keep the Sabbath, and it don't say anything about land or sea or what-not."

Unexpectedly it was Seth Selden the sanctimonious who found the fact of daily Bible readings irksome.

"Religion is for the home," he grumbled.

"You stand up, and you close your eyes when I say the prayer," said Adam Long, "or I'll break the bridge of your nose."

Seth had a hangover that first morning, but he grumped every morning pretty much the same way. In other matters he was unexpectedly cheerful. Adam had been prepared for whining, or maybe an attempt to assert his claim to the captaincy, but Seth seemed happy. A good sailing man, he came for nothing. He had not been signed on, so he rated no wages. Not only that, but Adam charged him fourpence ha'penny for the rum he had drunk—exactly what Adam himself had paid for it—and made a note to this effect under Seth's ownership account.

There were many cases of men, skippers and mates mostly, who were mild-mannered ashore but fiends once they got out of sight of land. Seth was almost the other way 'round. So far from complaining, Seth settled down cheerfully, the chirkiest hand in the forecastle.

How much of this was real and how much put on, Adam didn't know. He gave Seth no more than the usual reasons for grumbling; but there were times when he caught the "stowaway" studying him with a look that fairly dripped with venom. Seth wouldn't do anything—now. But he was not likely to forget.

Two days out Adam learned why Seth had been so eager to make this voyage, in whatever capacity.

28

He was awakened by the bosun Jethro Gardner, who had the grave-yard watch. Jeth, a compact old man in his forties, habitually wore an expression of disgust, and he was not given to idle chitchat.

"Two sail. French. We're smacketty-dab atween 'em."

Adam woke up all over, as a good sailor should, and a second later he was topside, thoughtfully scratching his rump and studying the sails.

"Aye, they're French."

Dawn had surprised the *Goodwill* in a spot almost exactly halfway between the two war vessels, a frigate and a sloop.

Adam sighed and went below and got dressed.

The lieutenant spoke English. He was young. The first thing he did was ask if there was any news of the war.

"Has it been declared? We've been twelve weeks at sea."

Adam shook his head..

"Left Newport yesterday morning, early. No news of it then."

The Frenchman shrugged. He looked around.

Goodwill to Men was trim and to her master's eye beautiful; but hove-to, close-up, she was not notably rich in appearance. The Frenchman all but sneered. His gaze was accustomed to brass and the varnished surfaces of a warship. There was nothing of that here.

"Let's see your papers."

Excepting the logbook and the "X"ed list of the crew, there was only one paper, a "Contrackt of Affreightment," actually nothing but a bill-of-lading. This had the cargo itemized and cleared out of Newport, but it didn't say where the cargo was to be taken—for the sufficient reason that nobody knew. There were some hoops and pipe staves, and some salted fish, too, but the greatest part of the space below was taken up with dried eels, and it was Adam's plan to peddle these around and get the best price that offered, no matter where. There was hardly a planter down in those parts, whether Spanish, English, French, or Dutch, who didn't have trouble finding fodder for his slaves. The blacks multiplied, and the land itself produced only coffee and sugar, no game, no grain, not much livestock. Food, food—they always needed food! And Adam planned to sell it to them, somewhere.

The lieutenant pointed this out.

"You'll probably go to an English place. By that time war will have been declared. So we'd better arrest you now."

"You can't do that!"

The lieutenant shrugged.

"We're making for Havana. The Spaniards are our allies now. Appeal your case there—in Cuba. If we've done wrong, you'll be released."

Yes, Adam thought bitterly, be released after we'd wasted months in the worst yellow-fever port in the world and given away all our coin in bribes; and by that time the eels would be spoiled anyway.

He put this into words, but the lieutenant only shrugged again.

"I'll send over a prize crew. Now if you only had evidence of destination—"

"Don't you reckon Denmark would take that unkind, Monseer?" said Seth Selden, who had appeared on the ladder. "Seems to me I'd heard your country's being mighty sweet toward Denmark these days."

This was in Adam's cabin, and Adam had known that everybody else aboard would be around the slide up there, listening; but he resented Seth's intrusion.

"Denmark?" said the lieutenant.

"That's where these eels is to go to. Well, Ostnabrueck. Which is a Danish colony. You want I should get out that paper, Cap'n?"

Adam grunted, more in amazement than assent, but Seth headed unhesitatingly for his, Adam's, own chest. Seth opened this and made as if to take a paper from it, though in truth he took the paper out of his own shirt, as Adam, who was nearer than the Frenchman, saw.

It was crowded in that cabin. There was scarcely room to unfold the paper, which was the most impressive document Adam Long had ever seen and fairly crackled with ribbons and seals. Adam couldn't read a word of it; but then, neither could the lieutenant.

A French *matelot* tried to climb down, but there wasn't room, so he spoke his message from one of the top rungs. Adam sensed that there had been a signal sent from the frigate, where they were waxing impatient. Whatever it was, the lieutenant gave a cross answer.

"See, there's Ostnabrueck," said Seth Selden, pointing.

"Never heard of it," said the lieutenant.

"It's south of the Leewards, a mite over Trinidad way. Danish."

"Oh."

"And this here, this's the list of cargo. See that word 'kivkeet'? That means 'eel'—in Danish, of course."

"Of course," murmured the lieutenant.

"And that word, see? That means 'April.' We're late now."

"Overdue," said Adam, catching on.

"Very well," the lieutenant said. "You're hardly worth seizing anyway. I must get back to my ship."

Afterward Adam looked sideways at the "stowaway."

"Just what is that thing?" he asked at last, pointing to the document that now stuck out of Seth's shirt.

"Don't rightly know, Cap'n. I bought it from a drunken Danish sailor one night. I think he said it was a fishing license."

"Oh."

"I got a lot of things like that, in different languages. Some of 'em I bought, some I wrote out. I'm a good hand with a pen, Cap'n."

"You must be. You got those things with you?"

"Aye. I'd've made you out a clearance for some French port but maybe this was better—my French ain't very good."

"By the way, why was you in such a hurry to get aboard?"

Seth grinned. He was a different man with a deck under him.

"My writing talent again. It gets me in trouble. Friends'd ask: 'Why do we have to go all the way to Contraband Cove to fetch off goods we don't want to pay duty on? We could take 'em ashore here, we only had a cocket saying the customs'd been paid.' So I'd make 'em out a cocket."

"I see. That's why business at the Cove's been falling off?"

"I'd do it just for friends. But I got a heap of friends."

"You ought to be ashamed of yourself—doing honest smugglers out of work like that. Pity the admiralty didn't get you."

"They damn' near did. There was a Queen's man looking for me with a warrant. Heard that the other night, at Blake's. That's why I slipped out. And these papers and seals, I chucked 'em into my chest and brought that aboard of here, where the warrant wouldn't reach. Then I figured I might as well stay. So I did."

"I see."

"I still got those papers and so-forth, you should ever want a handsome-looking document."

"I'll let you know if I do."

7   It was that way all through those waters, where no man's ship was safe. The best thing to do at sight of a strange sail was run. Sight and scoot; and the Devil snatch the skipper who didn't watch sharp. Some of the hands even concocted a chanty about it:

> Scaredy-Cat Sea;
> That ain't for me.
> Scaredy-Cat, Scaredy-Cat, Scaredy-Cat Sea.
> Lightning aloft,
> Breakers alee,
> While we go rolling
> Down Scaredy-Cat Sea.

Only once did they stop for a gam, and that, you may be sure, was after they had identified a Yankee rig. The other was small, a sloop, booming north, skittish, coy; but those aboard of her, when at last they were sure of themselves, were happy to heave-to.

"Put the longboat over. *Fast*—afore he gets his in the water!"

For if the other skipper came calling, Adam had only that half-bottle of rum. So it was Adam who went, taking with him most of his crew, who would fraternize with the crew of the sloop.

The sloop was from Stonington, Connecticut. Would Captain Wallis take a letter? Glad to, sir. Thereupon Captain Long wrote a report to his owners. There was little enough to say. He did make mention of Seth Selden, "a valued member of my crew," who, he said, sent his regards. Seth grinned, afterward, when Adam told him this.

Captain Wallis had been down in the islands five months.

"They're scared of everything down there."

"Scaredy-Cat Sea," muttered Adam.

"Eh?"

"Nothing."

"More wine?"

"Thanks."

"You say 'boo' they jump a foot. Sure, they want to buy. But they'd like to have credit." He snorted. "*Credit!*"

"Does seem silly," Adam agreed.

"One minute they're going to set forth and conquer every island in this part of the world, and they're slapping themselves so hard on the chest they like to knock themselves backward—and next minute a shark breaks water 'way out, and somebody yells 'the enemy'! and the whole population skedaddles for those dad-blamed dodans of theirs back in the hills, all loaded up with provisions and water." He snorted again. "Water! It's a good drink for them!"

When Adam made deck again, blinking in the rowdy-dowdy sunlight, the hands in the longboat were teaching the Stonington lads a song:

> I spit on you,
> You spit on me—

"And never loaf offshore," Wallis warned. "They come out in boats. Swarm all over you."

> Ain't no politeness
> In Scaredy-Cat Sea.

That was the first time Adam Long had acted the captain anywhere but aboard of *Goodwill* herself. The second time came only a few days later, when he went ashore to register at Kingston.

He was disappointed in the flat, scorched city. To anyone used to the

32

mellowness of Newport, a town almost seventy years old, *seven*-year-old Kingston was shudderingly raw.

The port authorities were arrogant, the townspeople suspicious, surly. Adam drifted from place to place, now and then trying, rather pathetically, to pick up a gam.

His freedom suit was too hot for Jamaica, too plain, too. He wished he had a brighter, lighter coat, maybe even a sword.

He drifted into an ordinary and took a table far in the rear. The sunlight outside, reflected by the white buildings, had been so bright that now he could scarecely see anything at all.

At last he made out another customer, a man with a twitchy nose, a furtive manner, mouselike.

"Could you tell me," Adam started, "if any of those that sailed under Thomas Hart are to be found around here now?"

He had decided that he would seek out old members of Hart's crew and get affidavits stating that he, Adam Long, had had no dealings with the pirate. But he'd made too abrupt a start.

The man at first did not seem prepared to answer. Then he said from a corner of his mouth: "Best not to talk about Tom 'Art."

"Sorry," said Adam, embarrassed.

However, after a drink the mouselike one relented; and while nothing further was said about Captain Hart he did introduce himself—Willis Beach—and did tell Adam something about Kingston.

Kingston, it appeared, approached a panic. Nobody knew when the news of war would come—it might well be brought by a French fleet. The colony had a few cannons, a small store of powder and ball, half a warehouse full of rusting muskets, but no real soldiers. Nine men out of ten were scared half to death. They bustled here and there with the pauseless persistence of ants. They whispered in corners. They shaded their eyes to scan the sea. They hoarded.

"Some wants to arm the blacks, other say it'd be worse'n 'aving the Frenchies 'ere. Now if they was to—"

He broke off. Coming in from the street were three Marines in bright blue coats and pipe-clayed belts. They were large coarse purposeful men. One had a hanger.

Though he had never before seen one, Adam knew instantly that here was a press gang. There were warships in the harbor.

The men made for Willis Beach. One grabbed the little Londoner's arms and twisted them behind him, so that he squealed in pain. One yanked him off his stool. The third, the midshipman, finished his ale.

"Let him alone," Adam said suddenly.

He didn't know why he did that. It was none of his business. He truly

33

didn't give a hoot what happened to Willis Beach, even though the little man was the only one who had said a civil word to him so far in this colony. It was probably the presser's manner that did it. Any man from Rhode Island might have felt the same way.

The men were puzzled rather than angry. One reached for a short wooden cudgel Adam had not previously noticed: it hung by a leathern thong from his belt. Adam punched him in the jaw.

The man staggered backward, making low blubbery sounds of astonishment. He tripped over a stool and sat down—hard.

The midshipman drew his hanger.

"O-ho! It's a fight our Yankee friend would like, eh?"

Adam looked at the blade. There was nothing he could oppose to that, physically. He sneered. He whipped a paper out of a pocket.

"And it's a court-martial our officer friend would like, eh?"

Wary, his point still raised, the midshipman looked at the letter. Adam could not be sure whether he could read; but if he couldn't he wouldn't admit this. In any event the signature and seal were sufficiently impressive. The message enjoined one and all to abstain from hindering Adam Long, who was doing some special work of a confidential nature for "Benbow, Admiral, R.N." They had learned the name of the admiral from bumboat women, and Seth Selden, with some such emergency as this in mind, had made a fine thing of the forgery.

"You might've let me know sooner," the midshipman mumbled.

"You might've given me a chance to," Adam snapped.

Willis Beach loudly admired the signature, when the gang had gone. "Better'n the real one!"

"What makes you think that this isn't real?"

"Just 'appens I know old Johnny Benbow. Used to clark on 'is flagship. You see, Cap'n, it just so 'appens I *am* a deserter from the bloody Nivy. If they'd 'ad me in, I'd've got fifty-sixty lashes."

He rose. He shook Adam's hand.

"I'm 'eading for the 'ills, and I'll stie there till these wessels've gone awie. Gawd bless you, Cap'n. Good-bye."

That evening Adam announced that there would be no shore leave in Kingston.

"Unless some of you got a hankering to join the English Navy?"

The hoops and staves fetched a fancy price, but nobody would touch the eels. It seemed that the Navy had impounded all the food reserves on the island, or had threatened to. A fleet was expected from Home, the admiral declared, and he must prepare to stock it. But the colonists had to eat, and what's more they had to feed their slaves, the governor had replied, adding that the admiral did not have the right to do any such impounding. The admiral rejoined that he certainly did, and any-

34

way he was doing it. Voices had been raised, tables thumped. The governor, beset by political enemies, was unsure of his position, for he held only an interim appointment, and word from the new monarch, Anne, had not yet been received. Neither had official news of the declaration of war been received. Something had gone astray, some ship had been sunk? Meanwhile nobody knew whether the admiral's order stood, or in fact just what it was; but the planters in from their plantations couldn't buy food, and Adam Long was not permitted to sell.

"You'd have to get permission from Admiral Benbow himself."

"All right," he said. "I'll go and ask him."

He waited for four days in an anteroom. Nobody paid much attention to him. He was not uncomfortable; but he never did get a glimpse of the admiral. All the functionaries he ever saw, aside from a few clerks who sometimes scurried in to check the spelling of his name or the tonnage of his vessel, were a couple of marine guards, changed too often to make it worth while to hit up an acquaintance with them.

Alone, then, and uneasy in mind, he fell into the habit of surveying his own clothes and wondering what folks thought of him here—either that or else gazing out of a window to where he could see *Goodwill* in the midst of a cluster of bumboats. The bumboats made more tolerable the confinement of those aboard the schooner, but all the same the captain didn't like them. They were dirty, like the men and women who rowed them, and he misliked to think of dirty people near *Goodwill*.

He had turned from the window, the afternoon of the fourth day, and closed his throbbing eyes for a moment. The sunlight was merciless, blaring off the roofs, fleering away from the palm trees.

"Is the admiral in, pray?"

Adam opened his eyes.

This was a willowy stripling in silver and blue, who carried one hand on his hip whilst with the other he waved a square of lace doused with perfume. He looked as if a good breeze might blow him away, and his voice was a cultivated screech, a macaw's.

Adam made a leg, mockingly.

"They tell me he is, sir. I wouldn't know. I've never seen him myself. But then, I've only been waiting here since Tuesday."

The stripling's mouth fell open, and he seemed to gasp, like a fish out of water. The hand with the kerchief became still.

What if anything this apparition would have replied, Adam was never to know, for at this moment a clerk bustled in, swirling with apologies, milording this and milording that, and offered the stripling his arm and conducted him to the inner chamber.

It was too much for Adam, who left.

He was thoughtful when he called the hands aft that evening. There were no bumboats then, and the harbor was quiet. Night would come soon, in a rush. The lovely birds that sought garbage were gone. The surface of the water was crumpled with catspaws.

"There's plenty want food but they can't buy it here. So we'll take it to them around the other side of the island. The customs folks won't let us deliver our goods at the front door, we'll use the back."

"That'd be smuggling," Peterson cried.

"Why, so it would," said Adam.

Jeth Gardner pointed out: "But we can't even leave this harbor withouten we have clearance papers!"

Adam patted the mainsail.

"*There's* our clearance paper. All right—now let's have the hook up!"

8   Mr. Pendleton was a worried man with worried washy eyes. His sigh rose full from his feet. Whenever he came to a stop there seemed to settle upon him, invisible until it landed, a gritty sediment, ashes mixed with sand perhaps, giving forth an acrid odor like dust from some discouraged volcano. He dragged, and drooped.

Conscientiously he conducted his visitor around the plantation. It was nothing to be proud of. In those parts you always had a sense of *rottenness*. You could feel the nearness, the emergence, like a stealthy miasma, of decay. But this place was worse than most. It was falling apart.

Mr. Pendleton was the third Jamaica planter Adam had tried. The first had only recently been visited by another Yankee with dried codfish and live horses—so *his* slaves would eat for a while. The second had wanted the eels, but couldn't pay for them. Four dozen coconuts in exchange for a cask of oysters, was the best that struggler could do.

Mr. Pendleton was not going to be any more profitable.

"Shall we have a drink, Captain?"

"Don't mind."

Not the suggestion but its tardiness was strange. The average planter produced liquor as soon as you hove into sight. For one thing, he welcomed news from outside, and hoped you'd be talky. For another, if you got a bit drunk you might come down in your price.

They were lonesome, these out-of-the-way planters.

Adam decided to try a Frencher next. He'd run over to Hispaniola. Meanwhile it was only mannerly to have that drink.

Mr. Pendleton led the way past a ramshackle garden and into a mouldering house. He clapped his hands. Nobody came. He shouted; but the

36

echoes of his shout chased themselves to rest. Muttering something about sickness, Mr. Pendleton said he would get the rum himself.

"Why don't you go out there under those roses, Captain?"

Adam bowed gravely and went out to a shabby little arbor and sat down. He could see the schooner from there, which was good. He reckoned he wasn't entirely shoved out of everything when he could command *Goodwill to Men*. He might own only one-sixteenth of her, but she'd obey him when he put over the tiller. And he would own the whole vessel some day. He was bound and determined that this should be so.

"Here we are. Sorry I took so long. Will you have a cigarro, too?"

They lit up. They sipped. Adam's drink was powerful.

"Shall we talk business?"

"All right."

Adam did not even look at his host but continued to gaze down at the schooner, from which the Moses boat was putting out. That was right: he had instructed Resolved Forbes to send the boat at this time.

He named his price. He heard a gasp. Then came the tale of woe. It was sloppy, slippy, the words like pewter plates with gobbets of food still sticking to them. Mr. Pendleton was willing to pay, but— When his next shipment came—

Adam shook his head. He took a little, not much, of his drink. The Moses boat was nearing shore. It looked absurdly small and toylike down there on the blue, blue bay.

Suddenly Adam caught a change in Mr. Pendleton's voice.

"What was that you said?"

"I repeat: I am not going to debase myself with any more pleading. Either you sell me those eels at a price I can pay, or I'll have you seized and sent to Kingston as a smuggler."

"Why, of all the Joe-fired—"

"I mean every word of that, Captain."

He did, too. He was a weak man, but a wildly desperate one. Pasty, skinny, he wasn't going to depend on himself alone. A huge quadroon, the biggest man Adam Long had ever seen, now was standing beside Adam's chair. He must have slipped out of the house, at a signal.

"Well?"

"Go to the Devil! I don't do business that way."

Mr. Pendleton was stubborn as only a weak man can be.

"Your boat's coming in now. If you'll just give the order to unload, I'll pay you everything I've got."

"Go to the Devil," Adam said again, "if he'll have you."

"It means Kingston, Captain. They're touchy about such matters, especially right now. I happen to have some influence there, and I think

I can promise that you'd be impressed into the Navy. It might be years before your story got out—if it ever did."

Here was no empty threat. The English Navy was taking whatever it could get, without asking questions; and the port officials at Kingston would be in a lather about *Goodwill*. They had paid him no mind while he was there, but when they found him gone without proper permission their rage would know no bounds. They'd splutter that he had offended against the dignity of the Throne, when in fact it was their own dratted dignity they thought of. If folks started laughing at port authorities, where would port authorities be? The times being what they were, and sent-out clerks what *they* were, a man in Adam Long's position might well lose his cargo and vessel, his liberty to boot. Be a smuggler if you must, a corruptionist, even a pirate, but for God's sake don't venture to sneer at the third assistant deputy custodian of the royal high colonial admiralty seal! It is a fact attested by men of sense everywhere that of all pompous asses in a world overcrowded with same, the most vindictive by far is the port official.

Adam rose.

"Reckon I'll go back aboard, where it don't stink so much."

The quadroon stiffened. Mr. Pendleton drew from underneath his waistcoat a walnut-and-blue-steel horse pistol.

"We had better step inside, Captain. You and Oliver and I."

They went only as far as the veranda, where they were screened by long let-down jalousies. Mr. Pendleton watched the sea. Oliver watched Adam Long.

The Moses boat had been beached and two sailors loafed beside it. A third man was walking toward the house.

"From his clothes, Captain, I take it that we are about to be honored by a visit from one of your mates?"

Adam nodded. He had recognized Resolved Forbes. It had not been a part of Resolved's orders to come ashore in person, and the fact that he had done so might argue that he was suspicious—or just that he was bored.

Mr. Pendleton waggled the pistol.

"This will make it the more persuasive. The skipper *and* the mate."

Resolved Forbes came on. His gait rolled, as a sailorman's should, and he had his thumbs looped into the top of his breeches.

A hundred yards away he halted; and for a long moment he studied the arbor, the chairs, ashtray, glasses, Adam's hat, the still-smoking cigarro.

Mr. Pendleton cocked the pistol, a loud sound.

Resolved Forbes stood as though in thought, then drew a small telescope from one of his pockets and put this to an eye.

After a while he turned back.

"Get after him! Bring him here!"

Oliver was away like a great ungainly ape, bounding with enormous strides across the lawn, down the path. The sailors by the boat saw him and shouted to Resolved Forbes, who turned.

Adam Long was proud of his mate in that moment. Resolved was tall but not thick-thewed, and he couldn't have weighed much more than half of what Oliver weighed. Nevertheless he knew what to do.

It happened very fast. The sailors had started to run up from the beach but it was over before they could get there.

Feet firm, Resolved Forbes swayed sideways, ducking the arms, and hooked his right fist into the pit of the giant's stomach. Oliver, caught off balance, gave forth a thunderous hollow gawp, and doubled over; and when he did this Resolved Forbes closed in, using his fists as much for pushing as for punching, using his elbows, his knees.

Oliver, screaming, went over backward, Resolved Forbes on top of him. A moment later, when the *Goodwill* mate rose, Oliver lay motionless.

Forbes waved back the sailors, who had started up the path.

He leaned over Oliver, with his left hand grabbed the quadroon by the hair, and lifted the groggy, pulped head. Twice his right fist punched Oliver in the mouth: they could hear each *"splap"* clear up on the veranda. Then, shaking the man's head, Resolved Forbes started to talk to him slowly, earnestly. At last he slammed Oliver's head down again, wiped the blood from his hand, and set off for the beach. A few minutes later he was being rowed out to the schooner.

After what seemed a long while Oliver rose and staggered to the house. He would have entered, not seeing the others, but Mr. Pendleton called out.

Oliver turned; and he was a horrible sight to see.

Something had been snicked out of his body, so that now he was all lax and limp, and he sagged woefully, his arms dangling like the arms of a cripple, while tremulous fear lit his eyes. His lips and cheekbones were puffed. But the thing that had been done to this man's spirit was the worst wound of all. He would never be the same again.

"He— He wouldn't come."

"Obviously. What did he say to you?"

Oliver was obliged to make a mighty effort to remember.

"Said to tell you if Cap'n Long wasn't down on the beach by the time he got aboard he'd bombard the whole plantation."

Mr. Pendleton wheeled on Adam, who gazed out over the lawn.

"I didn't know you had a cannon!"

"Likely there's a heap of things you don't know."

"Well anyway, he'll never reach us here—with a stern chaser. That tub down there couldn't move anything heavier."

Adam said nothing.

The *Goodwill* was moving in, propelled by sweeps—three long ash oars on each side. There was a good deal of stir aft. The Moses poked ahead, sounding. But the water wasn't shoal. At a point less than two hundred yards from the beach, the schooner was turned, and the men on the veranda at last had a look at the afterdeck.

"Good God! That's a twelve-pounder!"

Adam still said nothing.

Men had peeled a tarpaulin off a glittering black object. Somebody took a last swipe with a polishing cloth. Others were bringing up loggerheads, powder bags, wads, crows, sponges, a match tub from which smoke rose. Still others rolled black balls to a shot rack.

Mr. Pendleton broke.

"Get them away from here! Tell them not to shoot!"

Adam wasn't worried about them shooting that thing, whatever it was, but a mite of anxiety wouldn't do the planter any harm.

"I mislike being hurried," he drawled.

He sauntered across the veranda, onto the lawn. He was seen, and a cheer rose from the schooner, while the Moses put out for shore.

Adam paused at the table to take his hat. He picked up his half-finished cigarro. He finished his rum in two slow smooth swallows.

When at last he climbed to the deck he pumped the mate's hand with a vehemence that embarrassed them both.

"Best job of jury-rigging I ever saw!"

He beamed at the sawed-off spar, tarred and shiny, the carriage made of tarred barrel staves, the rickety "powder boxes," the wads improvised from undershirts. He whuffed out the light, a real one, in the match tub. He kicked one of the "cannonballs," which, trailing fresh black paint, clunked into several of its fellows: these were coconuts a planter had given Adam the previous day.

"Only thing I can't figure—why did you stop short of the house?"

"Saw your hat and thought I saw tobacco smoke, so I got out the glass," said Resolved Forbes. "Said to myself, 'If Adam Long leaves a half-smoked cigarro and a half-finished rum, then there must be something mighty queer going on, so I'd better fetch help.'"

"Tarnation! For that I'll give you a drink free! Come on!"

9 It was a wild coast and they had approached it with caution, which may account for the fact that nobody saw Eb Waters and Carl Peterson slip over the side.

Adam nearly resorted to profanity when they wakened him.

"Serve 'em right if I let them stay here!"

He looked at the land, a dark one, above which no smoke stood. There might be a plantation or two, or three or four, tucked away in the folds of those hills, but he could not see any. There would be coves and creeks along such a coast, ideal hiding places for the small-boaters Captain Wallis had warned him against.

"I expect they thought all they had to do is lie down and food'll fall right into their faces."

"Aye," said Jeth Gardner.

"While beautiful brown gals fanned 'em with palm fronds!"

"Aye. They've never been down in these parts before."

Adam sighed.

"Well, they'll be back. Won't be able to stand it. But maybe that'll be tonight and maybe not till tomorrow. I don't want to wait that long, a spot like this. I'll go after them. Prayers first. Bring me my Book. And the musket, too, long's you're down there."

He wanted the gun not for signaling purposes—it never occurred to him that he might need to signal—but for protection against snakes. Adam had always been deathly afraid of snakes.

"Stand on and off. See anything you don't like—run. Don't stay and shout for me."

"What if you're not back by dark?"

"I'll be back."

There was a skimpy shelly beach, backed by jungle that evidently had dismayed the runaways: their footprints showed that they had moved back and forth a little before plunging in.

Indeed, entering that jungle was like walking into a solid thing, a wall. Even Adam Long caught up his breath when he did it.

Then he paused, permitting his eyes to get used to the gloom. As he had expected, the trail was as plain as though made by oxen. Sailors ashore are the clumsiest of men.

But Adam was so busy watching where he was going, where he put his feet down, that he soon lost the trail. He might have turned back to the beach, but he'd be seen from the schooner then and would appear ridiculous. He kept on. He tripped over decayed stumps, sank calf-deep into holes. Creepers, pushed aside, sprang back to lash him from behind, and their spikes cut his neck and clothing. Several times he fell full-length, the heels of his hands squashing into the muck.

He was panting. It startled him to hear it. Aboard ship his wind always had been sound. In this close dank place he was all but stifled.

He cast to the right, taking it much more slowly; and when after a while he found no sign of the deserters there, he swung to the left.

It was some time before he confessed that, ridiculous or not ridiculous, it would be better if he went back and started all over again. Then he found, to his flabbergastment, that he could not even follow his own trail back. He did not even know the direction of the beach! He sniffed earnestly, holding his head back like a hen that drinks water. All he got was the rank wet odor of rot, no brine.

It outraged him, at the same time frightening him, to learn that this jungle, this sewer of suffocating stench, could blot out every trace of the sea near at hand, the clean sea. It didn't seem decent.

Once he thought he heard a slippy noise near his feet, and he shied like a colt.

There was another sound, a faint dripping; but when he moved stealthily toward this in the hope of finding a stream he could follow to the sea, it came from behind him; and when he turned, it came from one side or the other. Motionless, listening carefully, at last he decided that the dripping was all around him. It was almost inaudible—was in fact less a sound than a sense of motion, of disintegration, as though the forest were softly, wetly dropping to pieces.

He prayed. When he had finished—and he was brief—he looked up, already with an idea.

He would climb a tree.

He must be still near the beach. No matter how queer this place was, it couldn't screen off a whole ocean.

He placed his musket at the foot of the largest tree he could find, and started up. Vines and creepers came spewing down when he put weight on them. Some were too slippery to hold. Some had spikes. It was worse up there than it had been on the ground. It was thicker, trickier. He was never sure what was the true trunk of the tree and what parasite. There were mosses and twisted slimy flowers. Things came away in his hands, unclean things that made a soft sucking sound. Adam could clamber up ratlines as nimbly as any boy; but he knew when he was beaten.

Baffled, having seen nothing, he climbed down again.

He was within a few feet of the ground and about to drop the rest

of the way, when he looked down in order not to land on the musket—
and the sweat that larded his body turned cold.

A snake lay across the musket. It had been in motion and was curved,
but now it was still except for the raised head, which tilted slightly this
way and that like some delicate flower stirred by a breeze.

The snake was about six feet long, and very thin, and the head was
small. It was bright green in color, a luminous, almost a *phosphorescent*
green, with dark gray spiraling along its back.

After a while, still holding its head high, it slithered away.

Adam counted to five hundred, then dropped, snatched up his musket,
and ran.

When he had stopped, only because of lack of breath, he forced himself to be still and to think. Though he could neither hear breakers nor
see the sun, it stood to reason that he had not gone far.

He heard a high wailing behind him.

He whirled around.

He heard it again. It was some distance away, half a mile perhaps,
though that was hard to estimate in soggy air like this.

Now Adam Long was not superstitious. He didn't believe in ghosts
much. With no hesitation at all, as the howling came to his ears again,
nearer this time, he started to run toward it.

Even if it *was* a ghost he would prefer it to a snake.

At last he saw light ahead. He burst into a clearing.

The howl rose again, that wail as of a banshee, right in front of him;
and he made out the monsters.

There were two, collared, and to their collars were attached long leads,
the other ends of which disappeared into the jungle. In appearance at
least they were not fierce, these enormous dogs. They seemed tired, or
bored. One had already flumped in disgust to the ground; the other,
after a half-hearted growl, its snout tilted skyward, regarded Adam with
a bleak bleary gaze, the while absently scratching a flea.

Into the clearing, now, came a man in blue and pink. He stopped. He
hauled out a pistol.

Adam Long raised his musket.

After a while, but moving with circumspection, watchful, tense, the
men lowered their weapons a little.

The bloodhounds took no interest in these somewhat silly proceedings. The second flopped down beside the first; it grunted, then fell
asleep.

The man was thin, thirtyish. His own hair, unpowdered, was caught
behind in a sash of silk, unblushingly blue, and a blue velvet band
decorated his hunting hat.

"Zut, alors! Dites-moi, que cherchez-vous ici?"

"Can't you talk English?" plaintively.

"But to be sure I can! You are the English, then?"

"I hail from the continental colonies."

"Ah, a Yankee?"

He pronounced it "Yawn-*kee*."

"I reckon," said Adam.

"And you seek water, it could be?"

"Could be, but it ain't. I'm looking for two hands jumped ship."

The bloodhounds lay motionless, except that now and then one of them would twitch its hide in order to shoo off flies. The Frencher regarded them with a fond paternal smile.

Suddenly he remembered his manners.

"Maitrejean, Monsieur, Jules de Marigny de Maitrejean."

"Name's Long," said Adam. "From Newport."

"The 'ounds and I, we 'ave sport together."

"A runaway slave?"

"Ah, yes. They are incorrigible, *monsieur*. Scarce a week passes but one slips away. I—I confess I make it easy for them to do so. Not *en masse* but singly. It provides a diversion. And it is exercise for Castor and Pollux here, also for me. Sport. You are shock', *monsieur?*"

"Well, they say 'When in Rome—' "

"Assuredly, *monsieur*."

Only I don't think I'd ever hunt a man with dogs, even in Rome, Adam reflected.

"Your mariners, *monsieur*—it is likeliest that they will stumble out into one of my fields, and an overseer will then send them to the plantation house. Will you go there with me?"

"Your nigger—"

"Tomorrow will do as well."

"Don't you ever lose 'em for good?"

"Sometimes."

He was an odd one, for a planter. He must have been wealthy; but if he was wealthy, then what was he doing in the islands?

"In addition, *monsieur*, assuredly you need refreshment. The, uh, the forest has been unkind to you, eh?"

"Looks like *you* came through it all right."

"I am use' to it. I live here. Were we aboard a ship doubtless you would snigger at how I reeled."

Adam didn't expect he'd snigger at anything just then, the way he felt.

They came out of the jungle abruptly, to find themselves at the edge

44

of a cane field. There was no glimpse of the sea. Here Maitrejean paused to permit his guest to rest, though he himself showed not the slightest sheen of sweat, nor was he breathing heavily.

"A bath, some brandy, and *monsieur* will be a new man, eh?"

"Sounds good."

"*Monsieur* must stay a while—a few days, a few weeks."

"Whoa! I got work to do."

"Such as?"

"Got eels to peddle, somewhere."

The word was strange to Maitrejean, who said over and over, his brows knit: "Eels—eels—"

Adam tried to elucidate but he could think of no other word for the pesky animals. Unused to waving and waggling his hands, nevertheless he strove to make a manual explanation.

"Aha! But of course, *monsieur!* I will find you one!"

He darted back into the jungle and began to run from place to place, scanning the ground. It was some time before Adam could catch up to him and persuade him that it was not snakes he sought.

They returned to the edge of the cane field, where Adam tried with his hands again, this time however supplementing the mad motions with one of the few French words he did know, *poisson*, fish.

Maitrejean brightened.

"Ah, *les anguilles!* You carry a cargo of *anguilles*, Monsieur? But—it is for eating?"

"Can't imagine what else you might use 'em for."

"But—but this is sent by Heaven!"

"Might not think so, you smelled 'em on a hot night with the hatches open."

"You conceive, *monsieur*, I have seventy blacks, and more on the way from Guinea. They must be fed. But our Navy— You have 'ow many barrels, *monsieur?*— Ah!— And you demand?"

"Five pounds," Adam said glibly, raising the price on the spur of the moment. "That's English pounds, of course."

"But I do not have any English money!"

"Well, I don't know about French money—"

"I do not 'ave francs either."

"Then molasses. I'd have to sample it. Make sure of the grade. I can supply staves and hoops, you lend me a cooper."

"I have three coopers. You'll see their shop soon, when we reach the top of this rise. But I have not the molasses, *monsieur*."

"Umph— Well, I'll take clayed sugar."

"But I do not have clayed sugar. No, nor raw sugar either. At this

45

moment, alas, I am all out of both. Observe—there is my crushing mill, and there's the cooperage beyond it. We'll come in sight of the house itself soon. No, I have no sugar, *monsieur*."

Here we go again, thought an embittered Adam Long.

"But I do have silver, *monsieur*. Not gold, no, but silver. Spanish eight —real pieces. Would they suffice?"

Adam Long squinched shut his eyes to conceal the joy that must have leapt in them. Thunderation! Pieces-of-eight *suffice?* Why, they were better than sterling! He cleared his throat thoughtfully.

"Could be they'll do— Could be—"

Very light slaves, octaroons likely, *métis* the French called them, bathed Adam, while others dried and brushed and mended his clothes. He was shaved. He was even sprayed with scent. He must have smelled like a bawdy house when he rejoined his host on a terrace, but all the same it felt good.

It was mid-morning now and very hot. On the air hung thick sweet ribbons of smoke from the kettles. Back in the hills a road twisted, coming into sight, vanishing again; and they could see that a horseman was descending toward the sea; dust stood behind him.

"A courier from Gonave," Maitrejean said.

He clapped his hands, and slaves brought a brassbound box.

They were sure-enough pieces-of-eight, Spanish coins. Adam tested several with his teeth and clanked others on the stones of the terrace.

An overseer arrived with Waters and Peterson.

Now here was a pitiful pair, lacerated, bloody, muddy, too. When they saw their skipper the delight on their faces was touching. Once surly, now they groveled. They begged to be taken back.

"Don't know's I want you," Adam growled.

Inside, he felt bad about the business. Maybe he had been too harsh? What right did he have, after all, to be sitting in judgment? Who was he to be waited upon, a pile of silver at his elbow, while foremast hands cringed before him? His common sense repeated that these two were nogoods; but there is more to a man than common sense.

"Lash 'em?" asked the Frenchy.

"Eh?"

"I'd have it indoors then, *monsieur*. You, uh, you understand? The example—"

Adam shook his head.

"You islanders," he muttered. "Like living in a powder magazine."

"It is precisely like that, *monsieur*."

Adam said to the deserters: "You found your way here, now find your way back. And tell Mr. Forbes to get ready to unload."

"Do we have to go through them woods again?" Waters quavered.

46

"A fine pair," Adam said scornfully. "Take a little walk among the trees and you look as if you'd been run through Mister Maitrejean's crushing mill here. And scared half to death."

"It— It was like the Dark Place," Waters whispered.

"We'll have no blasphemy! Go back to the schooner!"

Adam and the planter discussed the deal. Maitrejean sent for his coopers. He caused hands to be called in from the fields.

There was no written contract—after all, this was an illegal transaction —but the agreement was perfect. The two men rose to seal the bargain with a handshake.

A servant announced the arrival of the courier from Gonave. Maitrejean excused himself.

Adam sat down again, his hand still unshaken. He was filled with relief. He had in fact fallen to thinking, after so many failures, that this voyage might be bewitched. There could be a spell over the whole enterprise; and if this was the case suspicion pointed at Deborah Selden as the raiser. Adam didn't like to think this of Deborah, a woman he admired mightily. It must be a terrible thing to be possessed by the Devil, your soul doomed to everlasting torment. But until a little while ago it sure looked as if that might be the case with Obadiah Selden's dark-eyed daughter; and Adam shivered at the thought. Now, however, everything was all right.

The planter came back, and Adam rose to greet him with outstretched hand. But Maitrejean's face was sober.

"I fear, *monsieur,* that we cannot complete our deal."

"Why in tarnation not?"

"You'll esteem me finical. Yet each must do as his honor tells him. I ought to seize your person, but you're my guest."

"What's got into you, man?"

"The news I just received from Gonave."

"Yes?"

"*Monsieur,* your nation and mine are at war."

The runaways were ankle-deep in water that stung their bare bleeding feet and they were waving to the boat that made for them, when Adam Long hurtled out of the jungle.

"Ye grease-bellies!"

He got Peterson with great force in the backside, a kick that fairly seemed to jolt the whole beach. Waters squealed, and dove in time.

"You swam ashore! Now swim back!"

10 WUMP-wump-wump! the drums went. WUMP-wump-wump!

There were not many other noises. Bees hummed indefatigibly. From a kiosk made of palmetto thatch came a faint apologetic spickle of glassware, silverware. The bay's unbelievable green met the equally unbelievable blue of the sea at a reef, smothered in foam now, flashing in the sunlight, and this hissed, steaming, mumbling with faraway impotent rage. But for the most part the drums, beaten back in the hills, had the air to themselves.

WUMP-wump-wump! WUMP-wump-wump!

Horace Treadway looked up from the paper he had been checking. In his thirties, he could have been fifty.

"Damned Ashantis," he muttered. "Never should have been brought over. Never did work the way these Angolans I've got now do. Kept slipping away. Scores of 'em up there. And how they breed!"

"Ain't you afraid of 'em?" asked Adam, wishing that some day some planter would talk about something else besides his slaves.

"Of course I am! They'll swoop, one of these nights. And then all this"—he moved his head in a circular motion—"won't be here any more."

He swallowed punch, then dabbed his lips with a Valenciennes-bordered kerchief. There was Valenciennes at his throat, too, as there was rosepoint over his wrists. This man Treadway would have been a head-turning sight anywhere. His coat, the color of cinnamon, was embroidered four or five inches deep with silver lace, and lined with sky-blue silk. There were silver buckles on his shoes, which had red heels. His small clothes fitted him as though they had been painted on. He wielded a toothpick with his left hand, whilst checking figures with the right. He belched elegantly.

"Oh, and one other thing, Captain. One last little matter."

Adam's heart went small and cold. He did not trust himself to speak. He sipped his punch, and solemnly bowed his head.

"Might I ask you to make a delivery in the continental colonies?"

Adam exhaled again, but a little at a time, in order to make no sound. So that was all? A delivery! He waved his hand.

"Anything," he murmured.

"You come from New England, I believe?"

"Aye."

"Is New York in that colony?"

48

"Well, it's near there."

Treadway nodded. Though they would destroy the papers afterward, he checked everything carefully. They had arrived at a price of four pounds three shillings a barrel, to be paid in molasses; and if these men did not snarl at one another, neither was there any real friendship between them; they came from different worlds. But they respected one another! Adam wondered what Treadway was doing here. The colonies, insular or continental, did not often get his kind. The ones they send us, Adam reflected sourly, are the sweepings, criminals, drunkards, cranks, the whimperers who can't fit in anywhere else, whom nobody wants, not even the Army—not even the *Navy!*

"That is agreed, then, Captain?"

Adam waved.

"Agreed, sir," he murmured.

The Englishman was to provide all the labor. He had even provided a lookout, armed with a large glass, who sat on the roof of the plantation house and swept the sea; at his side was a gong, with which to give an alarm if any suspicious sail was sighted.

Treadway gave another glance, a glance of pure malice, at the hills from whence came the sound of drums—WUMP-wump-wump!—and then returned to the papers. And Adam Long, who conceived it to be his part to look loafy and at ease, his eyes half closed, did exactly this.

Truly, Adam felt good. The sunshine, the scene, the murmur of bees, and the drowsy creak of the windmill, soothed him. He had a sense of returning, of reaching journey's end, his task completed. There would be another task to take up after that—there always was—but just at the moment he could stretch his legs and enjoy himself.

There are gardens and gardens. The ramshackleness of Mr. Pendleton's, the flamboyancy of M. Maitrejean's, were not to be compared with this place. The lush vegetation of the tropics had not been permitted to run riot here, but had been trimmed, pruned, trained. An immense amount of work had gone into the making of this establishment; and it was not just the work of slaves either, of bought muscle. A great deal of thought had been needed, and watchfulness. None of the sloth the climate suggested could be noticed. Weeds had been kept at a minimum. The buildings were painted and in perfect condition. The mill, the carpenter shop, the kennels, stables, field hands' quarters were models of careful upkeep. The kitchen garden was a triumph, with the homely French beans and smug heads of cabbage exactly spaced, serried, looking, in this strange setting, positively exotic. Years of skilled and loving care had gone into the making of the orchards. Since it was not utilitarian, though it was customary, the garden in which Adam sat had not known such special attention as the orchards, clearly Treadway's particular

49

pride; but the garden was clipped and clean, and here, as everywhere else, things were kept in their places.

WUMP-wump-wump!

All the same, he'd be danged if he'd want to live down here, Adam thought. It was too hot. It wasn't healthy. Folks were forever getting fevers; and even the ones without fevers appeared to have forgotten, if they'd ever known, how to step smart. Things *dragged*.

Also he did not care for those glowering field hands. It was not only the danger of an uprising; it was also the very idea of slavery. After all, Adam himself was the son of a slave. They called them indentured servants, but it came to the same thing. His mother had fetched six pound ten on the very deck of the vessel that brought her from Home. It was somewhat less than a healthy nigger would have been knocked down for, and of course it included the infant, Adam. She might have fetched more, maybe even seven pounds, if she had not been so haggard and gray-greenish in the face, being still seasick.

Adam was not crybabying. He had been well treated. Apprenticed to one Mr. Sedgewick, willed by him at death, along with sundry articles of furniture, to his brother, also a joiner, he had learned a trade, had been protected by colonial laws, had not been whipped often—not as often as many a son of free folks he knew—and had been taught his letters, as demanded in the paper. He had been brought up in the fear of God. He'd been given many advantages.

But he had never had a home.

This was not anybody's fault, and Adam was not down on the world because of it. But he was conscious of this lack as a deaf man of his deafness, a blind man of his inability to see. He felt that he wouldn't really live, and be whole, until he had a house of his own.

But it would not be one like this. It would be white and trim, and would have a little white fence around it.

Horace Treadway put the paper down. He came around to Adam, his right hand extended.

"I think we understand one another, Captain."

"Reckon we do," said Adam, and rose and took the hand.

Mr. Treadway summoned slaves and ordered more punch, and when overseers and superintendents came, obsequious silent mulattoes, he gave directions for the unloading and reloading of the *Goodwill*.

"I make quick decisions," he said when they were alone again, "and I have decided that you are a man who can be trusted. Now about that delivery to New York—"

"Anything," Adam said grandly.

"You will be paid a hundred pounds for the service, if this is satisfactory?"

Adam, who had been sipping, almost choked.

It was customary for the planter, after exacting a promise to make a delivery as part of the bargain, to offer to pay for this service, which offer it was customary for the skipper to refuse. No sum was ever mentioned. Certainly no sum like a hundred pounds was even dreamt of.

What was he being asked to tote—the crown jewels?

In any event, and rocked though he was, Adam had not the slightest intention of refusing the offer. The money would be his, not to be shared with any of the crew or with the owners; for this sort of service, by clear agreement, was one of the skipper's prerogatives.

"It'll be enough," he said casually.

"It would be more convenient to pay you here, leaving it to your honor, in case delivery could not be made, to return the money."

He was not buttering Adam. He did trust him, though until a few hours earlier, when Adam had put into this little cove on the north side of Jamaica, these two men had never before seen one another.

"I'll deliver it all right."

"This is a passenger," Treadway said.

"Oh."

That did not make the matter any clearer. Adam assumed that it was a slave he was to transport—a courtesy gift, somebody with some special talent for making something, or doing something, which would appeal to the New York acquaintance. Well, he could be put into the hold, where the incoming molasses would not take up as much room as the outgoing eels had. But what black in all this world would any man be ready to pay one hundred pounds transportation for?

"I have every confidence, though," Treadway added, "that you will get her there."

"*Her?*"

"Yes," said Treadway.

Now here was something out of a different bag entirely. Sure, it still could be some fat old black hag who happened to be an expert seamstress, say, or a celebrated cook; but something told Adam that the passenger was younger. A cast-off doxy? Some seductive coffee-colored *mustee* or *mustefino* whom it was advisable for private reasons to get plumb out of this part of the world? It sounded like that.

Not that for one hundred pounds Adam Long would have refused to carry her if she had been Satan's own sister, complete with horns and tail. It was the matter of discipline he was thinking of. Excepting Seth Selden, the hands, he believed, were of tolerably good character; but all the same, a loose woman in the listless heat of the horse latitudes—

"Is she in good condition? Reason I ask, it might be advisable to keep her below and have the hatch battened down, the whole trip."

"The person we are talking about," said Horace Treadway, "is my cousin, the Honorable Maisie de Lynn Treadway-Paul."

In those days politeness was not obligatory, but it was advisable. Adam leapt to his feet.

"Say, I'm sorrier'n all outside I—"

Treadway tossed a languid handkerchief.

"It is nothing." He rose. "Ah, here she comes now."

And Adam turned, and saw her, and his heart stopped.

It was not only that the lady was lovely: it was that she was *alive*. Most of the white females you saw here in Jamaica looked as if the climate had them licked. They looked pale, drawn, like persons who are suffering inwardly. Nothing stood out about them, everything drooped. The sheen of sweat on their upper lips and on the backs of their hands might have been unavoidable, granted, but assuredly it was not becoming. In short, you felt sorry for them but not impelled toward them. Likely enough they hadn't been any great punkins to start with.

This lady now was as alive as lightning, darned near as dazzling, too. She had a roundish face, perhaps slightly thick across the cheekbones for the most precious taste, but good, a clean face, and exquisitely tinted. She had a small nose washed with faint freckles. Her eyes were light brown with specks of green in them. Most dizzying of all was her hair. It was not powdered, though it was piled high in the formal fashion and surmounted by a huge "commode," a tower made up of rows of plaited muslin stiffened with wire, one above the other. The hair was dark red. It danced. It glistered. Never for an instant was it still, for its colors shifted constantly, so that it fascinated you like a fire in the fireplace, or the sea.

"I'm sure you two will get along well together," the planter said.

Maisie Treadway smiled; and the sun stood still a moment, ashamed.

"Oh, I'm sure we will," she said.

---◆---

PART THREE

Dangerous Waters

11 She interfered with his prayers.

Adam Long was not one of your foul-weather supplicators. He preferred to pray whenever he just happened to feel like it and got the chance. He liked to pray alone, prayers made up as he went along: set prayers he regarded as Romish, and anyway how could you expect the Lord to listen when all you did was recite words somebody else had written down for you? Adam would pray in adversity but he preferred to pray in prosperity, where maybe it meant more. By himself he prayed somewhat as a Quaker might; and it was true that he'd long had a sneaking admiration for that sect; but he was seldom moved to pray aloud, in public places. He would join in the Amens at meeting house but he was not a faithful goer. He insisted upon the service each morning on deck rather for the sake of the immortal souls of the others than for any personal spiritual benefit. Regularity in prayer might well have a good effect on the men, he thought. His own greatest satisfaction was derived from prayers that no one else heard, about matters just between himself and his Maker.

What's more, he did not like to have anybody see him when he prayed. He was not one to mutter a hasty Our Father behind his teeth in a moment of danger. He didn't even like to pray while lying flat in his bunk. He liked to get right down on his knees, the way a man should.

In the cabin this had been easy. He and Forbes kept it clean, and not often had they both been there at the same time.

In the forecastle, matters were different. It was a small forecastle in the first place, and Jethro Gardner, Eb Waters, John Bond, Carl Peterson, Abel Rellison, and Eliphalet Mellish had filled it before the unexpected arrival of Seth Selden. Now Captain Long and Mate Forbes were added to this company.

True, Peterson and Waters for the time being were on deck, for that's where the irons were; but even so, their chests remained in the forecastle.

The men took it well, at first. They even seemed amused by the spectacle of skipper and mate turned out of their quarters.

It was all a lark for the lady, and she sought to win the hands to her by circulating and smiling among them; and for a while she did.

Most of them had never seen anything like her, no more than had Adam Long. Her hair, the flecks of green in her brown eyes, the swift-striking warmth of her smile, the clothes she wore—these, even without her affability, would have dizzied the hands. She was obviously eager to please them, an attitude that flattered. "Lady Maisie" they called her. It could be that a shadow of gawkiness about her, as though she had not yet got used to the length of her own legs, touched their hearts. It certainly touched Adam's. What was she doing here? What was the matter with her friends, that they let her go off to a strange wild land alone? Why did Horace Treadway offer such a thumping sum when he booked passage for her on a small smuggling vessel whose skipper he had only just met? Now and then Adam would catch her when she was not smiling at anybody, not chatting, or even conscious that she was being watched: she'd stare out across the sea, not necessarily toward England, not back over the way she had come, but anywhere, and there would be an expression of unutterable loneliness in her face. She'd look so lost! She shouldn't be here. She ought to be back in London, dancing at a rout, pirouetting, flirting, not zigzagging in the company of colonial louts through some of the most dangerous waters in the world.

Treadway had come aboard to speak his farewell to her, but it was formal enough. The two had kissed, of course; and they had called one another "cousin"; but Adam, who had steeled himself to witness a tearful leavetaking, thought the business downright brusque. Nor had she stayed at the taffrail, waving an idiotic small handkerchief, for more than the few minutes it took to row Treadway ashore; and then she had gone promptly below, where her boxes, baskets, hampers, chests, bottles, bedrolls, and bundles had been put.

Perhaps an hour later the slide went back and the Honorable Maisie de Lynn Treadway-Paul's head appeared. She tossed Adam a smile.

"La, Captain! Would you be good enough to dispatch the *valet de chambre* to me, pray?"

He bowed—in part to hide his face.

"Sure will, ma'am."

The head disappeared, the slide was closed. Adam and the man at the wheel looked at one another.

"What in Hell's a *valet de chambre?*"

"There's no need for profanity," Adam said. "It— It's a kind of servant, I think."

"Didn't know she had a servant with her."

"Hasn't. Reckon it's up to us to supply one."

Thoughtful, he went forward. *Goodwill* carried no regular cook. Just abaft the foremast there was a sandbox made of bricks, and anybody who wanted to could cook anything he drew from the larder at any time he wished—subject, naturally, to regulations the captain might announce from time to time. It worked out well enough. Salt pork and Poor John and jerked beef, with bread when they could get it, and fish when they could catch any, made up most of their diet; and these things don't call for a fancy kitchen. It was understood that the skipper, mate and bosun did not have to cook their own food but could order anybody else to do so at any time; but in fact each of these officers took a hand now and then as circumstances suggested. There were no set meal times. They ate when they got hungry, that's all.

The whole crew was there this noon. There was a spitted goat Mr. Treadway had given them as a farewell gift. It had been roasted a luscious golden-brown. Yet when Adam was first offered some he shook his head. He was studying these men.

At first he thought of Seth Selden, who, in his middle forties, was, with Jeth Gardner, by far the oldest person aboard. Seth was spry, but no man at that age could nimble it like an ordinary hand. Which is to say, Seth could be spared, except in a blow. But could Seth be trusted in a lady's bedchamber? Probably not. Not off soundings anyway.

Adam then went to the other extreme, his gaze falling upon Abel Rellison, who at thirteen was really a boy and was only being paid a boy's wages, though often enough he did the work of a man. Abel was a good lad, earnest, not flip. Adam stabbed a finger at him.

"You!"

"Aye, sir," and Rellison rose.

"You're the *valet de chambre*."

"What's that?"

"I don't know. Go to the cabin and find out. Don't forget to knock before you go in. And after that do whatever she tells you to."

"Empty her pottie, I expect," said Seth Selden.

This was in plain truth what Abel was told to do, for Lady Maisie had brought with her, among so many other things, a private close-stool, a contraption that folded in an ingenious manner, not looking at all like what it was; but so long as he was there, she had set the lad about other duties as well, helping her ladyship to get the cabin straightened up. When he returned he was agog.

"Never saw so many bottles of perfume! *Shelves* of 'em! And there's all kinds of jars and bowls of stuff that looks like bear grease, only it don't smell that way. Now she wants the steward. Who's he?"

"You again, I guess," Adam said. "You seem to be doing all right."

"Sure!" And he raced aft.

"Why not take her a handful of goat?" somebody called.

She came up on deck two hours later. How all the unguents and ointments and patches and powder had been disposed, Adam was sure he did not know; for though she did smell sweet—it could have been her natural smell, at that—surely she had not painted her face like the wicked Jezebel, who got thrown out of a window for it. There might have been a smitch of powder, but there was no pigment. Adam looked.

She was dressed in drugget—a flaring bodice, a wide-spreading skirt, the color of salmon—and wore a white petticoat swagged with rosepoint. She wore dark green doeskin gloves. Her head was bare.

The Rellison boy had been sent away some time before. He was still telling the crew about it. Adam himself was at the tiller, for two reasons. He feared that a seaman stationed there might be tempted to peer down past the scuttle into the cabin, spying out the wonders Abel Rellison had prated of, maybe spying something else, too. The other reason was that Adam Long wanted to peer down there himself and see if he couldn't find out what she had done to his cabin. He believed he could do this without appearing to, but he didn't want any witnesses while he tried.

She had some difficulty getting up, what with the hoop-petticoat, and he helped her. She was wearing dark green stockings and small soft yellow shoes with crimson velvet roses at the instep.

She thanked him cheerily. He did not bow. He had thought this out. If he bowed every time he encountered his passenger—well, he'd be bowing a good part of the time. And bowing was not so easy when you were bowling along on a careless sea with a tomboyish wind behind you.

He was not accustomed to bare-headed women, and the sight fussed him even more than the sight of her stocking had done.

They stood there for a time, talking of this and that, Adam didn't rightly remember what. She told him that she was sure she was going to be comfortable and that she did hope she wasn't putting them to any inconvenience; and he cried "Oh, no!" She said that this seemed the pleasantest part of the boat, right back here where they were; and Adam said he would rig an awning for her here tomorrow.

Adam raised his eyes, but they encountered the upper part of the lady's bodice, which, very low, was trimmed with muslin, maybe not enough of it; and his temples pounded, and sweat sprang out around his mouth, so that he put his gaze down to the deck again in a hurry.

"The sailors—didn't I hear them singing a while ago?"

"There was a chantey, while they were having the hook up."

"It was a charming little thing. So— So *pastorale*."

"Well—"

"D'ye suppose they could sing it again?"

They did, and with glee. They sat along the taffrail and kept time with their hands, and for the most part they remembered never to start the verses that were not proper to this occasion, though at least once they slipped.

"*Magnifique!*" cried the passenger, and she laughed so hard that they all had to laugh, too. She and Adam were seated on the scuttle, and she put her head on Adam's shoulder a moment.

She had a mouth that seemed small in repose, though it was not often in repose; yet when she laughed it was seen to be large, but at all times it was well formed, full; and she had exquisite teeth.

"La, la, Captain, 'tis good for the gizzard not to have to be a lady of *ton* quite *all* the time!"

She pulled away, patting his arm and looking up at him, laughing. She had a mouth—

"Must be," said Adam.

"You there, Rellison. In my room you'll find a brace of bottles of French brandy, in the locker on the left. Fetch 'em up. I want you to give them to the boys, as a reward for their singing."

Oh, they loved her—that first night.

It was the next morning that the trouble started.

12   Adam was up at first light, his heart high in his chest. At dawn it was always like this. Given visibility, the *Goodwill* could keep away from anything that swam the seas—except maybe oared harbor boats in a time of calm—but each time the sky grayed, and especially if the night had been moonless, you looked around, staring so hard that your eyeballs ached, fearful lest some warship or worse should loom out of the murk all too close. Ships didn't show lights and they seldom struck bells when they were hunting. You might find yourself within gunshot of pretty near anything. You could even be in the middle of an enemy fleet. It had happened.

This morning the horizon held only a brig, but it was a large one, dead ahead. It was Spanish; and they fell off. The Spaniard, following them, was easily outpaced; but he was in sight until early afternoon. And no sooner had they made about on a northeasterly course again than they raised another vessel, a Frencher, which went for them with the velvety silent swiftness of a cat.

Between these raisings Adam was sent to take a look at Eliphalet Mellish.

Eli was a Newport boy, gnarled, never said anything, no beauty but a good worker. Now he had the fever, bad. His face was so hot it burned your hand, and it was steamed with sweat. He rampaged from side to side as though determined to break the bones of his own body. His eyes were shut. He didn't seem to hear anything you said.

Nobody knew when he'd been taken. He had stood his watch, night before. He'd attended prayers. But then, he was always a quiet one.

Eli had been ashore at Mr. Treadway's. But—here's the realization that douched them—they all had been, every man-jack of 'em.

His breathing was horrid to hear, a sort of rattle.

They washed his face and neck and they loosened his clothing. There wasn't much else they could think of. John Bond suggested burning one of the big sulphur candles, but Adam shook his head.

"They're for purifying the air, and it takes two-three days with everything battened down. They'd kill him, you burn 'em in here."

An hour later, when Lady Maisie came on deck, after having breakfasted below, Adam made no mention of Eliphalet Mellish. Some people, he knew, were superstitious.

She herself seemed in the best of health, though *Goodwill* was standing about a bit, the seas being tolerably high.

They chatted by the taffrail. She was not a high-and-mighty lady, really. She was easy to talk to. He let her hold the tiller, and showed her how to watch the compass, and how to make the schooner come around to the compass card rather than try to make the compass card come 'round to fit the schooner, as your landsman customarily did. This entertained her, and while she did it he rigged the awning he had promised.

Once she looked back. She couldn't have been wearing a heap of clothes under the gown, for just turning thrust out the curves of her breast and hips. Her neck was sheer cream and he wished he could kiss it. This morning she wore a black lace scarf over her head, tied beneath her chin, a Spanish-looking thing. A few strands of hair had leapt loose and were flipping and curling.

"What's that boat behind us, Captain?"

"Came from Petit Guave way. A Frencher. She likes the looks of us."

"We're not running *away* from them?"

"Sure are."

"By this compass it says we're going almost straight south?"

"That's right, ma'am."

"But New York is *north* of here, isn't it?"

"Yes, but that Frencher's north of here, too. We won't get back on our proper course till after dark. We can lose her then."

"Why can't we go 'way over to the east or west?"

"There's only just so far to go. I'll show you on the chart. Look— This is the Windward Passage here, between Hispaniola on one side and Cubie on the other. That's maybe fifty-sixty miles. And the French, they got havens at Leogane here and at Petit Guave. They're fast sailors, too."

"D'ye think there's any danger, Captain?"

He shrugged.

She asked: "These privateers—"

"Ain't so much the privateers I'm worried about. The hands—they sometimes call this place Pirate Alley."

"I see." She gave him a smile, the first real one that morning. "Well, with you managing us, Captain, I'm not afraid."

"Thank you, ma'am. I try to do my best."

She went below; and ten minutes later they came to tell Adam that the patient was dead. He had a hard time believing it. They all did. Crammed into the forecastle there, as many as could get in, leaning far over, they examined Mellish again and again, taking his shirt off, putting their ears against his chest. They could detect no heart beat, no pulse. The sweat was beginning to dry on face and neck, and indeed all over, but the skin was still furiously hot. The drying sweat, sort of slimy, stank.

They didn't want to dispose of him until they were stone certain he was dead, but at the same time they didn't want to keep the corpse here if it really was a corpse. It was late June now, and most prodigiously hot, even for those parts.

They were quiet, for they were all scared.

They worked some threads out of a shirt and held these over his open mouth, and the threads did not stir—or most of them *thought* that they had not stirred.

"If we only had a mirror," said Jethro Gardner.

Adam said to the boy Rellison: "Go ask her ladyship if I can borrow a mirror. Don't tell her what we want it for."

He was back in a few moments with a thing with a long handle, a cream-colored thing grotesquely out-of-place in the forecastle, the mirror part of it octagonal, the edges inset with nacre, the back an Arcadian scene, mostly shepherdesses, in pink and light blue. There were ribbons attached to it, for no ascertainable reason.

"She says to tell you that the next time the handsome captain wants to look at his reflection why don't he come and borrow this himself? That's what she said."

It was a harmless enough message—silly, yes, but given the circumstances, not in bad taste. It was only meant to be playful, you could even say gracious. After all, Maisie did not know that a man had just died up here. Adam felt like pointing this out to the others, who scowled; but he didn't.

The mirror, held a long time over Eli Mellish's mouth, showed not the faintest film. Adam sighed and sent it back.

"See he's sewed up. And seal his box. I'll get the Book."

Late that afternoon, when she came on deck to watch a sensational sunset, she commented on the quietness of the crew. They were so subdued! Not at all like last night, when they'd been gay.

Adam mumbled something. This was not because he was ill at ease. *Physically* she unsettled him; in her presence, even sometimes when she was not there, he suffered a prickling of the skin, all over, that could only be a yearning for the lusts of the flesh, and, recognizing this, he fought it. But *socially* he was comfortable with her. In the past he had more than once wondered what a lady would be like, to meet. He had pictured something formidable, difficult to approach or even to address. Maisie, now, was as human as your next-door neighbor. Her smile was genuine—it wasn't a thing to be fished out of her reticule and fastened on her face from time to time as the occasion suggested. It came from inside.

Adam guessed that she was not sure of herself. Sometimes she was shockingly bold, forward; but of a sudden she would come all over shy, and fall silent. No doubt she was forever reproaching herself about this. She wanted to be liked, maybe even loved. After all, don't most folks?

"Don't look too chirk yourself," he commented. "Thinking of home?"

Two things about her flummoxed him, being utterly different from what he had known, and these were her clothes and her manner of speaking.

Never had he seen such clothes, even the time he'd been to Philadelphia: frills, flounces, furbelows—ribbons and laces galore—velvet, chine silk, drugget, sagathy cloth, colebatteen, holland, muslin, drap du Barre— As for colors, there were colors he had not known the existence of: yellow and Nile green or yellow and vermilion were her favorite combinations. She was not narrow in her taste, nor yet timid.

He never saw her wear the same thing twice. He could not imagine how she had managed to stow all those stuffs and accoutrements into the one small cabin. They never showed mussed either, never wilted by the heat. It was an act of magic every time Lady Maisie came topside.

As for her speech, some of her words were strange, maybe French. But not many. And he could always understand her if he listened carefully. Her voice, her intonation, rather than any choice of topics, ringingly proclaimed her station; yet she was anything but high-and-mighty. She had a few tricks of speech, of an exclamatory nature, that Adam reckoned were fashionable—leastways he could see no other sense to them. For instance, she'd cry "La!" or "Oh, la!" or maybe "La, la!" every now and then, almost as if she did not know that she was doing it, as though it were an unconscious uncontrollable physiological act, like a hiccup. She'd talk very fast, in spurts, with silences that came suddenly, as though she were catching her breath in, being frightened to realize how she'd rattled.

This evening she was a touch bitter.

"Home? No. Nor is anybody there thinking of me. They're too happy to be rid of me."

He made no reply, and she stared at the sunset as though she thought it had no right to be as sensational as all that.

"Oh, la! 'tis still dear-Maisie this and Maisie-my-love that, but the truth of the matter is they've been shunting me around like a poor relation—which is just what I am, come to think on it—ever since I lost my fortune. Horace back there"—she jerked her head in the wrong direction but Adam knew that she meant Jamaica—"was just the latest. No, he couldn't do anything for me either. Lacked even the influence to get me permission to leave the island. That's why I had to be smuggled out like a criminal. Unless Horace was willing to settle my debts, which he wasn't."

"Oh," said Adam.

"So now I go to New York, which I take it is a barbarous hovel, and I'll appeal to another cousin, a mighty remote one, I can tell you—a man I've never met and probably wouldn't consent to meet in London."

She turned suddenly to him and put a hand on his arm. She looked right at him, close.

"Forgive me, Captain. La, sir, you'll think me a sniveller. It ain't that I mind losing fifty thousand pounds—never did learn where it went—it ain't that."

"No?"

"It's the way my friends behaved. It's a blow on the head for any infatuated fool like me."

"I can see where it would be."

"There was one was going to marry me. I believed him. I let him do things a lady shouldn't, Captain. And then he changed his mind. He forgot what he'd promised. That was one reason why I went to Jamaica."

She turned back to the taffrail, and was silent a moment, swallowing.

"I— I'm sorry, Captain. I won't do that again. Now let's talk about something else."

"All right," said Adam.

Hours later, after night had come, and Adam chanced to be alone on the afterdeck for a short time, he went to the scuttle and squatted beside it and cocked his head, listening. Yes. He nodded as he came away. Yes, she was sobbing down there in the darkness, the poor lovely woman, the lonesome one. She was sobbing as if her heart would break.

13 For more than a week they beat up toward or into the Windward Passage, only to be chased back each time. They took chances, doing things Adam Long would not ordinarily have authorized. They sailed close to the shore of Cuba, close to the shore on the other side, near Mole St. Nick, a corsairs' crossroads if ever there was one; and more than once they tried to make it right smackety-blank up the center. The result was the same in every case. They had to run, hard. There was always a sail in the wrong place at the wrong time. The nights were too bright, the seas too rough. Even the winds, which might have been expected to be regular, came and went erratically in short gusty chuffs: it was as though God coughed.

Captain Long, though he gave the necessary commands, was scarcely aware of this luck.

He told Maisie: "It's different where I hail from. There ain't any ladies or gentlemen there—only the men that have property and the ones that don't, and even the ones that have don't have much. And everybody works, all the time."

He told her: "Sure I quote the Book a lot. That's the best place to find an answer in. But even then you can't always be certain. I know *I* can't anyway. There's good on one side, there's evil on the other. That much I do know. What I'm not always sure about is, which side is which?"

He told her: "Times I think I'm scared to see England. I've thought so much about it, ever since I can remember. I reckon my mother told me a heap, though I can't recollect much of that. Must've been too little then. But I'm sailing there soon, now that I got my own command. And I'm heading straight for London, and I'm going to seek out this man, Sir Jervis Johnston—you let his name slip last night—the one that, well, that didn't marry you." He all but said "betrayed you," which would have sounded inexcusably dirty and vulgar, applied to such a lovely lady. "And when I find him I'm going to kill him."

" 'Vengeance is mine,' saith the Lord."

"Well, it's going to be mine, too, in this case."

"There are laws against murder in London, Captain."

"I'll do it fair. I'll call him out."

She started to laugh, but she sobered when she saw how much he meant it. She leaned even closer, dropped her voice, touched his arm.

"You must not even think of it. What's done is done. You know what they say—'You can't unscramble scrambled eggs.' You couldn't win me anything back, Captain, though it's a thought full of sweetness. Look at it that way. And besides, Jervis is an experienced swordsman. He's fenced all his life. While you—oh, it isn't your fault, I'm not saying that!—but probably you have never had a real sword in your hand."

"I'll learn," Adam muttered. "I'll take lessons."

They leapt into their acquaintanceship with an avidity that astonished both, as if they had been waiting years to get at one another. There was no reconnoitering, such as might have been expected; nor did either sniff the air, test the wind. They just sat down beside one another and talked —and talked.

He told her about his mother, "the Duchess," and how the townspeople had disliked her and still made fun of her memory.

"I asked you, a while back, if you was homesick. Now, the good Lord help us, I'm asking myself the same question." He waggled his hands. *"How can a man that's never had a home be homesick?* But I am."

One night he mentioned bundling, and she, piqued, asked for details. Adam had assumed that she didn't bundle, but he was amazed to learn that she had never even heard of the practice.

"It's mostly a matter of saving tallow. Firewood, too. It's for poor folks —but then, we're most all poor folks in Newport."

"But in the summer—"

"Summer's the worst. Ain't much sparking then. Days're so long. Sunup to sundown folks work—men, women, kids. That don't leave much time to sleep. Bundling's for winter. They sit up in front of the fire a while, and then the old folks say good night, and pretty soon the girl she gets up and says she's going to bed, too, and he gives her a little time, the young man that's sparking her, and then he blows out the candle and goes and gets in with her. But he gives her a little time first."

"To let her hair down? To get undressed?"

"Wouldn't know about her hair. I guess that's depending on how she feels. But she don't get undressed. I told you that. And neither does he. They just get under the blankets the way they are."

"Shoes, too?"

"Well, I wouldn't know. I reckon if they're finical they might take their shoes off. Can't see's it makes much difference."

"It might to the servant who has to wash the sheets."

"Don't have sheets."

"The blankets then."

"That'd be the girl herself anyway. If she don't squawk, no reason why anybody else should."

"And how long does he stay? All night?"

"If she lets him and he wants to."

"If she lets him what?"

"Lets him stay all night. But most likely he gets out around midnight. Depending on how far away he lives. If it's eight-ten miles, and he's got to walk, and get to work at sunup, he leaves earlier."

"That's real love!"

"Well, sometimes it is and sometimes it ain't."

"How does the swain keep his hands to himself?"

"He don't. But all the same, he's got to be careful where he puts 'em. Lots of girls tie their skirt and petticoat down at the bottom, over their shoes."

" 'Tis said love laughs at locksmiths."

"Course, she knows how to hold him off. She won't let him get in with her again, he don't behave."

"But what *do* they do, then?"

"Oh, hug and kiss. All like that."

"And what if it gets too much for both of them?"

"Well, likely enough, it begins to work up to that, the mother or father will call out and tell 'em to stop."

"From the next room, you mean?"

"If they're in the next room."

"If they're—"

"Might be in the same room, of course. We don't have so many rooms in our houses as an English earl, ma'am. Tarnation, they might even be in the same *bed!* Lots of times they are."

He could feel her scan his face then, and he knew what she was thinking. She feared she was being gulled. Of all matters not pertaining to fashionable London she was singularly ignorant; and being young, and alone, a woman, she hesitated. Indeed Lady Maisie often, even in the course of these little chats on the afterdeck, seemed tense as though to repel laughter—or to counterattack with it. The folks she was brought up among, the way Adam figured it, must have been forever trying to find some excuse for jeering at other folks. She did not have to worry about that with him, as she was learning. It could be that here was one reason she liked so much to talk with him. For she did like it. He knew that.

"I, uh, I don't want to sound libidinous, Captain."

"No."

"And I know this ain't maidenly. But—d'ye mind telling me if it ever happens that the mother and father are asleep, and that cord around the feet, the one that holds the skirt down, breaks?"

"It's been known to. But not so often as you might think."

This was night, which was just as well. The moon hadn't come up

64

yet. They sat close together on the bench Adam had constructed under the awning, backs to the taffrail, and spoke in whispers, so that the man at the tiller couldn't hear: it was John Bond. The day had been a scorcher, and the deck still glowed, throwing up heat like something made of metal.

"*Then* what do they do?"

"Well, just what you'd expect."

"Yes?"

"And then they wait and see if she's going to have a baby, and if she is, they get married."

"Always?"

"Pretty near. If they don't get married before she has the baby, they do right afterward. And the way folks figure, it's no sin."

"*Provided* they get married, you mean?"

"Oh, sure. They got to do that."

She studied this a moment, her head down, staring at the tar that still bubbled, if sluggishly, in the deck seams.

"Have you ever—bundled?"

It caught him off guard, though there's no reason why it should have. He gulped. He gave a short laugh.

"Me? Who'd want me?"

She said almost coldly: "I'm sure I don't know why not?" And it came to him that she didn't believe him.

"No money," he said, trying to make it sound light. "No property. I'll have it some day, but not yet."

"Lord ha' mercy! Must you shove your accounting books ahead of you, to prove you're solvent, every time you climb into bed with a wench?"

He came near to snapping at her then. He felt like shouting that it was all very well for her—that could talk about losing fifty thousand pounds—to make light of the need for money. Why, there wasn't as much as fifty thousand pounds in cash and property, he didn't reckon, in the whole Colony of Rhode Island and the Providence Plantations. And she could just mislay it, and yet—

But he didn't snap. He swallowed furtively, and even produced a laugh.

"Well, anyway. I never did bundle," he said.

"You certainly seem to know a might about it."

"We talk about it, back there. All sorts of folks. It ain't thought any sin or shame, not any more'n the way you and I're talking now."

"No," softer. "No, I see nothing wrong with the way we're talking now."

"Neither'n I do, ma'am."

He did not make any mention of Deborah Selden, not any more than he did of Elnathan Evans. Matter of fact, he scarcely thought of them these days.

Adam did not do all the talking. For long spells, for hours, she would run on about London. He had a heap of curiosity about London, and prodded her with questions; but he had to admit that though he listened to her carefully he couldn't make a great deal of sense out of what she said. She made more mention of people than of places, and she supposed, it'd seem, that he knew them well or at least had always heard of them. She caught herself up, apologetically, sometimes; and she would under-breathe of "Archie" that he was the Marquis of This, or of "Polly" that she was the Countess of That, rattling on self-consciously afterward as if she feared that he might think her condescending.

She seemed to know some pretty exalted folks, but she never mentioned the Earl of Tillinghast. Neither did he.

Though he tried, he did not truly learn much about the fifty thousand pounds. It, or property of about that value, had been left to her by her father, the late Earl of Ellison. She had no brother, no sister. The title, together with the seat, were held now by a cousin she didn't like—and who didn't like her. This cousin and certain others, a handful of dishonest lawyers, too, had somehow held back or grabbed the entire sum. "My fortune," she sometimes called it—glibly, immediately, too, as though it were a snuffbox or some similar small article, something that, having been misplaced, might at any moment be found again.

Adam pondered this, as he pondered many matters in those days and nights of trying to get up through the Windward Passage; but he noticed little else, so that late in the afternoon of the ninth day out of Jamaica when he saw the delegation coming aft to talk with him, he was rocked on his heels and not ready.

As soon as he saw them he knew what the trouble was.

14   Not only was there no manner of quarterdeck or poop, but the traditional "boundary line" of the mainmast was not respected aboard *Goodwill to Men*. Anyone who wanted to go aft for any reason at all, even if it was only to stretch his legs, was free to do so. Because their quarters were back there—or until recently had been—and also because the after end of the deck was the best place from which to give orders, it was thought of as primarily the domain of Captain Long, Mate Forbes, and to a lesser extent the bosun, Jethro Gardner.

However, there was usually a seaman at the tiller, and like as not he'd have another hand perched on the taffrail nearby in order to carry on a gam with him. This wasn't sacred, this territory.

All the same, when he saw the whole crew coming toward him, Adam knew that it was a deputation, not a coincidence. There was a purposefulness about the party that couldn't be mistaken. They might have been marching to music.

They were all there except Resolved Forbes, who had just been relieved by his skipper and had no doubt turned in.

Had they picked a time when the mate was asleep? Or was that chance?

They all nodded, and the Rellison boy touched his cap.

Adam didn't say anything.

How in Tophet could I've missed this? he was asking himself. *It must have been making up for days—and me bunking there!*

Abel Rellison went to the tiller, as he was in duty-bound to do at this hour; but it was plain from the way he had walked aft with them and the way he faced them now, that he was part of it.

Jeth Gardner was not part of it, though he was there. He stayed a bit to one side. He was troubled, and kept watching Adam, to whom it was clear that the bosun, though sympathizing with the men, still thought of himself as an officer and was not going to have any part of any remonstrance.

Carl Peterson and Eb Waters were there. They had been released after only a couple of days in irons. They were not obliged to work, though they could work if they felt like it. They were not drawing any pay now.

John Bond was there, shuffling from foot to foot, striving to look grim, actually unsure of himself, side-watching Seth Selden for a cue.

Seth was the ringleader. That was obvious. Seth ordinarily went out of his way to be informal with the skipper, taking advantage of his age and of the fact that he owned a lay in the schooner. But today he was angry. He cleared his throat.

"Cap'n, we want to speak to you."

Adam nodded. He glanced toward the scuttle. It was open a trifle. It'd have to be. There was no port in that cabin, and if the slide was fully closed for long in weather like this, Maisie'd stifle down there. Unless she was asleep now she could not help overhearing everything.

"Captain, we demand that you put back for Jamaica and discharge our passenger."

"Oh, you do, eh?"

"We do."

"You demand it?"

"Yes, sir."

"I am the master of this vessel," said Adam.

He should be seething. Instead he felt only sorrow—sorrow for the end of those talks here on the afterdeck. They had been such a comfort! Why was it that they had to cease? He looked around him, nodding thoughtfully, studying their faces; and he saw clearly that, come what may, he and Lady Maisie would never again be permitted the childish delight in one another's company they had known these past nine days. That's exactly what it had been, too—childish. It was innocent. He wondered whether these men, his hands, thought it was anything else. The Seth Selden who faced him had, again, a bobbing Adam's apple, an outjutting chin that suggested a pumphandle: this was the meetinghouse Seth Selden, not the scamp off soundings. Acid was in his eyes; flint clipped along the edges of his voice.

Adam hooked his thumbs into the top of his breeches. His feet were spread—though the truth is, *Goodwill* barely moved, having found a dead spot in the air just off the eastern tip of Cuba.

"When I need advice," Adam added, "I'll ask for it."

Nobody moved. Indeed, even the schooner, which had been shushing along languidly enough, as though striving to listen to this talk, slid to an utter, soundless stop; and the canvas, no longer spottily filling and falling, hung lank entirely.

Seth Selden took a step toward the skipper. Adam did not double his fist. With one blow he could have knocked Deborah's uncle clear into the sea; but he forbore.

Truth is, he admired Seth Selden in just that moment. Seth made him think of the screeching prophets of the Book, the men who were always scolding folks. Those men could not have been very pleasant company; you wouldn't want to pull up a stool and have a gam with any of them; but they possessed magnificence—Amos, Ezekial, Habakkuk Jeremiah, all the rest.

"*That woman*"—and a bony forefinger went toward the hatch slide as though Seth were hurling a javelin—"*has you bewitched!*"

Adam swallowed, holding himself. His chin rested on his chest. He did not look down at the deck, for that might have seemed cowhearted, but neither did he look directly at Seth Selden, afraid that a sight of the man's quivering face would cause rage to leap uncontrollably within him.

"*I tell you the woman's a witch! She's a slave of the Arch-Fiend, pledged to him with her blood!*"

"Speaking of blood—"

But Seth Selden was out of control now. He windmilled his arms.

"*She's put her sign upon you and upon this vessel! She's delivering us all into the hands of Satan!*"

"If there's any witch has anything to do with this," said Adam, still

68

tolerably mild, "it's your niece. *There's* somebody that's really possessed."

"You lie! There never was a witch in our family!" He jabbed his finger again, in that splendid Old Testament manner, at the scuttle. *"Do you deny that that woman has wheedled you and blinded you—as sure as ever Delilah blinded Samson at Gaza?"*

"She didn't. Delilah, I mean. All she did was cut off his hair. The Philistines blinded him later."

"Do you deny that she has cast a diabolical net over you and—"

Adam glanced at the scuttle. He shouldn't have let himself get into a word-battle like this. It was undignified, even indecent.

Coldly he cut in: "The Honorable Miss Treadway-Paul is our passenger. She'll require an apology. But not now. Go forward."

"The Honorable Miss Treadway-Paul is a Whore of Babylon!" shrieked Seth, whereupon Adam knocked him down.

I oughtn't to have done that, Adam thought right away. It made him a mite sick to look at the man, crumpled up in the scuppers there, limp as a rag, moaning. He had punched without meaning to, stirred by a word. It was true that he was the skipper of the schooner and faced with what might be the beginning of a mutiny. Something had had to be done; and Seth Selden, in his state of frenzy, never would have listened to mere words, no matter how loudly shouted. All the same, Seth was a smaller man than Adam and twice Adam's age.

Seth got to his hands and knees, and the moaning ceased. It was Adam's impulse to go to him, to help him up, tell him he was sorry, even conceivably to give him some of the second half of that bottle of rum. But a captain has his position to think of.

Adam cleared his throat, hooked his right thumb back into the top of his breeches. He nodded at Seth Selden, and said to the bosun: "Put him in his bunk."

Truculent, though troubled, afraid to look Adam in the eye but with his fists made, Carl Peterson stepped out.

"Ain't you going to listen to what we got to say?"

Adam looked at him.

"No," said Adam.

So that's the way they all stood, there in that space none too big for such a crowd, and each, frightened, was wondering what if anything he ought to do.

The Rellison boy had both hands on the tiller, though *Goodwill* lay in a dead calm with no way on her at all, and no doubt he was debating whether he'd have time to pull this out and get swinging it, in case of a fracas—or perhaps whether he'd have the nerve to do so.

John Bond looked more shocked than scared, as though at something sacrilegious.

Seth Selden rose, groggy; but his head was clearing. Left alone, he would recover his senses, might even apologize to Adam afterward—not that Adam cared about that, one way or the other. But the madness had not completely ebbed out of Seth. In a fight right now he'd be a maniac, finding strength no man should have.

Peterson glared at the deck at the skipper's feet, trying to screw up courage for a rush; and behind him his friend Eb Waters waited for the signal.

Jeth Gardner the bosun was trying to make up his mind whether to obey orders and take Seth Selden forward or to run forward himself and fetch the mate. Either way, he would leave his skipper unsupported for a spell.

Bewitched, eh? was Adam's thought. And they had been so happy, the two of them, sitting here talking about things.

Well, something had to happen, and happen fast. He was the skipper.

Peterson was the one to flatten—first. Then wheel on young Rellison, who was thinking of yanking out the tiller bar but who could be caught before he made up his mind. Jeth would leap on Waters—and hold off John Bond.

And of course yell bloody murder all the while, which would rouse Resolved Forbes.

Yet if Peterson didn't go down—

He took a step toward Peterson, a big man.

"Boats abeam us! Larboard!"

It would not be necessary to shout for Resolved Forbes. The mate had waked of his own accord; or it could be he had been awakened by some deep instinct, some seventh sense, signaling peril. Blinking in the late afternoon sunshine which goldplated the deck, he had emerged from the forecastle—to see something none of them had yet noticed.

From the dark low shore of Cuba, a few scant miles away, boats were putting out. They were small boats, and though some had masts, none spread a sail, for canvas would have been useless in that calm.

There was no town in sight on that shore, no sign of habitation, and smoke did not rise anywhere. But there were many of these boats—dozens of them, scores.

They were making for the schooner.

15

Nobody hesitated to obey Adam. The family fight was over, or at least suspended.

Adam ordered out the sweeps. Every inch of canvas already was spread, and it was *Goodwill's* lightest suit of sails, but there wasn't enough wind to shiver the reefpoints.

The sweeps alone would not move the vessel fast enough to get away from these coasters, who could swarm over it before the coming of night, or immediately thereafter. The best Adam could hope for was to get a movement that might help pick up some stray breeze and hold the schooner ahead of the coasters until after dark. Once the sun had gone down there was an excellent chance of a land breeze that would take *Goodwill* away from this shore.

There were six sweeps, ash oars long and clumsy. Adam ordered the Moses over, together with a cable, assigning Peterson and Waters, stout backs, to this pull.

The coasters got closer. They did not appear to hurry. They knew what they were doing, had done it before.

Six sweeps, five men. Adam hollered for Maisie, who came promptly. He pointed to a sweep. She made no fuss, wasted no time.

Though they strained mightily, the sweat rolling down them, *Goodwill* barely stirred. It rained; and they toiled on; and the rain went away; but they had scarcely moved.

The coasters, the wreckers, crept closer. More and more of them kept putting out—it was a large fleet.

Adam rested on his sweep, studying them. *They* were scarcely working, with their small boats, yet they would certainly overhaul *Goodwill* before the sun, smearing the sky with red right now, scrounched down behind Cuba. They knew these blind spots off their coast. They were sure of themselves.

"This won't be enough," Maisie panted.

"Aye."

Adam thought of, and winced to think of all those dirty beastly men on his schooner, scrabbling aboard of her, swarming over her. They were vermin; and *Goodwill* was clean, always had been clean. Doubtless they'd burn her after stripping her of all her fittings. But it was not this thought that chilled her master. It was the thought of them polluting her, making her all sticky with their nastiness.

He went to the gunwale. He couldn't even be sure that they were moving at all. He looked up at the canvas. Reddened, it still hung without life.

"All right, stop it," Adam called. "Jeth, have the boat in."

"What're you going to do?" asked the bosun.

To Maisie, Adam said: "Go below again. I don't want them to see you."

He pulled in her sweep and shipped it, as he had done with his own. He doubted that the coasters had seen those sweeps. The Moses, yes; but there would be nothing to indicate, from that distance, that the Moses was striving to tow.

"It's *something*," pleaded Jethro Gardner.

"Ain't enough," Adam said.

"But we can't *fight*'em!"

"No," said Adam. "We can't fight them."

He got out his glass and studied the coasters.

Here were no storybook characters. They did not sport earrings, bandannas, wide-topped boots. They did not aspire to roam the seas, never dreamed of capturing any big prize. Small pickings were what they lived on. Like carrion, like garbage-grabbing buzzards, they sat and waited until their intended victim was dead or all but dead—and then they struck. Yet petty though they were, and despicable, they were pirates. If they were caught, they'd be hanged—and they knew it. These men would not leave evidence.

They kept coming. There was no bravado among them, no show of ferocity. They acted rather like men on a picnic. They hailed one another, laughed and talked, brought their boats together in small groups, passed bottles. They did not get nearer to the schooner than about two hundred yards, and then only on the land side: they did not surround their prey.

No terms were offered; none were asked. No flags were flown or signals made. The coasters rocked where they were, obscene men in dirty little boats, their numbers growing all the time. The land breeze would not come until after dark. They'd strike before it came. That was what they were waiting for—darkness. Then, only half seen, they would creep in close. There might be a musket or two aboard of the schooner, possibly even a pistol, and this was why they waited for the darkness, not caring to take any more risk than was necessary. They were not dashing, daring fellows who loved danger for its own sake.

There were cutlasses among them and no doubt pistols and knives, but Adam saw no muskets. Muskets would be in the way. In most of the boats were knotted ropes, to one end of which were fastened steel hooks. These would be thrown to the deck when the boats came alongside, and then the human lice would swarm aboard.

They must have numbered a hundred and fifty by this time, with more coming. The word was out, there ashore. They were closing, slowly, for the kill.

"God in heaven, ain't you going to do *anything*?" Jeth Gardner cried. "They'll fire us afterward! They won't leave a plank!"

Adam nodded, and went on staring at the coasters. The holiday spirit out there was the more notable by contrast with the hush of the schooner. Here, aboard, nothing stirred. The sails hung slack. Nobody moved. The helm was untended. An air of hopelessness—almost, as though by anticipation, an air of death—hung over *Goodwill to Men*.

This was the way Adam wanted it.

The wreckers were a shabby scurvy lot, of all ages and complexions, scum of the scum of the seas. Most were in rags. There were even some women among them. Was it because the time was coming closer that there seemed a falling-off of the carnival spirit out there? Or was it something else? The coasters did not sound as chatty as they had. The bottles were not being passed back and forth now.

"Jeth!"

"Aye, aye, sir!"

"No—don't *run* to me! *Walk*! I want no running—now."

The bosun was flabbergasted. But Resolved Forbes, who was watching Adam carefully, seemed to sense what Adam was getting at.

"Those sulphur candles. Fetch 'em out—*slow*! I don't want anybody to move fast! Light 'em. One forward, one here."

Resolved Forbes said thoughtfully, when the bewildered bosun had gone: "There's one barrel of eels got left over. Spoiled by bilge. It's mighty far down. Only learned about it today. They stink."

"*Lots* of stink?"

"Make a skunk run."

"Good. Fetch it forth—and broach it."

Dragging his feet, his shoulders slumped, arms hanging before him, he made his way to the main hatch, the one on which in daytime the off-watch hands liked to loaf, where some of them slept nights, too, when the forecastle was unbearable. Peterson and Eb Waters were there.

"Do what I say—and I'll forget that desertion charge and you'll get your full pay when we get home."

They were not impressed. Whipped men already, they gazed glumly at the coasters.

"What makes you think we're ever *going* to get home?"

"Well, I'll tell you," said Adam; and he did.

It would be sacrilegious to use the Book itself, so he brought out his log. From that distance they wouldn't know the difference. Neither would they be able to hear what he said, so he determined not to speak any real prayers, though he remembered well the chapter from Second Corinthians he had recited last week when they slid Eliphalet Mellish overside:

"And as we have borne the image of the earthly, we shall also bear the image of the heavenly . . . for the trumpet shall sound, and the dead shall be raised incorruptible, and we shall be changed."

He could remember the splash, too. Well, he would never forget it.

He shivered. His head low, as though he lacked strength to hold it up, he bent over the log book. He stood amidships on the larboard side, in full sight of them.

"Mumble-mumble-bumble," he practiced.

Resolved Forbes, feet dragging, came to him. Resolved Forbes would not have made a good playactor; but at that distance it was all right.

These two were the only ones in sight aboard the *Goodwill*. The sagging mainsail, the boom being inboard, blocked off the starboard side of the deck.

"They're scared," Resolved Forbes reported, leaning droopingly against the wale, a position so unnatural to him that it all but caused Adam to giggle. "They want to know how can they be sure the stitches will give."

"Thunderation! Some men just won't let you save their lives!" Adam thrust the log book into his mate's hand. "Here, you conduct the first services. I'll demonstrate."

On the far side of the mainsail he found the rest of the crew. Carl Peterson and Eb Waters were stark naked. On the deck were two lengths of cut sail, seven feet by four, firmly sewed together at each end, while at each end, too, a weight was attached. The weight was conspicuous.

"All very well for you to say it'll be easy," Peterson blubbered, "but how can we—"

"All right—*look!*"

Adam stripped. He took a knife. He lay down on one of the pieces of canvas, the knife on his chest, his two hands over it.

"Go ahead, Jeth."

The bosun sewed the two sides together—not firmly but loosely, with large sloppy stitches it must have pained him to make.

Adam lay still while John Bond and the boy Rellison heaved him to their shoulders.

"*Stagger* more, you beefwits!" he scolded from inside the canvas.

So they lurched and stumbled aft on the larboard side to where Resolved Forbes slouched, making out like they were going to drop Adam at any moment. They put him on a plank balanced along the top of the gunwale amidships; and he heard his mate go "Glub-glub-glubbi-blub," which was *his* way of putting it.

Adam could not see anything, and when the plank teetered this way

74

and that it was might scary, so that he had all he could do to keep from screaming.

The mate stopped glub-blubbing; the plank was tilted; Adam slid off.

That was even scarier. He could feel himself falling—a sickish coldness in the stomach, a tightness in the chest.

He hit with a tremendous splash, on his left side, and started instantly to sink, pulled down by the weights. With his knife he slashed the sloppy stitches, and he wriggled out of the shroud.

His right big-toe got caught in some loosened thread, and pulled him down. He leaned over, pawing it, seared by panic; but it came free, and he started up. He put his knife into his mouth and began to swim. The *Goodwill* was unexpectedly beamy. It seemed to him that he swam hundreds of feet, and yet whenever he'd roll his head the gray cover was still above him, the schooner's bottom.

His ears hurt, his lungs hurt. But he made it. They were waiting for him, with a knotted line out, on the starboard side where he couldn't be seen by the coasters. On deck he started briskly to dress.

"Well, now you know. Make it look as if you was fetching 'em out of the forecastle each time. And remember to *stagger!*"

He took the log book back from Resolved Forbes and with head bent over it he could still look up through his eyebrows at the clustered boats of the pirates. Those boats were closer together, suggesting uncertainty, even fear. Now and then one would approach the schooner; but after a moment it would scurry back. The stench was truly terrible.

The sun lay red on everything. There was still no hint of breeze.

Swathed in canvas, sewed up, weighted, Carl Peterson was carried to the plank and placed on it.

"Mumble-bumble-bumble-bee-bumble . . . It ain't hard . . . Mumble-mumble . . . Remember, don't start slashing till you're under . . . And mind the barnacles!"

The plank was tipped. There was a splash. Seth Selden, unseen back of the mainsail, sewing up Eb Waters, caught the spirit of the performance and though uninstructed began to wail like a man in uncontrollable grief.

"Good," said Adam. "Mister Forbes—*crawl* to the cabin hatch and tell Lady Maisie to do that, too. Top of her lungs."

The boats of the coasters stirred restlessly.

Eb Waters was carried out, and Adam mumble-mumbled, and Waters was dumped.

Meanwhile Carl Peterson had surfaced on the far side, and he was being enshrouded again.

And soon Eb Waters came up there and was hauled in.

The Honorable Maisie proved to be a most convincing wailer, a banshee on a bad night. Just to hear her would have halted a rampaging lion.

Seth Selden tempered his own wails, saving his strength, only letting out a long low one every now and then. He was busy, of course. They were all busy.

Peterson had gone to his Maker for the third time and they were toting Eb Waters out for *his* third funeral when the coasters broke.

Somebody out there screamed. Boat after boat was turned.

The most Adam Long had hoped for was that they'd pull back a bit for a conference. He'd sought time, while he could pray for the coming of a land breeze and maybe think of something else.

But wild panic seized them. With a flash of oars, and bending low over the thwarts, they flustered away like a flock of shot-over birds.

An hour later, when the sun had set and a breeze had come at last, there was no sign of them.

"You have a voice of rare quality," the skipper told his passenger that night, "but I like it better up near like this."

"Maybe— Maybe what that man said is right."

"Maybe it is."

"We keep on this way, Adam—the two of us here every day, every night—" She was trying to make it sound frivolous, as became her training, fashionable; but when he swiveled his eyes toward her he saw that she was staring mighty hard at a horizon that had nothing notably interesting about it and in fact could hardly be seen. "La, sir, it could even be that on some tropic night, under the rich rolling Caribbean moon, you could—well, sir, you could conceivably seduce me into bundling with you."

"You bundle with me," Adam said sententiously, "and it won't be with your skirt tied down over your feet."

She tried to laugh at this, but the sound of a sob was heard, and when she started away he was afraid he had wounded her. But she came right back.

"No, really, maybe you'd better, Adam! Better return to Jamaica!"

He looked at her a long time, and it all but made his heart stop, she was so beautiful. Sitting next to her, occasionally brushing her arm or being brushed by a stray fluttering lock of her hair, perhaps watching her hands in her lap, was not like this now—gazing smack into her eyes. He seemed to rock and wobble. He felt that he might explode, blow up like a bombard, or else faint dead away. It was too much. He couldn't keep it up.

"*Please*, Adam!"

He cleared his throat. After all, he had his position to think of.

76

"I am the master of this vessel," he said, "and when I want advice I'll ask for it."

16 It tugged at him as a temptation, next morning while he lifted the Book out of his chest, to pick for a text at prayers something that would twit the doubting Thomases of the previous day; for they were fully through the Windward Passage now—though still in Pirate Alley—and pranced along handsomely in a sea they had all to themselves under a serene high sky in which there was not even the edge of a raincloud, though this was the season for rains.

"When the righteous are in authority the people rejoice?" No. That'd sound as if he was overfond of himself.

"Obey them that have the rule over you and submit yourselves . . ." "To obey is better than sacrifice, and to hearken than the fat of rams . . ." No, again. He wasn't quite sure of either of these, and it would take him some time to look them up.

Best thing to do was drop the whole matter anyway. The men were over it, no use embarrassing them. They deserved a rest, relaxation. No doubt they were a whit ashamed of the way they had acted. And Seth Selden was his old shipboard self again, eyes twinkling, mouth twisted to slip out some elliptical sarcastic remark. There wasn't a touch of the hysteria that had moved him yesterday, and he didn't even seem to have a spiritual hangover to remind him of how he had acted.

Seth was even unrepentant enough to put on, as he did so many mornings at prayer time, a mock air of piety. He was small-boyish about it, the old scoundrel. He simpered.

Yet even the irreverent Seth straightened his face when he heard the verses Adam read from the Book. For he remembered them, as all the men there did: they were the same verses Adam had selected for reading when Eliphalet Mellish's body was slid overside. They were among Adam's favorites. In the midst of life, he aimed to remind the hands, we are in death.

". . . when this corruptible shall have put on incorruption, and this mortal shall have put on immortality, then shall be brought to pass the saying that is written, Death is swallowed up in victory."

He did not feel that this was personal, so to speak; for he had already thanked the Lord in his prayers for having spared the schooner; and now he was able to make it a good show to see. He raised an arm, raised his voice too:

"O death, where is thy sting? O grave, where *is* thy victory?"

He finished on a quieter, more assured note:

"Therefore, my beloved brethren, be ye steadfast, unmovable, always abounding in the work of the Lord, forasmuch as ye know that your labor is not in vain in the Lord."

He closed the volume, and lowered his head and kept his eyes shut a moment—not in prayer but because he was overwhelmed by the eloquence. The Book often did that to him.

He opened his eyes, looking up, and saw, where a moment before had been clear blue sky, a storm.

This in itself was not unusual. Given the latitude and the season, you were bound to have storms—dark ones, noisy ones, not very dangerous storms, each brief. They came singly, also massed. Wall-like to see, some straight, others wobbling, they would march in a menacing manner clear across the firmament, to get, most of 'em, nowhere. There was nothing surreptitious about them: you could see them for miles, and hear them almost as far. For they were crammed with rain, these breathlessly low clouds, and set up a deafening clatter as they moved.

The limits of any one of these storms were most marvelously clear-cut. In this they were not unlike summer thundershowers at home, only more so. By no means all of them, or even all of the ones that started for the schooner as though drawn by an immense magnet, struck *Goodwill to Men*. The hands—though Adam frowned on the practice—used to sit on the main hatch and watch them approach and lay bets on whether or not they would hit. Sometimes one would pass within a few feet of the vessel, so that you thought you could reach out and get your hand wet, and the downpour would be such that you could not see the horizon on that side, though elsewhere the sea was smooth and bright; yet not a drop would fall on deck. When one did envelop the *Goodwill to Men* it would be in a gray hissing mist, and there was nothing you could do but hang on and wait it out: they never lasted for more than a few minutes. Even if somebody was standing right next to you and you shouted at him, he couldn't hear you. You could not see from gunwale to gunwale. Then suddenly it would all be gone—all except a frantic scampering of water in the scuppers, with the sun shining on it already, and the receding clack-and-slap of rain on the surface of the sea. Then there would not be even that, and you would find it hard to believe that there had ever been any disturbance in this exquisitely beautiful day.

What Adam saw now was a greater and more horrible thing: a wall or column of darkness rushing toward them, but no rain drops with it, only a low ominous moaning. Surely it was moving faster than any tropical rainstorm, for already it was almost upon them.

78

He had never seen anything like it. None of them had. The moaning swelled to a high howl. The air around them tingled, taut with expectancy, and got bright, even iridescent, like a swelling soap bubble just before it bursts.

The seas had been running short and even, satiny on the surface, showing no white. But now, abruptly, all around the schooner the water leapt high, the waves tumbling every-which-way, as though half a dozen swift ocean currents converged at just this spot.

There was a spitting sound and they saw flashes of lightning close and low, blue lightning, some of the hands said afterward; others said yellow.

Then darkness.

All hands were on deck, as they always were for prayers, and that was a blessing; for in such weather the forecastle hatch habitually was left open, so that when the storm hit it filled the forecastle almost instantly with water, and if any man had been in there at the time he'd have been drowned like a rat.

Everybody it seemed spotted the storm at the same moment, and they all sprang into action. Resolved Forbes and his skipper were shouting orders in the time they had; but the hands knew what to do anyway.

The boy Rellison ran aft for the tiller, where it was his trick.

Jethro Gardner had been doing some work on the long boat at the time of the call to prayers, and in consequence this was not lashed. Grabbing a line, Jeth ran for it. The long boat was heavy; and if it took over, in a blow like this, it could do a powerful lot of smashing.

The mate, shouting orders, made for the main halyards. Others went for the fore halyards or forward to the jibs. They were going to strike every inch of canvas—if they were given a chance.

As for Adam, he went for Lady Maisie.

Her cabin hatch was closed. He knew this, having closed it at her request—she complained that the wind would riffle her finery hung down there—when he was about to conduct her forward for prayers. They'd not have time to get to it, open it, stuff her down that steep ladder, make fast the hatch. She must be sheltered somewhere here.

She opened her mouth to say something, but he shook his head. He hooked a leg behind her legs and shoved her so that she sat down thuddingly, her back against the starboard grating. "Hang on!" and he started away; but he remembered the irons and turned back. It was at this grating that Waters and Peterson had been chained, and the irons still hung there. If they got to whanging back and forth, as they might well do, they could brain her.

So he made his passenger fast. Before she knew what he was doing, before even she had got over the jolt of being thrown down on her backside, he had locked two shackles on each ankle, two on each wrist. Good. That would hold both irons and lady in place.

He was racing aft when the storm hit.

It was incredible that any disturbance of nature could catch up to them so swiftly in the vast peaceful sea, equally incredible that its onset should be like an explosion. It slammed Adam Long against the starboard gunwale, tipped him up, came near to toppling him over. He hung, gasping, for a terrible moment. All he could see was a lather of water inches from his face. The schooner must have been all but on her beamends. Would she broach-to? She'd snap her sticks if she did, perhaps even turn upside-down, squashing the life out of all of them.

He wriggled back to the deck, fought his way aft. The Rellison boy desperately clinging to the tiller was being snapped back and forth like a rag. He was trying hard, he was sobbing. He just didn't have the muscle. Adam reached him barely in time. With their combined weight they got her over, and *Goodwill*, shuddering, righted herself.

Nobody remembered much about the actual duration of that storm afterward. It seemed long to most. But it might have lasted merely minutes. Descriptions differed wildly. Even the names of the storm differed: some swore that it was a waterspout, others called it a white squall, while Seth Selden was not the only one who was wont to refer to it as the Visitation. Some said it rained pitchforks, others that there was no rain at all. It was wet enough in all conscience, for the seas thamped over the schooner again and again. A few said that there was thunder. They were all agreed that there was lightning, closer-up than any of them had ever known, though there were many opinions of the shapes it took, the colors it showed.

Adam spent most of the storm hanging on to the tiller, bucking it, bracing it, side by side with young Abel Rellison, who, to give him credit, never faltered. Back and forth they went, back and forth, fighting. They lost all sense of time. They couldn't see much—no other men at all. They didn't even try to shout at one another but saved their wind.

And this, reflected Adam, is the same lad who a few hours ago was thinking of bashing my skull in—and this is the very stick he was thinking of doing it with!

He grinned at young Rellison, who grinned back. They struggled on.

The let-up was abrupt, and it was cruel, more of a shock, physically, than the onset. A couple of the men almost fainted. The boy Rellison flopped down on the deck. Adam went forward.

The sticks remained, also the bowsprit. Most of the standing rigging still stood. The long boat was gone, and it must have been its departure that had torn out a good fifteen feet of the larboard gunwale amidships, leaving nothing but splinters. The foremast boom was gone but the sail itself had been saved. The mainsail, too, had been saved; it must have been by a tremendous effort. Both jibs were gone.

John Bond had dislocated his left wrist. Jethro Gardner's right leg had been smashed, badly, while he tussled with the long boat. They were all banged and bruised a good bit.

Adam hiked Lady Maisie's skirt and petticoat down, then went for the key. It took some time, the forecastle being flooded. When he returned, and was releasing her, she nodded toward Jeth Gardner, in a swoon now.

"We must carry him to my cabin. He's a brave man, Adam."

"Aye," said the skipper, who would take such a thing for granted of Jeth Gardner. "Well, now you've seen what the sea can do, you'll understand why we all hate it so."

"La, 'twas exciting," said Maisie.

17   There, among the perfumes and pomatum, the spikenard and rice powder, where rosewater rocked in its jars, and from a score of pegs silk and satin and flimsy frilled muslin swung with the movement of the schooner, Bosun Gardner lay in a bunk until recently the domain of Resolved Forbes. It was there that Adam broke the news to him.

Likely enough Jeth was expecting it, but this was not the reason why he made it easier to say. Lying there, he had been grumping. Adam would have worried still more about the state of the bosun's health if he *hadn't* grumped. A Jeth who found the world satisfactory would be a Jeth on the very threshold of extinction.

"Been down here two days and nights now, and you got to get me out, Cap'n. Ain't no place for a man."

Adam grinned.

"What's the matter with this cabin?"

"Might've been all right when you and Mr. Forbes was here, but not now. Oh, she means first-rate! It was chirk of her to think of it, and I appreciate that and all. But I can't stay here."

"What's the matter with this cabin?" Adam asked again.

"Well, for one thing, it stinks."

"Coming from a man who's spent most of his life in forecastles—"

"I'm used to that kind of smell. I ain't used to *this*—" and he waved his hand to indicate the bottles, the jars.

They were alone. Three would have crowded the place uncomfortably, even indecently if the Honorable Maisie Treadway was one, and the rule was that whenever anybody wanted to visit with the patient, the lady, called down to, would come up first.

Of course they all did visit.

"They ain't fretting about me," the bosun growled. "They just want to get a look at them corsets hanging up there."

"Jeth," Adam said now, "do you think this vessel's under a spell?"

"No, not any more I don't. Did used to. But not since we come through that crazy storm without snapping a stick."

Adam said slowly: "We're losing the services of a crackerjack bosun."

"Not for long. I'll be ramming around again right soon, I expect." He looked up suddenly. "Or won't I?"

That gave Adam an opening in which to say what he had come to say, but it chanced that he wanted a little more palaver first.

"Do you think Lady Maisie's a witch, Jeth?"

"She could be, but I don't think so. *You* ought to know."

"I don't think so either. But I can see where anybody else might."

"Aye, she's a dreadful attractive female."

"Aye," said Adam.

Jethro hitched himself up in the bunk, or tried to, but gave it up, wincing, when a crash of pain reminded him of his leg.

"That brings me to the other reason I want to get out of here, Cap'n. I'm used to close quarters all right, but not with a woman, and especially a woman like this. Oh, it ain't her fault! She's been mighty kind with me and not pushy. Hangs up a couple of skirts for a curtain whenever she changes any of her clothes, which she's doing just about all the time. Talks to me, to keep me from thinking about things. But I do think about things just the same. Can't help it."

Jethro Gardner actually was blushing.

"It ain't healthy. Don't like to talk about a thing like this, Cap'n. But you understand. It's goldarn hard on a man, all the time."

"I understand," said Adam Long.

"That's the other reason why I want to get out."

Adam nodded.

"We'll get you out. Right away. We were going to anyway."

"Oh?"

Jeth was studying his face. Adam kept looking at the other bunk, his erstwhile own, piled high now with frilly fabrics, ribbons, kerchiefs. That was where she slept.

Jeth paused a moment, so's to be sure of his voice.

"You mean you don't like the way my leg is, then?"

"No, I don't, Jeth. Neither do the others."

"And you reckon we ought to—ought—"

"I think we should, Jeth. That's what the others think, too. They've all looked at it. Course, we won't do it if you don't say go ahead."

"But that's what *you* think, yourself?"

"Aye."

"Want another look at it?"

"Yes, I do."

A few minutes later: "Still feel that way, Cap'n?"

"I do, Jeth. I truthful do. Down here in this hot climate— And we certainly don't want you to die on us."

"Don't want to die myself, comes to that." He was silent a moment. "There's God's plenty of knives, but what about the bone?"

"I got a saw, in my carpenter's kit."

"Oh— You'll do this yourself, Cap'n? Personally?"

"I wouldn't ask anybody else to."

"No, you wouldn't. That's the way you are. All right—if you're going to do it yourself I'll say go ahead. But I wish you'd sprung it on me, sort of. It'll take some time to hot up an iron."

"One's all hotted up out there right now, Jeth."

"Oh."

Adam drew a bottle from under his shirt. It was half full of rum, the half Seth Selden had left. Adam took the cork out.

"You'll be using a bit of this?"

"A *bit* of it?" Jeth took the bottle. "You can just throw that cork away, Cap'n. Throw it right away."

"May God guide me," Adam said somberly to Maisie a little later. "And keep your hatch shut. He's sure to scream."

"You've never done anything like this before?"

"No."

"You'll need more courage than he will."

"Aye."

This was the first time he had ever been in the cabin with her, and it sure was close quarters, as Jeth had said, especially with all those things on the wall and piled around. It would have been impossible not to brush her, at least. He didn't try. He glanced up through the hatch to assure himself that only the legs of the man who was waiting with Adam's carpenter's kit were visible. Then deliberately he put his arms around Maisie and kissed her on the mouth.

It was more wonderful, even, than he had dared to hope. She had wanted him to do it. He knew that, felt it. Like him, she staggered back a bit afterward, as though the kiss had taken strength out of her legs, as indeed it had.

83

They didn't look at one another.

"G-God be wi' ye, Adam."

"Aye," he said, and went up the ladder.

The cutting itself was unexpectedly easy. But the sawing was hard, the bone. That round slimy surface slipped and splintered.

Jeth made moans, some he probably didn't even know about, but that was all. They had him spread-eagled on the main hatch, a man at each arm, a man at each leg. Not until the iron was brought over, spicking and spitting, fresh out of the fire, red-to-turning-to-white all up and down, did Jethro open his mouth as a signal that he wanted the stick of wood they'd whittled for him. They put this into his mouth, and he fastened his teeth on it, and he closed his eyes.

This part Adam did fast. He had to, because of the blood, which for all their precautions was gushing. But he had to do it fast anyway, if he was going to do it at all.

He didn't vomit afterward, nor did Jeth Gardner faint. But there wasn't much idle chit-chat aboard the *Goodwill to Men* that evening.

The skipper took the graveyard watch, seeking stillness, knowing that he wouldn't be able to sleep. Nobody was blaming him for anything; and indeed he had done a good job of it, considering; but he thought that he would never shake the feeling of that saw out of his hands, nor force from his ears the hissing of the blood when they cauterized the stump.

He had not seen Maisie since sundown. Her slide was open, her candle out. He stared thoughtfully at the square of blackness there in the deck, dwelling in his mind on how close she was. Was she asleep? This was an exceptionally quiet night; the moon was high, the seas low. He could hear the schooner working in her customary way, the sounds any sailing man hears without noticing them unless they change or cease—the squeal of timbers, occasionally the clunk of a block on deck, the hum of air in the shrouds, the shush at the bows, and the persistent, hollow, chuckling gurgle of the wake. Below these he fancied sometimes that he could hear Maisie breathing.

He rose, loosely lashed the tiller, which was steady anyway, and walked around the deck several times on bare feet.

When he'd pass it he would eye the black square that was the entrance to the cabin. What was she thinking of? Or was she asleep? But he believed that she was awake, lying motionless down there.

The jury boom kicked and fussed a bit, and he reset it, glad of something to do. *Goodwill to Men*, largely because of this jury job—a good enough job in its way but by no means what Jeth Gardner would have

84

turned out—under a greatly shortened foresail was not making her usual speed. Still she was graceful, and stepped daintily through the sea.

Nobody else was up and around. Adam, who had dismissed the tillerman, had the deck to himself.

He roamed.

Now here was that black hole before him again, the square of darkness. Seemed like he always came back to it, no matter which way he walked. He stood spread-legged looking down at it. Though the deck was washed by the moon, none of this appeared able to penetrate the opening, which looked packed with a darkness that was not merely an absence of light.

It suggested a pit. Was it a pit? *The* pit? Was that man lost who lowered himself into it?

Her voice was a whisper, coiling up to him like smoke.

"Is — Is that you?"

"Aye," said Adam.

A pause. Then: "Are you coming down?"

"Aye," said Adam.

He could not see her, when he turned at the foot of the ladder, stooping; and indeed he couldn't see anything down there; but he knew exactly where she was. He could not hear her breathing. He went to her, and her arms, all bare, slid past his arms and went around his neck; and her breast was bare, too, and when he started kissing it he learned that she was sobbing. She fell back, holding him tight, all her flesh trembling and twitching beneath him.

"We— We've waited so long, Adam."

18   The moon was low and large, and still bright, scattering sequins, and to the east the sky gave no hint of dawn, the morning Adam came topside to see the sloop chasing them. He started to yell.

He had lingered below at Maisie's insistence. Each night he took the graveyard watch, his own helmsman; and if the crew divined the reason for this—and he believed that they did—nevertheless they stayed in the forecastle and didn't snoop. Each night, too, he and Maisie had their quarrel: why didn't he remain a little longer? Their first, it was a pretty quarrel, and playful, yet it held an undercurrent of seriousness, for Maisie needed reassurance and she was getting annoyed by the haste with which Adam climbed back to the deck, almost as if he was eager to escape from her. Again and again he had pointed out that a ship should be handled, never neglected in any part. But it could steer itself, it could keep its own course, couldn't it? the lady had asked. True, the skipper had replied; and it was true, too, that there in the cabin, no matter what else he might be feeling at the time, he could feel instantly any change of the wind, any shift in sailing, or unusual activity or lack of activity of rigging or canvas—and get topside in time to correct it. But still it wasn't *right* to leave a helm unmanned, a deck unwatched, even for a matter of minutes, the skipper had declared. "Kiss me again, my pet, my lover," the lady had whispered, "never mind about that steering stick— kiss me."

This sailorman's instinct, this sense of duty, would have been sufficient reason for Adam to cut short his visits, precious and unforgettable though every moment of them was. But there was another reason, one he didn't mention to Maisie: he was no longer sure of his crew.

What might have been a mutiny, and certainly seemed the beginning of one, had been nipped in the bud by the visit of the coasters. Then had come the freak storm, and Jeth Gardner's injury. Lady Maisie had shamed the hands by her kindness to the bosun; and the weather was better now, too, and they weren't forever being chased. But suspicion persisted. Adam could see this not from the way they looked at Maisie but rather from the way they did *not* look at her, the way they dropped their eyes at her approach.

With a crew like that you did well to watch your deck.

Of the loyalty of Resolved Forbes there could be no doubt; but the hands knew this, and they'd be unlikely to talk in his presence, for the mate, berthed in the forecastle now, would stand for no nonsense. Jeth, too, would be loyal; but Jeth couldn't be counted upon, in case of a fracas. Eliphalet Mellish, devoted to Captain Long, was dead. John Bond and the boy Abel Rellison were well-meaning but they could be influenced. Peterson and Waters definitely hated Adam. Worst of all, the ringleader, a dirty man and a dangerous one, was Seth Selden. And Seth was sincere, unfortunately. Cynical in so many things, a scoffer, he had his passionate convictions, one of which was that Maisie Treadway had cast a spell over the schooner. The very force of his feeling in this respect would carry weight with the crew.

Then, too, Seth had been knocked down, and his was not a forgiving nature. He might grin to Adam's face, and outwardly, about his work, seem the same, but Adam caught dark glances now and then, and from all that Seth said privately poison dripped.

What's more, they were heading back for Newport where Seth did not dare go now. How grave had been his crimes and how much of them had been uncovered by the Queen's collector, Adam did not know; but the charges could hardly have been trivial if they caused Seth to sneak out of Blake's the night before the sailing and stow away aboard the schooner of which—though he didn't know this—he had just been elected captain. Had he planned to jump ship and refrained from doing so in Kingston only because of the press gangs? Or perhaps he hoped to fit the schooner up with guns and take her "on the account"? Could that be why he had been so eager to get the captaincy?

True, they were going to put in at New York first, but even New York might be too near home for the fugitive Seth Selden, decidedly a man to be watched.

All of this, however, Adam did not impart to Maisie when they had their hushed loving quarrels about his departure. Each night for four nights he returned to deck promptly; but on the fifth night he capitulated.

No man who is in love is wholly sane; but there are degrees of daze. Adam Long wasted no time when he saw that sloop.

She was fast. Water creamed sweetly at her bows, and she had everything conceivable cracked on—even studdingsails—everything but a spritsail, for she was going too fast and dipping too much for that. Her wake fanned out all turbulent behind her.

She was not much larger than *Goodwill*, but her hull was disproportionately high, especially forward: it looked even in this light as though false bulwarks had been built there in order to conceal something —or somebody.

There was no one in sight. The sloop might have been sailing itself, as until a moment ago *Goodwill* had been, a ghost ship. She showed no colors. She was dark.

Resolved Forbes was the first to tumble out, but Jeth Gardner was not with him, as once he would have been, nor was John Bond going to be of much use, with his left wrist still out of joint. Nevertheless the men moved fast. They did not need to be told how serious was their situation. All they had to do was glance astern.

"How in thunderation she ever get so close?" asked the mate.

Adam Long did not answer.

They had been running almost directly before the wind, making up the middle of the Old Bahama Channel, with the islands to starboard, Cuba to larboard, neither in sight. The moon would soon be down, but dawn was coming: there was no risk of going aground somewhere. Adam ignored the course, the compass and chart, and put her sharply about, yawing.

He looked back. The sloop had changed course as quickly and easily as though she ran in a greased groove and was being towed by *Goodwill to Men*. Her studdingsails had to come in, of course: Adam had counted on that. On the other hand, *Goodwill*, with her jury boom, found the tacking laborious.

The vessels, then, stayed about the same distance apart. It was a bit more than gunshot.

Adam tried half a dozen tricks, changing course, shifting rig. In ordinary circumstances he knew *Goodwill's* sailing qualities perfectly—knew what he could expect of her, just when she'd start to strain, when he ought to drive her. It was different now. An outside skipper, miraculously placed in command of *Goodwill* at this stage of the chase, would not have been so greatly troubled as Adam Long was, and wouldn't have felt the need to try so many sailing points. It was precisely because Adam *did* know this schooner so well, having assisted at her birth, having sailed her lovingly all the years of her life, that he found it difficult to adjust himself to the way she handled with that short foremast boom, the less-than-half foresail, the heavy coarse storm jibs. It was as if a man knew his wife completely, or thought he did, and understood and loved her, but then she got taken sick and fell into a fever and started raving, yammering things he should never have overheard. And what could that man do? He could only bear with her, tut-tutting and pooh-poohing her, not permitting himself to be drawn into a quarrel, and praying all the while that they'd pull her through. That man would love his wife the same way when she'd got well again, and try to forget the things she'd shrieked in delirium. But while she was feverish he'd have a hell of a time. It would be harder on him than it could ever be on an outsider.

This was the way it was with Adam Long and the *Goodwill to Men.* He looked back.

The sloop was having no trouble with spar or canvas. Her sails were white—not notably clean, but still white, refusing to be pearled by the dawn. There was never a furrow in them. Adam reckoned he had never seen sails like that. Linen all right. He wondered where they came from. The Low Countries? Folks who had been to New York told him that the Dutchers have the best canvas in the world.

For the rest, the sloop wasn't anything remarkable. She was a Bermudian, sure enough fast, with a raking mast, very tall, carrying a lot of topsail, precious little jib. The most remarkable thing about her were those high bulwarks forward, and the fact that no hands were in sight. Adam Long wondered if the men aboard of her truly thought that they were fooling anybody.

She was well handled. She came about and fell away as neatly and quickly as *Goodwill* herself: it was as though the two vessels were doing a well-rehearsed drill.

She was a trifle closer now.

Lady Maisie came halfway out of her cabin, the upper half of her. She awarded Adam a smile that was carefully polite—after all there were hands everywhere—but he thought that she was blushing a little; and his heart stopped.

"Get below," he said.

In the spreading light the faint sweep of freckles across her nose looked burnished. When she glanced astern her eyes were enormous, lighted a little with fear. Then she looked forward.

"Why are they throwing water on the sails, Captain?"

"Make 'em wet."

"But why should they be wet?"

"Speed."

"How can wet sails make a boat go faster?"

"I don't know, ma'am. But they do. Now—*go below!*"

He was satisfied that she had not been seen from the sloop.

It was afternoon before she addressed him again, and then it was in a quiet voice, from the depths of her cabin, while Adam stood on deck near the partly opened hatch.

"Is it truthfully pirates?" in a whisper.

"Aye."

"How do you know?"

"I know."

"Will they catch us?"

"Reckon so. Keep away till sundown, we might have a chance. But I don't guess we can."

"What's that rumbling sound I hear?"

"Hands hauling the cargo out of the hold. Hogsheads of molasses from your cousin's plantation."

"What're they doing that for?"

"Pitch 'em overboard."

"Oh— Isn't it rather a shame to lose the cargo?"

"If that's all we lose," muttered Adam, "we're lucky."

The sun in fact was large and low and just beginning to turn tawny when the following vessel, sure of herself, at last spoke. A flag was run to her top, a flag unequivocally black, without design or device. The false covering of a gunport, a piece of painted canvas at the starboard bow, was yanked aside, and a chunky brass culverin run out. At the same moment the false bulwarks were pulled down, and men rose to their feet all around the deck of the sloop, yelling, brandishing blades. Fifty or sixty of them by Adam's first count, but later he estimated there were nearer a hundred. The wonder was that such a small vessel could hold them all. Obviously she couldn't have taken them far. They were variously dressed, most of them gay, all of them dirty. They shouted and screamed, waving their weapons wildly. The plan seemed to be to show as much steel as possible, with a barbaric abruptness, in the hope of scaring the quarry into surrender. Most of the weapons were cutlasses, but there were also some pikes and harpoons, a few daggers, a smattering of muskets. Some men even had two weapons, one in each hand.

The culverin coughed. A great white blob of smoke appeared at its mouth, to be scattered by the wind. Forward of the *Goodwill to Men* a spear of sea water rose into the air. Much too high, that shot.

The corsairs set up an even louder clamor. A few even fired their guns.

"Must have plenty of powder," opined Adam Long.

The culverin was run out again, and again it coughed, immediately afterward being blotted out by whipped-away smoke. This ball fell too low; the sea gulped it. But the space between the vessels had lessened alarmingly, and there'd be no darkness for at least an hour.

The pirates weren't very good shots, but it was a fact that their gun would reach now. Sooner or later they would get the range.

So Adam sighed—and struck.

19 Adam swung *Goodwill* clear up into the eye of the wind, so that the jibs cracked and slapped, and then he dropped fore-and mainsail; and suddenly the schooner loafed.

A long boat, expertly handled, was manned by at least thirty pirates, most of whom scrambled aboard. They showed no discipline but ran here and there, stretching their legs, waggling their cutlasses, asking questions, looking at things, kicking things, obviously delighted to get away from the cramped quarters of the sloop. At first they seemed to have no leader. They might have been a group of excited schoolboys. They scarcely glanced at the open main hatch, the empty hold, nor did they go aft; but they showed great interest in the rig of the *Goodwill*, testing sheets and lines, rattling goosenecks.

"Fast! You nigh to getting away from us! What kind of a vessel you call this anyway?"

"In Rhode Island this is what we call a schooner," Seth Selden told them.

"Why?"

"Don't know. Reckon she scoons."

"'Scoons'? What's that? What's 'scooning'?"

"Don't you know what scooning is? Why, it's what a schooner does."

"Oh."

There was no scuffling. Possibly exhilarated by the chase, the pirates appeared in a holiday mood. Only one, a man somewhat older than the others, a man with a single eye, displayed any sense of responsibility. This one, a worried expression on his face, tried to quiet the others, who for the most part paid no attention to him. At last he accosted Adam.

"You the skipper?"

Adam nodded, not caring to commit himself any further than that.

"We'll take your cargo."

"No you won't," said Adam.

"Eh?" One-Eye bristled, backing a bit. His hands went to two iron pistols stuck in his sash. "You mean you'll—"

"I mean there ain't any cargo. Not any more." Adam glanced at the open hatch. "It's all in the sea."

"Look at me," commanded the pirate, his face working.

Adam obeyed, though only with an effort. The pirate did not wear a patch over his put-out eye, though he should have done so. Extraordinarily repulsive, he must have been sensitive about his appearance. He had seen too many men turn away, embarrassed, slightly sick. Now he put his face close to Adam's.

"Got rid of it all, eh?"

"Didn't want to."

"What was it—rum?"

"Molasses."

One-Eye cursed.

"You can't sell molasses down in these islands!"

"I didn't aim to sell molasses down in these islands," Adam pointed out.

If he was standoffish, his nose high, his voice edgy, this was because he feared tears. He was about to lose his ship, his first. Also he was about to lose the woman he had just learned to love. If he kept up this colloquy his temper would snap; so he turned away.

Nobody asked him, now, for the papers. Nobody gave a hoot. Pirates don't need papers. They just take whatever it is they lack, without all the botheration of signing and sealing and endorsing; and what they most lacked in these waters were small fast sailing vessels.

Is it the Devil himself ye've got by the tail?

Another man rose from the gig alongside. This was a very big man, massy, though not fat. The first that was seen of him was his loose full-bottomed black periwig; then his face, large, larded white, with a patch over each cheekbone; and his cravat of fine if dirty lace, tied in the careful-careless Steinkirk mode; and at last, as he climbed aboard *Goodwill*, his long blue brocaded waistcoat, his white silk breeches, his blue silk stockings, and the silver buckles and red rosettes that all but hid his shoes, which had red heels. This man displayed no weapon except his sword—not a cutlass but a small straight sticker, a court sword, showily scabbarded. He carried an enormous plumed tricorne under his arm.

Shrugging hugely, he took snuff. He had small eyes, large gross lips. He stood before Adam Long, looming over him, though Adam was no midget.

"I am Major Kellsen."

Adam only nodded. He wouldn't let on that he'd heard of the man.

"You move fast, Captain. We need speedy pilots. Come—no beating about the bush, eh? Join us."

Adam shook his head.

"Don't be a dolt," Kellsen rasped. "You can be forced, can't you? Let yourself be forced."

"I'll have no truck with piracy," Adam said.

One-Eye put in: "His majesty'd prefer to be marooned, no doubt?"

It was the classical piratical punishment. The freebooters avoided violence, fighting only when they had to, for they were in the business not for the fun of it but for the money. Their personal duels, though frequent, were as conventionalized as those of gentlemen. They never inflicted flogging, which would have reminded them of the days of discipline they loathed—for most of them were either Navy deserters or runaway white slaves, or both. Nor would they hang a man, since such an end might seem to foreshadow their own. A person they wished to dispose of, then, they marooned. That is, they left him on some bare, sunbaked, small island without any supplies; and there he could die of thirst or of hunger or even of sunstroke—*they* didn't give a hoot.

All the same, Adam shook a stubborn head.

The others of the crew were watching him. They had already been solicited. Members of the Brotherhood of the Main notoriously were disrespectful of authority, and in particular of authority at sea: that's why they were what they were. Wronged mariners, in their own eyes at least, they resented all skippers, and even mates, while they esteemed the forecastle hands to be natural allies, taking their sympathy for granted. Here aboard the *Goodwill to Men* they had already, in their irregular way, without method, asked Peterson and Seth Selden, Waters and John Bond and the boy Rellison to join then. They even asked Jethro Gardner, whose soggy stump they scarcely glanced at. Each of these in turn, without having conferred with any of the others—and of course Resolved Forbes did this, too—nodded toward Captain Long, indicating that he would do what the skipper did, not more, not less.

So now everybody was looking at Adam.

"Be forced," Kellsen urged. "You don't sign articles, you don't take shares. So if you're caught you don't get your neck stretched—maybe."

"Make up your mind," snarled One-Eye.

Adam buttoned his coat—he had put on his freedom suit for this occasion—and straightened his cap. He cleared his throat.

"I must seek advice," he said. "Excuse me."

Nobody made a move to stop him when he went aft. They watched him in wonder, but said nothing.

He paused at the scuttle, and looked around. Only the top half of the sun showed now, and the sea was gold. *Goodwill to Men* rocked and rolled, groggy, the tiller lurching like a drunkard. Scarcely a cable length away the sloop stood with flapping jibs, her deck crowded with watchers who no longer troubled to look ferocious, being by now just plain impatient.

Adam sighed, and pushed the scuttle fully open.

"Will— Will they kill us?" Maisie whispered.

Her voice wavered but it did not break.

Adam was impassive.

"Come up," he called gently, "and do just as I tell you."

She had been prepared. She must have readied herself to the last fluffy ruffle. How she could have done it in that small space—and having done it, how so garbed she could climb the steep ladder and emerge on deck with a genuine smile, a vision of loveliness in yellow and blue, ribbons and laces and furbelows, the neck of her bodice low and frilly over bare powdered shoulders—here was a thing that no man could know, a secret between the ladies and the Lord.

Adam Long made a leg. She dropped him a curtsey.

He took her hand and held it high as he turned her to face the men amidships, properly proud of her. *They,* and especially Major Kellsen, were all eyes.

"My wife and I," Adam announced, "have decided to join you."

PART FOUR

Life Among the Cutthroats

20 Is there anything dirtier than dirty snow, or more clumsy than a swan out of water? The man who called himself Carse had only two things to remind him, physically, of what he once had been: his right hand and his left.

With a sword he was lithe and precise, grace's very epitome combined with strength, brain running into muscle running into steel, so that no man could say where one left off and the other began. Let him scabbard that blade, however, and Carse became what he customarily was—a fellow with a slouch, a leer, shifty eyes. There was no spring in his step. Indeed he shambled. True, he avoided bluster, a negative virtue which yet in itself marked him off in Providence, a place where loudmouthedness was the rule, where men seemed to feel an obligation to wallop themselves on the chest, bellowing about their unbeatableness, and where a stranger might have assumed, with reason, that courage was measured exactly by the volume of the voice. When he spoke at all Carse spoke low. There were times when he even lisped.

Except for those hands, then—long, slim, exquisitely tapered—he was, when not fencing, a singularly repulsive person. Though long, he looked squat. You believed that beneath his clothes, in little crevices of his body, in his armpits, in his crotch, there were pockets of stale air. He was not more than twenty-five or -six, but he looked overripe, prematurely rotten. His hair, his eyes, held no color: his face was a watery pink. He looked as though he couldn't grow a beard. He is best described, if it be description at all, by a sound: he looked like the noise that your heel makes when you draw it up out of the mud.

"Now this is what Marcelli used to call a *mezza cavazione*. You're resting too much weight on your left leg, Captain. Now watch. I'll disengage from above down, in either line. And keep that foot pointed this way."

"I feel like a fool, holding a position like this!"

"Very well. Stand any way you wish."

Adam hunched his shoulders. He took a stronger grip on the rapier, easing his forearm by not being so careful to keep the palm up. He let his left foot get further back. He left his right toe steal inward.

"Now," he cried. "Now I can *fight!*"

"Good—we'll fight."

Emotionless, saving his breath, the Englishman called the touches. He came back into guard position and saluted after each. Then he'd say "Now!" and attack again. He did not press. He moved with a sweet smooth supple regularity, perfectly in control of himself.

"Now—*touch!*" The blades were buttoned, but nevertheless they were stiff steel—not just foils from an academy—and when they hit they hurt. Carse did not seem intent upon what he was doing, but casual, almost negligent; and surely he didn't bunch his puny muscles, or pant, or roll his eyes; yet each touch was the apogee of carefully collected, inswept strength, and it stung.

"Now—*touch!*"

Adam Long tried every engagement he knew—not many, truly—but he could not catch the other's steel. He even tried, in desperation, what Carse had called the "universal parry," a heavy sweep in seconde, from a high quarte, executed at full arm's length as he retreated. He swished only air; and then Carse's padded point rammed his ribs—"*Touch!*" and Carse dropped back into guard position, saluted, and began to attack again.

Panic slipped its hot fingers over the man from Newport. He had already learned that you cannot depend on your eyes—that a great deal of your *awareness* of combat with rapiers lay in the way you felt your opponent's steel against your own, whether you pressed or he did, or whether the contact was so light and silvery as never to be noticed by an onlooker. That tingle of touch that passed between the blades and into your arm and all down and up your body, was an absolute requisite. Without it you were lost—as Adam was lost now. Was this a wraith he faced? He couldn't catch Carse's weapon, even for a brief click, much less parry it.

"Now—*touch!*"

Adam was getting more and more up on the balls of his feet, a natural nervous reaction Carse had warned him against. He was gripping his weapon with a fury of intensity, as a man might grip a club. He leaned forward, his face streaked with sweat.

Then it happened. He never did learn how. He did not feel the other's steel, yet without being conscious of it he must have answered with his eyes and immediately afterward with his weapon a false lunge, a feint. He was wild, of course, by this time. He tried to recover, and teetered. He

95

waved his arms. He sat down—sat with a resounding thump on the hard sandy earth of Providence—he could even feel the sharp small chunks of coral dig through his breeches and gleefully get at his skin.

"Touch," said Carse quietly, without touching. He regarded a puffing opponent for a moment, then helped him to his feet. "And do you still fear to look like a fool, Captain?"

"All right," said Adam, who ached in every joint. "After this I'll keep my palm up, I'll keep my toe out."

"And that left hand—high, high."

"All right, I'll even do that. Now let's have that *mezza cavazione* again."

When he put his sword aside, Carse became not merely a different man but a different *sort* of man. It was a re-transformation not at all comparable to that of coach-and-four back into mice-and-pumpkin, since pumpkins, mice, too, are homely, familiar things; whereas Carse the bladeless would have repelled a jakes-farmer.

The first half-dozen lessons did not include any bouts but were devoted to posture, irking Adam, who cried that what he sought to learn was how to fight with a rapier, not how to strike poses with one. Carse paid no heed to this. He must have heard it before, often. "I don't think it will be necessary to teach you to fight, Captain," was as near as he came to comment. "I think you know too well already. Rage and a rapier don't go together."

More recently they had been having bouts, and for these they wore plastrons. Carse always laced his plastron carefully. Once, with some bitterness, Adam said that for the life of him he couldn't see why.

"The best swordsman in the world is not afraid of the second best swordsman," Carse replied gravely. "Nor is the sixteenth best afraid of the seventeenth. But any one of them would be frightened to face a man who'd had only a few lessons."

They practiced under a sizzling sun, some distance inland and blocked from prying eyes and the jeers of the camp by dunes. Now Carse as they sat down for a rest untrussed himself, for he was sweating. Not that it made much difference. He stank anyway.

"Beats me how a man like you is in a place like this, with all your skill," Adam said.

Carse shrugged.

"I am not so skillful as you think. I only seem so, here. I lack the most important quality of all."

"What's that?"

"Courage."

Adam stared at the man in amazement. Carse, forearms on knees, was gazing quietly at the ground. He waggled his long, beautifully kept hands in a gesture of hopelessness.

96

"That's a strange thing for a man to confess," Adam said slowly. "And to hear it from a Brother of the Coast—"

"Rapier fighting is lonely fighting," Carse said. "You are on your own. And I have always been afraid of my own company. I embarrass myself, and sometimes frighten myself. You think a pirate needs to be courageous? Not at all. Truly, Captain, not the way we of Providence here practice piracy anyway—and it's the only kind I know."

"But you board!"

"It's usually all over by that time. We've won before we started—or if we weren't going to, we wouldn't start. Let us get a sign of real resistance and we shy away. And even when we do board, we're shoulder-to-shoulder, all waving out weapons and yelling bloody murder. It's part of our technique. And I don't mind it, because there's a crowd. Then it's all over. And we're busy stealing everything we can lay hands on and telling each other what brave lads we are. Besides, I'm usually drunk then. That helps. But when you fight with a rapier you fight alone."

There was some silence.

Then: "Yet you like it well enough to teach bunglers like me."

"I like it well enough to teach bunglers like you, yes. It —It reminds me of certain other times."

"Where'd you come from, Carse?"

The pirate did not answer immediately, and this pause, though his face was expressionless, in itself was a rebuke.

"On Providence, Captain, we do not ordinarily ask such questions," he said at last.

"I'm sorry."

"It's forgotten. And my faith, I have to ask you a question—though it's about the future, not the past. I must know in what way to teach you. Now I take it that you are doing all this work for two reasons—correct me if I'm wrong. One reason is *not* because you are bored. We are seldom that here, eh?"

Adam grinned. This sink Providence, into which had been poured half the human garbage of the Caribbean, this crowded hot rat-hole, where escaped slaves jostled deserters, where pimps wheedled, corsairs swaggered, whether English, French, Dutch, Danish or what, and the purveyors of rum and the purchasers of fine silks plied a noisy trade night and day, where every man carried at least a dagger, which he was embarrassingly eager to use—this place Providence might do many things to a visitor but it was not likely to bore him.

"Seldom," Adam agreed.

"I take it then that the two reasons are, first, that you want to be a gentleman—"

"My blood, sir, is every bit as—"

"Now don't be touchy! Nobody's questioning your pedigree! But you know as well as I know, Captain, that a man who carries a sword and knows how to use it is far more likely to be accepted as a gentleman than one who might boast a whole bushel basket full of certified quarterlings."

"Go on," said Adam.

"The second reason—and this is the one I'm interested in—is because there is a man you want to meet some day with no buttons, right?"

Adam nodded.

"He's not here in the camp, that I know. Excepting me, nobody here can fight with a rapier at all. They esteem it silly. When they brawl here they use whatever's handy, and when they duel it's with pistol and cutlass. What I am teaching you won't help you a bit with a cutlass, Captain. You know that."

"He's not here," Adam said.

"I won't ask you his name. I don't care. But this I should know—is he a good swordsman?"

"I don't know. I've never even seen him."

Carse rose.

"In that case we had best assume that he is." He laced his plastron. "Now I'm going to teach you how to riposte. And I don't mean parry and then half a minute later lunge. I mean tic-a-tac! right away! at what Marcelli used to call the *tempo indivisibile,* you see?"

"No," said Adam.

"Well, get up there and I'll show you."

21 It was his custom after a lesson to saunter around the camp, stopping for a jaw here, a drink there, nodding, sometimes spinning yarn, now and then putting a discreet question about followers of the late Captain Thomas Hart. He'd check a few prices. He'd look over, from the beach, any craft that had recently arrived, being careful not to seem to study *Goodwill to Men* with any special attention. And at last, almost as though by chance, he would find himself back at the shack he shared with the Honorable Maisie de Lynn Treadway-Paul. Tarpaulin Hall they called it.

In truth it was not as fortuitous as all this, his walk. He was careful never to leave Maisie alone for long.

There was this to be said about the camp: no matter what its population—which indeed might shift from three hundred to three thousand and back again within a few hours—it must have been the noisiest place, per capita, on earth. It suggested an enormous turbulent outdoor tavern, where somebody was always drunk, and there was ever present, if not a brawl, then at least the boisterous beginnings of one. Night and day made no difference. The bay could be silent at night, and usually was, no matter how many the vessels there; for the Brethren of the Coast preferred to quit their ships as soon as possible and go ashore, where there was life and movement—and rum—and by habit they left not even watchmen, excepting always half a dozen cannoneers stationed at the fort overlooking the entrance of the bay. But among the tents and huts and in the marketplace there was an unceasing hubbub which knew no clock. Wine and bumboo flowed pauselessly; women wailed or shrieked in rage; men cursed their luck at the dice games and card games, bellowing, snorting like porpoises. The auction in the marketplace never faltered. Always somewhere somebody was singing, while somewhere else men quarreled.

There were no streets in the camp, which was a heterogeneous and messy agglomeration of tents made of sail and houses fashioned from odd ship parts—spars, planks, sections of mast—lashed together with tarred rope. There was no beginning or end, no set boundary. Even the platform that made up the marketplace, the community's only semi-stable structure, from which all sorts of articles were raucously offered for sale, was moved three times, and twice because of carelessness was partly burned, in the four weeks Captain Long and the Honorable Maisie Treadway had spent on Providence.

Nature alone was orderly there, and gentle. The bay, wide, deep, glittered a glorious blue. The sand, though so light and bright as to sting the eyes, was smooth, and it sloped and rolled languidly. There wasn't much vegetation—clumps of dry juiceless sun-scorched grass that clittered anxiously in the breeze, and everywhere, as trees and as scrub, the flashy twittering palmetto. There were no hills, but neither were there any low spots. The air was dry. The sky, kindly, leaned close. A breeze was always blowing, carrying away the stench of the camp.

So Nature was good, Man bad.

Woman was even worse.

It had astonished the *Goodwill* prisoners to find women at this outlaws' retreat, and for an hour Adam had fondly supposed that this might make the place safer for and more acceptable to Maisie. He was soon disillusioned. The women of the camp were all shrill, all thoroughly vicious. Not many belonged to pirates, though a few were pirates themselves, who went to sea in search of prizes. Most of the women were there for business —of one sort or another—and were attached not to buccaneers but rather to hangers-on, men who bought and sold, who haggled and cheated, the furtive men of labored jocularity, parasites, but astute in a low way.

99

There was an amazingly large number of these commercial-fringe men—fully half the camp, not counting their trulls, Adam had estimated.

It was these same trollops, indeed, who caused so much of the clamor, all out of keeping with their numbers. It is true that there was always a squabble somewhere, always a fight about to well up; but though the pirates were a touchy lot, unless they were too drunk to know or too angry to care, they ordinarily ceased to shout curses after a certain stage in any quarrel, and adjourned to another place, another island, from which at least one of the disputants never would return. Whether this was done out of respect for the women in the camp or whether it was because the pirates truly fancied themselves as something akin to quality folks after all, as they consistently pretended to do, and so aped their betters' ways, Adam Long did not learn—and didn't care. The women, on the other hand, wasted no time in cartels, challenges, seconds, least of all fair play, but were wont to fly at one another with teeth and nails bared, soon to be rolling, kicking, on the ground. Some pirates deplored this practice, though they did not venture to break up such fights—he'd be a stout-hearted man who tried *that!*—but others enjoyed them, and ran to it when they heard one making up, and watched, cheering, while they offered bets on first blood, first fall, final outcome.

Though he sought to be inconspicuous, if only in order to get more chance to look around for some possible means of escape, Adam found himself a much pointed-at man.

There were several reasons for this. One was Maisie, who, though he did keep her under cover as much as possible, would have attracted attention anywhere. The Providencers were dazzled by Maisie, and being human they gawped at the man who owned her.

Then there was the fact that Adam had helped to build a vessel of unusual design and prodigious speed, a vessel that even with a jury boom had almost heeled one of their own finest. The pirates took a great interest in speed at sea.

Another reason for Adam's popularity was purely fortuitous: the second morning he was on the island he was accosted by a personage into whose sash had been thrust no fewer than three pistols and two daggers, a sign of distinction at Providence. This man was older than most of his fellows, and clearly a personage. On his head was knotted a red silk kerchief.

"You're from Newport, Cap'n?"

Adam stopped.

"Aye," he said.

"Think I remember you. Used to work for a man named Sedgewick?"

"Aye. He's laid up now. Paralyzed."

The pirate kept staring at Adam.

"You were a heap smaller then. About this high— And Sedgewick's house was right near the public pillory."

"It's still there. Mr. Sedgewick's house, I mean. So is the pillory, for that matter."

"And you don't remember me, eh?" Slowly the pirate took the kerchief off his head. "Maybe this'll help you?"

His hair was scanty and long, and it was pasted hard to his head by sweat; but it wasn't remarkable. What caught Adam's eye were the holes in his ears—not those in the lobes, from which swung gold rings, but those in the upper part of the ear, small, old holes, scarcely more than pinpoints of white skin tissue.

"*Sharpy Boardman!*"

"That's right, lad. It was a long, long while ago, but I'll always remember the drink you brought me that night. It was the sweetest I ever drank. God bless you."

He held out his hand. There were tears in his eyes.

"I'll give you a drink now, lad, you come to my hut. It'll be the finest French brandy, but it'll never mean as much as the water you handed me that night fifteen years ago. Come on—meet some of my friends."

Sharpy had many friends. One of the oldest and richest of the pirates, he was a man of much influence on Providence, and he never tired of telling the story of how the little Long boy had brought him that jack of water when he was nailed to the pillory. "Stood to have the skin whopped half off him, they caught him doin' it. Mates, I tell you that took sand."

The shack assigned to Adam and Maisie, doubtless as a tribute to the first lady ever to visit this settlement, was, as Providence dwellings went, downright palatial. It had no floor, but the ground it enclosed was strewn with Oriental rugs. Walls and ceiling consisted largely of tarpaulins strung between spars sunk into the earth, but there was an actual, practicable, jalousied door, ripped, doubtless, from some once-gilded galleon. And when they ate it was from silver, and when they sipped wine or rum it was out of costly Venetian glass goblets. Certain of the amenities of civilization might have been lacking at Providence, but of loot there was always plenty.

As Adam approached it today he saw a man leaving this shack, a very large man who did not look back. Adam frowned. Major Kellsen was unmistakable, even at that distance.

The major had been much about, from the beginning. With some reason he considered them his personal prisoners; but it was not only this. The man was smitten with Maisie: his infatuation was obvious. And he was jealous of Adam Long.

Major Kellsen wished to be king of the colony, no less. Providence being what it was, a democracy, where each skipper and mate and sailing master was elected by popular vote at the beginning of each voyage, he sought personal popularity. Like a politician, he moved among the men making himself amiable. He had built up a following. He hoped to increase this.

The camp *as* a camp was more or less in a state of permanent anarchy. Easily its most powerful personal member, though he kept out of sight, was one van Bramm, a spiderlike figure, indefatigibly busy, though scarcely moving, a man who never sallied forth, seldom even raised his voice. Van Bramm had small dark reptilian eyes, and his skin, too, cold, shiny, dry, suggested a serpent. He smiled at all times—maybe even in his sleep, if he ever did sleep—a fixed meaningless half-smile that had thorns in it. As he was without warmth or wit, so he was without pity. He was no fool. He'd stop at nothing. If Major Kellsen was summoning forces with the purpose of snatching the leadership from Everard van Bramm—and it looked as if he was—then Kellsen was playing with sudden death. Kellsen himself must have known this.

A liaison or even the appearance of a liaison with the lovely Lady Maisie would go a long way toward building up Kellsen's prestige. And prestige was almighty important among the pirates.

Resolved Forbes came out of a neighboring shack. Forbes was always to be depended upon. Jethro Gardner, the bosun, had been left aboard the schooner as a sort of watchman, it being assumed that a one-legged man could not play much of a part in any plot to cut that prize out. Seth Selden, made much of as soon as his calligraphical accomplishments became known, had openly gone "on the account," and had given Adam a paper asserting that he, Adam, was the rightful skipper of the *Goodwill to Men,* to whom Seth was selling his one-eighth share for (though the price wasn't mentioned in the paper) twenty-five pounds. This was cash, gold, part of the money Horace Treadway had paid for the transportation of his cousin to New York. The reason Seth was willing to let his share go at such an absurdly low price was because he considered the schooner lost to the outside world, community property here on Providence now, where Seth intended to remain. Adam did not agree with this. Adam had plans to escape.

Carl Peterson and Eb Waters, too, while they had not gone over to the enemy as openly as had Seth, were fascinated by the life here on this Bahaman island, and it was clear that they'd sign on for a piratical jaunt one of these days. Good riddance.

John Bond was laid up with fever.

The Rellison boy, dizzied by the sunlight, blinking at the things he saw, was by no means sure of himself; and he couldn't be counted upon.

Resolved Forbes alone was there, reliable; and Adam never left Maisie at the shack without checking first to make sure that Forbes was next door, watching.

Now Adam nodded toward the departing giant.

"Been here long?"

"Not long. I didn't have any orders."

"Ten minutes, maybe?"

"About that."

Adam nodded. He didn't like it; but he did not wish to show his perturbation too publicly. To change the subject he shifted his gaze toward the *Goodwill*.

"Still no boom?"

"No, but it might come in any day now. They've got a shipment of timber expected."

"Looks like we're going to be here for quite a while yet."

"Aye."

Adam went inside. There he paused, had to, until his eyes got used to the darkness.

Fully a quarter of this shack was taken up by a huge four-poster bed. A massy, carved thing from which all tophangings had long ago been ripped, and the posts of which had been chipped and scarred by knives, it remained an impressive piece. And it was comfortable.

Adam could not see Maisie at first, but he knew, sensed, that she was on this bed, her accustomed place.

Her whisper came from right about in the middle of the bed.

"It's so hot—already. Lock the door, dear."

He locked the door behind him. He heard her stir.

"That Major Kellsen's been here. A bore. As soon as he went away I got into something cooler. Come over here, darling. Don't keep standing there."

"I want to talk to you about him."

He found the bed, sat on the edge of it. He was seeing things more clearly now.

"Don't scold me, Adam. It's too hot to quarrel."

"I don't think he ought to be allowed in when I'm not here. Even if it's only for a few minutes."

"Adam"—and she looked the other way—"you trust me, don't you?"

"Of course!"

"I wouldn't—I wouldn't've—let you do—what you've done—if I didn't think you trusted me. I'm not a whore, Adam."

"No, no! But this man—"

She rolled over. She took his hands. Her own hands were warm, dry. She held his against her neck, and he could feel the blood throb and course there.

"Sh-sh-sh! No quarrel! Adam—"

"Yes?"

"Uh, how was the fencing?"

"It was all right."

"You must forget about Jervis Johnston. I shouldn't have told you—And it was a long while ago."

"You know what I'm going to do."

"You haven't changed your mind about that, Adam?"

"I don't change my mind."

She had released his hands. Her breathing was loud. He could see her clearly now. Her hair tumbling every-which-way, she wore a yellow silk wrapper, and though the curves in her body were clear there was again about her, here, something of the girlishness, the long-leggedness he had known aboard the *Goodwill to Men*. It was touching, the sight; and it caught up his breath.

Now she turned her head again, facing him, and she smiled a little, her eyes almost closed.

"Let's not talk about that, Adam."

"All right."

"It's so hot— And I've been lying here waiting for you. . . ."

22 The strips of sunlight that were javelined in between the jalousies crept toward the center of the room, stealthy as thieves, as high noon approached, while the day drowsed.

From the bay side came the thin high *ree-ee-ee* of gulls, the closer, more querulous squeal of timbers as various vessels rocked, the rattle of blocks, the rubbing of hawsers, and through it all the lazy monotonous slap-slap of wavelets striking the sand, to hiss up, spreading thin, and slither whisperingly back.

From the other three sides came curses, drunken snatches of bawdy, the hullabaloo of the marketplace.

Inside Tarpaulin Hall the chief sound was a rustle of silks, though occasionally when Captain Long stirred, just to prove to himself how exquisitely exhausted he was, the bed creaked.

"Don't recollect that brown thing," he said sleepily.

The place might have been a shop. Though much larger than the *Goodwill's* cabin, it was even more crammed with stuffs, as though these had somehow expanded in the heat; so that wherever you looked there were petticoats, bodices, skirts, chemisettes, stockings, corsets, of muslin, sagathy, satin, drugget, silk, perpetuana, rich brocade. Ribbands serpentined everywhere; lace lay in piles; and the dressing table and each stool were heaped high with fleecy frivolous furbelows.

The brown thing he had mentioned was a hunting jacket, small, trig, made of velvet. Maisie wore it with a man's high broad-brimmed beaver, a man's lawn cravat passed through a ring of gold, a box-pleated green twill skirt. She canted a riding crop under her arm. She strutted the floor for the benefit of Adam's eyes alone.

A warmish outfit? True; but she wore nothing underneath it, not a stitch. And in a moment anyway she had whisked the whole business off and was fumbling for something else, bent over, her back to him.

She was putting on a sort of fashion show. It was these between-number moments that Adam especially enjoyed, and he didn't pretend not to. He gloated. He suspicioned that Maisie hoped for a renewal of their recent activity; and he wouldn't be surprised, he told himself, if she got it. Tarnation, what a body!

He dropped an arm over the edge of the bed and picked up the brown velvet jacket.

Now Maisie was wriggling into something more feminine, something yellow—her favorite color. Her head reappeared, frills and flounces cascading away from it, and she was smiling at him: she upcocked her eyes.

Shopping was Maisie's only pastime here at Providence, and she delighted in the bargains, dickering, making to go away, returning, all that. She would have spent three-quarters of her time at the marketplace, had Adam permitted it. Not because of the pirates, who stood in awe of her and punctiliously brought down their voices and scrubbed their speech when she approached, but rather because of the camp women, who understandably hated Maisie, he had forbidden her to go out unless accompanied by him. Somewhat scared at first, she acquiesced; but now she chafed under the restraint.

For a person in bankruptcy she was marvelously well equipped with cash. You could buy anything at Providence; and Lady Maisie, though wont to crow over the prices afterward, didn't care what she spent.

True, these things were stolen, and more than one of them no doubt had been stained by blood; but Maisie looked wonderful in them all the same.

"D'ye fancy this, m'lord?"

She dropped a curtsey, half in mockery, half in order to show off the yellow skirt.

But he was absorbed now in the brown jacket. Of all the multitude of small sartorial absurdities in the shack, this suddenly had become, to him, significant.

"Swogged if I remember it," he muttered. "When did you buy it?"

"And what if I didn't buy it? What if somebody gave it to me?"

He looked up quickly.

"Who?"

"La, I've been obleeged before this to make complaint of your possessiveness, Captain. Please to remember, sir, that we're not *truly* married." She giggled. "Though I'll grant that you showed wit when you named us man and wife on the spur of the moment."

She raised her arms and started to slip the dress off over her head. The fact that she wore no underclothing was made dramatically evident, there in the dimness of the shack where her skin shone. She moved her hips, and her shoulders, so that her breasts swung, as she worked the dress off.

Adam came off the bed with a bound.

"Who gave you this?"

She was angry, and it was a hot morning. She was out of the dress now. She held it in front of her, partly covering her nakedness.

"Ah well, if you must know—rather than have my eardrums burst by such unmannerly shouting—'twas Major Kellsen."

"That popinjay!"

" 'Tis a good thing he's far away when you say that, Captain."

He paid her no mind. Adam's blood was not the sort that is easily agitated by words alone; and this particular taunt he scarcely heard. For he was thoughtful, a whit sad, too. It was clear to him what he would have to do, and he didn't like it. But he could not pass a thing like this by. Kellsen would exploit the gift to the full, telling of it everywhere, trying to get Maisie to wear the thing, alerting others to watch her then, pointing, purring, pleased with himself. And on Providence, where so much depended upon prestige, if the men and even more the women fell to sniggering at you behind your back, then you might expect no favors, no leniency. On Providence, if they weren't afraid of you they despised you. It was not a matter of personal pride with Adam, though he had his pride, too, and he was angry; but it was rather a matter of getting a chance to escape.

Kellsen had taken an inch. If he wasn't pushed back, and that promptly, and with unmistakable force, he would try to take a mile. Then it would be too late.

Adam fingered the jacket. It was good velvet, expensive. He grunted. He thrust it behind his shirt, and went outside.

Resolved Forbes, as faithful as any cuckoo in a cuckoo clock, appeared at his elbow; and Adam, squinting, frowning in the sunlight, told him what he was about to do. The mate rubbered out his lips, shook his head.

"I don't like it, sir."

"I don't like it either. But it's got to be done."

"You— You ain't going to get *killed* now?"

"I hope not," Adam said soberly.

Nodding to acquaintances, right and left, as neighborly as all-get-out, Adam Long made his way to the marketplace; and there he came upon One-Eye.

Now this odiferous obnoxious cantankerous ugly man was disliked, but he was feared. He had standing as Kellsen's familiar. His bluster, his irascible, self-important squint, were not laughed at openly. He would carry any sort of tale, no matter how harmful, to the massive major, who, to do him justice, never failed to back this toady. Like the small fish that pilots the shark, One-Eye was nothing in himself, a great deal in what he represented.

"Where's your master?"

"We don't have masters here," said One-Eye. "We are the Brethren of the Coast. No man is the master of us."

"I can hear you, Parson. Stop singing hymns. Where's Kellsen?"

Men were gathering. It was easy to raise a crowd here.

One-Eye thrust his face close to Adam's face. It was a nasty habit he had. He grasped Adam's shirt.

"When you speak of Major Kellsen you will please give him his title, understand?"

"And when you speak to me, Mr. Skunk, you will please keep your hands to yourself," said Adam, and punched him in the mouth. "Understand?"

It was not a hard blow, scarcely more than a slap, but it brought a swift bubbling of blood to his lips. One-Eye gasped, his eye popping. His hand went for the hilt of his knife.

Then Adam stepped in and really did hit him.

One-Eye went backward, the crowd quickly parting to give him room to fall. One-Eye lay still.

Adam sighed.

"Reckon I'll have to seek the fool out myself," he said, and strolled on.

He was playacting, sure. He knew perfectly well that there was no need to hunt out Major Kellsen. The whole camp was abuzz by this time, jabbering, spitting, gesticulating, they were telling one another what had happened—and what would happen next. Kellsen was being informed, assuredly. And Kellsen would act. He'd have to.

They met in the middle of the marketplace—it seemed casually, informally, by chance—and the scene could not have been better set if they'd rehearsed it. Kellsen was all done up in what Bosun Gardner would have called his "damnation regimentals," a huge cherry-red coat with a vast amount of froggery, and trimmed with lace that was positively frivolous. He carried a gold-headed walking stick almost as tall as himself. His periwig was stupendous; it must have cost fifty pounds. Adam wondered whom he had stolen it from.

He came to a graceful halt, his right foot slightly forward, garter ribbons dangling almost to his shoes. He flipped a lace handkerchief negligently at Adam.

"You sought me?"

"It's about my wife," said Adam.

He slightly stressed the word "wife" for the benefit of bystanders. In the four weeks since the taking of the *Goodwill to Men* he had more than once congratulated himself upon the presence of mind which prompted him to claim marriage to Maisie. He couldn't have conceived a more telling lie. The sacrament hushed the pirates. Though they professed, publicly and noisily, to hate all authority, even the authority of God, of which marriage was so clear an example, they must have had their doubts in the very presence of it. Though they jeered, they were filled with uneasy awe.

Yet they would veer the other way at any shift of wind, any mishandling of the sheets; for if there was anything that could be said with certainty of these pirates it was that their emotions and beliefs, jiggled and jogged by this and that, were unpredictable; they were never sure of themselves. On Adam Long, then, ironically, rested the responsibility of standing for an institution of which in fact he was only a false representative. He must now defend the wifely honor of a woman who wasn't his wife at all.

"Ah, the charming Mistress Maisie! Charming!"

"Aye, but it'll be enough if she charms me. She don't have to charm you, too."

Nobody breathed. Kellsen's eyebrows started to seek his wig.

"You, uh, have some *specific* objection, perhaps?"

"Yes," said Adam, *"this!"* and he threw the brown velvet jacket into Kellsen's face. "My wife," he added, "does not accept gifts from a thief."

He turned and started to walk away.

He did not know what to expect. He might be slaughtered in this instant. But he did not think that Kellsen would discharge a pistol in such a crowd, and if he drew he would probably be restrained.

What came was no more than a voice, but it brought him up.

"A moment, pray, Captain Long."

Adam turned.

"Yes?"

Kellsen had not stirred. The brown velvet jacket lay in the dust at his feet: nobody cared about it any longer, for it had served its purpose. Kellsen might have been disappointed, having hoped for craven, exploitable compliance, rather than a fight. But he did not show this. His eyes were cast down almost shyly.

"It is my thought that we might pursue this matter further, Captain, you and I."

"Any time you say."

"Would, uh, would *now* be too soon?"

"Now's fine."

Kellsen nodded. He turned, leaning on his cane.

"On the beach, then, in a few minutes," he drawled over a shoulder.

He left the marketplace slowly, with his handkerchief flicking away flies.

23   For all the men save two the trip was a picnic. There was no touch of ceremony, and the scramble at the beach was a joyous one. Half a hundred longboats and dories and similar craft there must have been, each overfilled, overweighted, showing precious little freeboard. Everybody was laughing, splashing. All they needed was fireworks and paper streamers to make it look like the royal barges on the Thames when the court was out for a frolic.

Chattering, they rode out among the anchored vessels, virtually all of which were unmanned at the moment. They passed the *Goodwill to Men*, and it was then that Adam felt his chest get tight for the first time. He did not look much at the *Goodwill*, three-sixteenths his now, only a glance; but he did see Jeth Gardner, forearms on the taffrail, watching this mass of boats, doubtless wondering what it was all about. Jeth did not see Adam, who was looking down after his one glance. Adam had seen casks on the deck, forty or fifty of them, and he wondered what they were. Not from the hold: they were smaller than the barrels of molasses from Horace Treadway's plantation, most of which had been rolled overside during the chase anyway. But things up there had looked in good condition. Even with one leg, and the stump so raw, Jeth Gardner would keep the *Goodwill* shipshape. Jeth had his orders. The schooner was one of the furthest out, near the pass; and Jeth was to stand by, with everything squared away, ready at any hour of the day or night, until such time as Captain Long and Mate Forbes saw the chance to sneak aboard, axe the cables, hoist canvas, and be off. *Goodwill* still carried a jury boom on her fore, but even so, given any kind of start she could probably walk away from the fastest craft the pirate fleet could show. Beyond doubt it was that broken boom which kept the schooner in the bay here. Once properly equipped she would be taken outside in search of prizes. They'd pile some greasy guns aboard her first, of course. And they'd dirty her decks with their dirty feet. Meanwhile she waited, incomplete, for her master.

Adam had already learned that the outlaws of Providence, incorrigibly poor business men, suffered from certain chronic shortages. Gorged with rum and rare wines, they had difficulty getting fruit, and even ship's biscuit was sometimes hard to come by. Of gold and silver plate they had vast quantities; yet of simple ironwork of the sort so badly needed to equip their vessels—for clasps, clamps, and such—as well as lead sheathing, an imperative in those parts—they were rather more than likely, at any given time, to have none. Any one of them might have produced for you altar plates, a triptych, candlesticks, gem-studded chalices, each one a work of art, worthy of a velvet cushion in a museum; but none could have produced a single simple nail, a plank or spar.

So Adam held his head down, and they kept going.

They passed the reef, after waving to the men who manned the cannon up in the old rebuilt fort. Other men, men who had not been able to get boats, were running out to the end of the point, to the fort, in order to get the news sooner when the flotilla returned.

The sea was a lake, the sky hadn't one cloud. It was just after noon.

In the holiday spirit the boats came together, separated, came together again, while men shouted back and forth in half a dozen different tongues. The talk had largely to do with betting; and as far as Adam could gather—the Brethren of the Coast had their own cant, not easily understood even when it was supposed to be English—the odds were three to one on Kellsen.

Nobody questioned for a moment, everybody knew, that the fight was to be à outrance, to the death. They took this for granted.

When the boats approached Cay Cucaracha—Cockroach Key the English called it—a silence fell over them, not all at once but gradually. The company broke into two parts, the smaller, the one Adam's boat was in, proceeding around to the far side.

It was tiny, an atoll, scarcely more than a raft of rubble supporting a few seared palmettos. It was round, perhaps a quarter of a mile across. The center was somewhat higher than the shore, but even the center was so low that a good-sized sea might have swept right over it.

However, there were no seas. When they landed on the sloping beach, the keel grating small coral stones, it was as easily done as bringing a canoe to the bank of a pond.

This was the only boat in sight that had come ashore. The others stayed some distance out.

Adam walked up and down, stretching his legs, his arms. There were six or seven men with him, not all of them men he knew, though he knew that they were all favorable to him—friends he didn't notably want, for him largely because they were against Major Kellsen. Adam had no wish to lead a faction in this trouble-spot. Now he paid little attention to the men.

They had become serious, even grim. One had a musket, one a cutlass, one a pistol. The one with the pistol snapped it two or three times to make sure of the spark. It was huge, with a brass barrel, no sights, a fishtail butt made of Circassian walnut. It was heavy. The others watching, the man poured in a measurement of powder, cut a large round ball, dropped the ball in, little-fingered a chunk of wadding into the muzzle, rammed this home with a ramrod. He rapped the barrel smartly on his heel, so that powder fluffed out through the touchhole and into the pan. He handed the pistol to Adam.

"Use it careful. It's the only shot you'll get."

"Make a good club," Adam said, and took it by the barrel and shook it.

"'Sblood, beefwit! That's *loaded!*"

The man with the cutlass handed this to Adam, who took it in his left hand. It was exactly the same length as Major Kellsen's, the man said. They had measured them.

Adam asked: "Where is the major?"

"The other side of this island. He's got a pistol, too."

Adam looked around. The sun was almost directly overhead. The sand, the stones, the fronds of palmettos shimmered. The sea gave little love-taps to the shore at his feet.

A semicircle of boats, possibly twenty of them, was motionless a couple of hundred yards away. Other boats were coming around from the far side of the island, but staying well out.

"And where do we meet?"

"Wherever you run into one another. The major's right opposite here. He ought to be ready now. Are you?"

Adam wetted his lips. He did not have much spit. He wanted to swallow but was afraid that he couldn't. He looked toward the center of the island, where nothing moved.

He hoped that Maisie was all right. He hoped that if he was killed she would still escape. Poor girl! She'd had it so hard, she was entitled to a change of luck.

"Yes," he said. "Yes, I reckon I'm ready."

The musket went off with a bang, and in spite of himself Adam jumped, not having expected it. Immediately afterward there was another musket shot from the far side of the island. It sounded a faint thin *"pip!"* The men scrambled into the boat, and pushed out.

"Good hunting," they called.

They rowed away.

Adam Long stood motionless a moment. He thought that if only he could pray he would feel better, but he feared to kneel just now. He kept watching the middle of the island. Nothing moved.

After a while he began to walk sideways along the shore, still watching the middle of the island, though from time to time he flicked his eyes right and left, the way he was going, the way he had come.

He had some idea that Major Kellsen would do the same as he was doing—start circling the island, whether to right or to left.

But suddenly he realized that the major, not new at this, was more likely to take a bolder course and charge straight across the island, hoping to reach him before he had found cover.

In that case Adam would be utterly exposed, a sitting duck.

He started to run for the palmetto. He didn't care what the men in the boats back there thought of him. He ran fast, bending low.

What a fool he had been to waste that time!

Gasping, sobbing, he threw himself into the first clump of palmetto. His heart was going like a triphammer, but it was the only thing that he could hear.

He was more scared than he had ever been in his life.

When he got to his knees and peered around, in all directions, cautiously, he saw little enough. He was in a slight natural depression between two dunelike mounds. It was a good place, and he was in no hurry to leave it.

He prayed then. It was not an impassioned prayer. Simply and quietly he asked God to spare him a little longer, for the sake of Maisie, the hands, and the schooner, amen.

It made him feel better, as he had known it would.

He got to his feet, though he squatted, keeping his head low. Some of the powder had slipped out of the firing pan of the pistol, and he rapped the barrel with his left fist to joggle more through the touchhole. He wiped his mouth. He took up the cutlass. He started to prowl.

It was arduous work, and he felt a fool, though still frightened. He was not accustomed to stoop and crouch and bend, slithering from place to place like some obnoxious animal mankind sought to exterminate. Instinct screamed to stand up like a man, not skulk like a wildcat; but he crushed instinct and continued to crawl.

He was careful not to knock stones together, not to rattle palmetto fronds. Whenever he elected to break cover he looked around first in all directions; then made a dash for it; then lay still, listening, panting.

The ground was irregular, pockmarked like the surface of the moon. Adam sought out the low spots, avoided the high.

It was a strain on his muscles and often he stopped to rest; but he remained alert.

Was Kellsen doing the same thing? Was the Major crawling and creeping from place to place? Or was he a paragon of patience who could wait unstirring for hours until his opponent, restless, twitchy, exposed himself? Adam doubted this. The flamboyant clothes, the drawl, the insistence on supremacy, did not suggest a phlegmatic nature. Major Kellsen, Adam suspected, was out looking for him in exactly the same way he, Adam, was out looking for Major Kellsen.

It was like a game of blind man's buff in which *all* the players staggered around with bandaged eyes—and the forfeit was the loser's life.

Now and then he came in sight of the sea again, but it was impossible to tell on which side, so nearly round was the island and so much the same everywhere.

More than once it occurred to him that what he really should do was lay out the island in his mind, make a mental diagram of it, and take care not to retrace his own footsteps—in other words, plot this prowl mathematically, so as to be sure that he covered every yard. Yet, again, where was the sense of that? It could only be a useful tactic if Kellsen sat motionless.

They could of course go on creeping around like this for hours—Adam wondered what would happen when night came. Certainly he'd never dare to sleep.

The pistol in his right hand, the cutlass in his left held low so that it should not reflect the sun, he lifted his head out of a clump of palmetto —and saw a strange man.

This man was about fifty feet away and had his back turned. Clad in buff breeches and a brown shirt, neither of them silk, which would have glittered, and black wool stockings, he wore also a brown linen cap. He was large, but bent far over, apelike, his fists almost trailing the ground. His attitude suggested a steel spring: he was set to snap shut. His head jerked back and forth as he looked around. When he turned that head Adam's way, Adam ducked.

A moment later Adam looked again. And Adam came to realize marveling, that this was in fact Major Kellsen. Shorn of periwig, froggery, and bravado, this uncertain duelist, like Adam himself, tense, crept from place to place, fearful lest a finger, an unwitting toe, should turn over death.

Adam's pistol was a cannon in miniature. He had seen the charge poured into it, a heavy one. He had seen the ball they'd cut—tremendous. Though it would not carry far with any degree of accuracy, this brass-and-walnut weapon could smash a man's head open, tear a man's shoulder off, crush his chest. And Major Kellsen, all unaware, made a perfect target.

But Adam couldn't slay a man from behind. He had to say something, make some noise.

He cleared his throat. Kellsen didn't stir.

"Uh, *ahoy!*" cried Adam.

Kellsen whirled around, his pistol raised. Adam fired.

The explosion was terrific. The recoil threw his arm high. There was a great deal of smoke.

But when the smoke had sauntered away, Major Kellsen still stood there. He looked thunderstruck, his eyes bugged out. But assuredly he had not been hit. And in a moment he began to grin.

His pistol high, he started to walk toward Adam. He placed his feet carefully. He would be sure of himself when he shot.

And all this while he was grinning. He was a very happy man, teeming with the joy relief brings, a relaxation of the tension. For now he had won the duel.

His thumb cocked the pistol. It made a sharp *"click!"*

He came on, and on.

Adam Long might have turned and run, saving himself a few minutes of life, conceivably even a few hours; but where could he go? Kellsen, with but one precious ball, would hold fire until he could not possibly miss.

Yes, Adam could have run, dodging from place to place, from hole to hole, like a rabbit. To hell with that! He was going to die, but he didn't have to die whimpering.

He rose. He threw his pistol straight at Major Kellsen's face.

There was an explosion, as Kellsen's foot slipped. His gun, like Adam's, had been hair-triggered.

There was a great deal of smoke.

And Adam Long, with a gurgle of delight, a throaty sound, realized that he was alive.

He didn't grin. He *laughed.*

It was not often that Adam Long laughed.

He shifted the cutlass to his right hand. He fairly whooped as he made for the major.

Kellsen was strong, and he had long arms, long legs, a reach longer than Adam's.

This was a spirited fight, though a short one. It would not have gladdened the heart of a fencing master. The men were clumsy. But they were fierce.

Kellsen stood erect, hacking down. Adam went in low, crouching, his guard high above his head.

Three times they locked hilts, after a brave sparking and slapping of steel. Three times, by common consent, though without word of mouth, or even a grunt, each sprang back.

The fourth time Adam went in lower than ever, but with his blade also low this time. He didn't try to slash. He swept into a straight classic lunge, as though it was a Spanish rapier he held. For you can lunge with a cutlass, which had a point as well as an edge. That is, you can if you don't mind exposing your whole head. Adam ran a terrible risk. If Kellsen was fast—

Kellsen wasn't fast. His sword never came down—except that it slipped out of nerveless fingers. He was slow in falling, like some colossal oak. Yet he died rapidly enough, coughing up great gouts of blood, quarts of it.

Adam had trouble getting the sword out. He carried it, together with Kellsen's, down to the beach. It was a beautiful day.

"All right, ye dogs! Come and take me away!"

24   Adam knew from Newport how news travels fast in a small place; but the pirates of Providence had some system of their own for disseminating information, and it was a system that would have made the tongues of Rhode Island matrons seem slow. Long before the flotilla of small boats even got past the fort and into the bay the whole population of the island, including the Honorable Maisie de Lynn Tread-way-Paul, lined up along the beach, knew the outcome of the contest on Cockroach Key.

She had thrown herself into his arms with a fervor that took the breath out of him, embarrassed him, too, in front of all those people. Yet the others appeared to expect this, and there were even cheers for the lady mixed with the cheers for Captain Long. He put her aside, tut-tutting, near to tears because of what he saw in her eyes, the anxiety there, the love; and of course it wouldn't do to let anybody see him acting that way.

"You shouldn't have done a thing like that for me," she cried again and again. "I'm not worth it, Adam! You shouldn't have done it for me!"

Well, he hadn't done it for her, except maybe indirectly; and later on, in the comparative privacy of Tarpaulin Hall, he tried to explain this. He had done it for her, yes; but he'd also done it for himself, for the two of them, and for Jeth Gardner and Resolved Forbes and the others, and last but by no means least for the *Goodwill to Men*. It had not been a grudge fight, a matter of jealousy. It had been done, it had *had* to be done, in order to get his standing straightened out. Sniggered over, he could do nothing toward escape. Admired, he might be able to do much.

He had tried to explain to Maisie that when he went to England, soon, he would certainly seek out, among others—he did not mention his father the Earl of Tillinghast, who was high on his list of those-to-be-seen—her seducer, Sir Jervis Johnston. He had sworn that, and he'd do it. *That* would be personal: it would be directly and entirely for love of her. But this affair on Cay Cucaracha—

She'd have none of the explanation. His intent to call out Jervis Johnston she had never appeared to take seriously anyway, but she was impressed, and deeply touched, by the fact that Adam had killed Major Kellsen. That was immediate, undeniable. It was not part of a dream seated in the future: and Lady Maisie could understand it. His protests were swept aside as evidence of his too great modesty. She cried repeatedly that he shouldn't have done it for her. She insisted upon fussing over him.

So he let her. If a woman is bound and determined to believe something, he reasoned, it was better to agree. After all, it was pleasant. It was ridiculous in one sense, true—Maisie demanding that he lie still while she fetched him this and fetched him that, and washed him, and anxiously brought him things to eat and drink, quite as though he was near death, whereas he hadn't a scratch on him and wasn't even tired, not having had to row either way—but in the long run it soothed, it flattered. Besides, the attitude reassured Adam. Feeling sneaky, feeling disloyal, he had from time to time recently caught himself wondering if maybe the tropical sunshine had brought out in Maisie a certain crassness he had not previously supposed was there. She was not, or not always, the same girl he had known on the schooner. It was not just that her unconcealed and even exuberant enjoyment of their intimacy somewhat shocked Adam Long, who had more than once caught himself blushing, too, at her habit of exposing her body; it was also, and perhaps even more, the way she looked and acted in public—a note of shrillness had crept into her voice, a touch of tautness at the corners of her mouth. He loved her, and thoughts like this were a torture for him to bear. But now he felt better about it. Now he knew beyond doubt that she loved him. It wasn't only a matter of words: it was a lot more than that. It wasn't just the way she had thrown herself into his arms, down there on the beach. It was a feeling he had when he was with her. She had been stirred, a condition she couldn't have concealed if she'd wanted to. Through all her fussing, silly as some of it was, this truth stuck out. She loved him.

So he lay back and enjoyed it. A man doesn't get that kind of attention every day, and there was no reason why he shouldn't have a good time.

As far as his physical condition was concerned, he was able to prove to her beyond all doubt that it was excellent; and this, too, he enjoyed, though it was disconcerting to have that crowd surging and stewing outside, scarcely beyond reach, sometimes even causing the walls of Tarpaulin Hall to sway, and never quiet. But you can get used to anything, he learned.

Once in the night he woke up and lay for a time staring at a ceiling he couldn't see and thinking, unexpectedly, of Major Kellsen.

Kellsen was dead and you shouldn't think of him any more, Adam knew. Nobody else here did. He heard the sounds of the camp, where there was no respect for the clock and where a most prodigious celebration was going on. Those men and women out there, by no means unaided by rum, had worked themselves into a frenzy of admiration for him, Adam Long—admiration that almost approached, sacrilegiously, adoration. The fight on Cucaracha was the first part of the process of being built into a legend; and Adam was its hero. Liked before, now, by tarnation, he was fairly revered. This threw him off, for it was not at all what he had sought; and he wasn't sure that popularity was a good thing to have on Providence Island in the Bahamas this year of Our Lord 1702.

Kellsen had sought popularity and achieved a certain measure of it, and who thought of Kellsen now? Kellsen was the only man Adam Long had ever killed, but he felt no squeamishness about this. He was not proud of himself, but he wasn't ashamed of himself either. It had been a job of work, and he'd done it. He'd had his reasons. The results flummoxed him—all this clamor and praise—but he still thought that he'd done what he should have done, and if he'd had to do it over again he would do it the same way.

But Kellsen—didn't anybody think of him? Kellsen only a few hours ago had been a man of some magnificence. Something between a pouter pigeon and a peacock perhaps, but a man all the same, with a man's heart, a man's feelings. He, too, had risked everything. The only difference between him and Adam was that he had lost, Adam had won. And because Kellsen had lost he was forgotten. So far as Adam knew, nobody had even taken the trouble to go back to the middle of Cockroach Key and view the body, much less bury it. And when they landed on the beach here, Adam had spotted one pirate wearing that high full flamboyant periwig of Kellsen's, while three or four others wore coats that had belonged to the dead man. So early! It did seem indecent. They had a curious outlook on the matter of property here at Providence. Any man would snick his knife out in a dispute about sixpence; but that was cash, and different. The same man would gladly give you, or at least sell you for a song, weapons, articles of clothing, pieces of furniture, which indeed constituted something close to communal property. Kellsen's wardrobe, in other words, had become the possession of the men who got there first. But it did seem, all the same, as though they might have waited a little while.

Adam had despised Major Kellsen until he killed him. Now he was not at all sure that he didn't feel sorry for the man.

Maisie moaned a little in her sleep, and he looked at her, his heart going all jelly. He could be a hero outside: he was humble here. Loveliness like that, his to touch and take, lying beside him, was a heap of responsibility. Here was an angel! He swallowed, and that was hard to do. Yet when she moaned again stirring a mite, and gave a small sad sigh in her sleep, so that he saw the silk coverlet rise and fall over the outlines of her breast, he knew that he was going to wake her up. And sure enough, pretty soon he did.

25 The call came early, along with the dawn, a sudden sharp rapping on the door. Adam sat up, sucking in his breath. Maisie was awake, and she watched him. She, too, was frightened.

Sternly: "Yes?"

"Message from Captain van Bramm."

"That's what I was afraid of," whispered Adam.

For in camp the talk was all Long, Long, Long, the redoubtable skipper from Newport, the captain who had skewered—what was his name? This was not at all what Adam sought. He was willing to accept popularity if it meant power—in the right place. But he wanted no part in the politics of this pirates' nest, a settlement that was a stench under the nostrils of civilization and was tolerated temporarily only because the Dutch and English and French and Spanish navies were too busy with their war to stamp it out. He owed more than that, and much more, to Maisie. He owed it to Horace Treadway, whose passage payment he had accepted; and to the burghers of Newport, whose schooner he commanded. Yes, and by thunderation, he owed it to himself! He simply couldn't afford to be an idol.

It was not too be supposed that Everard van Bramm, hearing all these hysterical shouts of praise, and doubtless many lower, more serious, but equally fervent whispers as well—for the man heard everything—would permit such a state of affairs to continue. But what would van Bramm do? Adam had seen the man only once, and then briefly, for van Bramm seldom came out into the open air. In those moments Adam had sized him up as a man not easily sized up. Would van Bramm, who himself cared nothing for praise, though he did care for power, make Adam an offer—suggest, say, that Adam go on being the man on the pedestal while he, van Bramm, manipulated the machine? Or would van Bramm simply strike? If he struck, there would be no warning. That much Adam was sure of.

These men at the door right now might be ready to rush him when he opened it, knock him down, beat him to death, or perhaps hack him with their cutlasses.

Adam got out his sheath knife. Each man from the *Goodwill* had been permitted to retain this weapon, or tool, presumably because the pirates took its existence for granted and would no more have thought of taking it from a prisoner than they would have thought of pulling his teeth or tearing out his fingernails.

Adam held this behind him. At the door he looked back. Maisie was watching him wide-eyed, but when he frowned at her and made a motion commanding her to cover her shoulders, she couldn't restrain a giggle. Maisie always found his prudery amusing. But she did cover her shoulders.

Adam opened the door, stepping back and a little to one side. He did not display the knife.

There was only one man before the door, though others, idly curious, hovered in the background, for a courier from van Bramm's headquarters always drew a crowd.

"A message from Captain van Bramm to Captain Long."

Adam held out his hand.

"I'll take it."

The man was not to be cut short like that. He was tall and gaunt, and the skin of his face, heavily lined, had the cretaceous quality of chalk: you thought, looking at it, that you could have chipped some of it away with your thumbnail. He was very earnest, conscious of the audience.

"Captain van Bramm's compliments to Captain Long, and he says to come to his house."

"Now?"

"Why, of course," cried the courier, off guard for the moment. Adam shook his head. He smiled.

"I'm sorry. I have an appointment to have breakfast with Mistress Long this morning, and after that I am expected for a rapier lesson by Master Carse. But after *that*—say, in about two hours from now?—I would be glad to call upon Captain van Bramm. Will you give him my compliments, please, and take this message to him? Thank you."

And he closed and locked the door.

Maisie was looking at him. She nodded.

"Good," she said. "But I still don't like it."

"I don't either."

"I'd feel better if I was with you when you go for that fencing lesson."

"Why don't you come along then?"

She got up, and started to turn over dresses and skirts.

"Perhaps I will, but I have nothing to wear."

It was a triumphant procession, which again Adam hadn't wanted. He would have been followed, and cheered, whenever he went out, after the events of yesterday; but this march might have been interpreted to look as if he intended to create excitement, as though he asked for applause. To be sure, it would have been impossible to go out anywhere at any time in the company of Lady Maisie and not attract attention. This morning she looked superb. She was all done up in yellow and silver, and, under a sunshade yellow as buttercups, her fine brown eyes gleamed, her red-brown hair danced and glittered, as she smiled and nodded right and left, gracious, a queen. Maisie did not personally, physically, fear the pirates; she only feared what they might do to her lover. Maisie did not fear any men. She had learned from experience that all she ever had to do was smile. She smiled today.

Though Carse of the beautiful hands apparently was unaware of the crowd that trailed Adam and Maisie out to the fencing strips, and showed no self-consciousness during the lesson, as an Adam Long not yet sure of himself did, the master was uncommonly if unobtrusively kind. He gave few instructions, and those in a tone that implied that he was only reminding Adam of them, rather than giving them for the first time. He did not permit Adam to win any of the bouts—that would have been too obvious—but there was none of the harshness that sometimes featured their meetings alone, nor was there any disarming, or seating Adam with a thump on the ground. Afterward the two men shook hands, thanking each other.

Taking off his plastron, Adam strolled over to the bag of blades. Nervously he whipped a few. All were buttoned.

"You, uh, you didn't happen to bring a *workable* sword with you today, did you?" he asked quietly.

"I didn't happen to, no. I did it purposely. Here. It is conceivable that you might need it. You deserve it anyway."

There it was, scabbard and all, a somewhat Italian-looking weapon, slightly archaic, but a beauty—silver-hilted, with bell guard, with long fancy quillons. He drew it slowly, thrilling to hear the whisper of the steel. The blade itself was true Toledo, damaskeened with gold in a folageous design near the hilt. A handsome thing, surely; but no toy! He whipped it, smiling. It had perfect balance. The point was stiletto-sharp, and each edge might have been a razor.

"But, man, this is valuable!"

"Keep it," Carse said carelessly. "It can serve as a souvenir of our lessons."

"You talk as if I was leaving."

"It could be that you are. It could be. In any event, Captain, it might give you confidence to know that you've got steel at your side when you answer van Bramm's summons in a little while."

Adam, buckling on the sword, looked at him.

"You know about that?"

"Everybody on the island knows about it. Excuse me, Captain—"

Maisie had come over, and she thanked him graciously for helping her husband keep up his rapier work, and gave him a hand to kiss. A moment later she looked curiously at him.

"Haven't we met before, sir? La, your face is familiar! In London?"

"Impossible, ma'am. I have never been in London."

Adam rested his left hand on the hilt of the sword, and felt the point go up behind. That was a good feeling. He had never before worn a sword. He thought that he would always wear one now.

Resolved Forbes was by his side, speaking low out of a corner of his mouth.

"It'll be tonight."

"Good! Does Jeth know?"

"I'll tell him. But still no boom."

"We'll use the jury."

Forbes started to drift away, but hovered.

"Don't get killed now, Captain, when you call on van Bramm."

"I won't get killed."

"It would spoil everything," Resolved Forbes pointed out.

26   From his name you would take it that the tyrant of Providence was Dutch, but in appearance he might have been of any nationality; and he spoke, it was reported, every known language, each with an accent. Some there were, even in that ungodly company, who branded the question pointless anyway, saying that Everard van Bramm was not a man at all but a devil.

To these freebooters the bizarre was a delight, the barbaric a condition to be cultivated. As vain as women, if scarcely as neat, all of them were besmudged, most were lousy as well; and they had a childlike fondness for color. As though to make up for their lack of inward strength, the way their emotions wobbled, the instability of their existence, they favored not only gay apparel but also anything *metallic* they could lay hands on. That they were overarmed—ludicrously so, it seemed at first—became understandable when their method of taking prizes was learned. A great sudden show of weapons was a part of this technique. Yet they loaded themselves with cutlery and firearms in camp, too, when there was nobody to intimidate. Each fairly clanked as he moved. Adam Long had seen pirates here with as many as five pistols stuck in their sashes—though it might be that few or none of these would work. They went in, too, and very heavily, for large belt and shoe buckles, flashy cutlass hilts, and all manner of bijouterie—not just ear ornaments but finger rings, gold and silver chains, even in some cases bangles.

Into this pattern Everard van Bramm fitted perfectly. His was an ugliness that fascinated.

Though the figure of a spider persists, it is not altogether accurate. A spider has no force, being dependent rather upon guile or venom, or on both. Van Bramm had the guile, the poison as well, and, a chunky silent man, he did give the impression of one who squats in the middle of a web. But he was a person of great bodily strength. He bulged with muscle. He was more than surface; for he had in him, even beyond his horrible appearance, immense reserves of brutality.

When Adam Long was ushered into his presence, van Bramm was puffing on a long pipe, and the clouds of smoke that blurred his features lent him an additionally diabolical aspect: he might have been some overfed fiend, spikily asmile, who peered up through the smoke from the brimstone while he greeted a freshly damned soul into Hell. In that light the smile, never amiable, seemed rather a leer.

The man was stripped to the waist, which waist, a large one, was enwrapped in four or five heavy, raw silk sashes of various colors. It was *not* stuck with daggers and pistols, in the Providence mode: there were no weapons about van Bramm at all. He wore short black flannel pantaloons, very wide, which did lend him a Dutch air. He wore soft slippers, red leather exquisitely tooled, somewhat Moorish in manner. His ankles were bare. The torso was tremendous, but though there was fat, it was not sloppy fat: van Bramm would never have waddled. His head was large—and as bald as an egg. He had so thick a neck that it seemed no neck at all. There were many rings on his fingers, even a ring on one of his thumbs. A plain flat band of gold encircled his left arm just above the biceps. A heavy chain, the links of which were thick gold triangles, hung against a chest as innocent of hair as the head. From his ears were suspended silver crescents set with small diamonds, rubies, emeralds. These quivered as he puffed on his pipe, and the gems, shaken, caused a swarm of tiny bright reflections to swing back and forth on the top of each massive, slightly oily, satin-muscled shoulder.

With it all, Everard van Bramm's most compelling feature was his eyes. They were the eyes of a snake.

Adam's first thought was one of gladness that he'd refused to bring Maisie with him. She had pleaded to come, bring afraid for him. Well, Maisie had a strong stomach, and especially for a young woman seemingly so slight; but Adam doubted that she could have looked upon van Bramm without swooning.

Resolved Forbes was keeping an eye on Maisie; and this need was regrettable, for Forbes had a great many other things to do today.

"Sit ye down, Captain. Rum? Bumboo? Madeira?"

"Thanks," said Adam, and flopped upon a cask and spread his legs, the sword hiked around to fall between them.

Nobody mentioned the sword, but it was certain that they all saw it. For there were others in the room, four or five others, though van Bramm was the only one who counted. A man named Cark did a great deal of the talking, but he watched van Bramm's face all the while as might an interpreter.

There was no palaver, as Adam had expected. They went right to the point.

"You come armed, Captain—" with a waggle of his pipe to indicate the sword. "Are you a prisoner here or one of us?"

Adam chuckled.

"That's just what I was going to ask *you*."

Van Bramm chuckled. He raised a blond eyebrow toward Cark, then returned to his pipe.

"The late 'Major' Kellsen, so-called," Cark said sententiously, "had given us to believe that when you and your shipmates and your esteemed wife were captured, Captain, you expressed a willingness to go on the account. Did he get this straight?"

"He did not. I expressed a willingness to go with them."

"But there was nothing else you could do!"

"That's right."

"Kellsen reported that you had agreed to join us."

"I said nothing about going on the account."

"That was his understanding."

"I can't help it what his understanding was. His understanding up till yesterday was that he knew how to fight with a cutlass, but it seems he was wrong there, too."

Cark was deadly serious, but van Bramm here took the pipe out of his mouth and chuckled. Van Bramm looked appreciatively at Adam.

"What about the others?" he asked Cark.

"Selden, Peterson and Waters will join. Gardner, Rellison, Bond and Forbes will do whatever the skipper says."

"So you see, Captain, how many lives you take when you refuse to become a pirate."

"I didn't say I refused to become a pirate."

"You will join us then?"

"I haven't made up my mind yet."

"Bloody well time you did," somebody muttered.

Now this was true. What Adam had been banking upon was the Providencers' clear propensity to let things slide, their slovenliness, laziness, lack of attention to details. The very phrase, "go on the account," meaning to become an out-and-out pirate, an avowed pariah, was an odd one—or was it ironic?—to apply to these men who couldn't keep anything straight, in their minds or on their books. What Adam had hoped was that he and his fellows from the *Goodwill* after a while would be taken for granted, more or less forgotten. Then when the right time came they could slip away. He wished to do everything he could to give the appearance of settling down, not talking about the outside world, never letting himself be seen to gaze wistfully at the *Goodwill*. However, being inconspicuous was difficult when you were paired with a woman like Maisie Treadway. And since the fight on Cucaracha he might as well resign himself to the fate of being a folk hero, a still-living myth.

Van Bramm leaned toward him. There was never a moment when the man didn't smile.

"We have your cargo, which we don't want, Captain. We have your vessel, which we do. We'd like to have you. What's your decision?"

Adam paused.

"After all, Captain, you're a man of sense. You have your fortune to make. Well, join up. The way they feel about you out there"—with a wave of the pipe toward the door—"you're sure to be elected captain of any enterprise you undertake. That's a double share."

"If I get it."

"I think you'd get it. I think you're the kind of man who would. And remember there's a war going on. We're free to roam the seas and nap anything we can nap."

"And remember this, too, that the war ain't going to last forever. And once it's over they'll be looking around for people to hang—people they didn't have time to hang while they were fighting."

"Afraid?"

"Not of hanging, no. But maybe I am a mite afraid of going into a business I've got no control over and can't say how it might end. If we had a guarantee that this war would last so-and-so-many years, that would be something else again. But we haven't. We didn't know when it was going to start, any more'n we knew why. And we won't know when it's going to end—not until they tell us it's all over—and we won't know why *then* either."

"Meaning you think piracy's bad business?"

"Well, there's a power of folks don't care for it."

"When the pirate's small, yes. But look at Drake. He was the one said, 'Who ever heard of being a pirate for a million pounds?' "

"Well, a million pounds, that's different," Adam conceded.

"Did they hang Drake? No, they knighted him."

"That was a long while ago."

"Henry Morgan wasn't such a long while ago," one of the other men said. "And they knighted him, too."

"They didn't knight Brandish. Or Kidd."

"Kidd was a fool."

"And what about Thomas Tew? Blown to bits. And Avery? Buried in a pauper's grave after they stole all his money from him and he didn't dare squawk. And Tom Hart? He hangs in my home town right now. Been hanging there two years. It hasn't done him any good."

Van Bramm shook a reflective head.

"Witness Tom Hart's turning-off, did ye, Captain?"

"Aye. Did you know him?"

"I was his sailing master. And Newport—never thought they'd get him there. We had a good agent in that town. Man name of Evans."

For a moment Adam was too frightened to speak. He didn't dare let eagerness sound in his voice.

"Zephary Evans?" he asked after a while, sounding casual, offhand.

"Could be. Long lank man with a long thin nose. Looked like a crane —like he ought to be standing on one leg." He put the pipe aside and leaned forward. His earrings went back and forth, making a kaleidoscope on the top of each shoulder. "Well, Tom Hart swung, though he was a slick 'un, I'll grant you. Ask me, he was sold out by somebody—maybe your smug Mister Evans. But that's no porridge for this meal. What we want to know now is: Will you sign up?"

Adam paused.

There was a knock on the door. For a moment, startled, they ignored this; but the knocking continued. One of the men went to the door.

"Captain Long's mate." He made the announcement to van Bramm. "Wants to speak to him."

"Why not?" said van Bramm.

Adam went to the door. Relief leapt into the eyes of Resolved Forbes, who stood there. Forbes had been sent by Maisie—Adam saw this right away—to make sure that he was alive.

Behind Forbes, too, though a respectful distance behind, a worshipping crowd was pleased by the appearance of Adam. It was as though he were royalty. There was a glad bumble of greeting, even a few cheers.

One of these men seemed vaguely familiar; but Adam did not permit himself to look at them; the last thing he wanted just then was cheers.

"It's still tonight?" he whispered to Forbes.

"Aye. Bond and the boy, too. You all right in there?"

"I'll get through till dark—somehow."

"Just one other thing—"

"Yes?"

"Man named Willis Beach wants to join up. Says he knows you."

"Willis Beach?"

"Says you saved him from a press gang. Wants to serve under you, the way they're allowed to pick their skippers here."

"Oh. Well, sign him on. We sure need another hand. But keep him aboard. Don't trust him ashore."

"What about Lady Maisie, sir?"

"She mustn't know, of course."

There was a great deal of silence when Adam turned back into the dim room, closing the door behind him. They all looked at him. The talk about who'd hanged and who hadn't was all very well, but the issue was clear enough. Was he or wasn't he joining them?

"Well?"

"You have been patient, gentlemen, but I'm going to ask you to wait till tomorrow morning. I want to talk it over with my wife."

They snarled at that, and moved toward him, reaching for their knives, for they supposed that he was jeering at them. But Everard van Bramm, the only one who mattered, raised a hand.

"You others get out," he said.

Soon these two, alone, faced one another.

Van Bramm took the pipe out of his mouth.

"Captain, you're planning to bolt tonight."

A blow in the mouth couldn't have startled Adam more.

Van Bramm still was smiling, even chuckling a little, down deep.

"No, nobody's betrayed you. I just put two and two together, Captain. I've been watching you. You didn't see me, but I was there. You don't want to join up. But you don't want to die either."

Adam said nothing.

"So you think to escape. You could probably do it alone, in a small boat. But you want to take your crew—those of 'em who want to go with you—you feel you owe it to them. And you want to cut out your own vessel. You love that schooner, Captain. I've watched you look at her. You just couldn't leave her behind. Well, tonight's the logical time. That mock trial ought to draw almost everybody in camp. You hope it'll draw Senac and Williamson from the fort, too, don't you?"

He was guessing, but he guessed with an uncanny accuracy. Recovered from his first jolt of amazement, Adam was silent, watchful.

Van Bramm waved his pipe stem.

"Good, good. Why don't you escape then, tonight?"

Adam might have looked puzzled. Was he being played with, cat-and-moused? Van Bramm shook a sleepy head.

"I could have you killed, but—they like you too much." He waved the pipe stem to indicate the crowd outside, unseen but audible. "*Today* you are their hero. Tomorrow it may be different, but *today* is the day we live in, no? If I kill you now, I might have trouble with them. If I let you stay, I'm sure to have trouble. Kellsen was a fool. You're not. You'd be heading an uprising in no time at all."

"I see," softly.

"I'm sure you do. By all means, run away. I'll miss that bonnie boat of yours, but it's worth it to be rid of you, Captain. I'll even go so far as to promise that Williamson and Senac won't be out at the fort tonight—and if they're not there nobody else'll be. Oh, there might be a few shots from the beach, but only musket fire. You can clear the Point before the cannon's manned."

"How do I know this ain't a trick to get me out there, sink me?"

"You'll see Senac and Williamson at the trial. Besides, how can you lose? If you *don't* go, Captain, I'll have no other choice—I'll *have* to kill you."

Adam nodded. It made sense, admittedly.

"There's only one other thing, Captain. When I call Cark and the others back, I'll tell 'em you've agreed to go on the account. You don't have to take any oath! Simply hear me say that—and don't deny it. That will be my justification for calling in the gunners. If you're one of us, we don't have to watch you. The others, afterward, they might think I was too trusting—but they won't suppose I helped you to get away. Understand?"

"I think I do."

"It would seem to make you a traitor to the brotherhood—and you know what that means, if you should get caught—or if you should ever come back to Providence here. But I don't think you ever will, eh?"

"It doesn't seem likely," said Adam Long.

27 Atop a tun in the middle of the marketplace sat a fat man wrapped in a rich red robe trimmed with ermine—real ermine —and he wore three wigs, one above the other, through the topmost of which a sea gull's feather had been thrust. He walloped the tun with the flat of a hatchet, his gavel. He hiccupped.

"Oyez, oyez!"

Somebody emptied a jack of rum onto the wigs and it soaked through these to zigzag in erratic rivulets down the face of the fat man.

"Order in the court!"

A dumpy fellow with the pocked face of a frog now rose. An inverted thundermug was over his head. He wore the handle on the left.

"If your honor please— If your honor please—"

"I don't please! Sit down—before I order the sergeant-at-arms to knock you down!"

This was very funny. There were roars of laughter. The torches spat and hissed, and smoke coiled out of them to hang in aerial hanks around the camp.

Adam Long loosened his sword in its scabbard, his knife in its sheath. He sat quiet, but his eyes were busy. It looked as if almost everybody in the colony was here in the marketplace, excepting van Bramm himself, who never showed up at such affairs. Certainly the company's best gunners, Williamson and Senac, were there. All the same, Adam was uneasy.

"If your honor please, we have a very serious case here tonight. A very serious case indeed. If your honor please, this is the very serious case of a man who is in love with his wife."

"Oh, no! Not that!"

The Brethren of the Coast, here assembled in all their tatterdemalionism, and for the most part drunk, thought a great deal about the law. When they were not defying it, they liked to deride it. This, now, was their way of celebrating some special occasion, their favorite form of amusement, a mock trial. They were hilarious.

Adam was in a conspicuous place, necessarily. Nearby, Resolved Forbes said, as usual, nothing, seeing, as usual, everything. Jeth Gardner with his one leg, John Bond with his touch of fever, and the not-trusted Willis Beach, the Londoner, were aboard the schooner in the bay. Maisie of course was at Tarpaulin Hall, unguarded, alas, just for the moment.

Peterson and Eb Waters, like Seth Selden, had outspokenly joined the pirates. Adam could see them now, laughing. Seth with his Adam's apple gleefully abounce. Adam wished he could see Seth apart, if only for a moment, to ask him about Zephary Evans' connection with the late Thomas Hart: but there'd be no time for that now.

"Think of it, your honor," the man under the chamberpot was declaiming, "he is in love with his wife!"

"Hang him," somebody shouted.

"Bastinado him!"

"Burn him in oil!"

Adam glanced at Resolved Forbes, who slipped away unnoticed.

"Order in the courtroom!" The judge used his hatchet. "This here is a very serious case, as the worthy prosecutor so worthily said. Prosecutor, produce the dastardly person who is accused of doing this dastardly deed. Order in the court! Oyez!"

Adam Long rose with a reluctance he tried to conceal.

"Let the prisoner be sworn in."

"No swearing around here," cried the judge. "God damn it, I won't stand for it!"

Adam was caused to place his right palm upon a bundle of stolen ships' papers, whilst his left hand was raised.

"Do you solemnly swear that you will tell lies, the whole lies, and nothing but the lies, so help you the Devil?"

"I do."

"That's a lie! You don't at all!"

Through the applause Adam kept a sheepish smirk fastened on his mouth, but his eyes were still busy. Yes, the entire population of Providence must be here. The beach, a scant half-mile away, no doubt was deserted. Likely enough all the ships were deserted, too. And the moon wouldn't rise for more than an hour.

He hoped that Maisie was all right. Maybe it had been wrong of him to fail to tell her what he planned; but she'd have wanted to take this piece of goods and then that piece of goods, and skirts and stuffs, and more and more and more—and anyway he did think that the fewer as knew a secret the better.

"Prisoner at the bar, you have heard the heinous offense of which you stand accused. What say ye? Are you guilty or not guilty?"

"Well, comes to that, I reckon I'm both, your dishonor."

"Order in the court! The prisoner will please display some sense. God damn it, you can't be both guilty *and* not guilty!"

"Why not? This is a free country, ain't it?"

He was a success. Oh, he was the star performer! Conceivably, he thought with bitterness, I should have become a strolling player? Perhaps the stage lost a distinguished ornament when I took to trade?

When at last he could make himself heard again, the judge asked Adam what he had to say for himself. Not only was he accused of loving his wife, but it began to look as though his wife loved *him* as well, which was a pretty state of affairs. Why else, asked the judge, pointing with the hatchet, should she have followed him into court?

Adam wheeled.

The Honorable Maisie de Lynn Treadway-Paul came toward him, murmuring apologies as she weaved in and out among the pirates, ignoring the black looks and fruity obscenities of the whores. Such of her hair as escaped from under a muslin cap showed a brighter red than ever in the red light of the torches. Her eyes were huge. She was smiling, though it was a mannered smile, a fixed, ceremonial one.

"What have you got to say to that, prisoner at the bar?"

"I've got *this* to say to it, your dishonor—"

He drew. He ran toward her. Several of the men in that vicinity reached for their cutlasses, sensing a brabble, but Adam only used its flat to clear a space and capture a cask. He sheathed then, and made for the cask with Maisie, resisting furiously, in his arms. She had tried to say something to him in a low voice, but he was too angry to heed. He sat on the cask and threw her across his knees, face down.

She kicked and screamed. She clawed at his legs, and even tried to bite him, while the pirates roared with laughter.

Adam laid it on hard, resoundingly. Eight, nine, ten times he whammed those buttocks with a big flat horny right hand. The crowd went wild.

He rose, Maisie in his arms still struggling.

"If your dishonor pleases, I've got other business—"

"The court excuses the defendant temporarily and I only wish I could have some of that business myself," shouted the judge.

Carrying her, trying to hold her still, while she beat his breast and reached with fingernails for his face, he ran through the cheering crowd. He was given plenty of advice, but nobody followed him.

Clear, he ran among empty tents and huts. He passed Tarpaulin Hall. He put Maisie down.

She slapped his face, first right, then left. He shook his head impatiently.

"No, no! Don't waste time! We've got to—"

"*Before all those ruffians!*"

"Why'd ye come then? I told you to—"

"*You're one of them! You're the worst one, yourself!*"

She slapped him again.

"Tarnation," muttered Adam. "We could go on like this all night."

He swept her up into his arms again. He ran to the beach.

It was dark. He had picked the place well. He raced around the end of the island's only warehouse, a ramshackle structure one end of which was right at the edge of the sea, and found the *Goodwill's* tender there, as planned. Resolved Forbes also was there—but he wasn't alone.

"You are leaving so soon, Captain?" asked Everard van Bramm.

28 They can be mighty odd, the thoughts you have in an instant of peril. They can shame you with their incongruity, their triviality.

Adam Long's first thought as he faced van Bramm, who was backed by Cark, each of them with a pistol in his fist, was: Well, I'm glad he's got a shirt on at last.

He heard Maisie gasp. Until now—as had been the case with Adam until a few hours ago—she had but glimpsed Everard van Bramm from a distance. To be in the very presence of the monster was a shock.

Adam made a low mocking bow. A bold approach, he'd learned, was the best for van Bramm. Also, he could use time to study the situation.

"Surely you wouldn't seek to detain me, Captain van Bramm. Haven't I always been told that a gentleman never imposes his company upon another gentleman? If either of us could be called that."

The pistol van Bramm held was a large brass one. It was cocked, and there was powder in the priming pan.

The man went on smiling. But then, he always smiled. The Spaniards, who knew him too well, called him El Sonriso, The Smiler.

"Detain you, Captain?" His voice made you think of something scaly slithering across the stones of a cellar floor. "Certainly not! Indeed, sir, I am delighted to have you go."

Just then, as though at a signal, it began to rain. Here was no torrential tropical downpour, but a warm clean easygoing rain that fell with a tinkly sound on the bay and chuffed apologetically into the sand at their feet, kicking up small silvery spears. There was a land breeze, just right for the schooner.

Van Bramm was wearing a broad-brimmed yellow hunting beaver. He pulled the pistol in close to his body, to protect the powder under that brim as roof. His hand was utterly steady.

Cark, slightly behind him, had turned a bit so as to face Resolved Forbes, who stood right where he had been surprised by these two, ankle-deep in water, the painter of the Moses in his hands. Cark was not so sure of himself.

It was dark. There was nobody else in sight. There was no sound from the settlement save the distant rumble-bumble of laughter and shouting at the mock trial, none from the bay excepting the thin discouraged squeal of timbers as this vessel or that lackadaisically rocked. The rain prattled, pert, gay.

"There is only one thing I feel I should object to," said van Bramm.

Adam flicked a glance at Resolved Forbes. The mate, motionless, was not looking into Cark's face but at Cark's pistol, staring not as though fascinated but as though he aspired to fascinate *it*. The pistol wobbled. Resolved Forbes, seemingly so relaxed, in truth, Adam knew, was taut as a bowstring. Adam was glad that it was Forbes here. There wasn't any man he'd rather have on his side in a fight.

"Didn't you tell me this afternoon, sir, that I could leave with all my men who cared to go with me?"

"I did, Captain. I did indeed."

"Thank you." They were both being excessively polite. "Mister Forbes, will you haul that tender up a bit further, so that milady won't have to get her feet in the water?"

He turned, and gallantly offered his hand to Maisie. She wetted her lips, gave an absent nod, put a hand into his; but all the while she was looking at van Bramm.

They started for the boat.

"I said your vessel and all your *men*," said Everard van Bramm.

Adam stopped. Maisie stopped. Resolved Forbes was still staring at the pistol Cark held.

What van Bramm said next was so appallingly brutal that for a moment they found it hard to credit their ears. Yet the man was serious.

"I must be paid *something*. Leave the lady. I'll take her."

Had this been accompanied by a leer, had van Bramm moved toward Maisie or even extended a hand in that direction, doubtless Adam would have been unable to control himself. As it was, Adam did very well indeed. He even managed to produce a smile.

"Indeed, Captain, you do me a great favor in taking her off my hands. And may I wish you—happy nights?"

He took a step toward van Bramm, who tensed. Adam reached for his hat, like van Bramm's a broad-brimmed one. He swept it off his head. Most elaborately he made a leg, bowing low.

The hat swished through the air a good eighteen inches from the muzzle of the pistol, but so great was its force that its wind blew the powder clear out of the priming pan.

Van Bramm cursed, stepping back.

From the bottom of his bow Adam jumped.

Van Bramm pulled the trigger. He got a spark but there was no flash. He started to slam the side of the pistol with his left hand, meaning to jar powder up through the touch-hole; but by that time Adam was upon him.

The other pistol, the one Cark held, exploded stunningly. It was like a cannon shot. The jumble of sound from the marketplace instantly ceased.

Cark had been wild, seemingly. Adam never did learn where that ball went—nobody ever did—but he knew that Resolved Forbes wasn't hit, for though he couldn't spare a glance he could hear the scuffle of a struggle back there.

He punched the pistol and the hand that held it, not van Bramm's face. He treated the pistol like a living thing, to which the pirate himself was no more than an accessory. Van Bramm kept stepping backward, swinging the gun away from Adam's rush. He stumbled. Adam's fist caught his right wrist, stinging it. Van Bramm dropped the pistol.

The pirate then didn't punch, didn't back up any further. He simply threw both arms around Adam, fighting as a bear would. He was immense and very strong. Adam got a short hard left punch into the belly, but the man didn't even grunt. Then the arms tightened, and Adam could no longer move. From the first touch of that embrace he became light-headed. Soon the blood thundered and banged in his temples, and his eyeballs, furiously hot, seemed to be striving to spring out of his head. Small warm greasy blobs of sweat meandered down his face, down his neck, tickling him.

Yes, like drowning. Soon he would have to let go the breath he held. And he'd never get another.

It was no gallant way to die, he thought—just standing there on a dark beach, not being able to move, not making a sound, even a moan, simply being hugged to death.

Then van Bramm slipped and fell. Adam had enough strength left to push against him, so that he fell backward, Adam being on top.

There was another great stroke of luck—the pirate's head hit a rock. The steely arms were loosened a moment—not much, not enough to permit Adam Long to get his fists free, but he was at least able to hunch one shoulder up smartly, catching van Bramm under the chin, slamming the man's head back against that rock again and again. He grunted noisily each time he hoisted that shoulder. Somehow it gave him relief to grunt.

Everard van Bramm never made a sound.

The arms, slippery with sweat, flopped off right and left like a couple of seals from a slimy rock. Adam wriggled away, got to his knees, to his feet, swaying. He was afraid of a trick, so he stepped away. But van Bramm was not playing 'possum. A moment later, shaking his head to clear it, Adam rushed at him again and kicked him three times in the jaw. The head was slammed back against the rock each time. Van Bramm did not stir.

Not until then did Adam look around.

All this had happened fast. Through the echoes of the pistol shot, and through the tinny clatter of rain, he could hear the shouts of men who were running down from the marketplace.

He sprang to Maisie's side. She stood as though she'd never moved, too startled even to be frightened. While he bustled her into the boat and shoved her toward the sternsheets, she moved like a sleepwalker. He clambered in after her.

Resolved Forbes rose from a dark figure on the beach, and he was wiping his knife on his breeches.

"Kill him?" Adam asked.

Forbes shrugged.

"Might have."

He seized one pair of oars. Adam had the others, the stern oars. They pushed out.

Suddenly the beach was black with men. There was a splatter of musketry, but the distance was too great. Boats were put out, meaning pursuit, but they didn't get far. There were still oars in those boats, but the thole pins had all been removed: the *Goodwill's* mate, on order of the distrustful skipper, had seen to this.

"And right—right before all those—beasts!" Maisie whispered.

She started to weep.

Some of those on the beach were running out to the point, to give the alarm at the fort.

Goodwill to Men was in fact under way when they reached her. Jeth Gardner had sacrificed both anchors, but the vessel was moving.

They were through the pass before the guns of the fort finally spoke.

The first three shots were wild, each one worse than the previous one. Evidently they couldn't see the splashes from up there in the fort.

The fourth slished the air just forward of the bowsprit, uncomfortably close.

The fifth actually hit. It screeched along the deck amidships, virtually *caroming off* that deck, showering splinters everywhere. It missed by a few feet the clutter of barrels the pirates had loaded aboard the schooner and hadn't got around to stowing below. It tore a hole in the larboard gunwale and plopped into the sea.

"If I was one of them Roman Catholics, I'd be crossing myself licketty-split right now," said Jeth Gardner to Captain Long. "That was hot shot. Tell by the smell. They know what's in them barrels."

"What is?"

"Gunpowder."

Half an hour later they had the sea to themselves, and the rain had ceased, and the moon began to ooze over the horizon.

Only a few minutes earlier, when it got between his legs and all but threw him flat, Adam had suddenly remembered that he was wearing a sword. It made him feel a fool, having plumb forgotten it in the first fracas he'd been in since strapping it on.

There was a subdued sobbing in the captain's cabin below.

"You all right, Jeth?"

"Sure I'm all right. You could cut the other leg off me and I'd still be all right."

"I believe you would, Jeth. I truly do. Well, take the deck." He nodded toward the hatch cover. "Reckon I'm needed down there."

PART FIVE

The Shortest Way Home

29   The sea sloo-ooshing along the side on its way toward the hurly-burly of the wake, the doleful clunk of blocks on deck, the squeal of lines and squeak of timbers—these noises, to which Adam awoke, may not be dear to a sailor's heart, since he takes them for granted; but their absence can make him mighty uneasy. Adam heard them before he opened his eyes to gaze with gratification at the sun's rays reflected from off the sea, shimmering and wavering above him.

He rolled his head. In the larboard bunk, so close that he could have reached out and touched her, lay Lady Maisie. She had an air of sweet childishness, the girl he'd first known. Her mouth was a little open, she was sleeping well. This was natural. They'd had considerable of a quarrel here last night, but it had been followed by an unforgettable making-up.

Adam watched her for some minutes, thinking how lovely she was, swearing that he would always protect her.

He remembered Deborah Selden, as sometimes he did when he lay like this, and he was glad, again, that'd he'd eluded her ruse. He supposed that she was getting ready to have her baby by now, and he wondered whether she had been able to trick or bribe some other man into playing the part of a father. Well, no matter. Adam had almost heard the clack of the cage door closing on him that night. Just when he'd been freed to grab his place in the world, too.

As though to remind him of this, his freedom suit, hanging from a peg above his head, swung with a movement of the schooner and brushed his face. Maybe it wasn't as easy as all that—just getting handed a statement that your apprenticeship had expired and stepping into a linsey-woolsey suit? Maybe there was a heap more to it? He was not so sure that he was free, even now.

Maisie moaned a bit, stretching. The movement brought out the curve of her hips under the sheet, and Adam, swiftly stirred, for a moment was almost in pain. He reached out. But tenderness overtook him, and he fished for and found his Book instead.

It fell open to the Song of Solomon; but clearly that wouldn't do, if

Maisie was to be permitted to slumber; and he leafed back a bit, coming to rest at last, as he so often did, on Job. He didn't know how many times he'd read Job. Sometimes he read it, as you should read any part of the Book, with devout attention, going back over certain parts that he wasn't immediately sure of, pronouncing each word in his mind, pondering the meaning of that whole story. At other times he would read it rather with his ears than with his eyes, caring nothing for pronunciation and not at all concerned with what God was getting at, but just plain enjoying himself, the way he might have enjoyed himself if he'd leaned back against something and listened to lovely music.

When he put the Book down, then, he felt better; but still he deemed it prudent not to venture another peek at Maisie. He picked up his ledger.

It was Adam's habit not to enter anything in the ledger until he had rehearsed it in his mind. The figures he finally set down were no more than a recording. The calculations themselves, by steps and in the whole, were mental. Adam was not quick at figures but he was thorough.

So that now he did not touch a quill, only stared at the pages, while his mind weighed possible insertions and amendments.

On the whole, he was proud of the report so far. He recapitulated. He'd lost a couple of jibs, the longboat, the foremast boom, a great deal of molasses.

The widow of Eliphalet Mellish would be paid his wages up to the day he died, of course. Adam already had this money put aside, in a place the pirates had not found. Seth Selden, carried as a stowaway, never rated wages, and Peterson and Waters had quit all claim on theirs. The new man, Willis Beach, would not have to be paid until he was officially signed on—if he was. To be sure, this left the *Goodwill* seriously undermanned, and Adam would have to pick up some hands. But even allowing for this, he was keeping the payroll down first-rate.

Thanks in part to the weather, in part to his decision not to run all the way down to the Leewards, but chiefly to good stowage, very few barrels of eels had gone bad. And he had sold the rest at a record price.

Only a quarter of the one hundred pounds he had taken as passage money for Maisie had been spent for Seth Selden's share of the schooner, a notable bargain.

He'd had another purely personal windfall—those twenty-nine hogsheads of gunpowder the pirates had piled on his deck. Gunpowder was something you could always sell. This rated as a fortune of the sea, something like an act of God. It was, legally, all Adam's. It had been put there by pirates, who enjoyed no standing, being outlaws; and this was the same, in the eyes of an admiralty court, as if it had been thrown up there by the sea.

Well and good. But there remained the matter of the missing molasses.

The hoops and staves and the fish had been paid for in cash, and this he had still, hidden away. But of the molasses from Horace Treadway's plantation fewer than fifty barrels remained. More than three hundred had been rolled into the sea.

Adam feared that he was going to have to ask somebody for a loan. He shook his head, clucked his tongue.

"Are you bankrupt, too, my chick?"

He grinned, slapping the ledger away, slipping out of his bunk, and knelt beside her, and they kissed. They kissed for some time.

"La, what an importunate lover," she laughed when she got the chance. "I do declare, I think you'd beg me for it if we was in a hurricane."

"It'd be a delight then, too."

"Damned undignified though. Not that it ain't always. The position, I mean."

He sighed, with a seriousness not wholly mock.

"Some day, sweet, we'll be alone. And we'll do whatever we want, as many times as we can, without worrying about storms or mutinies or pirates or anything else. Some day."

The smile slid off her mouth, which desire now was tugging tight.

"Some day," she whispered as she pressed closer. "And in the meanwhile, my Adam—"

While he was dressing she said lazily that she supposed they were at last making a course direct for New York? No, he replied, they were heading back to Jamaica. She sat up.

"Why?"

"Different reasons," he replied. "Get more for the gunpowder there. It's no safe cargo anyway. Best to get rid of it as soon as possible. Then we need a real boom. And a longboat. And a couple of hands. In Kingston we can get niggers or deserters from the Navy for next to nothing. But most of all it's credit I'm after. To replace that molasses. I'd thought, uh, of going back to your cousin."

"Oh— Horace again, eh?"

"I'd hoped maybe you might talk him into taking my note, on my share of the schooner."

"I see. Well, I'll try, Adam."

He was about to start up the ladder when she spoke again.

"Adam—"

"Yes, dear?"

"What my poor weak womanly mind still can't encompass is: why do you have to make up for that jettisoned cargo? You were lightening the ship in the hope of escaping, isn't that right?"

"That's right."

"Well, wasn't that your best judgment? You're bringing the boat itself back, which is more than most skippers would do."

"The Providencers should never have been allowed to get so close. The man on watch should have spotted 'em earlier."

"Who was the man on watch?"

"Me."

"Oh."

"And I was the only one. And I was down here."

He turned back to the ladder.

"But, Adam, who *knows* that you were down here?"

He looked at her, open-mouthed. He had been about to blurt: "Why, God does." This seemed to him prefectly natural. It might not seem so to Maisie. It might sound sanctimonious to her. Some folks had odd notions about God and how you should think of Him.

"Well— Well, anyway, that's how it is."

The slide was pushed back. Resolved Forbes was there, discreetly upright, not bending forward to thrust his head in.

"Sail on the starboard quarter. Over Cubie way. A two-sticker."

"What rig?"

"She ain't got no rig. She looks—well, sort of *lost*."

30 When a knave has kissed you (goes an old saying), count your teeth. A skipper becomes cautious down there in Scaredy-Cat Sea; and Adam had his nose atwitch, ready to smell a trick.

On this fine clear morning there was no land in sight, though as the mate had said Cuba would be off the starboard bow, which is where the derelict, if it was a derelict, was.

It was riding high, as if empty. It might have been fifty feet on the waterline, and didn't look fast, being somewhat puffy at the bows, while its two masts, though stout, were not notably tall. These sticks, all unsparred, were about the same height, so that the vessel at least was not a ketch or a schooner. The only canvas showing was a jib, but half-sheeted home, which flopped to this side or that, as though the vessel had its own whims, couldn't make up its mind, or did not care.

Nobody was to be seen aboard. The tiller flumped listlessly.

Adam would study this sight for a while through the glass, then with his naked eye. Then, like as not, he would search the seas elsewhere with a suspicious scowl. He couldn't help thinking that somebody was aiming to trip him up—that if he reached for this purse in the pathway it would be yanked away by a string, if he kicked this old hat, he'd sprain his toe on the rock inside.

It was just too good to be true.

He began to tack. He wouldn't take in an inch of canvas. He wanted to be ready to get away when the trick was discovered.

Maisie appeared at his side and asked to borrow the glass. Breakfastless, she yet was bright, and there was not a wrinkle in her frock. She studied the strange sail with delight, uttering little cries. It might have been a new dress model, a latest-mode bonnet.

"Can it really go on sailing itself?"

"Until some weather makes up, or it drives aground."

"And if nobody's there, who owns it?"

"Whoever brings it in. It's not the vessel that finds it, it's the vessel that brings it in."

"Oh— The owners get it all, then?"

"Depends on what the skipper's arrangement is. In this case, no. In this case the owners'd get only one-tenth, all of 'em together."

"And you're three-sixteenths of the owners, after all."

"Aye. Then the mate gets a tenth and the crew gets a tenth. All this is after expenses have been taken out. And provided the towing vessel ain't had her hull strained coming in. In that case her owners'd have a claim for more."

"Who gets the other seven-tenths?"

He couldn't help grinning.

"I do."

She kissed him right then and there, smacko on the mouth.

"Adam! Then you'll be rich!"

"Well, not exactly rich. You got to accept the admiralty's estimate. And the lawyers'll get a big share, of course. But I ought to clear enough to keep your creditors quiet for a while anyway."

Tears came swiftly to her eyes. They didn't fall, but they glittered there.

"You think of me—first."

"I think of you all the time," he pointed out matter-of-factly. "Just can't help it."

They did a deal of hallooing as they approached, but there was nothing to show that they'd been heard. Twice they passed the stranger, in real close, one on each tack, but they saw no sign of life. Not until then did Adam give the order to heave to.

He still didn't like it. He kept expecting something to explode in his face.

The other sail trailed no line, and neither did it show any anchor, spar, or gig. Its deck, what they could see of it—for the other vessel was the higher-sided—was as clear as though swept by a hurricane. Yet there was no hint of damage about this idle saunterer of the sea: nothing showed stove in, the sticks were upright, the bowsprit jaunty.

They kept hallooing—and getting no answer.

They did pick out the name, *Quatre Moulins*. It was a French name, Maisie said. Did it mean anything? She shrugged. "Four Mills"—that was all.

There was nothing else on the counter. No home port was given. But since to give the name of such a port was the exception rather than the rule, they thought little of this.

"Put over the Moses," Adam said.

"Who'll go?" Resolved Forbes asked.

Now this was exactly what Adam had been asking himself for more than an hour.

Jeth was out of the question because of his leg. Resolved Forbes might be thought the logical one, but Adam was determined to go himself and one of these two should remain. Maisie pleaded to be taken, but Adam shook his head. John Bond still burned a bit with fever. The new hand, the tiny Londoner Willis Beach, might have been willing, but Adam didn't know him well enough to trust him. That left the boy, Abel Rellison. Adam nodded to him.

"Take the oars."

There was no port through which they might peer, and even by standing in the sternsheets Adam could not see anything of the deck.

Rellison rowed clear around the vessel, but there was no movement except the groggy swing of the tiller, the flap of the jib.

There was no line, no ladder, but Adam had prepared against this with a length of knotted line to which had been tied a grappling hook. He threw this. It caught the first time. He tested it.

He drew his sword, the beautifully damaskeened Toledo that Carse had given him, and put it between his teeth. He might look tarnation silly, scrambling up the side of a strange sail with that thing in his mouth; but there was nobody to see him—he hoped—excepting his own men and Maisie.

As soon as he'd dropped to the deck he took the sword out of his mouth and held it in his hand.

He looked around.

The deck was singularly clean—that is, not clean as though it had only just been holystoned, but clear of gear, unlittered. Except for the shrouds and the single jibsheet, the vessel was all unrigged. There wasn't so much as a single block knocking around. There was no line coiled or laid. Not only were there no halyards, there were no bits for halyards to be made fast to. It made Adam think of unrigged ships he'd worked on in the yard where *Goodwill* was built, though this vessel was not as clean and fresh as all that, nor was there any odor of just-sawn wood, just-planed chips.

It did not take him long to search the deck. He did this alone, having commanded Abel Rellison to stand by in the Moses.

The poop was only a bit higher than the waist. He went there. The binnacle was smashed, the only sign of damage. He examined it. The compass had been ripped out. This must have taken a good bit of work, his carpenter's eye told him. If it was done before the ship was abandoned, that event couldn't have been marked by much haste.

Then he saw the stain. It was on the deck, in the waist, near the larboard rail, a few scant feet indeed from the point where Adam had stepped aboard. It was a large stain, roughly round, perhaps eight or nine feet across. Adam knew right away that it had been caused by blood.

He couldn't have said how he knew this. Bloodstains are not necessarily red—in fact, they seldom are—but can be brown, black, blue, purple, depending on how long ago the stain was made, the nature of the material stained, the condition of the blood itself, and temperature, moisture, half a dozen other things.

This stain was a darkish brown, and it was beginning to peel at the edges and in a few places in the middle. But it was blood all right.

It wasn't just the blood of any one man either. One man doesn't have that much.

He went forward. He could walk anywhere on this deck without being obliged to pick his way, for it had been stripped clean. It would never have been taken to sea like this, and he doubted that it would have been so stripped even at anchor or alongside a dock. From various marks on the masts and from the nature and condition of the chafing gear on the shrouds Adam deduced that it had probably mounted three square on the fore, a fore-and-aft and a square topsail on the main: a brig then.

The forecastle hatch was open, though it slid back and forth with the unenthusiastic pitching of the vessel. Adam wetted his lips.

"Ahoy down there!"

There was no answer.

I croak like a tarnation frog, he told himself.

He looked around. Everything was still. Holding the rapier point low, his hand sticky with sweat now, he stepped into the hatch and started down the ladder.

Not much sunlight, and none of it direct, got into the forecastle. He had a hard time even seeing the bulkheads, at first.

There were six bunks. Allowing that there was room for two men to sleep on the deck between the rows of bunks, and allowing, too, for two watches, that could mean a crew of sixteen.

Four of the bunks he could see clearly, once his eyes got used to the gloom. They were utterly empty—no bedding, nothing.

He had started toward the two darker bunks, which were located far up in the bows, one on either side—when the slide was slammed over the hatch.

It was as if a lamp had been blown out. The forecastle was thrown into utter darkness.

Adam scrabbled up the ladder, hurled himself against the slide. He might have been screaming. He'd lost all control of himself.

The slide went back, and once again he was bathed in sunshine.

The slide opened, closed, opened again, as the brig lolled in a warm and friendly sea. Aboard of the *Goodwill* they saw him again, and waved.

He exhaled, sobbing, exasperated. He wiped his face, sheathed his sword. If it had been possible to march down a perpendicular ladder he would have marched back into that forecastle; but anyway he did go back there, and searched every inch of it.

And he found nothing. There wasn't so much as a shred of clothing, a grain of tobacco, a candle stub.

Going aft, the cargo hatch was next, amidships; but though it was not battened down, it was in place, and too heavy for one man to move, so he passed it by and went to the cabin.

This hatch was small and opened like a door, for a foot or so of the cabin was above the level of the deck. The hatch was not fastened, but it was stuck. It came free at last with a clack.

It was not until then that he realized what had happened.

His nose told him, and then his stomach, which wambled. There was no smoke to see, yet the cabin reeked of smoke. There was no flame, but it smelled of burnt wood. The air that came out was hot, angry, and it caused him to cough, and stung his eyes.

He did not go down, being afraid that he might keel over, but he did hold his breath and stick his head in. The cabin was not so dark as the forecastle, and being square it was easier to scan. It was black—black from smoke, probably, rather than from fire, though there had been a fire. The only objects were a table, which being fastened to the deck couldn't be moved, and some charred corners of mattresses.

Adam withdrew his head and gratefully breathed real air. It was, he reflected somberly, like coming up out of Hell. He closed the hatch. Let air circulate in there and the fire might yet break out again. It should be thoroughly wetted down first.

Well, it was plain what had happened. Coasters had caught this brig off Cuba, as a few months ago they had almost caught *Goodwill*. They had butchered everyone aboard and tossed the bodies overside. They had stripped the vessel of everything movable, except, inexplicably, that one jib. They had set fire to a pile of bedding in the cabin and had departed for their own shore, confident that the flames would eat all traces of their crime.

The jib, gallantly if not speedily, had carried the brig away from the shore at the same time that their oars had pushed the coasters in. When no flames showed, the coasters must have deduced what had happened: the hatch had been rocked shut by the motion of the vessel, had got stuck there, and had kept air from the cabin, so that the fire smudged itself out, choked. By the time they learned this it had been too late for the coasters to do anything about it. It had probably been night then, and the brig had been standing well out to sea; while the coasters, already gorged with loot, and possibly not liking the looks of the weather, did not care to venture too far from their beach.

"Are— Are you all right, sir?"

Adam went to the gunwale and looked down at the honest anxious face of Abel Rellison. It touched him to see the boy there. He swallowed.

"I'm all right," he muttered. He nodded toward the schooner. "Tell 'em we've catched a prize. And fetch 'em, one by one. And fetch writing materials, too.

"What happened to the crew, sir?"

"It's best not to think about that."

31 The man from London saw his skipper come up, strapping on a sword, and he swallowed in nervousness. He was a lonely little man, this Willis Beach. Slum streets had been his hearth, his parents pickpockets, and he'd begged and stolen—and run away from things—as long as he could remember. He was good at escaping, at wriggling out of trouble. He'd sneaked out of the English Navy itself, by God! And now if they napped him he wouldn't be lucky enough to get off with a hanging. When you're hanged, you die. Beach, who had never found life a song, was not afraid to die. What he was afraid of was the cat. He had taken twenty-four once—he could still feel the welts when he wriggled in his hammock—and he was damned if he'd take any more. Never again would he let them rip the shirt off his back and drag him to a grating, while marines stood wooden-faced, and the officers in their fancy uniforms looked solemn on the poop, and your messmates

and the boys and like enough everybody else aboardship stood around watching you and making bets on which stroke would start you screaming. He wasn't going to have the quartermasters seize him up, so that he hung from his wrists; or look in horror over a shoulder to see some monstrous muscular bosun's mate take the cat out of a red baize bag and run it through his fingers, caressing each of the slugs that soon would be all sticky with blood and shreds of skin. No. He would kill himself first. He meant that.

A natural fugitive, Willis Beach was not a man to look far ahead or behind, being concerned always with an immediate dilemma. When he saw Captain Long coming toward him, he began to wonder whether he had done right in trusting himself aboard this colonial hooker.

It was the sword. Beach had liked this Yankee skipper when he met him in Kingston; and that he was alive now, indeed, he owed, beyond all doubt, to Captain Long. But now the skipper had taken to wearing a sword, and Beach didn't like that. A man with a sword was an officer, and an officer was somebody to avoid—to defy if it seemed safe, to buck, to bewilder, or betray—but best of all to avoid. Beach looked upon a man with a sword as his medieval ancestors had looked upon a man on a horse, or the naked savages of America had looked at first upon the plate-armored conquistadores. These were creatures of a different species, and it was but the part of wisdom to whine before them as it was to disobey and if possible to hamstring them when their backs were turned. There could be no friendship with a man who wore a sword. Make no alliance with him, even for an hour! You could no more understand him than he could understand you, and it was better not to try.

Beach touched his cap. The skipper nodded. He looked at the compass. He scanned the sea. For three days and nights they had towed the *Quatre Moulins* brig, an axe being right here beside the helmsman to enable him to cut the cable in case of trouble. And hour ago, now that they were off the north coast of Jamaica, and after leaving the mate and the boy, together with some spare spars and canvas, aboard of the brig, they had cast her off. The *Quatre Moulins* was to proceed around to Kingston and report herself a prize, while those aboard the schooner were to conduct—well, some other business.

The skipper turned suddenly. He drew. Willis Beach swallowed, shifting his feet. He glanced over the taffrail at the wake, God knows why: they were a good twelve miles from shore and he couldn't swim anyway.

The skipper shook his head.

"Dad-blamed smoke! I can smell it still, seems as if."

Beach swallowed again, and turned his gaze toward the brig. The skipper had been commendably careful there. Not a one of them was to get ha'penny—the skipper got it all—but he'd had them take a good look around the brig first, one by one, and then he had each one sign or make his mark under a statement of what he had seen. Willis Beach approved. You couldn't be too careful when you were dealing with port officials, admiralty lawyers and affiliated vermin. As for the stink of the scorched cabin, Beach hadn't much minded it, not any more than he had minded the stain on the deck. He supposed that he was sorry for the poor blokes who'd had their throats slit; but that had been some days ago, some miles back.

"Aye, aye, sir," he said, all the time eying the sword.

The skipper pinned a fluff of wool to the top of the taffrail, and then from a considerable distance he began thrusting at this. It looked gawky, the way he lunged, his palms up, his head back, feet flat on the deck; but he was good; he skewered the thing every time.

He was still breathing easy when he straightened.

"Why do you hold your left hand over your head like that, before you rip loose?" Beach asked.

Immediately afterward he gasped at his own temerity. Aboard a man-of-war had he dared to ask so flip a question of any officer the dreaded cry "Start that man!" would rise, and a bosun's mate would came on the double to beat him all about the head and arms with a rattan. It could be almost as bad as the cat. Beach had seen a man's left wrist broken that way once, and he'd heard of a man who had one of his eyes put out when he looked up to plead for mercy. It was against regulations; but it was done all the time. Not only the officers but even the bosun and bosun's mates, the master-at-arms, the marine sergeant, the ship's corporals, were just as likely to light into a hand they didn't like with a cane or a knotted rope.

Captain Long, however, answered mildly.

"Balance. Grant you it *looks* daft, but you throw that arm out and down when you lunge and you get in quicker."

"Looks awkurd. Ever fight a man with one of them things, Cap'n?"

"No."

"Ever going to?"

"Yes."

The skipper sheathed. He spread his legs, fisted his hips.

"Now let me ask *you* some questions—"

Beach nodded. He had expected this.

"You deserted from the Navy?"

"I told you that, in Kingston."

"Why?"

"I'd been pressed, beat up, near broke me bloody jawr. After that they treated me crool. Not enough to eat, no rum at all. The quarters was wet. They worked you to the bone. They 'eld up your wiges. Didn't like my mites, either. Scum. And there was other reasons. But most of all I was afride of getting the cat again."

"Flogging?"

"Aye."

"What had they flogged you for the first time?"

"Last man down."

"Down from where?"

Puzzled, and as always suspicious, Beach looked at him.

"Why, from the tops. I was a topper. We always riced mast aginst mast when there was any canvas to be mide or shortened. 'Smart' they calls it. 'Ad to be bleedin' acrobats, we 'oped to go on living. 'Op around like fleas up there, with the wessel rolling. Then when you'd worked an' pounded yourself barmy, with all them officers screechin' at you, then last one down rited two dozen. Every day. 'Cept Sunday. Our captain was a religious man."

"But the last man down had probably been the first one up!"

"Didn't mike no difference. 'E got two dozen. Wonst I saw a topper smash both 'is ankles, 'urrying to get down. Another time a messmite of mine get killed. But they still did it."

The skipper glanced at the cabin hatch, which was closed, no doubt to assure himself that that juicy ripe redhead he had down there wasn't listening to all this rough talk.

"How did you get to Providence?"

"Why, aboard of a wessel."

Adam Long looked at him. "Ax" for "ask," "fit" for "fought," and such possessives as "ourn," "hern," "yourn," and "hisn" he was familiar with, while other expressions this Londoner used were not wholly strange —for instance, Beach would say, "I wouldn't do it without I had some help," whereas a Rhode Islander would have said *withouten* I had some help"—but the transposition of "w"s and "v"s never failed to bring him up short.

Beach, who didn't fancy the look, stared at the horizon, and he swallowed yet again, making his Adam's apple fairly leap.

"Well, I didn't expect you'd *swum* it," the skipper said at last. "But what boat? And where did you find out about it?"

"At Walter's. The plice that press gang tried to nap me. It's where you go when you wants to find out anything about the lads that're on the account. That's what I was doing there. Looking for transportation. Thought I was sife, specially in the daytime."

"I see," slowly. "You seem to have picked up a lot."

"I got big ears. Always 'ad."

Beach, prodded, told him something about the political situation in Jamaica. The governor, General Selwyn, had died, and soon after that had come the fleet under Benbow, and then the news that William was dead and Anne was Queen. But the *official* notification of this had not yet arrived, any more than had the *official* news of the declaration of war. This was why nobody knew for sure whether the lieutenant governor, a rich and disagreeable planter named Beckford, who held his appointment of course from the late King William, had any right to be acting as governor. Beckford had many enemies; and it was customary for the local assembly to be at loggerheads with the governor and council anyway; but what really threw things nine ways from the middle was the arrogant attitude of Admiral Benbow.

"What's this Benbow like, personally?"

"A disey, sir."

"Yet you served on his ship and they flogged you."

"Not the admiral didn't! That was the captain! When my back was patching and I couldn't go aloft they used me for a clerk—because I can write, y'know. *Then* there wasn't no flogging. Not that old Benbow wouldn't 'ave 'ad your 'ide off, 'e thought you was sodgering! 'E's a lamby, that 'un. When 'e gives a command it's thunderbolts, and when 'e grits 'is teeth there's sparks fly."

"I see— And now you want to go to the continent?"

"Aye, sir."

"Providence too rough for you?"

"Too dishonest, sir. I don't mind a bit of thievery now and then, but they was thieves *all the time!* It don't seem right."

"It ain't," Adam agreed. "Some one of these days somebody's going to stamp that nest out. Maybe it'll be your Benbow. He'd sure like to! It's costing him warships for convoy. And yet if they go clear around the other end of Cubie they're likely to run into Spaniards."

He saw the cabin hatch move, and he straightened.

"Well, you seem a good enough worker. Stay aboard of us—if they don't get you in Kingston."

"I won't go ashore, sir."

"And no wages. By rights I ought to make you pay for transportation, but we'll take that out in work."

"Thankee, sir."

The hatch cover slid open, and the lady emerged, wearing a blue that shamed the sea, smiling a smile that shamed the sun.

"You've met Admiral Benbow," Adam said to her a little later, as they strolled the deck. "What sort of man is he?"

"A duck, my dear. Gentlest, sweetest thing you ever met. Why?"

"I'm thinking of a scheme," Adam said. "But it can wait."

"Money?"

"Money."

32 The mist writhed as though in agony, its ribbons butting without sound against the *Goodwill*, tumbling away baffled. It did not blot out objects—Jeth Gardner in the Moses was visible—but it blurred and distorted them. It was not fog; you don't get fog off Jamaica. As near as Adam could make out it must have been a ground mist wafted out from the low mucky land back of the plantation at the foot of the hills, the swamp into which slaves sometimes escaped. Yet it didn't smell of rotting vegetation. There was an acrid nip to it. Pearly —for this was before dawn—it was tinged with blue.

". . . twenty-two," Jeth called. "Twenty-one and a half . . ."

The lead flashed high, tumbling mist away from it, and fell after a clean lone loop, "*sploosh!*" into the water.

"Twenty-two . . . twenty-two . . ."

"What's the bottom?" Adam called.

"Sandy. Gray."

Across the deck, trailing mist, creating tiny whirlpools of it, a whispy wobbly wake, came the Honorable Maisie. She wore a long, light blue mantua, and her hair was caught behind with a yellow ribbon. She said no word to Adam but leaned, as he was doing, on the larboard gunwale.

". . . twenty-three and a half . . . twenty-three . . ."

Goodwill barely moved. The whisper at her bows was the sort of "shush" made by somebody who holds a finger to his mouth.

"Adam—"

"Yes, dear?"

"I hope you ain't counting too much on Horace lending us money. You know, he—he's a very hard man."

"I know that."

The mist wandered past. It could have been smoke now. Adam shook an impatient head. Danged if he wasn't obsessed by the thought of smoke, always seeming to smell some, ever since he'd boarded that brig.

"He'll drive a hard bargain."

He smiled a little, and put a hand over one of her hands.

"I'm used to hard bargains," he said.

"But I mean—maybe he'll ask for security?"

Where was the profit in trying to explain to her? On the not infrequent occasions of the past when she'd needed money she had of course obtained it by simply taking it, or else by giving in exchange a smile, a glib promise, the wave of a hand. The idea of *working* for it had never occurred to her.

But nobody had ever given Adam Long anything for nothing. Nobody, that is, until Maisie Treadway gave herself—wholly, gladly—and the thought of that gift humbled him, clobbering his throat.

"And I've no jewels left at all, Adam. What could we offer?"

"The derelict, if the admiralty will clear her in reasonable time. If not, and if I have to, my share of the schooner here."

"Adam! It would hurt you horribly to risk that!"

"It would."

"Why mightn't you collect on the derelict right away?"

He hawked, and spat.

"Admiralty courts don't work like that. But if you was just to speak to your friend Benbow—"

"I'll speak to him."

"Eighteen and a half," chanted Jeth Gardner. "Seventeen . . ."

The shore was visible now, a broken blue line not far away. The first rays of the sun were jabbing the mist, striving to scatter it.

"Sixteen and a half . . . *fifteen foot!*"

Adam slightly squeezed her hand.

"Soon," he whispered. "It may take us a little while to get everything cleared up, but we'll do it. And we'll be together—soon."

The sun then suddenly succeeded in prising up the white-blue stuff that floated in the air. As if by means of a stage trick, the shore, fuzzy a moment earlier, became clear in all its details. It was as though a gauze curtain had been lifted.

Just at first, for half a minute there, Adam supposed that he had somehow found the wrong cove. This made him angry. He had a shore-line memory that he liked to think was infallible; and the very act of putting into such a small obscure place without waiting for sunup was a bit of bravado that might have backfired.

For this could not be the Treadway plantation. Where was the house? The kitchen kiosk, slave quarters, mill? What had happened to the lovely gardens and the orchards? The warehouse? Well, yes, there was something there yet, where the warehouse had been. Not one stick of the building itself remained, but some of the cane that had been stored in it still smoldered sullenly.

Now they knew the nature of that "mist." Now they knew why no pirogues had put out to guide them through the pass.

Adam turned quickly to his companion and tried to get her away from the gunwale, but she'd already seen.

"We— We've got to go there," she said in a small voice. "He may still be alive."

"He won't be," muttered Adam.

He wasn't. They found his grave, a cleared space in what had once been his garden. Somebody had stuck a wooden cross over it:

"HORACE TREADWAY, GNTLMN. Bn. 1668 Kld. 1702"

While Maisie knelt, sobbing, Adam looked around. Decay and desolation lay everywhere. Near what had once been the house a large mass of charred chunks of furniture and scraps of bedding and of clothing had been piled, stuff that had long since ceased to send out smoke. The same men who had buried the planter—neighbors? soldiers from the capital?—clearly had made some attempt to clear up the garden. The flowering vines, representing years of loving work, had been slashed, uprooted; and the trellis over which they once trailed had been torn down. The rose bushes were flattened. What had been a hedge of hibiscus, the bushes so spaced as to alternate the different-colored flowers—ivory, pink, salmon, white, red—now was no more than a jagged trench. Even the seed sheds had not been spared; and the very garden gate had been ripped from its hinges.

Over everything hung the dank smell of death itself.

Adam looked back at the hills, which suddenly spoke.

WUMP-wump-wump! *WUMP*-wump-wump!

The Ashantis had paid their visit at last.

33 Even Kingston, close to the stroke of midnight, with only a few lights showing, could look lovely. Four-fifths of the time the town was dust, the other fifth it was mud; but right now it was moonlight.

The garden was fragrant with jasmine, and shadows were packed into it like jackstraws in a bowl. Flagstones zigzagged down to the gate in the wall. Even while Maisie and Adam stood there on the veranda, arms around one another, clinging, reluctant to part, a quartet of marines click-clacked past just the other side of that wall. The marines had been particularly active since the fleet under Admiral Benbow cleared out, the very day *Goodwill to Men* returned to town. The departure of that fleet, it had been accurately predicted, would lure down from the Blue Mountains and in from distant plantations deserters who hoped to sneak away in unconvoyed merchantmen.

"I'll make it back a-booming, you can count on that," he promised. "But there's a heap of things to do first."

"Not including, I hope, sir, the solacing of some dewy-eyed Newport beauty?"

He turned. He looked at her in amazement, and after a moment he laughed. He drew her to him, very gently.

"The man that has you ain't a man to go around looking for somebody else," he said. "You've got everything that's good and fine and beautiful and true, right here"—he shook her affectionately—"so why should I go out seeking a smitch of it here and a smitch there, when you've got the whole thing? Even if I didn't love you already, that would be reason enough to."

She didn't answer this with words, but looked up, her lips trembling, eyes shining with tears; and they kissed for a long time.

After the kiss: "If there's any worrying to be done, I reckon it's up to me. You'll be bored here. Kingston ain't London."

"I'll think of you all the time. That's what I'd do anyway."

Never having officially left the colony, Maisie had not officially returned. Smuggled out, she had been smuggled back in. The same legal restraints remained upon her. These were complicated, having to do with a multitude of unpaid debts, and Adam did not essay to understand them; but he did know that money would cause them to evaporate, and he hoped to have money soon. He had borrowed enough to buy a full cargo for *Goodwill*, getting this at twelve per cent on the security of Maisie's expected inheritance—for it was known that she was one of her cousin's heirs—from Maisie's lawyer, Mr. Cartwright, "the jew who isn't a Jew," as he liked to call himself. Mr. Cartwright, too, was to handle the *Quatre Moulins* matter, though nothing could be done there until either a true unquestioned governor was commissioned and confirmed and sworn in, or Admiral Benbow came back. In addition, Maisie had recently had still another paper served on her, this one forbidding her to leave the colony until such time as she had appeared before a yet-to-be-appointed court of inquiry into the death of the late Horace Treadway. That inquiry would be an intense one. The massacre on the other side of the island had shaken the colony, and while three or four parties were still out, with bloodhounds, beating for the fugitives, traders and officials alike realized that in spite of the war and the confused condition of the local government, something had to be done about the present slave system—a general study and overhaul was in order. Though it might be embarrassing to explain why she was not at the Treadway plantation when the blow fell, Maisie did not greatly fear this court of inquiry; and she reasoned that if she avoided it she might hold up still longer the settlement of the estate and conceivably even jeopardize her own share. This was why they had rented the house out on the road to Constant Spring.

Yet Adam Long couldn't live there with her indefinitely. He had business in Newport, business in England, too.

"And when Benbow comes back, you play every trick you know to persuade him to clear that prize. Don't forget one single wile."

"I'll enthrall him, my chick. I'll seduce him."

"Well, no need to go's far's that. If he's taken du Casse I reckon he'd clear the whole thing for a smile. If not, maybe not."

"Will he take du Casse?"

She often asked him questions like this, as though he owned the ocean.

"Well now, that's something only God and Admiral Benbow know— and maybe only God. Be a great thing if he did. Come close to ending the war right then and there."

"Why?"

"Du Casse is convoying this year's Spanish treasure to Europe. They do say he's got six million eight-pieces in that fleet. Even Spain couldn't take a loss like that—and stay in the war. And if Spain drops away, France will, too."

"Won't du Casse fight?"

"Oh, he'll wriggle and run, but if he's trapped he'll fight, yes. If Benbow attacks him. And from what I hear tell of Benbow, he will."

"He seemed like such a quiet little man."

"From what I hear tell of him, he'll attack all right."

Her forehead rested on his chest as she leaned toward him, and she poked tentatively, teasingly, with a finger.

"Let's not talk about Admiral Benbow. Or, in fact, about anything."

"Darling!"

It could have been the moonlight, or the fragrance of the jasmine, or conceivably even the tilt of the garden away from the house, the zig-zagginess of the path, but anyway Adam Long felt plain outright drunk as he made for the gate half an hour later. Positively he staggered—though he'd had no more than two or three noggins of rum since supper.

He turned in the gateway.

Maisie still stood on the veranda, the light of a hurricane lamp silhouetting her. It made him want to run back up there. He could not see her face. She lifted her right hand a little when she saw him turn, but she dropped it quickly, as though afraid otherwise to move, afraid of tears.

"I'll be back," Adam muttered as he went out, "sooner'n you expect."

PART SIX

◆

Home Is the Sailor

34 It was raining, a chill irascible rain that seemed to hurl itself diagonally at you no matter which way you faced, when they raised Montauk, and, immediately afterward—for though it's further to larboard it's higher—Block Island. These looked cold.

The place Captain Long called Home and had always thought of as Home, a land he'd never seen, was England. All the same, he decided not to stay on deck while they raised Judy. His eyes did not water easily, no matter what the wind, and the hands, seeing him the way he was, might think that there was something the matter with him. He turned over to Resolved Forbes.

"The east passage, sir?"

"Aye. And don't have me up till we're in."

His tiredness—he'd been on watch a good part of the night, an ear constantly cocked for breakers—did not bring him sleep. Yet he didn't toss, only lay there and stared with a flat dry-eyeballed disbelief at the deck planks above, or sometimes rolled his eyes to take in the rest of the cabin, while his muscles without prompting accommodated themselves to the movement of the schooner. There was no port, so he couldn't look out. He didn't need to anyway. He knew every foot of the way. As for the cabin, on this return passage he had for the first time been struck by its smallness. Resolved Forbes, that neat man, was as admirable a cabin mate as he was an officer: he had few possessions, and what he did have, like the coverings of his bunk, always were shaken out, folded, snugged away. This was as it should be, at sea. Dresses and laces and scarves and stockings scattered everywhere, so high sometimes, and so thick, that you had a hard time finding the ladder—that was *not* the way it should be. All the same, Adam was lonesome.

Resolved Forbes was a crackerjack mate; but he didn't do much to help pass the time away.

Was Maisie a witch? He doubted it. A witch, he reasoned, being surcharged with evil would show this overload exactly when her mind was least upon it. Actually employed in weaving a spell or concocting some philtre, he supposed, a witch might well dissimulate, holding back all outward sign of malice, the ability to do this being one of the gifts the Old One had granted her; but it might show when she least expected it —when she was thinking about something else or was asleep. The girl Maisie standing at the taffrail gazing upon the emptiness of the sea, or asleep over there in that bunk which now held only Forbes' tucked-in blankets and his Book—*that* person was all innocence, he knew.

If he'd become entoiled, he told himself, it was willingly; and he was not sorry.

Adam indeed would have been utterly sure of his position if the accuser had been anybody else but Seth Selden; for though in most matters he had little respect and no fondness for the uncle of Deborah Selden, he did esteem Seth expert in all that appertains to the Devil. Coarse, jocose, Seth nevertheless had much about him that was feline, suggesting less a witch than a witch's familiar. His eyes gleamed with an agate iridescence sometimes, and probably would shine like that in the dark as well. His nose twitched.

Adam sat up, bumping his head. Was it possible that *Seth* was a witch? He might have caused his niece to act as she had simply in order to get Adam into trouble, to clinch the captaincy for himself. For after all, Deborah, to give her her due, didn't seem like that kind of female. Seth, if he was possessed, naturally would do battle to Maisie Treadway, too; he would be obliged by the nature of his contract to try to discredit any person who brought out so much goodness in others. And when he'd been foiled, and had fallen back cursing, hadn't Seth Selden seized the first chance he got to desert?

But—no. Adam lay back, good sense reasserting itself. In the first place, it was known that the Devil seldom struck hands or exchanged the sealing kiss with men, for obvious reasons preferring to work through the weaker sex. In the second place, if any such forces had been seething in Seth the fact would long ago have been discovered by certain of his fellow townsmen. For there were men in Newport who knew a great deal about the Devil, a personage who there, too, because of the multiplicity of faiths, could scarcely be expected to escape detection, being viewed, as it were, from every angle; for whereas in a one-church community, or one with only two or three organized beliefs, Satan, notoriously cunning, might so accommodate himself outwardly to local opinion as to conceal his true purpose and power, in Adam Long's town *somebody* was sure to sniff the brimstone, to expose the hoof. (This was in a manner of mental speaking, for Adam did not believe that the Prince of Darkness any longer had a cloven hoof, but would certainly by this time have used some magical means to change this, as he would also in some manner counteract the distinctive odor associated with him.) No, the Devil would never rampage around Newport as only a few years ago, for instance, he had done in Salem, a town up in the Massachusetts Bay Colony. Newport was safe.

Having decided this, Adam at last went to sleep.

The rain continued, unrelenting, late that afternoon when Resolved Forbes stuck his head down and shouted an awakener.

Adam put on the coat he had bought in Kingston. It was not a stunningly fine one, not of the sort he would soon be wearing, but it was a considerable cut above the coat of his freedom suit. It was sober without being somber, a rich dark blue, and of course slitted for a sword. He had white woolen breeches and white woolen stockings to go with it, and the waistcoat, appropriately gay in order to offset the seriousness of the coat proper, was ivory in color and all shot with silver thread. His hat, a wide-brimmed felt, somewhat Quakerish in aspect, seemed glum and shabby in such sartorial company; but it was the only one he owned —and the rain still came down.

The first person he encountered when he stepped ashore was Zephary Evans.

35   This man Evans was slabsided and long. He had a muddy complexion, a conscientious if unconvincing smile, lackluster eyes, and a habit of shoving his face close to yours when he talked: his voice was always low, nigh onto a whisper, and he seemed anxious that everything he said should be clearly understood. When he walked it was with a jointy movement that reminded you of some tall wading bird, a crane or flamingo; and when he came to a standstill this same impression prevailed, for he seemed to lift one leg underneath him—though he didn't actually do this—and to stand on one foot. He was much older than Elnathan, his wife.

He took Adam's hand in both of his, greeting him gravely. Adam was not touched, and took his hand back as soon as he could get it. Adam had not expected any committee of welcome. He knew his Newport. Even if *Goodwill to Men* had been spotted off Weeping Point the sight would scarcely justify a messenger to the village. After all, the schooner, though phenomenally fast, and well remembered because of the disputation that had attended her building, carried but a small crew, and those mostly foreigners—that is, men not from Newport.

"You're looking well, Captain. Aye. Aye. And we're all the same here. All of us still."

"Well, not quite all—"

Adam looked over toward Goat Island, then back at Zeph Evans' face. There was no twitch of guilt, no pallor, as he'd hoped.

"Ah, yes. You miss Hart? He blew down one night. Chain broke."

"Good riddance," murmured Adam.

"Amen," said Evans.

"Odd thing, they never found out who it was was his agent here."

"Go hard with him if they did. Dudley's fair panting after that charter. I do hope and trust *your* record's clear, Captain?"

"Sure," imperturbably. "Y'know, down in the islands I met a man'd been Hart's second when Hart was operating off this coast: Name of van Bramm. I ought to've asked who Hart's Newport agent was."

"You should have, aye."

"Meet him again, I will."

They stood there looking at one another, Zeph Evans smiling. The rain was ardent. No folks passed. Blake's was only a short distance away, but did Evans, the old skinflint, make a move toward suggesting that they have a noggin of rum? No.

"Reason we ain't more surprised, Captain, a brig put in t'other day from Jamaica. She told us you was fixing to come back."

"That'd be the *Artemis?*"

"Aye. Told us about that prize you took, too. Congratulations."

"Derelict. I ain't commissioned to take prizes."

"You must have made money, then?"

Adam shrugged.

Zeph Evans harrumphed, rubbed one side of a hawklike nose with a finger that wasn't too clean, and in a few additional words jolted Adam so that his heels thudded the cobbles and his teeth clicked.

"Would you be interested in buying my share of the schooner?"

It was like a flash of pain, it was so intense and burny. Adam Long lowered his head lest joy show in his eyes. He spat thoughtfully.

Zephary Evans owned a quarter of *Goodwill*. Seth Selden's eighth, at a bargain price, had been a windfall for Adam, who now owned three-sixteenths but who had assumed that it might take years to buy more. With Zeph Evans' share he would own almost half.

But—why did Zeph want to sell?

Adam stood there watching the rain wash his spittle off a cobblestone. He scratched the back of his neck.

"Mightn't it be best you heard my report first?"

"Don't need to. Tell from what the *Artemis* officers said. Y'understand, Captain, I ain't aiming to *give* my share away!"

"Didn't suppose you was."

"We'll figure it out on the basis of your report. All I want to know right now is: *You didn't bring Seth Selden back, did you?*"

Adam shook his head. "Seth went on the account."

"Out-and-out?"

"Public. He's at Providence. Lives there."

Evans exhaled slowly. He leaned even closer, and put a hand on Adam's arm, an attention Adam did not like.

"Lucky thing for us you did what you did, Captain. You was the man for the job. I voted for you in the first place."

Aye, thought Adam, because your wife made you.

But Adam said nothing about this, only asked if Seth's peculations were so bad then?

"Captain, 'twas a scandal. The whole town knew of it, the whole colony, before you was twenty miles below Brenton's. Why, that Seth, he was mixed up in everything. Forgery, smuggling. Everything except being Tom Hart's agent. He wasn't even in Newport at that time."

"So it must have been some other man."

"The custos is hoppety mad. He'll be shouting at you sure."

"Mr. Clark? He wouldn't be persnicketty."

"No, this is a new one. Captain Wingfield. Not a pleasant gentleman at all. Dudley's been making a heap of changes, and the customs folks're bearing down on us." He nodded out toward the schooner. "Seth aboard of her, they might even seize her."

"Well, he ain't."

"A hypocrite, sir! That's what that man is!"

"Tut, tut," said Adam.

"Even stole funds from his own brother. I feel sorry for Obadiah. It's been a great disgrace for his family."

"That the only one?"

"Eh?"

"I mean: Deborah had her baby yet?"

Evans shook his head.

"She ain't with child," he said. "Never was."

"Oh," said Adam. "I thought she was."

He moved away from the older man, meaning to pull his arm free; but Zeph Evans, whose breath smelled like low tide, moved with him.

"Things like that scare me," Evans whispered. "Seth'd sailed in command of that schooner we'd never've seen it again."

"That's right."

"Thank God, Captain—and I say it reverently—thank the good Creator in Heaven above that you did what you did!" He stopped, and Adam slipped free. "Why not come up to my house and we'll talk it over, after you've reported to Wingfield?"

"That'll be right chirk."

"You'll be there then?"

Adam looked at the *Goodwill to Men,* which sat apart, clean, sweet of line, all loveliness, resting in the water as though she was doing the bay a favor, light as any bird. Tears came to Adam's eyes, while across his mouth a series of small smiles slid like catspaws touching a satined sea early in the morning.

"I'll be there," he promised.

36 Adam looked out the window and told himself that he must not explode. Ordinarily he found it easy to keep his temper. If the other fellow wasn't worth a fist in the face, Adam turned away. If a fight looked likely, he preferred to start it—and finish it. In either case the business was soon over with.

This did not apply to collectors of customs. Assuredly it did not apply to Captain Arthur Wingfield, whose rudeness was more than just professional—was something extra, heavy, labored, loud.

This Wingfield was of course a Queen's man, a Dudley man, and new in Newport, a place he clearly considered beneath him. He was large, long, young, and arrogant with an arrogance that was not interesting, only crass. You knew what he was going to say next, though the vehemence with which he said it never failed to offend.

In the nature of his calling, Adam Long was obliged to hear a deal of blasphemy. He thought that he knew the meaning of the Third Commandment. He sure hoped he did. But the mere mouthing of the words themselves didn't seem to him to make up much of a sin, no matter which way you looked at it. That is, the sound of swearing sanded him slightly but didn't shock him. He simply couldn't see why men cussed. They *said* that it relieved them, but in Adam's observation it only made them hotter, just as Wingfield here, who a bit earlier had been but simmering, now, like a man fascinated, unable to help himself, was approaching boiling point.

"I'll see everyone of those whoresons in Hell first before I'll let her Majesty's service be diddled! Now if—"

Pompous officials, men filled with a sense of their own importance, Adam Long had met and could endure, though not blithely. After all, a windbag may bore but it can't prick.

With the official who goes on the assumption that the *un*official world is peopled exclusively by sneaks, cheats, thieves, liars, Adam was likewise, unfortunately, familiar. As much as possible he ignored such people. It was not good business to let yourself get huffed up. A man can't think clearly when his fists are clenched. It is hard to add a row of figures with a hand that itches to slap a certain face. And after all, the ass in question might be decent and even a good companion outside of his office. A skipper has to make allowances.

Captain Wingfield was something special. He overdid his part. He sounded as if he really meant it.

"—take this man Selden, Seth Selden. Now God damn it, Long, are you going to sit there and tell me—"

So Adam stared out of the window, trying to think of other things. Though it was still raining, more and more men came to a stop before the customs house. Wingfield's voice carried well.

"—and I tell you that this attitude that it's bright and charming to cheat the Queen's customs has got to *stop!* It's got to *stop,* mark you, man! Now about this van Bramm—"

Was this planned? Was he trying to provoke a fight?

Adam wasn't evasive. His answers were brief but they were straight, and if he didn't look at the custos while he spoke, this was only because he was afraid he would knock the man's teeth out. He admitted that he knew about the orders in forged cockets Seth had filled, but said what was perfectly true, that before the sailing he had never even heard of this trade, much less associated Seth with it. He denied that he might have done more to keep Seth and Peterson and Waters from joining the outlaws of Providence. He refused even to consider a suggestion that the money from the sale of the gunpowder should be divided among the owners of the schooner and therefore become subject to taxation; but he did remind Wingfield that he had referred to this matter, as a point of information, in his report to the owners, a copy of which the custos had before him.

Save his anger, Adam had nothing to hide. His report was in order. It was clear and it was complete, and he expected to be commended for it. The voyage had been a success. His own commission was in good order, too, and still a matter of record, as he had learned indirectly. Whether the men of the Adventurers' Table had been reluctant to admit publicly that he'd made fools of them, or even more reluctant to admit that Seth Selden had, Adam did not know—and didn't care, now. Whatever the reason, no complaint had been lodged against him, and it was not even a matter of public knowledge that he had virtually stolen the schooner.

Wingfield indeed was not so much bringing charges against Adam as he was hurling hard words at him in the hope of causing him to blurt out in anger something that in a cooler moment he'd conceal—something useful to Colonel Dudley.

Or was it more than that, the reason for this spate of abuse? Could it be that Wingfield, uncertain, seeing that he was not well liked here, had taken refuge in bluster for bluster's sake, and now hoped to make an example of this whippersnapper Long? Could he have been told—there were plenty to tell him—that Adam had always been too big for his breeches? Had he resolved to take the wind out of Adam's sails before Adam could get a mite of way on?

Whatever it was, it was becoming intolerable. Adam couldn't listen to it much longer. And the crowd outside was really large now.

"I guess that's all we need to talk about." Adam turned on his stool. "You want to know anything more you know where to find me."

"Now damn it, no bastard of a Newgate whore's going to come in here and tell me that—"

Adam did not spring to his feet, but he got up right fast.

"All right, that's enough." He drew. "*Draw!*"

Here it became patent that the custos had not been trying to start a fight. His amazement was genuine. Though he had seen that Adam carried a sword, surely he had not dreamt that Adam knew how to use it.

It was equally evident that, though flabbergasted, he was not frightened. He, too, rose, and with alacrity. He, too, drew. When the astonishment had faded from them, there came into his eyes a glint of joy. Adam could all but hear the man say to himself: "Oho! now I can really teach the whelp to heel!"

In fact Captain Wingfield bowed—a very small, stiff bow, scarcely more than a curt inclination of the head. He glanced at the door: there was only one, and he stood near it.

"Can't fight here. Ceiling's too low. Go on outside."

"Not while you're standing there I won't."

"What's the matter—don't you trust me?"

"No."

That really riled the custos. The anger of his tirade had been in part simulated. Then he'd been astounded and immediately afterward amused and probably pleased, being sure of his own swordsmanship. Now he was sore. His chin went down, his small dark eyes blazed.

"I'll go out my own way," said Adam, and threw the stool he'd been sitting on through the window. "Meet you in the street!"

It was a tall window, though narrow, and he sprang to the sill and jumped backward, not looking where he was going. Bits of broken glass chickered around him. His blade was in position all the time, in case of a rush; but as he jumped he saw that Wingfield was racing through the door.

Adam landed easily; it was only a few feet. Men fell away from him. He ran around the corner of the building.

Wingfield was coming, sword high.

Adam's first emotion, when they engaged, was one of chuckling triumph. He didn't think then of the position of his feet or how he gripped his blade. Nor did he even do any feeling-out, as he should have done, or plan an attack, howsoever elementary. He simply sailed in.

It was a minor advantage he had, in the beginning, but it could count; and it amused him. For Wingfield not only had not expected him to draw but never supposed that he would know how to hold his weapon, much less that he would attack.

They had for footing wet rounded cobblestones. Adam slipped, in a lunge, and went to his right knee, his sword hand down; but he was up again swiftly. Wingfield slipped, retreating; but he was back in position before Adam could close. Wingfield retreated further.

There were men on both sides of them and likely enough these men were yelling. Adam didn't know. They told him afterward that he'd laughed aloud throughout the engagement, as though he was having a wonderful time; but he didn't know this, then.

Wingfield retreated. This might have been wholly because he was startled, as Adam supposed, or it might have been because he knew he was backing toward the wharf, where the footing would be better.

The wharf, a town property—simply *the* wharf to Adam, though it had recently been named Queen's Wharf—was packed gravel between planks and pilings. Wet, the gravel would be firm, not slippy.

Wingfield might have wished he could turn and run to this, but he didn't dare. But the moment he felt the gravel underfoot he made a stand. He caught Adam's blade low and clacked it off, and his own was in for a riposte that almost reached. Then he was back in position, grim.

Adam thrust again. Again he missed—and Wingfield stepped back several paces and lowered his point.

Adam stopped, panting, puzzled. But he kept his point in line.

"You're hit, sir," Wingfield shouted. "An affair of honor ends when one party's been hit!"

There were men on either side, yammering. It all sounded like clickety-click-click.

Adam had known nothing, no burn or pain. He was breathing short but feeling fine. He was remembering not to grip his sword too hard. He looked past its point now, at Wingfield's face.

"This ain't an affair of honor. It's a brawl. *Guard!*"

He went in again.

Now he, too, was off the cobbles and onto the gravel. It felt good. He catstepped, his blade steady, threatening, threatening. Wingfield retreated with a dainty sure step, a watchful fighter no longer flustered, who believed that his chance would come soon.

Now they were near the end of the wharf, not a long one.

Adam lunged again, full-length. He was very low, stretched close to the gravel. He had aimed for the right armpit, meaning to slip under the other's guard. Wingfield did not even try to riposte, but arched in and went high on his toes, straightening his sword arm.

Adam's point fell short. Wingfield's was not accurately thrust, by inches. Otherwise Adam would have lost his right eye, perhaps his life, too. Adam *sensed* the steel go past his ear, though he couldn't have said whether he felt it, it was that close.

For a split-second then Adam knew fear—a tap, a touch, no more. He shook it off.

In fact, the advantage was his. He couldn't go further in—he was stretched full—but as he brought his left leg up for another lunge he knew that Wingfield would have to retreat further.

In the position he was in, Wingfield, about to be attacked again, had no choice. He jumped back—and his left heel struck the stringpiece at the end of the wharf.

That finished the fight. The stringpiece was only a few inches high, but the contact spilled Wingfield's balance. He had to parry, and he did; but he couldn't risk a riposte; and Adam pressed in.

Wingfield teetered. His right hand went high, then quickly low. His point was badly out of line.

Adam swept his blade up, no longer threatening with the point. To those who watched it must have seemed a brilliant stroke, but in fact it was easy. Anybody could have done it, just then.

Falling backward, waving his arms wildly, Wingfield no doubt had started to release his grip on the sword. Adam's rapier caught it full in the middle, threw it up, took it out of Wingfield's hand; and Wingfield went over backward into the water.

The sword, after pinwheeling high, fell at Adam's feet. He grinned at it quietly, and picked it up.

Men were all around him, babbling at him, laughing into his face. Other men were reaching down for Captain Wingfield, who made an almighty big fuss there in Narragansett Bay.

"You're hit, Adam!"

"Punctured your shoulder!"

"Look, Captain, he got you right in the—"

Adam felt the place. It was wet, but then he was pretty wet all over, nigh to being as wet as his late opponent, what with the rain. But when he took his hand away and looked at it, there was blood. This astonished but did not dash him. It couldn't have been serious.

"A smitch of rum'll set that right," he said. "Come on, everybody."

"A souvenir for you, Blake," he said soon afterward, when he tossed Wingfield's weapon on the bar. He dropped some coins there, too. "And drinks for my friends—all of them!"

37 All lumpy with lemons, he slowed his step before the home of Obadiah Selden. There was a light in the big room but none in Deborah's bedroom beside it, and he stood a moment looking at the bedroom window only a few feet away. There was enough light from the large room—the door must have been ajar—to show part of the bedroom wall, and he made out a sampler, marvelously neat, hanging in a frame:

> Young Obadias,
> David, Josias,
> All were pious.

The rain had ceased only recently, and the late afternoon was overcast, dark as night. A breeze shivered the leaves of the maples, shaking loose a shower of raindrops which pittered all about him. He had climbed the hill fast, and what with this, and what with the ale at Blake's, he was a bit winded.

It was inevitable that his thoughts flew to the previous time he had paused at this spot. *Then,* a clear night, he had felt very pleased with himself, all the world being, as he supposed, just ahead of him. *Now* he was inclined to be somber. He rolled the lemons around in his pockets, rubbing them against one another, pleased with their sleek dry smoothness.

A shadow came to the window. It was Deborah. He could not tell whether she was facing him or had her back to him, and he didn't know whether, if she faced him, she could see him. But the lower pane was up, and on impulse Adam crossed the patch of grass.

"Deborah," gently.

She did not gasp, did not turn. She must be facing him. Yes, he could see more clearly now: she *was* facing him.

"I, uh, I'm glad you're not going to have a baby after all."

She didn't say anything, nor did she move. The town, for this hour, was singularly quiet. Lightning bugs began to appear, doggedly battling the breeze. Shaken, long-suspended raindrops thupped into the ground.

It was creepy, saying things to a shadow that didn't answer, or even stir. Maybe she did not hear him? He could have been mistaken about that window. He reached out. No, the pane was raised, sure enough, and his hand went right through and came to rest on the sill an inch from hers.

Now he heard a quick intake of breath, which made him feel more comfortable.

She cleared her throat, and that was a very small sound. It could be that she wasn't sure whether she could make any voice at all come.

"I never did think I was going to have a baby, Captain. How could I, when I've never been near a man?"

He shook his head, bewildered. Deborah Selden would not go skittering here and there in her talk, saying one thing when she meant another, flirting with words in order to flirt with him or whomever.

"Why'd you want to get married then?"

"I—I didn't just want to get married. I wanted to get married to you."

"Well—"

"Have you forgotten that I asked you, right here, before I—I tried to play a deceit?"

"No, I ain't forgotten."

"You shied away. Oh, you was polite about it! But you thought—well, what you just said. That's only natural. And you didn't want to take another man's leavings."

"Aye," guardedly.

"So you went on down the hill. And you was to sail at dawn. And Father was just about to go down and meet with you and with the rest. So I went to him and—and lied. Must've hurt him something dreadful."

"Likely."

"Hurt you, too. But I counted on I'd make up to you by being such a good wife and—well, warm."

"I see."

"I never thought you'd do what you did."

"Nobody else thought so either. Didn't myself. Hard to know how you're going to act sometimes, till you're right there facing it."

"Mine was a wickedness. Not just because I broke the Ninth Commandment—"

"You sure did that."

"—but because it was such a cruelty to you and Father both. *He* believed me, and it wounded him. *You* didn't, and it embarrassed you. I misdoubt you still believe me?"

"Well—"

"Never mind. I'm glad you stopped. I was going to seek you out and tell you how sorry I am, but that might've been hard to do without

165

causing talk. But now I can tell you. I can say, 'Thank you, sir, for being so kind.' You *were* kind, Captain. You were polite and had sweet manners."

The lightning bugs rocked. The grass, wet, gleamed up at him.

"Guess I couldn't think what else to do," he muttered. "First time anybody'd ever asked me to marry 'em."

"It will be the last time I'll ask you, now that you know how I feel."

"Expect you'll find somebody else easy enough, with all you got to offer."

He was thinking of her breasts when he said that, though she might have supposed that he was thinking of her father's wealth, for she stiffened a mite. Then she relaxed. She put a hand over his, on the sill.

"Reckon I won't," she whispered. "If you won't take me, Adam, nobody's going to get me. I got to go now. Father's calling. Good night."

The pressure on his hand was gone, and he looked up and Deborah was no longer there, only the blank window, the far wall blank, too, except for the framed sampler, the exquisite needlework.

> Young Obadias,
> David, Josias,
> All were pious.

He sighed. He was vummed if he knew what to make of the whole business. Well, she'd hear about Maisie soon—the whole town would—and then she might feel different.

All the same, it shook him, knowing that she had been like that all this time.

He drifted away, scarcely moving any faster than the fireflies. Not until he was off the grass and into the mud of the lane again did he remember the lemons. He'd meant to give her some. Indeed that was why he had gone to the window.

He took three of them from his pocket. They were sleek, bright, hard, a virulent yellow. He had brought them up the hill for Elnathan, truthfully, but he calculated she would not miss what she hadn't known she was going to get. It was a politeness: put it that way. Lemons were formal. There wasn't a housekeeper in town wouldn't squeak with delight, you handed her a lemon. They were thought of as gifts. If you had just come back from the islands, like Adam had, you were virtually expected to fish them out and pass them around among the womenfolks; though of course you could show favoritism, and if you were sparking some certain girl, she naturally got the most of 'em, or even all, for the town always jabbered, when a vessel was fresh in from the sugar islands, about who would get whose citrons and how many.

166

Adam had six of them now, and he put three on the window sill. He even considered a plan to put four there, giving Elnathan only two; but after all, he was on his way to the Evans house right now, and old Zeph hadn't signed that agreement to sell his share of the schooner yet, so it was best to play safe.

From the lane he looked back at them. They looked bright in the darkness, and firm, and hard. They were good lemons.

He had knocked once on the door of the Evans house but hadn't had a chance to knock a second time, when it was flung open and he was jerked inside and the door was slammed shut and Elnathan had both her arms around him and was kissing and kissing him.

38 Now here—it looked as if—was to be an evening of shocks. Adam, not without difficulty disengaging himself, was horrified; and also he was scared. For the room was a blaze of light, and he and Elnathan had not been in the habit of embracing in illuminated places. Theirs had been a sneaky affair—an affair of violent, hastily snatched squeezes, their hearts thudding harshly together, or fluttering in panic like newly caged birds, in closets or dim corners, and of the more nearly satisfying but still by no means leisurely pawings in her bedroom when Zeph was abroad on business. Furtiveness was of the marrow of their relationship. Except when they spoke to one another in public, Elnathan a touch condescending toward him, Adam a shade deferential toward her, their talk was in whispers. To tell the truth, though the whole sum of reasons for their getting together was the enjoyment of what is sometimes called the Ultimate Intimacy, they didn't actually know one another well. Their interest in one another could be, at times, intense: it was never informed. The beloved should be studied as well as adored. Adam, had he words, could have described in detail every far, tiny, tucked-away corner of Maisie Treadway's body; but put masks over their faces and he wouldn't have known the naked Elnathan from a naked any-other-woman.

He darted glances right and left. No, they couldn't be seen here, close up to the door, from outside. And surely Zeph wasn't home, though Adam already had run beyond the agreed-upon hour.

Nevertheless Adam had been affrighted. He swallowed, trying to smile. Elnathan, beaming before, now fairly glowered. She was a handsome rather than lovely woman, who ordinarily held herself in; who, if she seldom smiled, seldom really frowned either. It must have been that she saved most of her tempests, of one sort or another, for her lover. It was pretty safe Zeph Evans didn't get many.

"La, 'tis a fine way to greet the lady of your heart!"

Now where in Tophet had she picked up that silly little Frenchy "La!"? This was the first time he'd ever heard it out of her mouth, and it flustered him.

He achieved a smile. It could have been that the effort showed. Anyway Elnathan disapproved.

"Took the breath out of me, just seeing you again."

"You sure hurried here!"

"Ain't been ashore an hour and a half. Come rushing up here, what'll folks think? Ain't even reported to the owners yet. Look—"

He handed her the three remaining lemons, which softened her, though she failed to utter any cries of delight.

"Elnathan—"

"Yes?"

All the voyage home he had been dreading this moment. He didn't want to dirty Maisie, even in his thoughts. She was too clean and good a woman to be treated that way. Yet that Elnathan Evans would expect him back in her bed soon after his return seemed certain. Elnathan might be a wicked woman, and indeed she was, as by the same token he was a wicked man, but nobody could say of her that she wavered. As far as Adam knew, she'd never bedded another man, always excepting of course her husband. Their affair had not been of long duration, and it was hardly likely that one voyage to the Windwards would do anything to decrease her hunger and thirst for him.

"There's, uh, something I want to tell you—"

It was only decent and right. Far as that went, 'twas only common sense; for she'd soon find out anyway.

"What is it, chick?" She still was looking right at him, and standing close, but her eyes had gentled. Oh, she was fond of him! "You want to tell me you missed me?" She was not quite his height, and now as she lifted her face to him her eyelids drooped. "What's the best way to tell me that?"

Next thing Adam knew he had his arms around her and he was kissing her mouth and then kissing her neck, while she pushed herself against him, sobbing gently.

This time it was Elnathan who common-sensed them apart, though her very shove was loving. She moved toward the middle of the room, murmuring for him to follow.

"Anybody passing, they see this light they'd look in."

He nodded. Where they had been standing, near the door, they could not be seen from a window, but every other part of this room could be seen; and why should anybody stand, and keep standing, right up close to the door? Folks would be talking in no time.

Even a passer-by not ordinarily snoopy, and there weren't many such in Newport, assuredly would be set to wondering by the great light from the Evans house. It had smashed against Adam's eyes when he entered.

In a real silver branch on the table were no less than five candles, wax ones, too, and all of them lit.

In his right mind Zephary Evans would never have lit that many candles.

Adam took off his coat and hung it over the back of a chair. He took off his sword and sword-belt and clapped them on the table. He sat in the chair, stretching his legs.

Elnathan opened her eyes a bit wider at the sight of the sword, but she said nothing. She put a log on the fire.

"Knew you was coming."

"Figured you did." He forced a chuckle. "Never saw a door flung open so fast in my life."

She didn't respond with any manner of smile. She was not much of a smiler at best, and there were always those windows to think of.

"Mr. Evans saw you coming up the bay, this morning, from upstairs."

He nodded. He knew that a glass was kept in a rack next to the bedroom window. Like any other merchant, Zeph wanted to know what was coming and going, likewise whether it was worth while to make for the counting house.

"He went to meet you. Later he sent a boy up, tell me you was coming here on business and for me to fix flip."

"Good," said Adam, who had noted that the poker was in the fire. "How 'bout some of that flip right now?"

"Wait'll he comes. Look better."

"Aye."

"That's him now. I know the step."

She went to the door, threw back the bolt. Here was an entrance different from Adam's. Zephary Evans didn't sing out any greeting to his spouse, or even so much as peck at her face, but addressed himself promptly and with unaccustomed geniality to his guest. He apologized for being late. He'd been listening to the story of the duel.

"Brawl," Adam said incisively.

"Tell me about it," begged Elnathan.

"Woman, brew us flip," said Zeph. "I told you to have some ready."

All the same, and while Elnathan fussed with mugs and rum and spices, Zeph did relate what had happened down on Queen's Wharf, and he embellished the tale with touches of an imagination you wouldn't have supposed him to have, making Adam out quite a hero. Elnathan was goggle-eyed now; but she went on working. The poker hissed once, twice. The flip was ready.

Though the telling of the tale embarrassed him, Adam Long was to remember that scene, different from any he had known. The fire, the candles—though Zeph had snuffed out three of these—the steaming mugs of flip, the platter of injun muffins Elnathan had fetched from the kitchen, the low ceiling, rain slashing the windows: these combined to make a deep impression upon him. The Evans house, if comfortable, could hardly have been a cheery place on an average evening; but it was a home, something to which Adam Long was not accustomed.

He stretched his legs, leaning back in the chair; and though he did for form's sake now and then mumble a protest against the overvividness of the narrative—second-hand from Zeph Evans, who had missed the fight itself—for the most part he thoroughly enjoyed himself. The flip was excellent, the injun, too. The story of the fight gave Elnathan an excuse for gazing at him with eyes held wide in admiration instead of holding to her more usual expressionlessness; and when she served him—for her husband had not told her to sit down—she leaned far over, so that he could peek down the neck of her dress. At other times Adam stared at the candle branch.

It was real silver, that branch, and in any Newport household in the year 1702 an article of silver was something mighty special, something to be set out only on extraordinary occasions. Adam wasn't thinking of this, or wondering whose idea it had been to lug the branch out. His mind was on another and far fancier branch, one made of gold adroitly etched. The man who called himself Carse had been wont to fill the seven holes of this bit of booty with candles originally intended no doubt for the altar of some Papist church, and light these, and then set for Adam the task of putting them out one by one, in quick succession, from a goodly distance. Lunging his full length, Adam could barely reach a candle with the tip of his rapier. The trick was to put out each flame without ripping the wick or spilling hot wax. It was not easy. He'd had to come back to full salute position after each lunge, too. Only once, sweating, panting, in that sun-drenched hollow back of the settlement, had Adam put out every candle: but he'd seldom got fewer than four.

Well, he was a long ways from Providence island now. He smiled a mite, listening to the rain, sometimes sneaking a look at Elnathan, only half hearing the story of his own prowess.

The change-over from sociability to business was barbarously abrupt. The flip was extremely strong, but as soon as Zeph Evans saw that Adam was minding it he ordered his wife out of the room, ordered her, too, to close the kitchen door after her, and then turned to Adam and went right to work.

"You'll be sailing again, Captain?"

"Soon's I can catch a cargo. Anything about?"

"Spars and staves for London. But they're not the best cargo for a boat like *Goodwill*. But there's heaps of coasting."

"England, that's it. Two men there I want to meet."

"Now about my share—"

"Aye."

It was clear at once that Zeph was eager to sell, though Adam couldn't guess why; but it was equally clear that he meant to get a good price. These two knew one another. There were no fancy phrases, yet neither was there any thumping of the table. They went at it harshly but in low voices, not looking at one another. It was a full hour before they settled. Adam was to pay rather more than he'd meant to; Zephary was not getting as much as he'd thought to. It was a sound bargain. The merchant got out writing materials and they wrote an agreement and then made a copy of this, and each man signed each document.

They did not shake hands afterward, for Zeph was not a demonstrative man. Nor did Adam get another glimpse of the lady of the house, or of the flip.

It was still raining. He turned up the collar of his fearnought. He heard the door closed and bolted behind him, and he glanced back to make sure that nobody was watching from a window. Then he crossed the plot of grass to the window of Deborah Selden's bedroom. He couldn't see much, there under the maples—nothing of the girl, scarcely even the sampler on the wall—but he could see the sill.

The lemons were gone.

◆

PART SEVEN

Nobody Lives in London

39 The wide rolling river he had dreamed of so many times, the Thames, proved to be hardly a creek. The city itself showed at first glance an overgrown, dirty Newport.

Ashore, though, he began to catch a notion of London's bigness. Tarnation, what crowds! And the place stank, a sewer.

"Nobody lives in London," a doleful innkeeper was to tell him. "Nobody, anyway, that can get out into the country."

It seemed to Adam that half the people in the world lived there, all scrounched together as though afraid of the surrounding landscape, wherever that was, the way sheep in a gale huddle with their heads toward the middle, pushing and being pushed. Yet sheep, when buffeted, at least keep busy; whereas the Londoners stood or sat or sprawled to study with a sardonic eye the activities of others. In Newport this would have been unthinkable. Idleness was taken as a matter of course here; in Newport it would have been esteemed a sin.

There was no lack of laughter, but a lot of this was derisive. Newport folks, Adam reckoned, might well be thought solemn alongside these English; yet he didn't sense any large measure of happiness here, much less contentment. It must have been more than a frame of mind, it must have been a physical misalignment, that made Londoners look so sour. Even their smiles had acid in them. Even their grins canted. Two out of three persons you passed might have been suffering from some mild but persistent stomach trouble, a disorder encasing all their thoughts and impulses in a thin fibrous film of suffering.

And the noise! Men tramped on his feet, jogged his elbows, or pushed their faces into his, thrusting things at him, the while they shrieked "What d'ye lack?" Folks dropped things on him from windows, rolled things in front of him. Twice, jostled against a wall, he lost his footing and slipped to hands and knees; but nobody paid him any mind.

Here was the oddest part of it all: the attitude of these Londoners, who could loaf in the midst of turmoil and wouldn't trouble to turn head for anything less loud than a scream for help, if then. Had Adam been caught up in a mob clamoring for the blood of some miscreant he might have caught from his fellows some touch of their hysteria. Yet no common cause united the members of this teeming world, no purpose inspired them. It took Adam a good while to accept the all-but-unbelievable truth that these folks weren't flying around in any frenzy, that *this was the way they acted all the time.*

You were given no chance to take offense. You were bumped from behind, or butted, or shoved, and before you could whirl around and demand an apology the offender had hared off, leaving you to confront some totally different person, who had no interest in you. But then, nobody had any interest in you. Adam had known lonesomeness most of his life; but he had never before been as lonesome as this.

He had seen kicked-over ant heaps; nor was he one to disremember what the Book says about going to the ant, thou sluggard; but ants knew what they were doing, and they worked for one another.

He issued from out of an alley narrow enough so that he might have touched the houses on either side, and emerged into a street comparatively broad; and he saw a coach approaching.

Now Adam Long had never before seen a coach, though he recognized it from descriptions. This street was spacious only in comparison with the alleys he'd recently roamed: in itself it was scarcely wide enough to accommodate the coach, a yellow monstrous lumbrous contraption drawn by four fat horses. Most of the folks near him flattened themselves against walls or squeezed into doorways, but Adam stood staring, head cocked.

The coach was all over small wooden steeples and tassels, some red, some silver. Out of its center, high, wobbling precariously at every lurch of the coach as though it were going to break off, rose a flat wooden triangle on one side of which—Adam couldn't see the other side—were painted two diagonal white stripes, their edges clipped like the edge of a pie, against a background of red.

There were two men sitting up in the driver's seat, which didn't seem necessary. Only one held the reins. They wore red coats with silver froggery, the same sort of coats the two men who rode the left-hand horses wore. Adam couldn't for the life of him see a kernel of reason in those two men. They didn't do anything, just sat there.

Before the coach and on either side, behind, too, marched soldiers. There must have been twenty of these. They carried muskets, holding them out, away from their bodies, in readiness to use the butts as clubs. Folks faded before them. But Adam Long loitered a moment out from the line against the wall, rubbering for a peek at the person or persons within the coach. A soldier struck him in the chest.

"Out of the way, bumpkin!"

This was not a push but a substantial blow. Adam was slammed against the wall. He bellowed, reaching for his sword.

Instantly another soldier stooped low to slap *his* musket butt sideways across Adam's shins.

The pain was an explosion. The first blow had dizzied him but at the same time enraged him. Now all he could do was double up. He might have toppled into the path of the coach itself had not a third soldier kicked him in the mouth. That held him straight until the coach had passed. It also caused his mouth to bleed.

The coach gone, then, a final quartet of soldiers marching backward behind it, the street resumed its clangor, men tumbling about like water in a wake. Only one man, a pursy fellow of merchantlike mien, took the trouble to help Adam to his feet.

"Tut, tut! Lucky it isn't raining today. Might have ruined this." He was feeling the material of the coat as he brushed it. "Where, uh, did you buy this, if I may be so bold as to ask, sir?"

Adam had started to lug out his blade.

"No, no!" The pursy one grabbed his arms. "They're down to the river by now. You'd never even get near his lordship. They'd beat you to a pulp."

Adam licked his lips, tasting the salty blood. He shook his head, clacked his sword back.

"Thank you, sir," he said as quietly as he could.

"You're an American colonial, sir, I take it?"

Adam looked at him in amazement.

"Now how'd you ever know that?"

The pursy one summoned a water-seller, gave her a farthing for a can, proffered his own kerchief, and wiped Adam's mouth.

"Tut, tut! But you're lucky. I've seen men get all their front teeth smashed in, they didn't jump back fast enough."

"I was never taught to jump out of the way."

" 'Tis a good thing to know. There. Take care of that coat. You didn't buy it in Boston, I'll wager. Philadelphia perhaps?"

"Kingston, Jamaica."

"Ah," slowly raising and lowering his head. "Ah, yes. I see. Well, good-bye, sir. Your servant."

"Your servant, sir. And—thank you a bushel of times."

Still stunned, unsure of himself, struggling to hold his rage in, Adam must have walked half a mile after this before he as much as looked up —to see a sight so strange that in a wild moment he wondered whether he had been knocked unconscious and was dreaming this.

40 It was an open space, large for London, roughly round, the sort of place, as Adam later learned, though he was never to learn why, that was called a circus. There was a considerable crowd, in the center of which stood one of the largest persons Adam ever had seen, a man with immense shoulders, an ape's arms, black lank hair, a mouth continually atwist, hands that might have been hams, bare feet. This creature wore only a shaggy tuniclike affair seemingly made of the pelts of small animals, tasseled in unexpected places, and more than a little motheaten. He rumbled and growled pauselessly.

Prancing and capering around, and waving a branch of spruce, was a thin short man with the eyes of a malicious old monkey. He wore an extremely tall conical hat made of some sort of paper, on which had been crayoned pictures intended to represent (as near as Adam could make out) bears, birds, and bushes. He talked all the time.

". . . and the soil's rich and black, thousands of acres for any man wants to take 'em . . . and he don't have to *work!*" Grimacing, he pointed to the pictures on his hat. "The fruits of the orchards and the vegetables of the field, they're hisn for the picking!"

"Speakin' of vegetables," cried somebody, and threw a rotten turnip. It missed the talker by inches.

"Out to 'eave a *paving stone* at 'im, that's what," the man next to Adam muttered.

"What in Tophet's he talking about?" Adam asked.

"The American plantations. 'E's a bleedin' spirit."

"A what?"

"A spirit. Recruiter. We calls 'em spirits because they spirit men awie. They'll tike anybody—out of prisons, poor'ouses, anywhere."

The crowd itched to learn what that Samson in the patched pelts was supposed to be, and it was permitting itself to be entertained, and conceivably edified, but it was by no means co-operative.

"Four years of bloody slavery they gives you," somebody shouted. "Then they adds a couple more every time you let go a belch."

"Not so, my friends," cried the man in the dunce's cap. "A few years of easy, restful study, just so's you can look around and get used to being in that wonderful land—that's all. You wants time to pick your own plantation, don't you? Well, that's all it is. The contract don't mean nothing. Mere matter of form, my friends."

"He's a liar," Adam said, low.

"For sure. They all are. But there's a few as'll follow 'im, and 'e'll turn 'em over to the top uns of the gang and *they'll* really pour the lies on like clabbered cream on berries."

The bleedin' spirit was thrusting the spruce first into this face, then into that, all the time dancing around.

"Ever sniff anything so delicious in your life, my friends? The true *sequitur fugientum,* straight from America."

"Don't smell like nothing to me," one man said.

"Didn't leave it under my nose long enough," another said.

"If the talk-talk-talk don't do it," said the man standing next to Adam, "then they buys 'em ale—spiked with gin."

"And if that doesn't work?"

The man shrugged.

"They 'its 'em on the 'ead."

The recruiter was losing his crowd. He whipped from a pocket three glass balls, which he began to juggle. He wasn't a very good juggler.

"You just lie there and watch the corn grow. And in the daytime you listen to the mooing of the kine, and at night to the—well, the nightingales."

"The roarin' of the tigers, I reckon," somebody shot out.

The recruiter shook a vigorous head.

"No tigers or lions left there any more. The first settlers killed 'em all off when they cleared the land."

"Bad enough they net nitwits, the only kind'd want to go to the plantations anyway," the man next to Adam said, "but when they grabs children it's a caution."

"They take children? Kids?"

"Aye. They're napping kids all over town. Offer 'em sweets, anything. Or just plain break into your 'ouse and steal 'em. Kidnappers—ain't you never heard of the kidnappers, sir?"

Adam slowly shook his head. The very word, he reflected, had an evil sound. Kidnappers. He shuddered.

"You never even *heard* of them? Say, where'n 'ell do you 'ail from, if a man might ask?"

"The American colonies," replied Adam.

Next time he looked the man was not there.

The man in the center of the circus remained, however, and he was working harder than ever. His glass balls were not getting much attention; his audience was walking out on him; so he played his trump card —the dark-haired monstrosity they were wondering about.

"Where else in the world except a place where the air's so pure and the climate's so balmy, where else would you find a specimen of the human race like my friend Cyossetta here?"

176

He thumped the big man's chest.

"It's the wonderful air, my friends!"

"This one of them red savages?"

" 'E don't look red."

" 'Ard to tell what color 'e might turn out, somebody worked him over with soap and water awhile."

A pitchman doesn't dare to permit his audience to participate too freely, lest they take the show away from him.

"Cyossetta here, gents, happens to be a full-blooded Narragansett."

"That's a lie," Adam said loudly.

"Eh?" The recruiter peered at him, squinting, as though through smoke. He saw the sword. "Ah well, your lordship's right. I spoke too hasty. What I meant to say is, 'e's a full-blooded *Indian*. Matter of fact, 'is mother was a Massachusetts. So 'e's only *half* Narragansett."

"He's no more an American Indian than he is the man in the moon," declared Adam.

He couldn't have said why he broke in. He had nothing against the redskins, though he was no notable admirer of that race either. All the same, he didn't like to see the Narragansetts maligned.

Hands on hips, he surveyed the giant.

"He may be a Turk, for all I know, but he's no American. And everything else you've said here is a passel of lies, too."

Adam would have walked away then, had not the pitchman, fearing that he planned to linger, tried to scare him off.

Raising his voice: "Maybe if my fine jack-a-dandy here would like to swap a few buffets with Cyossetta he'd prove that a city-bred Englishman is physically superior to this product of the colonies?"

It was a threat. He was saying: "Be off—or I'll sic Samson on you!"

"I might, at that," Adam said.

Once again, there was no reason in it. This wasn't his cause, or shouldn't be. If the authorities of London permitted such goings-on, what was that to Adam?

Maybe he just felt like fighting? Maybe his blood still boiled from that encounter with the coach guards?

Anyway, he unstrapped his sword belt. He looked around for somebody to take it.

There was a thin, fragile-seeming youth, himself sworded. He was dressed in blue and silver, mighty jaunty, and on his mouth and in his eyes was a quizzical smile. Adam went to him.

"Would you be kind enough to guard my effects, sir?"

"Don't be a fool, sir," the young man said in a low voice, but smiling all the while. "That clod could crush you flat."

"I thank you kindly, sir," said Adam, "but I think I'll fight."

The man shrugged. He had thin shoulders. He took snuff from a gold case; but he also, in a moment, took Adam's sword, coat, hat. Adam had learned something about lace in Providence, and he'd have bet sixpence that that was real point d'Alençon at the young man's throat.

"God be w'ye. You'll need *somebody's* help."

"I don't think that this is any time," Adam said, "to be taking the name of Our Lord in vain."

The man opened his eyes very wide.

"Well, I'll be damned," he whispered.

Adam smiled, to show him there was no hard feeling, and then Adam turned and strode to the center of the circus.

41   It would not be like hitting a man. This was not a man, truly. It was some beast curiously manlike in appearance. The recruiter was more frenzical than ever, bobbing and leaping about, sweat bright on his face, while his wicked little eyes glittered. He spoke to Cyossetta, who gave over his yammering and came out with a real remark, his first, though nobody could understand anything either of them said. Likely enough they spouted a prearranged gibberish calculated to awe most listeners, or it could have been thieves' cant. Anyway, it wasn't Narragansett. Adam Long knew Narragansett.

Swinging his arms slowly, purposefully, Cyossetta shambled forward. Adam's breast tightened, his scalp tingled. Inside the hug of those arms any man would be crushed.

The brute stopped. He reached out, hands open, palms up. It was the gesture of a lazy Goliath. He seemed to be saying: Come here and let's get this over with; let me squash you like a melon, little man.

Standing his full height, Adam went in between those arms—but he went in fast. He punched right and left. He sprang back.

Cyossetta grunted. Blood stood out on his mouth.

"Clout 'im, yer ludship!"

"Bash 'is beak in!"

"First claret's yourn! Now catch 'im a conker!"

Adam's fists hurt. Cyossetta seemed the same, except for the blood. He came shuffling in, his hands a little lower now, his shoulders hunched forward. His head was low, too, the chin on his chest. From somewhere behind that tangle of hair two small eyes regarded Adam: they might have been serpents watching from a bush.

Adam sprang again. He struck but one blow this time, a rounder with

178

the right fist, but he landed it just where he wanted it—a trifle to the left of the point of the chin. Then he danced back.

Any other man on earth, he thought with a sob, would have been stopped by that punch. It stung all down Adam's arm, and the fist itself had been set aflame. But Cyossetta came on in.

Adam retreated. He had to.

He ducked low, and went in with head down, hooking right and left. He butted the belly, swung for the groin, missed, slipped. Something that could have been an elbow struck the back of his head, and a knee came up and caught him on a cheekbone. He was down, but his head was clear. He had time to spring to his feet and scrabble away from Cyossetta's charge. Baffled, Cyossetta came to a stop. Adam jumped in and plopped a fist spang on the nose. The blood fairly gushed out, slobbering all down over Cyossetta's fur togs. Cyossetta paid it no mind. He simply shook his head, the impatient gesture of a man who has walked into a cobweb in the dark, and came shambling on.

Did the brute have no point of vulnerability? Adam backed away, backed away— He tried to maneuver himself to a point behind Cyossetta, or even to one side of him; for the giant, waving his hands the way a lobster waves its claws, like a lobster again could only hold off a head-on attack. If Adam couldn't knock him down, perhaps he could throw him, spill him suddenly? Once Cyossetta was down, his head could be kicked against the cobbles.

Whether from instinct or reason, Cyossetta did not permit this. He turned as Adam moved.

When Adam would stand still for a moment, Cyossetta would start toward him. Cyossetta never appeared to be in a hurry.

Adam retreated, felt a wall behind him, stepped to one side, felt another wall. Then he couldn't swallow; for he realized that he had let himself be cornered. Intent on the giant's face, performing a series of quick retreats, never worried about the onlookers, who were careful to keep out of his way, he had given no thought to what might be behind him. It had appeared, initially, as though they had plenty of room. But though the houses that made up this circus were close together, in most cases touching, and though generally they presented a smooth wood-and-plaster front to the pavement, there were projections, irregularities. And Adam was in a corner now.

He took a deep breath. He bumped his buttocks against the wall, pushed forward with a foot, too, and hurled himself against Cyossetta.

It was like pummeling a tree, trying to make it go down. Adam swung from side to side, evading those enormous hands, hooking in punches as hard as he could—and as fast.

He couldn't have told you, afterwards, when it was that he missed Cyossetta. Men cooed and chittered reassuringly at him, a whit afraid to reach out and touch him, and after a while he caught himself stumbling around looking for the face he was to punch, not finding it.

Once he had seen a cock, a shakebag, hackles high, gaffs wet, one eye torn out while the other was flooded with blood, stagger around the pit, furious, tearing the air, blindly seeking its enemy—which lay dead. Adam must have been something like that.

He stopped, feeling a little foolish. He looked around.

Cyossetta the oak tree had been felled at last, and lay motionless. The spirit kicked him twice in the side of the head.

"Y' bleedin' fool," he screeched, accurately enough. "Yer carn't even *fight!*"

He kicked Cyossetta again, then slipped into the crowd.

Adam Long went to the young man in blue and silver, and bowed briefly, murmuring thanks.

"You were right, sir. It was more than I'd bargained for."

" 'Twas a damned fine show, sir. Here—permit me to help you on with the coat. Will you share a bird and a bottle with me, sir?"

"Well— Do you know any place we could go?"

"La, I know 'em all."

Together then, the slim and elegant young man carrying his hat, which was cocked all around and had blue feathers, they departed daintily from the circus. Their swords swung at their sides.

42 The young man's name it turned out was John Chumley, and it was necessary for him to carry his hat because he wore so big a periwig, a massive full-bottomed affair.

At the Crimson Cockatoo the host fairly slavered, and half a dozen customers bowed and called greetings.

"You are from the American colonies, sir?" politely.

Adam stared at him.

"Now how did you know that?"

Chumley smiled, and talked of something else.

He spoke slowly, indeed he drawled, yet it was not easy to understand him. His speech sounded to Adam even further from straight English than that of Willis Beach. In some respects, and notably in the use of "a" for "o"—he said "lard" when he meant "lord," for instance—it reminded Adam of the speech of Maisie Treadway. It had been purposely perverted. It was a class mark.

"What do you think of London, then?"

"Well, it seems mighty—crowded."

He stole a look at his companion, who, having demolished two partridges and a bottle of St. Julien, was picking his teeth.

"You must know a lot of folks in this town."

"I know everyone worth knowing."

"There are two men I'd like to meet. Something I want each of them to explain. I want satisfaction."

"What a bloodthirsty one it is! Invades our fair isle for the purpose of skewering a couple of gents he don't fancy, and the first morning he's here he pummels the guts out of some Whitefriars Hercules with a name like a sneeze—just to keep in trim, I take it? 'Struth, Captain, is it really that wonderful air the spirit spoke of?"

"Only one of them I'd fight," Adam said mildly.

"Now would it be unmannerly if I was to ask the names?"

"No harm. One happens to be the Earl of Tillinghast."

"Why now, dip me down a jakes! You'd call out a fuddyduddy like that, a man old enough to be your father?"

Adam flushed.

"He ain't the one I'm going to call out. Uh, I take it he don't live here in London? Out in the country, in his own castle maybe?"

"Well now, I wouldn't call Tillinghast a castle. Damned handsome shack though."

"I mean, he's not here in the city now?"

"Not now, no. He was, an hour ago."

"Eh?"

"Right this minute I'd say his lordship is just wondering what part of the river to heave his breakfast into. He just embarked. Ambassador extraordinary and minister plenipotentiary with love from Anne to Louis. What's that? We're at war with France? Why, so we are, man! And Tillinghast's being sent to Versailles exactly because Sarah Churchill wishes to be sure that we *continue* at war. There's been ugly rumors of a possible peace."

"He—just sailed—you say?"

"'Bout an hour ago. I saw his coach trundling down toward the river just before you came along and started tilting at the dragon."

"Is it— Is it yellow, that coach?"

"Why, 'tis, truly."

"Has it got a device on top—two wobbly white lines slantwise across a field of red?"

"Dexter?"

"Well, I guess so."

"Must be. Hardly be sinister. Why, that's gules, two bendlets invested argent. Aye, the Tillinghast 'scutcheon."

Adam touched his chest. He winced.

It had been a memorable welcome.

"The other one," he said, "is Sir Jervis Johnston."

"Oh now, see here, you're not proposing to fight *Jerve Johnston?*"

"I sure am. Reckon you could arrange it?"

"La, I'd be an accessory before the fact in a murder case if ever I did. Why, Jerve'd *carve* you."

"Well, he'll get the chance."

"Yet you could call him out right enough, yes. All the formalities. Go to the field. Then an apology, last minute. It's been done."

"I mean a real fight. I won't settle for anything less."

"Tut, tut, Captain."

"Can you arrange it?"

"I could, yes," said Chumley, and put his toothpick back into its case and pocketed the case, "for a fee."

He looked at the ceiling.

"Why, uh, what I had in mind was an affair of honor."

"Quite."

Adam gawked. Chumley's eyes were opened very wide and a faint fond smile still touched the corners of his mouth.

"Damn me, Captain, the surgeon'll get a fee. Why shouldn't I? I'm as much a specialist as any surgeon. A thing like this needs expert handling. But cheerily, I come cheap. Twenty yellow-boys. Twenty golden guineas, coin of the realm, eh?"

"That's a lot of money."

"Damn me, it's a lot you're proposing to buy with it, sir. Jerve Johnston's no frippery fop, I can tell you. A *rencontre* with a blade like that, why it'll be talked about in every coffee house from St. James's to the Tower for quite three days. Every detail will be discussed. Such a matter needs careful handling."

"I see."

"There'll be other expenses as well. The surgeon I just mentioned. Chair hire for both of us: it ain't thought genteel to go to the field mounted, don't ask me why. Other items. But first of all, a new coat for you, Captain. La, I say nothing against the one on your back now! Don't call *me* out! But we must get you something special and splendid. You lack friends, you must make it up with finery."

"That's the last thing I should have thought of."

"It's the first thing *I* thought of."

"Does so much depend on your coat, in this town?"

Chumley took snuff. He flicked a speck of it off his cravat. "A hell of a lot depends on your coat in this town," he said.

43 It has been said that the kind of person who always remembers everything seldom remembers anything worth remembering. Resolved Forbes was an exception. No man ever had a better mate. Adam Long signed the document he had written, sanded it, waved it, and then glanced up through the hatchway to where the *Goodwill's* second-in-command was supervising the unloading of the spars.

It had not taken Captain Long two hours to sell the spars. He reckoned it was because of the war that things cost so much. He could hardly believe it, the price he'd got. That was the last of the spars, being bumped out up there on deck right now. The schooner hands had been permitted to loaf at least half the time because the wharfworkers, though twice as numerous, couldn't keep up with them—or didn't want to. Adam was not paying for the wharfworkers, thank the Lord. They wouldn't be fiddlefaddling around like that if he was!

The reloading would not take long, in part because it wouldn't require any Londoners, in part because the cargo consisted of small items. Adam had been choosey. The average skipper who touched at Newport tended to fetch whatever gimcrackery he could lay hands on, assuming, as he did, that the Americans were glad to get anything at all. Adam Long knew better. He had, had had for years, his own ideas about what would constitute the ideal westbound cargo. First: well-built things, solid things that would last. Not fine furniture, for it occupied too much space and anyway might take too long to sell. Not fancy clothes, for folks were ashamed to buy those from somebody they knew; and then there was the matter of fit, and the further very important matter of fashion, which could veer crazily. But to Adam's knowledge there had never been enough iron nails in Newport, and from what he'd overheard the women say there had never been enough needles either. So he bought a lot of these, and a lot of knives. Axes, too. An axe always had a certain value in a place like Rhode Island, where you seldom saw any actual cash. It was almost like money; and a Newport man would take it instead of a coin, even though he already owned a perfectly good axe, for he'd know that he would never have any trouble selling or trading it. Adam had also bought some luxury notions like candle snuffers and sad irons, but not many such. All these things, again because of the war, were hard to get; and in America anything made of metal was a prize. In physical bulk, though not in value, the greater part of the cargo would consist of assorted cloths and dress materials—not silks, satins, or crepe de chine, but plain perpetuana and plenty of it, deerskin, felt, camlet, linen, sagathy, drugget.

In the profit from the sale of these articles, Adam as skipper would share. Additionally, he was filling personal commissions for fellow carpenters—augers, cleaving planes, molding planes, bench hook hammers, jointer planes, all sorts of saws, chisels, gouges, wimble bitts— There were never enough tools in Newport.

Adam's own flyer, a rare bargain, stumbled into by chance, was four gross of real wax candles. These wouldn't go bad or go out of fashion; their price would not grasshopper around; and they'd be easy to store. If it was necessary to raise money on them, they should serve at least as well as nails. Wax candles were a luxury in Newport, where most folks used tallow or just bayberry; but they were a *sound* luxury, a *respectable* one. Man or woman might hesitate to buy silk stockings in Newport, and hesitate even longer about wearing them in public. But wax candles, while symbols of a solid financial position, were not extravagant, not ostentatious.

There was another purchase that was personal to Adam, though it came out of the ship's fund—two suits of Dutch linen sails. *Goodwill's* canvas was dark, coarse, heavy, easily split. Dutch linen was not obtainable in America; and *Goodwill* deserved the best. Had Adam asked the Adventurers for permission to buy these, they'd raise their hands in horror. So he just said nothing—and went ahead and bought them.

Adam, however, was not thinking of this when he sanded the document. He was thinking that he'd properly ought to leave something to the faithful and efficient Resolved Forbes.

For this was Adam's will he had just written.

It had never previously occurred to him to make out a will, and that for at least two reasons: 1) he hadn't had anything to leave to anybody; and 2) he hadn't had anybody to leave anything to. But now his duty was clear. After all, he could get killed. And he did own seven-sixteenths of one of the sweetest little sailing vessels in any man's ocean. Zeph's shares had been paid for only in part, but Adam's personal profits from this voyage would make up the rest. It was little enough that Maisie had, there far across the sea, lonesome on that hot, disagreeable island: a basketful of bills, bitter memories, some claim to part of a ruined plantation, and the sworn word of a lover. That word at least was going to be good.

So Adam had not needed the urging of John Chumley to make out a will, though Chumley *had* urged.

184

"Ain't challenged Johnston yet," Adam had grumped. "Tarnation, I ain't even *seen* him yet."

"You will, my chick, you will. Besides, 'tis fashionable. All the bloods have done it. So now—hie you to a lawyer."

Well, Adam had not gone to any lawyer. After all, expenses were bad enough in this besmudged Gomorrah without adding a solicitor's fee to 'em. Adam could write the Queen's English passing well; and the testament was simple—it merely stipulated that after his just debts had been settled, and his body, if available, had been given a decent Christian burial, all that was left of his estate should go to the Honorable Maisie de Lynn Treadway-Paul. Even a lawyer would have had a hard time finding something to get confused about in that.

But there was Resolved Forbes, up on deck there. And—Adam suddenly remembered it—there was the new coat.

The coat was kept at the Hearth Cricket, where Adam had a room, it being altogether too spectacular a garment to be worn down by the river here—it would invite stones and muddy sticks. The serious abstemious Forbes, Old Sobersides himself, could not have been forced at pistolpoint to don such a coat. But it would fetch a fine price. Resolved Forbes, though he might disapprove of such pieces of frippery, would hardly be likely to overlook their value.

Adam seized his quill and in a moment had added a codicil:

"Save only my new coat, together with the waistcoat thereto, also the cocked hat, wch I give and bequeathe to R. Forbes, mate."

Feeling better, indeed humming, he went up on deck. Forbes saluted him; and the two stood watching the completion of the work.

"They're a good crew," Adam said after a while.

"Aye."

They were. The new bosun, Holyoake, if louder and less sure of himself than Jeth Gardner had been, was young—and he was spry, he was brisk. Abel Rellison still was with them, making a man's wages now, three shillings a month, which put him and John Bond into a position of great lordliness over the sailors from English ships. The two Negroes from Jamaica still were aboard, earning almost nothing, not caring, tolerably good workers, if slow. Then there were three strapping Newport boys, each the worth of any man. The *Goodwill* forecastle these days was a cheery clean place.

> Skipper's gone balmy,
> Mate's on a spree,
> Running in circles
> On Scaredy-Cat Sea.

Adam harrumphed.

"You should have all the new cargo aboard inside of three hours."

"Aye, but not stowed, sir."

"Take her out in the stream, do your stowing there. No sense paying wharfage. Leave the Moses and one hand."

"Aye, aye, sir."

"Have only one hook down. That's if the water allows it."

Resolved Forbes looked sideways at him.

"Might leave in a hurry, sir?"

"Aye. I might have just killed a man."

He said it matter-of-factly; and Mr. Forbes only nodded.

"Shall I have somebody summon a chair, sir?"

Adam shook his head.

"I'd admire to walk. I'll have to chair around later."

"I, uh, if it should happen that this man kills *you* instead—"

"There's a paper in my box, on top."

"Aye, aye, sir."

44 The cuffs alone must have been eighteen inches deep. Heavy with gold braid, they were stiffened inside by wire. The coat itself, where it was not brass buttons or braiding or turned-over yellow, was the red of a flame. It was made of moiré silk. Getting into it, when you were already encased in a waistcoat that reached to your knees, was much like what getting into a suit of armor must have been.

Adam was spared the crowning glory of this costume—the periwig.

"Run you anywhere up to fifty guineas," Chumley had explained. "Spend your money like that, you won't have any left for me."

So Adam had his hair cropped short and bought one of these new three-cornered hats. At Clark's of an afternoon, Chumley had said, almost nobody was bewigged. They wore instead little linen or velvet caps, not unlike nightcaps, or tricorns; or some even sat down bare-headed. It was a highly informal place. And the circumstance that his hair was close-cropped would make Adam appear a man relaxed, a man who had left his fifty-guinea peruke at home.

"La, but you couldn't go out that way at *night!*"

"Of course not."

Now he gave a last loving pat to his cravat and toddled cautiously downstairs, the boniface having shouted that his chair was ready. Clark's was scarcely half a mile away, but nobody save a fool would risk it afoot in a coat like this.

"'Ail the conquering 'ero comes!"

This was Hal Bingham, making a to-do, as he did each day, about Adam's descent. The Hearth Cricket was patronized largely by seafaring men, not many of whom customarily sallied forth each afternoon in a coat that would have shamed Joseph's.

Adam liked the Hearth Cricket, as he liked Hal Bingham and his wife, their daughter Lil, the customers, the neighbors. Adam's day, this past week, had been divided sharply into three parts. In the morning he had gone about his business, chiefly buying, checking prices, being insulted by port officials, perhaps dropping in at Edward Lloyd's place in Abchurch Lane to look over the "ships' list" that enterprising proprietor posted. In the afternoon he would sit at Clark's, chatting with John Chumley, now and then meeting sundry meaningless minor toffs, and sipping wine, while he waited for Sir Jervis Johnston to appear. In the evening he sat before the fire at the inn. This was best. Back in his freedom suit, he would stretch his legs, hoist his jack, and talk and laugh. Except for their accent these folks were such as he might have known in Newport. Adam liked them, and it made his heart warm to see that they liked him. Indeed it got Adam all throat-lumpy every time he contemplated this coziness.

Today, however, the air of the ordinary was strained. Mine host and his wife clucked around Lillian, who was weeping.

Lil ran to Adam. He mussed her hair with one hand, giving her a smack on the backside with the other. Still blubbering, she giggled. She was six.

"They won't let me play outside!"

Hal said quickly: "She can run far's Loo Lane upstreet and the Thatched Roof downstreet, but only in daytime. She knows that."

Adam considered.

"'Tis a short span, sure."

"Aye, and a few steps further," Goodwife Bingham cried, "might take 'er clear to the other side of the sea!"

"Bad as that?" Adam asked. "Even in daytime?"

"Bad as that," said Hal. "They'll be climbing in our windows pretty soon, snatching the babes right out of bed."

"Al Lamson's tyke, just about Lil's age here, she took a stroll last week —and they ain't seen nor hide nor hair of her since."

"Hardly seems possible— Where's the watch?"

"Wherever it's not needed. Don't you get Cap'n Long's coat all smeary there now!"

"She's all right," said Adam, an arm around her.

"Our one chick, y'see," said Hal. "Keeps up, we won't dare let her out-doors at all. Must be a gang of 'em working this neighborhood."

His wife sighed.

"Asking your pardon, Cap'n Long, but there's times I wish nobody'd ever discovered that America of yourn over there."

"Mary!"

"No harm," Adam said. "But we ain't all stolen nippers there, ma'am. We ain't all slaves. Folks in New England never even heard about these kidnappers, far as I know."

"You tell 'em, when you go back."

"That I will, ma'am. I sure will."

He cupped Lillian's chin in a hand, and raised her face, and grinned down at her. She grinned back, tears and all.

"Now remember what your mother and father said, or I won't bring you a sugar bun today. *Don't ever trust a strange man.*"

"I'd trust you," the child cried, and hugged him, "because you have on such a beautiful coat."

"A Londoner," said Adam.

The city seethed around his chair. Women screeched indefatigably, and men fought. Why? As always, the great number of idle appalled Adam. The streets and the places of refreshment that led off them were crammed with men who sat or stood all day doing nothing. In Newport when two or three were gathered together they worked while they talked, if they talked at all, and the subject of their conversation in such a case was likely to be, say, corporeal immortality, or perhaps the doctrine of moral inability in a fallen state. *Here* they droned of wenches, horse races, the price of gin.

All the noise, the fuss, the banging and slapping and kicking and stamping, the hubbub, the clamor—yet in a few hours, when night fell, an uneasy silence would fasten itself upon London; and the dust, if the day had been dry, would settle; while these brash boisterous persons, stricken dumb, scared, would disappear like worms that crawled back into the woodwork, leaving the streets still. It couldn't be, by Adam's reasoning, that all these persons had made themselves so uncomfortable in crushing so close together, in such a small and smelly place, purely for the purpose of *safety*. This, he'd heard, had been suggested by cer-tain wiseacres. He did not believe it. He reckoned that nobody who had walked the streets of London after dark would ever believe it either. They frighted even him.

Yet he shouldn't whine. He was Home, wasn't he?

The chair was put down, the door opened.

"Clark's, your worship."

Now this, though a wooden pot was fastened above the door, was no typical coffee house. Technically it was public; it was licensed. You went in unchallenged, and paid your penny at the bar, but when you sat down you weren't served—not unless you were known. Clark's atmosphere was different, as was, too, its very appearance. There was no sand on the floor. No advertisements were pasted on unpainted walls. Spittoons were not scattered about. The ceiling wasn't low, grimy. The barmaid—barmaids and the nasty English habits of spitting and of picking the teeth were what most shocked Adam about London—was not called Phyllis, as she was virtually everywhere else. At Clark's there were no readings of the public prints, nor were there auction sales conducted by inch of candle. Nothing vulgar like that.

John Chumley was in his accustomed corner.

"Just sent for a bottle. You're in time to pay for it."

Adam nodded. He was getting used to this.

Chumley took the churchwarden out of his mouth, and yawned.

"Old Clark's pressing a bit for a couple of quid I owe him. Settle it up, won't you, my sweet chicken, my chick?"

Adam took the coins from a pocket, and he spun one on the table.

"We've been doing this for a week," he reminded Chumley.

The latter's smile was sleepy.

"I know, I know. But I've not doodled you, my dear, believe me. This sort of thing is much the best when it appears to be done by chance, so to say. If we sought out Jerve Johnston 'twould be too crude—and not public enough. A man likes to get credit, among his peers, for the number of times he's called out. You see?"

"But when is Johnston ever going to *be* here?"

"He's here right now. Came in five minutes ago."

45 What Adam saw at first was not the man he meant to kill. He saw a mist, through which gleamed the green-flecked eyes of Maisie.

"The longish one in blue, with the Mechlin cap."

It is the traditional delight of the lover in separation to keep the memory of the loved one fresh by turning it over and over, regarding fondly but attentively every aspect of it, seeking out each detail. Adam Long was not concerned with tradition. He loved Maisie all right, and he was sick for the sight of her again; but that was just it—he couldn't afford to be sick. As much as he was able, he must keep Maisie out of his mind. She was bad for his work.

Yet he saw her now as he looked across the smoke-filled room to the place where his mortal enemy sat. He saw her as first he'd known her, the long-legged lass who used to stand at the taffrail and look wistfully across the emptiness of the sea.

He shook his head to clear it. He wiped his mouth.

Summoned by that effort of will, like a genie invoked by carefully concocted magic, Sir Jervis Johnston came into focus.

He was stick-thin and tall. His hands were beringed, his throat be-laced. He spoke in a high-pitched drawl. He waved his kerchief, and negligently took snuff. He rolled his eyes.

At a glance, then, a fool. But as Adam studied him, the man's restless strength somehow showed through. Johnston twitched with trivialities; yet despite these, and despite the fact that his every word and movement were thought out, he was a person to fear. How Adam sensed this he couldn't have said; but he did sense it.

Even at Clark's, where to be listless, to be languid, was almost a requirement for entrance, Johnston attracted attention. Though there was nothing so common as a craning of necks, Adam's ear, sharpened by a week's practice, caught the slight but significant change of tone. Jack-a-dandies in corners yawned in one another's faces and wearily swapped gossip; but they were out of eye-ends gazing at the newcomer.

Sir Jervis Johnston couldn't afford to gamble, had no interest in the life at court, wasn't military. There were two places where he shone, where his exploits were fabulous: on the field of honor or in a lady's bedchamber he was, they tittered, without a peer. His every triumph in each of these chosen fields was known to his fellow customers at Clark's —the only public that interested him.

"What do we do?" asked Adam in a voice that seemed to come from far away. "Do we pull his hat down over his eyes?"

"No, no, no, no! After an hour or so you and I'll drift over to his table, and I shall introduce you. Jerve'll undoubtedly ask us to have a glass of wine, and then when you fall to chatting you'll say that positively you don't swoon at the sight of his coat or that you would be glad to have your servant instruct his servant how to make up a proper cravat. That's all."

"I ain't got a servant."

"It doesn't matter."

"But will he know he's been mortally insulted then?"

"He'll know. He has a very keen ear for such things. Then we'll drift back here, and after maybe half an hour Jerve'll ask the waiter to fetch

190

writing materials and he'll compose a note to you, asking you if you wouldn't care to retract your remark. You'll read this and toss it aside. Then later *you'll* call for writing materials and—" Chumley broke off to grip Adam's arm. "See here, you *can* write, can't you?"

"I can write."

"Good. So you simply tell him that you don't feel you should modify your remark, and you subscribe yourself his worship's most humble and most obedient servant—and send it by the waiter."

"Then what?"

"I take care of the rest. You don't have to do any more."

"Except fight the man."

"You won't fight. You'll *meet* but you won't *fight*. Remember that."

Adam nodded. He had no intention of making an apology, but neither did he have any intention of telling Chumley this.

"Then what do we do?"

"Then we all share another bottle of wine—"

"I pay for that one, too?"

"—and it's finished."

"Tarnation silly, if you ask me."

They sat in silence. Adam glared at the table. John Chumley made bread balls for a while, then caught himself and called for a pipe. When the waiter came, Adam, resisting the temptation to look again at Sir Jervis, ordered a sugar bun, which he pocketed.

"You do that every day," Chumley said accusingly.

"For a friend of mine, a lady."

"I take it not the same one you're meeting Jerve because of?"

"Who said anything about a lady there?"

"Forgive me, my dear." The fribble, for once, was sincere. "The challenge of course will be because of taste in clothing."

"Of course," said Adam.

Two pipes later John Chumley yawned and announced that he was going to what at Clark's was called the necessary, not the jakes.

Alone at last, Adam permitted himself to turn. Sir Jervis Johnston screeched on in that mincing high drawl. Watching him, Adam began to rage. That this simpering coxcomb, a disgrace to his sex as well as his class, should be the first—

Before he knew what he was doing he had crossed the room.

"Sir Jervis Johnston, I believe?"

The man looked up. His brows had been touched with something dark. The whole face was painted. A white paste larded it, while a triangular "shadow" had been made beneath each eye.

"May I speak to you privately, sir?"

Astounded, yet with a mechanical and not unpleasant smile, the man nodded and rose—and led the way to the corridor to the necessary. It was a narrow place, where they were unseen.

"Captain Long, schooner *Goodwill to Men,* Rhode Island colony."

"I am honored, sir, I guess."

"Sir Jervis, you once knew the Honorable Maisie Treadway?"

For a moment the man looked almost human.

"Extremely well, sir. You have a message from her?"

"Yes. She asked me to give you this—"

And he punched Jervis Johnston on the nose.

46   It was not properly a punch, and the truth is that Adam had designed to make it no more than nominal—though unmistakable. Perhaps he was over-tense? Certainly he had not sought what street crowds called claret; but as certainly he got it.

Johnston, holding his head high, and blubbering something that sounded like "barbarous," turned and ran—not in the direction of the common room but in that of the necessary.

Adam wavered half a moment, then went back to the common room. He sat down. He knew that he was trembling but didn't think it showed. He might have circled the room with his gaze then and never caught an eye. Nobody changed the pitch of his voice or slowed his speech, not any more than he would point with an ill-bred finger. Yet they were all talking about Adam. Knowing this, he glowered. He recalled to mind the great burst of popularity he had enjoyed, endured rather, after having disposed of Major Kellsen, as well as the changed attitude toward him after he had bladed it out with the custos at Newport. And now—Clark's. The pirates of Providence, the burghers of Rhode Island, here these pomaded popinjays, all were the same. They wanted to see a fight, from a safe distance.

John Chumley, back, fumed.

"I get you accepted, I get them used to the sight of you, and you have to spoil it by clouting the man!"

"I didn't clout him," hotly. "I clouted him he'd've gone down."

"I tried to explain to Jerve that it's an American custom—"

"More or less is."

"—but now I'm afraid we've lost our chance for an understanding."

"I don't want an understanding, I want a fight. I'm tired of all this prissy-go-pink-toe business. If he won't fight me polite, then I'll just draw and pitch into him. If he—"

"Sh-sh! Here he comes back."

They saw no change in the bedaubed visage when Clark's most talked-of customer passed them on his way from the necessary. He bowed to Chumley as though seeing him for the first time, and his mask was unmarred, no blood. He was lackadaisically picking his teeth.

"He *may* pass it off," Chumley whispered. "More likely he'll challenge me, for having brought you here. And I'll apologize."

"Why shouldn't he challenge *me?*"

"How can he? He hasn't been introduced to you."

"I bloodied his nose. Ain't that introduction enough?"

"Not in Clark's," coldly.

Everybody knew what had happened, though Adam was danged if he could see how: there had been no witness. The buzz of talk never rose above a level befitting the gentility; but it was significant that nobody left.

After perhaps half an hour Sir Jervis Johnston did ask for plume and paper. Everybody pretended not to notice.

Similarly never a head was turned when the waiter bore the missive to the table where Chumley and Adam sat. The waiter handed it to Adam.

Though this was against tradition, Adam couldn't help tossing a grin of triumph at John Chumley, who languidly sipped wine.

Adam unfolded the paper. The hand was round, firm, good.

Esteemed Captain, sir:
The person whose name you mentioned would sure not relish the thought that two of her friends were bickering like fishwives. Doubtless you have an explanation that in my unmannerly haste I didn't hear. If this be true, pray correct me.
I remain, sir,
Yr Worship's most humble and most obedient servant,

J. Johnston, Bart.

"Now I call that handsome," Adam cried.

"He's had a plenty of practice."

"Get me some of that paper. I'll write him an answer."

"You'll do nothing of the sort. You put the matter into my hands now. You ignore this message."

"But *that* would be unmannerly!"

"At this stage of the proceedings you're supposed to be. Don't touch the note any more. Don't even glance at it. When I go to Jerve's table I'll pass the fire and drop the note in. That in itself will announce my intention of insisting upon a duel. It's customary," Chumley added, "to destroy all correspondence before a *rencontre,* lest the crown seize the survivor on a charge of murder."

Adam sighed.

"Well, why don't you go then?"

"Not yet, man! We must chat a bit. I'll go over in half an hour or so, as if I'd just remembered it. My dear, my dear, will you never learn that in polite society one never does anything in a hurry?"

"In polite society one never does anything at all," Adam muttered.

That was it—you waited and waited. You sat doing nothing, seeing nothing, getting nowhere, hour after weary hour. It fair gave Adam the creeps. When he visited the ships' chandlers or shopped for nails or needles, when he sat in Edward Lloyd's place listening to nearby conversations, or simply walked the streets of this celebrated sewer, he was learning something, or at the very least exposing himself to the chance of learning something. When he sat before the fire at the Hearth Cricket, telling little Lil a story, or dipping his nose into a jack of ale, he was enjoying himself. But at Clark's all he did was wait.

Even after John Chumley had sauntered over to Johnston's table, dropping the note into the fire as he went, there was nothing to indicate that those two men would reach an early decision. Stealing a look at them now and then, as everybody else in the coffee house was doing, Adam saw that they appeared to be chatting indolently about matters that bored. Yet they bowed politely enough, if somewhat offhandedly, when Chumley at last rose to go.

Back opposite Adam, Chumley ordered a pipe.

"What'd you agree, man? Tell me!"

"Tut, tut. Don't lean forward like that. You're being watched."

"But what'd you decide?"

"He'll meet you. He deems it condescending, but he's in a good mood. The cockpit back of Birdcage Walk, in the morning."

"What time?"

"Dawn. That's the hour that's fashionable for duels. The only thing it *is* fashionable for, damn me, in this town!"

Adam rose. It was late afternoon. Chumley objected in a low voice, but Adam had listened to Chumley too long. He wasn't going to sit around any more. And Chumley at last shrugged, and accompanied Adam, walking slowly, hand on hip, to the door. They bowed as they passed Jervis Johnston's table, and he bowed in return.

John Chumley leaned in the window of Adam's chair.

"I'll call for you, of course. Before it's light. I'll have two chairs. We'll need link boys, too. And whatever you do, *please,* my chick, my sweet, don't get coarse on the field."

"What's that got to do with it?"

"Do that, and Jerve might refuse to accept your apology. Then you'd have to fight him." Chumley shuddered. "And he'd *carve* you."

Adam said nothing.

"And get a good sleep," Chumley urged.

"I will, my chick, my sweet," Adam snarled.

"It's thought bad taste to have a drawn countenance when you go to the field of honor."

"Mine won't be drawn," Adam promised.

He was not so sure of that when, ten minutes later, he re-entered the Hearth Cricket—to find Goodwife Bingham on her knees sobbing, while her husband the host stood stunned.

"My Lillian! My one child! Lil, Lil, come back to me!"

Hal Bingham, no color in his face, looked at Adam.

"The kidnappers got her," he whispered.

47 It was well that Adam was not a blasphemous man, else now surely he would have taken the name of the Lord in vain.

"Then what in thunderation are you doing on your *knees?*"

The blow must have fallen only a moment earlier. The air tingled. There was another person in the ordinary—a lank, knotty-throated youth named Lamson, brother of that same Anne Lamson who had been stolen off the streets a week ago. Adam pointed a finger that might have been a poniard.

"You! Did you see her napped?"

The young man gulped, nodding.

"Two men was walking with 'er. Over in Loo Lane. Just now. She saw me and she started to call out somefing, but they 'ustled 'er along. They was 'olding 'er 'ands each side."

"Why didn't you go up to her?"

"I made out to, but one of the men chised me awie."

"What with? A regiment of lancers?"

"No, sir. But 'e doubled up 'is fist as if 'e'd 'it me, so I 'urried back 'ere. I was afride 'e'd 'it me."

"You mean—'it you like this?" asked Adam, and hit him.

"Ow-w! Please, Captain—"

"Or like this?" asked Adam, and hit him again.

Adam turned back to Hal Bingham.

"We'll go to that place and start asking questions. There's still a smitch of daylight left. You got a weapon?"

"Got a cudgel back of the bar."

"Fetch it out."

He turned back to the cringing Lamson, on the floor.

"You'll take us to the spot," he said.

"Not me! You couldn't get me to— *Please, Captain!*"

Adam had drawn, and he lashed the lad's legs, right, left, rhythmically, almost as though he were swinging a scythe. He was careful to strike with the flat, but he struck hard.

"Look at me, Lamson," caressively, as though calling a kitten.

Lamson opened his eyes. The point of the sword was two inches from his nose.

"You are taking us there, Lamson."

"Y-Yes, sir."

Adam glanced at Hal, armed with the club now. "Come along." He flung open the street door—and Lillian Bingham fell into his arms.

Much must be allowed a mother in moments of stress. Hal Bingham wept, and freely. It was the first time Adam had ever seen a Londoner weep. Adam himself was not sure of his eyes for a while. Nevertheless it was Adam who broke up the scene. Kneeling before Lillian: "Let's have the story once more, before we go out."

"*Out?*" cried Goodwife Bingham. "There's nobody in this family ever goes out after dark again!"

"Let's have the story once more," Adam said gently.

It was a simple story. Lillian was fully recovered now, had her breath back. She looked straight at Adam while she talked.

She had been playing at the intersection of Loo Lane, the upstreet limit she was allowed, and it was not quite dark. She'd been about to start home. She insisted that she had not gone further than she should have gone or stayed out later.

"All right, all right!"

She did not know from which direction the two men had come. They were just suddenly there. Did they call her by her name? No. They'd only called her "little girl" and things like that.

"You know—silly things."

"Go on," said Adam.

She had not at first felt frightened when each of these men took her by the hand and started to walk her, for indeed it had been in this direction, toward the inn, which seemed natural to her. Hadn't she just been about to start this way herself? She had not recognized either man but she'd not remarked anything unusual about them. Their dress was neither a peacock's nor notably mean. She remembered that they had walked faster than she liked to walk; but grown-ups usually did that. She had assumed that they were occasional customers at the Hearth Cricket. She met many such. She was vaguely obligated to smile upon any man in this neighborhood who acted as though he knew her. She always had been.

But these men, after a short distance, had turned, turning her with them, and soon were moving *away* from the inn. It could be they hoped that in the gathering darkness the girl would not notice this. They stood closer to her now, and walked a bit faster, and when she pointed out that they were going the wrong way they hadn't answered with words, only tugged her along.

"They didn't hold my hands very tight. It didn't hurt. But I couldn't let go."

Yes, she had seen and recognized the Lamson lad, and she'd called out to him, she didn't know what. One of the men had snarled at him, and he'd scampered away.

It might have been at about this time that she started to cry. But she hadn't cried much, she assured them now.

The men had hurried her along. They kept telling her that they were taking her home, that they'd only gone for a little walk and were near the Hearth Cricket now. Yes, they'd named the inn.

She hadn't really believed them, but neither had she fought hard to get away. She'd only held back as much as she was able, dragging, purposely stumbling and falling to her knees. The men had not been rough when they pulled her to her feet, but they'd been quick about it—they weren't wasting any time.

"Weren't there people around? Why didn't you scream for help?"

This had not even occurred to Lillian, she freely confessed. Then, too, she had been out of breath: the men made her move fast.

Not until they came to the house had she really balked. Walking the open streets, even while the light failed, was one thing; entering a strange house was quite another. Lil had torn herself free and turned and ran. Perhaps because she had been so "good," her revolt took them off guard. She didn't know whether either or both followed her. She'd never looked back. She had run up one street and down another until at last she recognized some shops. She had never stopped running until she fell into Adam's arms.

"Now about the house, my beauteous. This is important. What was that house like?"

Well, it was three stories, she thought. It was plaster-and-lath, not stone. It stood flush with the street, a cobbled one of average width. The door, which was wide, was dark brown in color, or it might even have been black. There was no knocker. She didn't think that there was a fanlight. Two or three stone steps led up to the door, she thought.

Now this description might have fitted any one of hundreds of houses within a mile of the Hearth Cricket.

Hunkered down before the girl, Adam remembered the sugar bun and brought it forth. Lillian grinned shyly.

"What do you say?" prompted her mother.

"Thank you, sir," said Lil.

"Now about this house," serious, confidential. "If we was to take you to where these men first came up to you, your father and I, and if we was to walk next to you, one on each side, the way *they* did, do you think you could walk us right to that house?"

"I— I might."

"It might come back to you, don't you think?"

"Maybe."

"That can wait till morning," said Goodwife Bingham. "Lillian, back to the kitchen. We're going to have a wash."

"No, no," Adam cried. "Tomorrow morning may be too late. We must get this while the memory's fresh. I think Lil could walk right there— now. She'd never be able to do that tomorrow."

"Now see here, Captain Long. We're monstrous grateful for all you've done, but Lil don't go out in the dark any more—not even if she was to be escorted by a company of the Queen's horse!"

"I'll go, sure," said Lillian.

Adam rose.

"Ma'am," softly, "it's not a time to hide under the bed. We've got a chance to break up this gang, if we act fast. We won't be long. And once we've found the place we'll bring Lil right back."

"She don't go out," said Mrs. Bingham.

Lillian, munching her sugar bun, looked from one to the other.

"Ma'am, if nobody ever does anything about this, if they don't ever do more than that cowhearted Lamson, you'll have it all over again. We're near 'em—let's get 'em! Your own husband told me this morning, right here in this room, that if that gang ain't cleared out soon they'll be snatching the babes right out of bed!"

"He's right, Mary," Hal Bingham said. "We got to go now."

"She don't leave this house!"

"It ain't just Lillian, ma'am, though it's her we're thinking of first. But there's others. There's other mothers, too. We may not get these villains, ma'am, but we're bound by our faith in the Lord to try."

"He's right, Mary," Hal said.

The woman gave in suddenly. She sank to a stool, and for the first time she wept. Elbows on knees, head in hands, she rocked a bit, while the tears streamed down her face. She began to moan.

Hal Bingham put a hand on his daughter's shoulder and he leaned close to Adam.

198

"Come on," he whispered. "Before she changes her mind."

The last to leave, Adam Long looked back from the doorway. Good-wife Bingham still sat on that stool, her shadow enormous on the wall beyond. *She* only rocked or swayed a little, but the shadow swung half-way across the room and back. Her moans were low.

There were few to see the curious walk these two men took with the child, no one really to watch it. Respectable London had shuttered itself in. The streets were deserted. There was no fog, and it was warm for that time of year. The air was oddly light and unsure of itself. It would stiffen erratically, waxing ominous, slamming a loose shutter, kicking up a whirlpool of dust and tiny sticks; then immediately afterward it would die, leaving silence.

They stayed close to Lillian, who was clear-eyed and cool. Lillian mostly looked down as she walked. She had probably looked down while walking with the strangers. She did not hesitate. The thing was so fresh in her mind that she could follow her instinct, not talking, letting her body take her. She did not go fast, but neither did she waver.

They had walked perhaps half a mile, and had made a dozen turns, some right, others left, when in the middle of a small somnolent street Lillian pointed.

"That's it."

She appeared not to have the slightest doubt, and the house fitted her description.

There was nobody in sight up or down the street. No light showed.

"What d'ye think we ought to do?" Hal Bingham breathed.

"Knock up the nearest magistrate. Who is he?"

"Man named Nixon. A right 'un, they tell me. But he might not be willing to smash in the door just on a little girl's say-so."

"If he won't do it," said Adam, "I'll go down to the schooner and order my whole crew up here, and *we'll* do it."

He examined the door closely, to see if he could make out any sort of name or number. There was none. He stepped back.

"You're positively sure now, Lil, my beauteous?"

"I am pos-i-tive-ly sure," Lillian said with great aplomb. "They got me all the way up on this stone before I broke away. I was standing here—"

She had passed in front of Adam and stood between him and the door.

Then this happened: The door was opened a few inches, and a hand came out. The hand grabbed Lillian by her dress. The door was opened a little wider, and Lillian was yanked in—out of sight. The door was slammed shut. There was the sound of a bolt being thrown.

Lillian had not made a squeak, hadn't had a chance to. The thing had happened in the blink of an eye.

Adam threw himself against the door. He couldn't so much as quiver it. There was a latch, which he rattled frantically. There was no keyhole, no opening of any sort.

"Go down to the schooner and get the men! All of them!"

"The magistrate—"

"Blast the magistrate! Take too long to make out warrants! Tell Forbes to bring a spar!"

Hal Bingham ran away.

This street was paved, if somewhat sketchily. Adam had kicked a loose stone a moment before. He found it, prised it fully free. Holding it high in both hands, he started for the door again.

He stopped, dumbfounded. He lowered the paving stone.

The door stood open. Nothing but darkness showed beyond.

"Won't you come in?" said a voice from that darkness.

Adam looked up the street, down the street. He was alone. Yet minutes might count. If he ran he could be chased, hacked to pieces.

He dropped the stone. He drew.

"Now d'ye know, I think I will," he said.

48 He walked with his sword held before him at arm's length. The street was dark, but the darkness massed inside the doorway was deeper and seemed *solid*, like a wall, or a pile of some black material—sand, loam.

The instant after the point of his sword had passed the threshold Adam jerked it back. Yet he himself sprang forward, crouching.

Something hit the floor with a thudding shock, just inside the threshold, about where his hand would have been had he followed the sword as he'd started to. The miss, he calculated, came from the right. So he skittered around that way, plunging into the dark as though into water, and stabbed blindly—once, twice. His steel met something soft. There was a high thin, piglike sound.

Adam whirled around, still crouching. Something slished past his left shoulder and touched his left elbow with as dainty a sting as a bee might have made. He cut, but hit nothing. There was a gasp—and the door was slammed.

Previously there had been at least a drizzle of light from the street. Now there was no light whatever.

Adam didn't move his feet, and he resisted an urge to reach out with both hands. He did not know this hall; but the man who had closed the door, the man with the club, did. Adam swished the air—right, left, high, low—with his sword. He had a long reach.

A door was opened upstairs. There were steps up there. On Adam's right, high, a feeble light appeared.

"Henry! You get him?"

From a few feet in front of Adam: "No! 'E got John instead!"

"*Look out, Henry!*"

Adam had lunged instantly at the sound of the second voice, the one near him. As someone upstairs walked a hall holding a candle, the shadows of rail palings flicked erratically across the wall, one by one; but none of the light, yet, reached the entrance hall.

Adam's point met something, he couldn't tell what. He tried to retrieve the blade. It was stuck.

There was a screech of either pain or fright, probably fright.

Adam got the blade loose.

There was a scrabbly sound on his right, like that of a very large rat. Adam advanced in that direction.

He stumbled, but did not lose his balance. The man upstairs rounded the head of the staircase, the newel post there, and was holding his candle high. For the first time Adam could see something.

It was a lower step he had stumbled over. Immediately around him there was nothing. The door was shut, and there were no windows. There was no furniture or arras behind which a person might hide. Adam shared this space with a single man, or perhaps it was no longer a man, merely a corpse. John, the one who had tried to sandbag him, sat in a corner, hunched forward, his head averted, his hands, palms up, limp on either side. There was a great deal of blood.

The stair before Adam was steep but it was wide, and the railing on his right—there was a wall on the left—was low.

Halfway up this stair, sidling like a scared crab, was a smallish man, presumably Henry.

At the head of this stair stood the man with the candle. He was a very large man, even allowing for the tricks of light and for his altitude, allowing that is, for the fact that Adam looked up at him. He held the candle in his left hand. In his right was a rapier.

"You beefwit! Here—hold this!"

Henry had reached the comparative safety of the upper hall. He squirmed around behind the big man. He took the candle.

"Hold it," said the big man, "while I carve the whoreson."

There were three things Adam might do now, and he reviewed them in as little time as it takes a flea to jump from here to over there.

He could run. But he could be overtaken, even supposing that he got outside. Nobody would interfere with a brabble in a London street after dark, unless the watch happened along, one chance in fifty. And the big man would doubtless be reinforced.

He could wait for the big man to start down the stairs, as in fact the man was about to do, and meet him halfway. Here he'd be at a disadvantage.

Or he could rush to the top of the stairs and meet the man there. This was what he decided to do.

Four at a time he went up.

He had reached the third step down before his steel met the other's. Adam cut in low, raising his blade as he straightened it into line. This forced the other point high. Not giving the man a chance to disengage, Adam went up another step. Both blades were out of line now, the points high. The hilts clacked together.

The men were so close that if either had had a dagger he could have finished the fight with his left hand. Neither did.

Recovered from his surprise, the big man pushed hard, trying to force Adam down the steps. But Adam made the top. He slithered his buttocks around the newel post and sprang backward, disengaging.

The big man attacked. He was fairly fast and had a long reach, but he was wild. He fought contemptuously—not as one who puts no value on his own life but rather as one who puts none on the skill of his adversary. That is, he fought like this at first.

Adam's riposte caught him high on the right arm, near the shoulder. It couldn't have hurt much, but the big man stepped back. He was panting.

"Get that candle over here! How can I see to slice the bastard!"

This upstairs hall was wide and the ceiling was high. When Henry got closer, timorously placing himself about midway between the men as far off on Adam's left as he could get for the railing, Adam for a wild moment thought of snuffing the candle. But he would not be lunging here under the watchful gaze of the man who called himself Carse. This candle was not held in a golden stick stolen out of a galleon, but in the hand of a highly nervous man who might and probably would move it or even drop it if he saw Adam switch his attack. Besides, what if Adam did put it out? What then? Even if in the dark he slipped past the big man and got downstairs and out, how would that help Lillian Bingham?

Adam thought of Lil's mother, the shadow that swung across the wall of the Hearth Cricket ordinary while the woman wailed. He attacked.

He did not go in full-length. He had plenty of time—and indeed the longer he could make this last the better—and he wanted to feel the big man out.

The big man's defense was weak. It could be that he wasn't accustomed

202

to parry, having always been the aggressor. When flustered, he really only had one counter. It would be easy to double-counter.

Adam nodded, and stepped back. Deliberately he put his blade under his left arm, undid all the buttons of his waistcoat, hiked up his breeches, took the sword again, and fell back into guard position.

He attacked.

He made the double-counter neatly enough and hit the big man again on the upper right arm near the shoulder, a much deeper wound this time. But the big man did not give ground. Instead, his blade straight-out, his arm stiff, he attacked.

Here was Adam's meat and gravy. Carse on Providence had spent many an hour teaching him various ways of disarming a man who attacked in this fashion—because, Carse had said, so many of 'em do, especially when they get excited.

Adam smiled. He might have been making the moves in time with directions called out by a master. In low; point high; catch the steel far down on your own; cut out and high until your point's in line again; flip it up.

Obedient as any goshawk to a whistle, the sword leapt from the big man's hand. It turned twice in the air, and fell on the floor at Adam's feet. Adam stepped on it.

The big man was no fool. He hesitated not an instant, but turned and ran.

Henry dropped the candle and ran after him.

There was a door at the end of the hall, a door Adam had not previously noticed. The two kidnappers went through this, fast.

Adam got his foot in the doorway and pushed.

He might have forced it open, but the candle, on the floor, was guttering out. He ran to the candle, and the door was shoved shut and he heard a bolt thrown. He got to the candle barely in time.

He was about to pick the sword from the floor—not that he wanted it for himself but he didn't care to leave weapons behind him while he explored this house—when a sound from above caused him to straighten, his head lifted.

It could have been the crying of a child, perhaps a small girl.

Sword in hand, holding the candle high, he went upstairs.

He found nothing in the hall above but four doors, each locked. He heard the sound again—from a place still higher.

He went up to the next floor, the top one.

Here the crying was clearly audible, and it *was* that of a girl. It came from behind a heavy door that was bolted on the hall side.

"*Is that you, Lillian?*"

The sobbing ceased.

He pushed back the bolt. This could be a trap. He footed the door open, then stepped back, the candle held high.

What met his gaze was surely one of the strangest sights any man ever beheld.

49 This was a large room: it must have taken up the entire top story. Along three sides crumpled figures lay, figures that might have been piles of poked dust except for the faces.

You have looked into a bird's nest soon after a hatching to see that the little ones are all mouth, their eggshell heads, the scrawniness of their bodies being mere appendages to the overwhelmingly urgent part presented—their bills? So it was here with the eyes. Adam scarcely saw the pale cheeks, the trembling lips, the hands each like a rickle of sticks, much less at first the leathern thongs, the staples, the pails, all the accumulated filth. He only saw the eyes—eyes that screamed in fear.

There was a dry rustling. The faces retreated from Adam for as far as they were able, and beat and bobbed against the wall, giant soft moths that, unlike ordinary moths, battered themselves in an effort to get *away* from the light.

There was a gibbering such as might have been made by monkeys. No words were distinguishable. This could hardly have been human speech: it was frantic, whittled thin with fear; and it ceased abruptly when Adam, his heart pounding, stepped into the room.

Something was thrown around his knees, locking them together. Something batted his thigh.

"Captain Long, it's me! It's Lillian!"

He knelt by her, and put his arms around her, babbling words of reassurance.

Lil had been through hours of hysteria, possibly twelve minutes of true time by a clock. Thrust here by one who from her description must have been the man Adam had just disarmed, the big man, she'd had no more than the briefest conceivable glimpse of the room and its occupants. Then the door had been slammed and locked, leaving her in a darkness crowded with sibilant whispers, with soft squeals and scuffling. She had cringed beside the door, as far from those chittery sounds as she could get. An adult might well have gone mad then.

"I—I'm glad you're here."

"I'm glad I am, too, my beauteous."

"Where's Father and Mother?"

"Your father's gone for help. Your mother's baking a special pie for the party we're going to have when you get back."

He rose, and together they surveyed the prisoners. For these cocoons of squirming rag and skin were no nightmare: they were children. They were not many, or not as many as had at first seemed. Lillian had supposed that there were scores, perhaps hundreds; and even Adam had estimated them at thirty or more. By actual count, now, there were eleven. The oldest might have been fourteen, the youngest about Lil's age, six; though it was difficult to make estimates here, so shriveled were they, so sunken their cheeks, while their eyes watered and blinked, red in the unaccustomed light.

They pressed against the wall, against the floor, whimpering, curs that had been kicked and expected to be kicked again.

Lillian moved, if with timid step, toward them. She held out a hand. "Don't be afraid," she pleaded, though her voice did quaver. "This is Captain Long. He's from America."

She couldn't have said anything worse. Oh, the cackling that came! Some of the children hid their faces, seeming to strive to dig a hole in the floor. Some, kneeling, wringing their hands, pleaded piteously not to be taken to the plantations.

Adam had placed the candle on the floor, and from its light their shadows swooped, bobbing, twisting, suddenly collapsing, to rise again, a grotesquerie of thin heads, bone-thin arms, shoulders that could have been porcupine quills. Those shadows suggested witches making queer invocative contortions.

"No, no," Adam called. "I'm not going to take you to America. I'm going to take you back to your mothers and fathers."

They did not believe him. They whimpered.

"Let's cut 'em loose first," Adam whispered to Lil, who nodded.

Now these children, weak though they were, feeble from their confinement, all were fettered. At regular intervals along the baseboard of three sides of the room—the door by which Adam had entered bisected the fourth wall—iron staples had been fixed. Each child had a small iron ring on his or her left ankle. Not chains, as in a dungeon, but tough round leathern thongs connected the irons with the staples. Each thong went through one staple and each end of it was fastened to a leg iron, so that when one child moved away from the wall the child at the other end of that thong was pulled closer to the wall. This allowed them a certain amount of liberty if they worked together. Either, for instance, could reach one of the wooden buckets or even the large wooden tub in the center of the room, provided that the other permitted it. But in no circumstances could any of them have reached the door.

The room was bare, and it looked uncommonly solid. The two windows, which were high, were strongly boarded. Even a man with a crowbar, and with something to stand on, would have required hours to open them. There was a second, much smaller door in the middle of the wall facing Adam—leading out, it would appear, into space, for here must have been the very back of the house—but this was bolted with a bar held in place by a huge padlock. There was no furniture, except the tub and the buckets. It was dry in the room, but cold.

When Adam started for the nearest child, a girl, she screamed and beat the floor. She must have supposed not that she was about to be killed but that she was about to be beaten. She'd been beaten before, and recently. Not daring to look up, with one hand she stripped off her sleazy dress—she wore no underclothes—and pointed to her back. It looked like raw veal. The welts crisscrossed, some coiling up over the spindly shoulders, others reaching as low as the bum.

"I won't hurt you— Tell her that, Lil," as though the Bingham child were an interpreter. "I just want to set you loose."

Done up in his flame-colored coat like this, he did not carry a sheath knife. He had only his sword, an awkward tool for a task like this, since the edge went scarcely one-third of the way down from the point, making it hard for Adam to get leverage without cutting his own hand. He sawed at the thong; while the girl, her eyes squinched shut, bent over, quivering, waiting for the first blow.

"*Look out!*"

Henry had crept into the room. He carried a long, lean, very bright knife. He didn't give fight when Adam turned. He simply ran. But he had the door closed and bolted before Adam could reach it.

"Now that was a fool's thing to do, to forget that—"

Louder, forcing a smile, he said: "So you see, now I'm locked in with you. But it's all right. We're all going to get out."

"My father's going to come and save us," said Lil Bingham. "Captain, here's Anne Lamson!"

"Good," said Adam. "Now let's cut these cords."

The thongs had been clawed and gnawed, and run back and forth through the staples, in an effort to sever them. It was for this, Adam was told—for they were beginning to talk now, beginning to look up, blinking, and especially since Anne Lamson had introduced Lillian—it was for these attempts to free themselves that they were most often whipped. Sometimes the men didn't even come into the room, the children told Adam. Sometimes they just stood on the threshold and pitched food in, or shoved in a water jug.

Didn't they ever empty those buckets or the tub? The children shook their heads. None of them had ever known this to happen.

Hacking the bonds away took a long time, and Adam fretted inwardly while he toiled, though he tried to keep a cheerful face, talking, encouraging the children to talk, promising them again and again that he wasn't going to drag them off to America.

What had happened to Hal Bingham? So many things *could* happen to a man alone in a London street near the river at night.

Nobody but Hal knew where this house was.

Now and then Adam would shush the children and stop his sword-sawing and hold up his head and listen. But there was no sound. The children told him that they never heard sounds from the street and seldom from the house itself. More than once, they said, they had tried screaming and yelling in chorus. There never had been any sort of answer. The kidnappers had not objected to these tactics, which argued that the kidnappers were sure of themselves here.

So Adam worked, sweat rolling down his body, a lump of fear in his breast, but trying to keep up light talk.

Even after the children had regained confidence it was impossible to learn how long they had been here. They had no way of telling day from night, and apparently their feeding was not regular. Most of the newcomers were so badly scared, or sometimes so bruised and beaten, that they weren't sure what time it was, or even what day.

Two, Freddy and Phoebe, brother and sister, had an undisputed claim to seniority. They figured that they had been in this room for at least a month. They had been the only children here when Bully Bill was brought in, the one who caused all the trouble. Bully Bill, a small fellow, but fierce, had charged the kidnappers every time the door was opened. It didn't make any difference how many times he was bashed, he always fought back. And when the leathern thongs and the staples were introduced, Bully Bill again and again tried to cut himself loose, though he knew what the men would do to him. Two other children had been in the room when Bully Bill was given his last beating, and they remembered it as clearly as Phoebe and Freddy did. The men had taken turns, hitting and hitting Bully Bill long after he ceased to move or to make any sound —for at least an hour afterward.

"Two hours," said Phoebe.

Adam, who had just cut the last thong, thought that he heard a noise downstairs. He went to the door. No. He had thought he heard a steady thud, a pounding sound: but he couldn't hear it now.

"What did they do with Bully Bill?" he asked quietly. "But don't tell me if you don't want to."

They wanted to all right. Bully Bill, they told him, had lain there for a long time—several days, they reckoned it—never moving or making a sound; and he had long before ceased to bleed.

"We used to call out to him and ask him to speak to us, but we couldn't get to him. He was on the other side of the room."

After a long while, after several more feedings anyway, the men had come into the room again instead of pitching the food in, and they'd examined Bully Bill. They had said some mighty dirty words, and looked scared, and they'd carried Bully Bill away.

"One of his eyes was hanging out," Freddy reported. "It'd been dug out by one of the sticks they hit him with, and it was hanging down from his head, swinging back and forth like a marble on the end of a piece of string."

"You— You reckon he was dead?" asked Phoebe.

Adam had gone again to the hall door. Truly he heard that thudding now. The sound seemed far away, and it was rhythmic, heavy.

"This the door where they carried him out?" he asked.

"No, no! It was that one over there. Where the padlock is. It goes out on a roof and they can get to a different house on another street. You're *sure* you ain't taking us to America, mister?"

"I'm sure of it," said Adam.

It occurred to him that unless the kidnappers had already decamped, abandoning their treasure of small slaves, they would try to escape by means of this route over a roof.

For by now the thumping was unmistakable. Somebody was smashing in the front door. Adam heard a familiar voice:

"*Ho* again, *ho* again! All right, lads, let's have a chantey!"

> I spit on you,
> You spit on me—

By this time Adam himself had joined in:

> Ain't no politeness
> On Scaredy-Cat Sea!

Adam smiled. He took off his coat and vest. He cleared away the buckets and the tub. He placed the children along the wall on either side of the hall door. He rolled up his sleeves.

"I think we're going to have visitors," he explained.

"You going to kill them, Captain Long?"

"Well, I'm sure going to do my best to."

The door flew open. The big man came in roaring, wild as before. He'd picked up his rapier. He charged.

"Good," said Adam.

Never had the Hearth Cricket been so crowded. It was after closing hour, too, indeed near dawn. But as Hal pointed out, the bailiffs, who were everywhere, in and out, wouldn't break up a private party.

Adam Long felt mighty ashamed of himself, standing there naked to the waist while Goodwife Bingham washed his cuts.

"Good thing I took that coat off," he grumbled. "When I think of what I paid for it—"

"They was anchored out in the river, that's what took me so long," Hal Bingham said for the fourth or fifth time.

Resolved Forbes was staring at his skipper.

"You told me you might kill a man, sir. *A* man? You didn't say you were going to tackle a whole gang!"

Adam started, looking for his shirt.

"Tarnation, I forgot all about that! Must be near sunup. Ought to be a chair here for me soon. I got to get shaved."

"*Shaved?* What in Tophet are you going to do at this hour?"

"Fight," said Adam.

50 A sliver of moon hung over the field. It was cold; and even before he was obliged to take off his hat Adam regretted that he'd let them crop his hair. He could see his breath. He would have hopped about, stamping, had not John Chumley forbidden this.

" 'Twould look as if you was nervous."

"I am."

Sir Jervis Johnston and his party arrived in Birdcage Walk a scant two minutes after Adam and his second. Some men, Chumley whispered, believed that it was bad luck to be first in the field; yet it would be bad manners to keep your enemy waiting.

If Adam must stay still, Chumley was a jumpingjack. Whether because they smelled trouble or because they had overheard informative talk on the way, every one of the chairmen and linkboys lingered; and they chattered like magpies—until the busy John Chumley shushed them.

"Now remember—gravity, gravity!" he'd tell Adam.

"I'll do the best I can."

Even on the way, Chumley, having hopped out of his own chair, electing to walk beside Adam's, had fretted and fussed like a mother at her daughter's first ball, a spate of instructions and advice. He made it clear, for the first time, that Adam had been accorded the honor of blading it out with Johnston chiefly because Johnston had difficulty finding opponents.

"Y'see, he's got this reputation to keep up. All he does is seduce

209

women and skewer men. But he's running out of men who'll meet him in the field."

"I take it he's not running out of women who'll meet him in bed?"

"You never run out of them here."

A bee, Chumley buzzed about, conferring with this man and that, peering into the surgeon's bag, pacing the ground, studying the sky, measuring the swords, hefting the long heavy saber the referee would wield as well as the thick leather sleeve the referee would wear, in general assuring himself that everything was correct. Adam was left alone. He had been informed, and most earnestly, that it would be strictly *de trop* for him even to glance at his adversay until the time came to fight. Nevertheless, as was natural, he did sneak a look; and despite himself, despite his memory of Maisie, he nodded approval. Sir Jervis Johnston here in the watery light of dawn cut a far better figure than he had in the coffee house. He stood straighter; and though still affecting the languid wave of the hand, the deprecating lazy shrug, he was alive and alert. He smiled and chatted with his friends, as though sharing a bottle with them, and scrupulously refrained from taking any part in the preliminary arrangements or even showing any interest in these.

Adam sighed. He forced himself to look away.

London was still. Not even a beggar prowled, not even a whore. The only light that showed was at a window of the Brown Tun a short distance away. The Brown Tun, being obedient to the municipal regulations, was officially closed; but arrangements had been made to keep its back door unlocked for the benefit of the spectators' thirst, perhaps that of the principals, too, or one of them, after the affair of honor was ended.

Chumley minced back. He looked as though he was having a hard time to keep from clapping his hands in excitement.

"Now remember—be grave!"

"When do we start?"

"Everything is in order. At this stage it's customary for each second to make a last-minute plea with his principal, to see if he can't talk him out of it. That's what I'm supposed to be doing to you now. But nobody ever takes it seriously."

"I see."

"Now in a minute Dr. Russell'll address *both* of you, formally asking you if you can't settle your differences in some other manner than combat with arms—that's the usual phrase, or something like that. Nobody pays any attention to this either, ordinarily. It's just ceremony. But this morning when he makes that announcement I'm going to step forward and say 'Gentlemen, my principal has something to say.' Then you speak up. You express your willingness to apologize. It'll be expected, this morning. I hope you've got it prepared? I, uh, I wouldn't want it to be anything uncouth."

"It'll be in perfect English," Adam promised him.

"Then the Brown Tun. They've ordered some of this new wine from Champagne. It's charged with bubbles of air. A new process some monk invented. Frightfully expensive stuff."

He helped Adam off with his coat and waistcoat, and folded these, together with Adam's hat and his neck band, in a neat pile. He shook his head at the cuts in Adam's shirt.

"La, you look as if you'd been fighting already."

"I have. But this is the only shirt I've got. I mean, that's lawn."

"Well, it'll have to do— Ah, here we are!"

The surgeon, a lumpy man, took the center of the field. As though addressing a vast throng he made a speech calling for reconciliation. It was full of pompous inanities but at least it was short. At its end he looked at the man who stood next to Sir Jervis Johnston—all the others had withdrawn—and that man shook his head. Then the surgeon looked at John Chumley, who stepped forward, clearing his throat.

"Gentlemen, my principal has something to say."

Adam, too, stepped forward. He and Jervis Johnston for the first time this morning looked directly at one another. Sir Jervis was appropriately serious, a model of decorum.

"All I've got to say," said Adam, "is, 'Let's get on with the fight.' We've wasted too much time already."

Chumley was white with what Adam assumed was rage, and he trembled when he brought the sword.

"You broke your promise, sir!"

"I made no promise."

"I'll repudiate you! I'll walk away!"

"You don't dare, now. You'd look too silly."

"But— But, damn me, Captain, I never thought it'd come to this! Truth is, I— I can't stand the sight of blood!"

"Then you'd better not look," said Adam.

He took the sword and swished it. It was lighter and somewhat less whippy, somewhat stiffer, than his own; but it was a good blade, exquisitely balanced. He nodded.

"All right."

Chumley wetted his lips, straightened his shoulders.

"My principal," he announced in a fairly steady voice, "is ready."

Then he quit the field, and Johnston's second likewise quit the field. This left, besides Adam and Johnston, only the referee, a tall man Adam did not know, who carried the long heavy cavalry saber and wore the leather arm guard. Adam paid not the slightest attention to the person of the referee, though he did hear his voice as he called out the few and simple rules for this meeting. Adam was gazing at Sir Jervis Johnston, who, dignified if stern, was gazing at him.

They stood about twenty feet apart.

The baronet was stripped of his finery. Like Adam, he was bareheaded. He wore gray stockings, dun-colored breeches, a dun-colored shirt. Nothing about him glittered now, who was by ordinary such a resplendent figure. There was nothing, that is, to catch and guide the eye. There were no buckles on his heelless shoes. No rings flashed on his fingers, no brooch at his throat.

This was as it should be. Sir Jervis Johnston might be the best swordsman in London, as some said, but there was no reason for him to take unnecessary chances.

The referee waved the saber and called out something about the spectators keeping back. Then he left the field.

"Gentlemen, *advance and engage at will!*"

51 Adam went right in. He had planned this. For one thing, he was nervous and he didn't fancy the audience: the less fencing, the sooner the fight was over, the better. More important, an immediate, uncomplicated attack would be the most unexpected move he could make. Johnston, with his reputation, would look for a timorous approach. If he was attacked at all, he'd reason, it would be only after a considerable feeling-out period, and certainly the move would be preceded by at least a simple *cavazione,* whether inside or out, or a *mezza cavazione,* or some manner of disengagement or counter.

So Adam, without making any attempt to meet Johnston's steel, without trying any pass whatever, swept into a lunge.

A gasp rose from the crowd.

Johnston parried. Without retreating—he didn't get a chance to retreat —he flicked his hand, an instinctive movement. Adam felt no resistance to his blade, but the point had been deflected. Though the lower half of the sword was out of sight, he didn't think he'd hit flesh.

The quillons clanged together. The two men, their faces close in that instant, Adam's being the lower, regarded one another gravely. Johnston was impassive, but in his clear blue eyes Adam Long read respect, even admiration. It had been a near thing.

Neither dared to move.

The referee's saber came between them.

"*Disengage, gentlemen. No cut or thrust till the signal's given again!*"

They stepped back into guard position, Adam's sword emerging from Johnston's shirt. Johnston stood easy, not swaying. There was no sign of blood. The surgeon hurried to him, while the referee took the center of the field. After a moment the surgeon stepped back.

"He's not touched."

The referee lowered his saber.

"*Advance and engage at will!*"

Again Adam attacked. But his chance had gone. He would never get near Jervis Johnston now.

Johnston retreated when it pleased him—when he sought to calculate Adam's reach, for example—but he never was flustered. He parried easily and almost absently. There was no excessive motion. Adam could scarcely feel the man's blade.

It can be a dreadful thing not to be able to feel the other's steel. It can induce panic. Adam began to get wild, and he was gripping his sword too hard.

Johnston stopped retreating. He had learned all he thought he needed to know. He was neither cutting this fight short, as he might easily have done, nor permitting it to drag unnecessarily. His movements were sweet and sure, but spare, not flashy. Not once had he made any riposte. His blade had always been in line, excepting when he parried Adam's first attack, and its point had constantly threatened Adam's face; but Johnston had not thrust, or even feinted.

Now he nodded. He did not gloat, for he was concentrating; but when he nodded, probably not knowing that he did so, it was as though he had said aloud: "Very well, now we'll go the other way." And he attacked.

Not catching the blade, Adam retreated. He retreated again, as Johnston, stepping with tiny catlike steps, advanced. Johnston didn't hurry, he didn't beat.

Adam made a wild wide counter, sweeping his point far out of line. He caught nothing.

Johnston came on in.

Never in his lonely life had Adam Long felt so alone, so frustrated. He had no chance, and now he knew it. He had stepped far out of his class. There was no such thing as beginner's luck in rapier play, and men like Jervis Johnston did not stumble or make mistakes.

Carse of Providence at his most brilliant wouldn't have been able to hold off his master, who coldly and exactly advanced.

Adam might just as well have thrown his sword away, for all the good it was doing him.

Well, he thought, *this is it.*

He retreated.

Now, he thought, *I'm going to die.*

He stood; for it occurred to him that he might better get killed while going forward than while going back.

He held in a sob so violent that it shook his chest. He attacked.

"Disengage!"

The referee's saber was between them, then the referee himself was. The surgeon came padding over.

The outside of Adam's right forearm showed a thin red line about six inches long, which presently began to fill with blood. The blood broke, some tumbling to one side, some to the other. There wasn't a great deal of it.

Adam stared at it, dumbfounded. He felt nothing there.

The surgeon started to swab it and to squeeze the edges.

"Tut, tut, man. Not deep, and it's clean. You're lucky."

He was lucky indeed. He looked across at Sir Jervis Johnston, who stood with lowered guard, his face grave, eyes attentive and polite. There was the man Adam had almost killed, a minute ago. There was the man who could have killed Adam half a dozen times over, during that minute. This touch was enough to end the fight, since it drew blood. It had been the lightest possible hit in the safest possible place.

Adam shook his head.

"That cut's nothing! I'm not satisfied!"

"Please address your remarks to the field only through your representative," the referee said sternly.

"Can't do that," somebody called. "Poor Chum's damn' well swooned, b'God!"

"I repeat," said the referee, "I declare this combat ended."

Johnston passed his sword to his second. He went to Adam, hand out. Adam did not hesitate. He dropped his sword.

They shook hands.

"Damn it, Captain, that was fine fencing! Thank you, sir, thank you! Had me frighted half to death for a while there!"

"Nothing to what *you* had *me,* sir!"

Johnston laughed. Everybody laughed, excepting Adam Long. The surgeon was bandaging his arm.

"Our, uh, our little disagreement, Captain— It was about a waistcoat, if I recall correctly?"

"No, sir, it was about a woman," Adam said. "But it's all right now, far as I'm concerned. I guess I don't want to fight you any more."

214

52 In the Brown Tun, in the first confusion, before they'd found their places and the wine had been poured, a nondescript man sidled up to Adam and touched his elbow.

"You are Captain Long of the Rhode Island colony?"

"That's right. Why?"

The man handed him a paper, which Adam accepted without stopping to think. It was a legal paper, crickly with seals. Adam supposed it to be some legal formality in connection with the duel, which after all, as John Chumley had pointed out, *was* against the law. The nondescript had vanished. Adam thrust the paper into a pocket.

The wine from Champagne tasted dry and sharp. It pricked the inside of your mouth. It had little bubbles in it, as Chumley had said. They raced up to the surface and pipped, flicking you under the nose as you sipped, making you sneeze. Adam didn't think he liked it.

Passers in the street, still dark between the buildings, must have marveled, as they yawned and blinked, that any all-night revelers could sound so spirited. Again and again the glasses were filled.

Of them all, Adam Long alone was not bright. But he was conscious of his manners. After all, he had no complaint. He'd been treated well. These men were fools, but they were fair. They kept pumping his hand, then quickly dropping it, to blurt apologies, and he kept assuring them that the arm, bandaged and hidden by the coat sleeve now, was comfortable.

They would ask what part of the American colonies he came from and did he know So-and-So who lived near Philadelphia or maybe it was Charlestown?

Every one of them, at some time or other, asked him what he thought of London.

"Well, I'll tell you," Adam would answer. "It's all right to visit, but I wouldn't live here if you gave it to me."

Nevertheless they toasted London, as of course they toasted the Queen, and as they toasted also, at Johnston's suggestion, "the Colony of Rhode Island and the brave men it sends forth!" There was a lot of cheering.

What with the wine, and the fact that the party broke up rather abruptly, and also what with Adam's realization that he was something of a guest of honor, and as such had certain obligations, he found himself one of the last to leave.

The boniface leaned close to him, carefully taking him by an arm, the left arm. He held something out.

"Excuse me, your worship. I was told to give this to you."

It was the bill for the wine.

Magistrate Nixon had a ferret's face, which because of the length of his periwig looked even more lank than in truth it was. The periwig was cocked slightly to the left. The steel-rimmed spectacles were cocked to the right. Notwithstanding these and a few allied oddities, Magistrate Nixon presented an appearance sufficiently terrifying as he studied Adam Long.

Adam was sore. He wanted to be back in the Hearth Cricket, relaxed among friends, where he'd had as yet no fitting chance to discuss in detail the events of the previous night. It was there, at the inn, that he'd remembered the legal paper, and had examined it.

A good part of the Hearth Cricket clientele, and also the proprietor, indignant, had trailed Adam here. They stood in back of the courtroom now, their hats off, silent, yet frowning, for like Adam himself they were sore.

"What am I here for?" Adam demanded.

"Say 'your honor' when you address the judge," said a tipstaff.

"Your honor, what'm I here for?"

Magistrate Nixon hawked, and spat.

"You can't read?" he asked.

"I can read all right, my lord. Sure I can read. But only English. This thing"—he rattled the summons—"I don't know *what* language *it's* writ in."

"Lawyers must live," the magistrate said mildly.

"I don't see why."

A titter escaped from the spectators. The tipstaff wheeled, gripping his truncheon. Magistrate Nixon, however, paid no heed.

"What are you here for? Why, murder, I should think. How many men did you kill last night, Captain?"

"Only two that I can count for sure."

"You're a saucy fellow."

"This is the first time I've ever been in a court."

"If I am any judge of physiognomy, Captain, it won't prove to be the last."

"I sure hope it will, my lord."

"You don't call me 'my lord.' I'm not a lord, only a beak. You call me 'your honor.'"

"Your honor."

Magistrate Nixon leaned forward.

"I sent for you for two reasons, Captain."

"Because of the duel, too?"

"Have you been dueling? Damn it, man, then don't tell *me!* That happens to be against the law, too, just like murder is."

"I know it, my lord. I mean, your honor."

"Two reasons," the magistrate resumed. "The first was, to thank you for saving the Crown a very considerable hangman's fee. The second was, I wanted to see what you look like."

"Well— Well, here I am, your honor."

"Your honor, sir!" The magistrate came down off his bench, down to where Adam was, and he grasped Adam's hand. *"Your honor!* Damn me, Captain, if we had a few more like you in this city there'd be no need for so many of me! I want to hear about last night, every little thing about it. But we'll not have the tale here in court. We'll go to some more quiet place, eh?"

"We could go to the Hearth Cricket."

"Good! But right now I want to thank you. I want to congratulate you. I only hope you're staying with us here in London?"

"Thank you, sir, but I'm sailing tomorrow."

"Good luck, Captain." He put his left hand on Adam's right forearm. "And a good voyage. Come back whenever— Oh, Lord! I've pressed one of your wounds!"

No doubt Adam had winced involuntarily. He smiled now.

"That one don't hurt, your honor. Not any more."

Mistress Bingham had baked a partridge pie—a special pie, as Adam had promised Lil—and they had it, with trimmings, washing-downs, too, not in the ordinary, where they might be intruded upon by any customers, but in the kitchen, which was more private.

It was one of the best times Adam Long ever had in his life. They treated him like a member of the family, and he had to blink hard to keep the tears from breaking out of his eyes. When anybody spoke to him he had to swallow several times before he could be sure that his answer would come out clear. He grinned foolishly and fondly at everyone. Lillian sat on his lap, and if she spilled food now and then it did no great harm, for he wasn't wearing his fancy clothes now, only his freedom suit.

It was mid-afternoon when a drawer came in from the ordinary with a message that Mr. Chumley was waiting outside with two sedan chairs and asked that Captain Long go with him to Clark's coffee house.

"No," said Adam. "I don't have to go there any more, and why anybody'd go there who didn't have to is more than I can see."

But the drawer was soon back.

"He says to tell you, sir, that after the way you handled yourself in that affair of honor off Birdcage Walk this morning they're clamoring to meet you. He says to tell you you'll be the toast of the place."

"I don't like being a toast," said Adam. "It costs too much money."

"What shall I tell Mr. Chumley then, sir?"

"Tell him to go jump head-first down a jakes. Excuse me," added Adam. "I mean, down a *necessary*."

PART EIGHT

—◆—

A Man in the Middle

53 An aspen, a poplar, a beech will get to whispering in any old breeze that should saunter past; but it takes something to make a maple talk, even more for an oak. The Queen's majesty as represented in New England was perturbed. Adam Long sensed this the moment he faced the new custos.

Mr. Macgregor was a far more effective official than Captain Wingfield. He had none of Wingfield's bowwow. Blusterless, never sneering, he went over Adam's papers with the painstaking thoroughness of a weevil.

Adam sat at a window, the same window he'd once jumped out of. Today as on the previous occasion a crowd had collected; but the other time the men had been caught by the sound of angry voices and the possibility of a fight, whereas today Mr. Macgregor was not going to make the mistake his predecessor had made. Mr. Macgregor had been selected indeed in large measure because he was a different kind of man —watchful, wary, above all thorough. He checked every figure, then checked his own check.

The other time it had been raining. Today it was bright; the sun was out; the town glittered, cold, windy, but somehow gay.

Adam paid little attention to the custos. He'd heard of the change as soon as he landed, an hour ago. That man Colonel Dudley up there in Boston, folks said, was a slick one. He never should have sent Wingfield in the first place, for what he wanted was a functionary who would keep his eyes open and his mouth shut, collecting not only the duties but information as well—information that might enable the royal governor of Massachusetts and New Hampshire, vice admiral of all New England, to prove to those highly placed in London that this Rhode Island was too brazen a breaker of laws to be permitted to keep its charter as an independent colony. Mr. Macgregor was that. It was not astounding that he was here. What astounded was the swiftness with which he had been sent, the abruptness with which Wingfield had been recalled once the news of his brabble with Captain Long had reached Boston. Joseph Dudley was keeping his eye on Newport.

Adam nodded, smiled, or waved to acquaintances. His fame, granted, was only local; and it was vulgar, being based on nothing more than luck in a street fight; but he enjoyed it all the same. This morning his hand had been pumped and his shoulder clapped at least a dozen times in the hundred-odd yards to the customs house. That warmed him.

Mr. Macgregor handed back the papers.

"They're in perfect order," he said, a man amazed.

This riled Adam, who was proud of his bookkeeping.

"What'd you expect?" sourly.

"Is your vessel in as good order, Captain?"

"Come aboard and find out for yourself."

"Well, I might do that."

And, by thunder, he did! He climbed over *Goodwill to Men* from astern to stempost, scrutinizing, poking things, his fox's eyes alert. The skipper, slightly asmile, for a time wondered if this curiosity might not be rather more personal than professional: Mr. Macgregor as a newcomer would have heard of the schooner. However, when the custos went below, it became evident that he was in truth seeking something. He'd displayed little enough interest in the only-slightly-steeved bowsprit, the almost-level deck; but the hold, the sail closets, the lockers, forecastle, cabin, Mr. Macgregor sifted as though through linen. What in Tophet was he looking for? Whatever it was, he didn't find it. So far as Adam was aware, the only hiding place aboard the schooner was that in a beam just above his own bunk, where he kept the *Quatre Moulins* affidavit, Everard van Bramm's deposition that Zephary Evans had been the Newport agent of Tom Hart the pirate, and some extra let-passes Seth Selden had made out for him before deserting—a Dutch one, a French one, to keep against capture. Mr. Macgregor did not find that hiding place, which had been made by Adam himself, quietly and alone: even Resolved Forbes, who shared the cabin with Adam, did not know of the existence of that secret panel.

"Satisfied, sir?"

"For now."

The first person Adam met when he took Mr. Macgregor ashore was Obadiah Selden.

These two, weeks before, had agreed without word of mouth never to mention the scene that night back by Ben Blake's well. The truth is, they were embarrassed by the memory. When Adam—all in the flush of his triumph over Captain Wingfield, hot with the knowledge that he had done a good piece of business in the islands, and determined that these money men should not again dictate sailing terms—when Adam had pounded the Adventurers' Table and shouted that he'd have none of coasting, he was for England, Obadiah Selden had voiced no objection. Had Obadiah demurred, Adam might have been overruled.

Adam felt no tug to crow. Once he had been afraid of this man. Now he felt sorry for him.

Obadiah was large and cut square. Dignified, assuredly he was not graceful. When he moved he seemed to be pushing against a great weight. Habitually he kept his chin on his chest—not from truculence, as you might at first suppose, but from shyness.

They bowed but didn't shake hands. Adam wished that they had shaken hands, and he suspicioned that Selden wished this, too.

"You've had a prosperous voyage, Captain?"

"Aye, thank you, sir. And you've been well, I trust?"

"I have, thank you."

"And Mistress Deborah?"

Obadiah colored, and his bushy brows twitched.

"She—is in good health."

Out of sheer nervousness Adam took off his hat and looked into it, then clapped it hastily back on his head. It was a cocked hat, his first, the one with the ostrich feathers. He knew that a description of it was being bruited about. The first time the Long boy had returned as a skipper he wore a sword; the second time, a cocked hat. Well, well. Yet Adam did not wear his flame-colored coat.

"I'll meet with the owners this afternoon," he said suddenly. "I'm through customs now, and I'll be at Blake's in—say, two hours. Please tell the others."

It was not the way to talk to a person like Obadiah Selden. It was overheard, too. Persons passing dragged their feet.

"Will Mays has opened a tavern on the street the tannery's on," Obadiah answered meekly. "Most of the men meet there now."

"We'll meet at Blake's," said Captain Long.

54 As he set out for Eaton's Point, the small sad voices of the gulls above him, the bay clucking and sucking at his left, Adam wished that he had been less abrupt. He had long ago resolved to check any move toward dominance on the part of the money men, being determined that he'd have no repeat performance of that night at Blake's when they had coldly voted to relieve him of his command. Pounding the table was the trick to use. It had worked before, it would work again.

But he believed that it was important that *he* pound before any of the other owners got a chance to. That should not be difficult. With Seth Selden and Zephary Evans bought out, there were, besides Obadiah Selden, only John Richardson and John Saye, who owned one-eighth each, and the cooper, Phineas Monk, who owned a sixteenth. Adam knew these men. They would ordinarily follow Obadiah Selden; but they'd been bullied before and could be bullied again.

All the same, Adam had been unneedfully harsh with Obadiah.

There was that which was crablike about the way Willis Beach scuttled off as Adam approached. Sharply Adam called him back. He'd never liked Beach, or trusted him.

"Where's Jeth Gardner living?"

Beach told him—up the hill a piece, back of Eaton's Point.

" 'E's 'ad a stroke. Don't talk much."

Adam all but winced. Even weeks of the howling North Atlantic had not washed from his ears the rasp of Cockney voices.

"Does he need anything?"

Beach shrugged. His eyes were searching the bay.

"Don't rightly know. Never see 'im. Cap'n, you didn't speak any Nivy ships on your way in, did you?"

"No."

"I'd 'ate to 'ave 'em come and tike me awie."

Jeth had had a stroke. Zeph Evans, as Adam had learned earlier, was ailing. Yet here was a lovely chill day, bright with sunlight, a day for capering and cavorting, the kind that should make you prance. Adam Long had never felt better. He fairly ran up the hill.

The sight of the bosun was a shock. Jethro would never ship before the mast again, even if he got his leg sticked. He was, of course, an old man—he must have been near fifty—but in addition, now, he was slack, pale, actually unsteady. His hands shook. His lower jaw trembled, his lower lip.

It gave him joy to see Adam, even brought tears to his eyes. But Jeth had none of his old disagreeableness. The overweening air of disgust with which he had once surveyed the world was gone now. He tended to whimper.

" 'Tain't the leg, Cap'n. No, no! It's something else. Reckon I ain't got long to live."

They sat there in the sun, Jeth in a chair, Adam on a stool, and looked down over the bay and talked about folks and about vessels. Jeth approved the plan to carry flour down to the islands, rather than go Guineaing. But, he asked, would the owners?

"They'll approve," Adam said.

Jeth tired. He who had more than once kept the deck through thirty-odd hours of gale, toiling, shouting, finding fault, now sagged perceptibly after less than an hour of murmurous talk. Yet he hated to see Adam go. He held Adam's hand for some time.

"You'll be here awhile, sir?"

"A week, ten days."

He sought out the landlord, and left some coins.

"They'd ought to do something about that man, the owners."

"They will," Adam promised. "I'm going to see to it right now."

Walking back to Blake's, his legs swinging, the gulls still uttering those plaintive squeals, the bay on his right now, he determined to take no nonsense from Obadiah Selden, John Saye, John Richardson, and Phineas Monk, the cooper.

So he was angry and his jaw was out when he swung into Blake's. He was acting and feeling as if his wishes had already been flouted.

Only one man sat at the Adventurers' Table—Obadiah Selden. For all his bulk, he looked shrunken, sitting there alone. He was not drinking anything or eating anything.

"Where are the others?" Adam asked. Then, without waiting for an answer, and remembering that he had promised himself not to be harsh with Obadiah: "Will you share dinner with me, sir?"

"Thank you," said the merchant. "I was just on the point of inviting you to go up and have dinner with my daughter and me. We're having venison tonight. And an oyster pie."

Something caught in Adam's throat, and he turned his head away. The Duchess' brat was not used to being asked out.

"Now that's right chirk of you, sir. But would Mistress Deborah have enough food?"

"She'll have enough."

"Even though she don't expect me?"

"She does expect you. She was the one told me to ask you."

"Oh. She, uh, she knows I'm back in Newport then?"

"Known it since seven this morning when she spotted you coming up the bay. She's always at the window with that glass, ever since you been gone. Spends most of her time there."

"I see," said Adam Long. Embarrassed again, he looked around. He wasn't being dominating, imperious, as he'd planned. "But oughtn't we have our meeting here first? I've got some matters to bring up."

"We can have it at my house with less ado."

"You can't bring *four* men home!"

"No need to. We're all here, all the owners. I bought out John Saye and John Richardson and Monk, the cooper," explained Obadiah, "last week."

"Oh. Meaning that now you own nine-sixteenths of the schooner?"

"Aye."

"While I own seven-sixteenths."

"Aye. And I shall admire very much to hear those suggestions you have to make, Captain."

Adam rose.

"While I shall admire very much to eat that oyster pie, sir. I always have been partial to oysters."

In the gathering gloom lightning bugs were being buffeted about. The leaves underfoot went clicketty-click. In the house across the street, the Evans house, a light shone where Elnathan no doubt sat up nursing her husband. Adam, glancing that way as he turned with Obadiah, for a moment had the unchristian thought that Zeph's illness was lucky for him, Adam, inasmuch as it kept Zeph's wife at home. Not for the smallest part of an instant, though, did Adam suppose that he was finished with Elnathan Evans—or, rather, that she was finished with him. Sooner or later they were going to have to have it out. He just couldn't carry on with her the way they had been doing before he sailed for the islands. It would not be right. Well, it had never been right, far as that goes; but he had Maisie to think of now.

Nor did Adam delude himself with the notion that Deborah Selden would quit. What she wanted, being the woman she was, she would try her dad-blamedest to get; and likewise her father here was going to try to get it for her. Adam was, of course, flattered; he was delighted; but also he was more than a mite frightened by the directness of the attack.

Of the two, he calculated that he had more to fear from Deborah. Elnathan was a tasted sweet. She could not aspire to marry him while Zeph lived; and an adulterous relationship, even without the appropriate trimmings, would sure as snakes be known to everybody in town. Liberal though Newport was—of course everybody knew about Maisie, for instance—it would not tolerate this. Fornication afar and fornication at home, right in sight of everybody, were two different things.

Deborah Selden, on the other hand, clad in all the might of her virginity, might be hard to hold off.

Adam took a deep breath before entering the house.

55 Manners can come in handy. The Seldens, indoors, were a touch formal in their treatment of Adam, who gratefully was formal in reply.

Adam was jolted when a girl he had once pursued with japes, being halted only when she turned to stick her tongue out at him—when such a one, Deborah, swept him a practiced curtsey. But Adam caught himself and made a leg Londonwise, his cocked hat held over his heart.

Deborah was wearing French gray camlet. There was white linen, thin and crisp, narrow, too, at the neck and cuffs. There was no cap and not even a suggestion of that tottering monstrosity the "commode," as affected by ladies of *ton*.

They talked a few minutes, proper but not stiff. She congratulated him on a successful voyage. He replied that it had yet to be voted a success, since his report to the other owner was not yet in; and it could be that he put some slight stress on that word "other." She said that she was sure it would prove a success; and then, directly, womanlike, she started to pump him about the dress materials he'd brought. She was worked up to hear about the wax candles, and told her father promptly and decisively that they should buy up a large stock of these. Obadiah, doffing his cloak, nodded. There were five candles in the branch on the table right then, and every one lighted. It made Adam feel like a duke.

Deborah excused herself and went back to the kitchen.

There was a poker being hotted in the fire.

Obadiah wasted no time on amenities. Even while he made flip, he was asking questions. He listened carefully to the answers. He approved the cargo and agreed to handle all of it, including Adam's own share, without any charge to Adam. With no hesitation he agreed to the payment of four pounds a month for Jethro Gardner's room and victuals, this to come out of the ship's fund. Concerning the few Dutch sails, though he bugged his eyes a bit at the cost, he said only that this was in the captain's province.

"That extra smitch of speed," Adam pointed out, "might save everything, the seas down that way being what they are."

"Well, well, I trust you, Captain. I think you know best."

"It'll be mostly your money this time, sir. Mine's going to go over there." And he nodded in the direction of the Evans house.

Obadiah studied the brim of his mug.

"I wonder if you'd tell me, Captain—that is, if you care to—how much, uh, how much you paid Zeph Evans for those four-sixteenths?"

Adam told him.

Obadiah's eyebrows, very bushy, were the only expressive feature of a face ordinarily impassive. Now the eyebrows leapt. Obadiah looked at Adam Long with interest and admiration.

"That was a bargain. Zeph try to get you drunk first, did he?"

"He tried."

"Want me to tell you what I paid Saye and Monk and Richardson?"

"I'd admire very much to hear, sir."

Obadiah told him.

Adam stared, aghast. Highly as he esteemed the schooner, who knew her better than anybody else, he found it hard to believe that more should be paid for five-sixteenths of her than was put out for the building of the entire vessel a year ago. Yet Obadiah Selden, never a boastful man anyway, surely was not boasting now.

"I had a good reason for paying that price," he said.

Deborah appeared.

"Dinner's ready."

After grace the talk took to less commercial matters. Adam's previous return had been so brief and withal so eventful that he was not well posted on conditions in Newport, any more than the Seldens were posted on conditions as he'd found them in Jamaica.

The kitchen was wondrously bright, and the conversation matched it. Obadiah himself didn't talk much, but Deborah was downright chatty. As for Adam, he became a clam only when they asked him what he thought of London.

"Well, it's different."

"You mean, better than you expected? Or worse?"

"Well—different."

The meal itself lived up to the earlier odors. In addition to the vension, with potatoes, they had baked fresh pickerel; and the oyster pie, served with some creamy meat sauce, was a masterpiece. Adam said as much, roundly.

He looked at Deborah as often as he dared. Not only was she mighty handsome, she had always been that, but her trimness flummoxed him. She'd had nobody to help her—Adam several times had peeked into the kitchen—yet when she sat down, after putting the food on the table, she was cool and trig. No hair was loose, her hands weren't red, there was not a fleck of spilled gravy anywhere on her. Adam liked things that way, shipshape.

Still the girl wasn't at ease. Though there was no scrape in her voice to show the strain, Adam was sure she was holding herself in. She didn't tremble, but she darn' near *shook*.

Adam would not have mentioned Seth Selden, but Obadiah himself brought up this subject, asking what had happened to his brother. Obadiah knew, of course; but he wished to hear Adam say it.

Adam was blunt. He said that Seth was now, to the best of his knowledge, on Providence island in the Bahamas, a nest of piracy that might last through the war or might get wiped out at any time, depending on Admiral Benbow. But that camp would certainly be flattened immediately after peace was declared, Adam added. He said he doubted that Seth would ever come back.

Obadiah nodded, and changed the subject.

The meal was sumptuous by Newport standards, yet Adam, watchful, sensed that this was the way the Seldens ordinarily ate. He was impressed. The table was covered with a linen cloth, and they were even given individual small squares of linen to wipe their hands on. There were no trenchers: everything was served on pewter. As head of the family Obadiah Selden even sat in a chair. *He* seldom picked his teeth during the meal, and Deborah never did, so Adam didn't.

They had a sweet pudding, and then the men returned to the parlor, where the biggest surprise of all awaited Adam. He and his host had brandy, real French brandy, and they had it not in leather jacks or in mugs but in cups made of *glass*.

They talked again of trade. Obadiah Selden was a sound merchant, one who knew his market, and he asked a great many questions.

"I don't go in for smuggling any more'n I have to," Adam told him. "But you can't get away from it for all." He dinged his glass with a forefinger. "I'll warrant this very brandy came in at the cove, sir?"

Obadiah said nothing.

"Some of the owners wondered how I got that molasses so cheap. Well, it was French, that's why. The French planters used to throw their molasses *away* until a little while ago."

"It came in English barrels."

"Aye. I bought the barrels already branded, only empty. Then I arranged through a friend of mine down there, a Mr. Cartwright, who's a lawyer, to get assigned to a flag-of-truce fleet that was going over to Guadeloupe to dicker with the Frenchies—I never did find out what about. It cost me twenty pounds to get that assignment. I put it on my list as entertainment expenses."

"But—I don't understand."

"Guadeloupe's French. The way they see the law in Jamaica it's not dealing with the enemy if you do some business while there's a flag-of-truce talk going on, provided you're a part of the official party. That's why they have so many of 'em there, to exchange prisoners and all like that. And that's why it costs so much to get assigned to one. We went as a supply vessel. I don't know what we was supposed to supply."

"And—you bought molasses?"

"Fleet was only there half a day, so we had to move brisk. But we got all the barrels filled—a thruppence a gallon, about half what we'd've paid in Kingston. I just mention this to give you an idea of how they do things down in the islands."

"I see."

"Why, down that way Englishmen buy their own wool from Frenchies.

227

That's right! There's French vessels that stand off Dover, and the 'owlers' run out and stock 'em with woolens. You've heard of the owlers?"

"Aye."

"Then they take the bolts to Jamaica or the Barbados and spirit 'em ashore. First the stuff's smuggled out of England, to avoid the export duties, and then it's smuggled into an English colony to avoid the import duties. Sometimes some of that stuff gets smuggled out of Jamaica again and into one of the mainland colonies here. That makes three full sets of smuggling, as you might say. And *still* it's cheaper than if you bought it legitimate. Though not much cheaper by that time," Adam added. "Not enough to make it worth the risk."

"I am glad to hear you say that, Captain. The penalties for violating the Navigation Acts are getting more severe all the time, and that man Dudley up to Boston means business."

"I'm perfectly clear!"

"I'm sure you are. And I'm sure you'll stay that way." He put a hand on Adam's shoulder, an act in him as astonishing as a kiss. "Our fortunes are tied up together now, and you must watch your reputation."

"Just because I bladed with that collector—"

"It ain't that. I'd say most folks think the better of you for that. There was lot out in the street heard what Wingfield said. But you mustn't forget that these are touchy times. The Lords of Trade over there can do pretty much anything they want with us, if they get to supposing we're a rabble of pirate lovers. And you're vulnerable, Captain. You've never denied that you've helped unload, out at Contraband Cove."

"I had heaps of company there!"

"Sure. But there's still those who say it's odd you jumped right from apprentice to invester."

"There was no coin involved! I got an interest in the schooner because I worked so much to build her, and everybody knows that. And I had the right to collect. Only I can't prove that now. Mr. Sedgewick is dead."

"I don't question a thing you say. I'm only reminding you that there are folks who'll go right on whispering that you might have been Tom Hart's agent here—that that's how you got your start."

It graveled Adam to hear that old charge. There'd never been an ounce of truth in it. *He* knew who had been Thomas Hart's agent here! If he ever fetched out that deposition— But he said nothing.

Deborah, skirt rustling, eyes downcast, came in with some needlework and sat at the other end of the bench before the fire. Obadiah picked up the brandy bottle and went to the back of the house. Soon Obadiah returned—in nightrail, nightcap, dressing robe.

"Bed's turned over but it's cold."

"Oh, I'm sorry, Father!"

228

She put down the needlework and sped out, to return with a warming pan into which she scraped embers. She went out with this.

Obadiah came into the room, walking with that peculiar widespread walk of his. He looked mighty silly in the nightcap, but that robe, Adam reckoned, must have cost sixteen shillings.

"We must talk about this some other time, Captain. This—and other matters. Good night now."

"Good night, sir."

Deborah came back and picked up her needlework and sat down on the bench, the same bench Adam sat on. The needlework was something fancy, Adam reckoned. Anyway the needle made a hollow bouncy "pong!" each time it went through. Now and then a flurry of leaves would click against the window, or a piece would fall off a burning log, to sink sheepishly among the deeper embers, and a shower of sparks would go spitting up the chimney. These were the only sounds.

56 Adam stared at the fire. The logs were mostly red cedar, well dried. Each was bottomed by small pink flames that strove to reach its top; and now and then a flame, stretching, would get up there, and expand, waxing blue, and leap in glee, and waver, then abruptly, as if spat at, die. But the flames underneath kept licking away.

"Pong!" went the needle. "Pong!"

Adam stared at the backs of his hands, but they looked pretty much the same as they always had, so, after a while, he stared at the fire again.

Deborah asked him about the voyage. What had the weather been like? He answered a shade impatiently. You didn't talk about sea weather except to sailors. If there was a lot of it, then there was a lot of work; or if not, not. And in any case the weather Deborah Selden asked about was gone now.

She asked also about London, though cautiously; and it was with caution that Adam answered. The truth is, he did not care to admit even to himself how disappointed he had been in what he used to call Home. What good things about it he could find in his heart to say, he said; but those weren't many. And he finished—remembering his mother, though not mentioning her—with the bitter observation that it was hard to see why folks had to be dragged out of jails or made drunk or hit on the head in order to persuade them to quit a place like that for a place like this.

"But I thought you didn't like Newport, Captain?"

"Never said that. I just figured Newport didn't like me."

"Do they really do those things to enlist people?"

"Worse. They steal 'em."

Without making any mention of his own exploits, he told her about the kidnappers. She was horrified.

"Why, there ought to be a law against that!"

"Probably is. There's laws against pretty nigh everything."

Their voices trailed off; and soon there was again only the sound of her sewing and the spit of sparks in the fireplace.

Some time passed in this way.

Then Adam rose. He waggled his hands. When he did succeed in speaking, his voice was louder than it had any reason to be.

"So you still want a husband, even though you don't have to have one, is that it?"

She did not look up from her needlework, and indeed she bent over it a little lower.

"Captain, I don't think that's very kind of you. I never said I just wanted a husband. I wanted you. So when I got a chance I asked you. And when you said no, I still wanted you. So I tried to trick you."

"You sure did."

"Any other girl would have done the same. Only she'd get a better chance. She'd let you walk out with her, and if she could, she'd bundle with you. Then you'd get all fussed up, and you'd beg her to marry you, and you'd think you was lucky when she said she would, not knowing she'd planned it that way. With me it wasn't the same. I had to ask straight-out."

He looked at the fire, and then he looked at the top of her head and down the back of her neck, where her dress stood out a bit.

"You never wanted anybody else, the same way?"

"No, Adam. I can honestly say I never did."

"But you did want me—like that?"

She had ceased to do the needlework. She dropped her hands to her lap, it could be to control them. Otherwise she didn't stir.

"I did, and I still do."

The voice was tiny. Slowly her head was lowered even more. Downy black hairs clustered at the nape of her neck just beneath the bun. Her shoulders were hunched up a bit.

She did not stir. He put out a hand and placed it on her shoulder, and at the touch she fairly jumped. She was quiet after that, but rigid. Her hands were pressed down white in her lap. Her feet shoved the floor.

"If I'd known that was the way you felt—well, things might have been different."

"You always seemed to be afraid of me."

"Maybe I was. I was afraid of most folks then. After all, I don't know who my father was, for sure. And my mother I don't remember well. Mr. and Mrs. Sedgewick weren't much help, though they didn't beat me much—I guess not as much as they should've."

"You— You used to jeer at everybody."

"I reckon that's because I *was* scared. Then the better work I did, the smarter I got, the more it seemed folks disliked me. I guess I just imagined that. But naturally I never even dreamed that you—well, I never even gave myself a loose to think about that, that's all. And now it's too late."

Her shoulder leapt under his hand and her head went back, so that he retreated, truly thinking for an instant that she was about to spring at him and claw his face with her fingernails.

"You didn't *marry* that red-head down there?"

She looked lovely. Her eyes were flashing. Her chin was up, and the way her head was lifted it showed the lines of her neck. Her hands were at her sides on the bench now, and her feet were drawn underneath her, as though she was all readied to spring.

Fascinated, he moved toward her.

"Don't you touch me, Adam Long!"

He stopped.

"*Are* you married to her?"

He shook his head.

"No," he said.

Her head went down, and the muscles in her shoulders and arms slacked off. She slumped.

"I'm sorry," she whispered. "I didn't think even you would be fool enough to do that. But I had to ask."

He just stood there looking at her; and he was the one who was doing the trembling now.

Color rose in her neck, in her face.

"You can touch me now, if you want, Adam," she whispered.

Eager leaves tinked and scraped at the window, then turned out of sight, sinking.

Adam did not touch her. He was afraid to.

"No, I'm not married— But it's sort of the same, in a way."

"How do you mean? No, I'd rather you didn't tell me! But you—you're not really married?"

"Not really, no. But I got certain obligations. I've done certain things and I reckon I can't back out of 'em now. I reckon that in the eyes of God I am married. God's got it all wrote down, in the Book. You know that."

She rose. Head averted, she stood right close to him. He could smell her hair.

"Reckon I'd better get back to the schooner," he muttered.

"You don't have to go, Adam."

"Reckon I'd better."

The air outside, unexpectedly cold, grabbed him like so many hands. He realized that he was all drenched with sweat.

A shadow sprang from behind a maple. Arms went around Adam's neck. He forgot his sword, and brought up a knee, hopping back.

"Ow! Adam, you hurt me!"

"Thunderation! How'd I know it was you, out in the dark like this?"

"You take me for a footpad? We don't have 'em here."

"I've just come from England, and they sure have 'em there."

"Just come from England, yes, and where do you go?"

"Selden's the only other owner now. I had to make a report."

Elnathan came closer. She had a long woolen shawl over head and shoulders, a shawl the size of a comforter, and when she let this fall partly open, Adam saw that she wasn't wearing a great deal more. She must be cold, he thought.

"Forgive me, my chick." She slid an arm around his neck, pressing close to him. "It's been so long—"

"We're in a public street, woman!"

"Yes. Let's go inside. That's what I was waiting to ask you."

"Zeph—"

"He's asleep. Won't wake up for another hour, we can be quiet."

She laid her cheek on his chest, turning her lips up. Her eyes were closed. Her breath came fast.

"Come on, Adam. He won't hear anything. Come on."

He wrenched himself free, choky noises in his throat. He didn't say anything at all, just ran on down the hill.

It was as well for him that he did not see Elnathan Evans' face, the way she looked after him.

PART NINE

———————◆———————

Said a Spider to a Fly

57 A sailor gets used to long separations, though it does not follow that he likes them. No matter what the poets may sing about absence making the heart grow fonder, any man whose skin is more sensitive than pasteboard knows that it's better to have your darling lying alongside of you, preferably with all her clothes off, than to dream about her from a distance. Well, the waiting was over now. Adam had claimed a cavalier's reward—and would claim it again. He should have been happy. He wasn't.

He could no longer tell himself that this was a real home he had established in the house on the hill just outside of Kingston. He had been overeager, trying to delude himself. He knew this now. Jamaica was no place for an orphan like him to roost. He didn't belong here.

He resented Jamaica. He had never liked the place, now he hated it. From the veranda, while Maisie mixed him a drink, he looked over the garden wall, over the town of Kingston, to the harbor, which was crowded. The fleet was back—seven warships, fourth- and fifth-raters, together with their attendant vessels of supply. A great deal had happened in these parts since Adam's previous visit. Admiral Benbow had caught up with du Casse off Santa Marta—ten vessels, only four of them warships, loaded to the gunwales with treasure. Benbow himself had sailed in with all guns blazing, but he'd not been followed by his captains, who despite orders had lingered in the background, making excuses. Eventually these captains had even presented the admiral with a round robin begging him to break off the chase. By that time Benbow, semi-conscious from wounds, was barely able to curse them. The English Navy was indelibly disgraced; while the luckiest man in the world, du Casse, escaped.

Benbow was still laid up—one of his legs had been smashed by chain shot—but he was going right ahead with his plans to bring charges of cowardice against the captains, two of whom had already been sentenced to death. Benbow's was not a forgiving nature. His rage made itself felt throughout the colony. There was no shore leave. He'd hear no complaints from civilians. Bumboatmen were roughly handled. More marines than ever tramped the streets of Kingston and Port Royal. The press gang and the requisition squads had never been so busy.

Nearer, the prospect was more pleasant, consisting as it did of a garden all stippled with sunspots, of zigzagging flagstones set in the bright green grass, and gardenia and hibiscus, roses, jasmine, cereus, and, pert and pretty, and startlingly simple amid those lush tropical blooms, great masses of periwinkle.

Nearer still, in fact in his lap, lay the real causes of Adam's perturbation. For he wasn't just emotionally upset. There were touchable, material reasons why he was in the dumps.

"Pish, my darling! Adam chick, you're not going to stew over tradesmen's bills at a time like this, sure?"

She gave him his punch and knelt by his chair, and put her hands over his left hand, her cheek against his left arm.

He smiled at her, but only from a distance. He shook his head. The husband who comes home to find himself inundated by evidences of his wife's extravagance was, he knew, a comic character. He didn't care. If, as some folks said, it showed a mean nature to worry about money matters, well then he had a mean nature. These papers in his lap were not funny, they were real. They might even prove tragic. Where was his Tillinghast blood? A true aristocrat would have swept them aside with a sneer. Adam couldn't. He was a mercantile man, a trader, and he took such things seriously.

He did not blame Maisie. In the circumstances she had behaved with a commendable moderation. It was his own fault, a result of his dereliction of duty, that they had been captured by the pirates and kept for a time on Providence, where of necessity all Maisie's clothes had been left. As she herself had pointed out, she had to have *something* to wear. And prices had gone 'way up, partly because the war had made for a shortage of fine clothes, partly because Maisie, already deeply in debt here, was a marked woman when she asked for more credit. Poor girl! Alone, with no one to guide her, spied on, tittered at, resented, she had consoled herself with change after change of costume here in their own house. She had pirouetted before a mirror, oh, yes! Adam was a lucky man that this was all she'd done. Kingston had not been kind to her. He didn't like the way she looked. When she smiled it was the same, warming his heart; but sometimes, when she didn't know that he was watching her, lines of worriment and of harshness crimped the corners of her mouth. She was paler than she'd been. Even the glory of her hair, it could be, was a touch dimmed.

More than ever it was advisable that she get away, that they both get out. But—how? Adam, who had maybe overstrained himself in order to

234

buy Zeph Evans' share of the schooner, had precious little ready cash. Mr. Cartwright, "the jew who wasn't a Jew," was pressing for his money, with twelve per cent interest. Nothing had been done about the Treadway plantation case. Nothing had been done about the *Quatre Moulins*.

Even if they had been willing to let both these suits go by default, they couldn't have sneaked away. Adam had not told her this, but *Goodwill to Men*, careened for a scraping over at Port Royal before Adam had learned how serious was his financial situation, was in no condition to sneak anywhere. What was worse, Adam's seven-sixteenths of the schooner, defenseless now, might at any hour be attached. Even to think of it was a poniard into his heart.

"We've got to take desperate measures, my dear," he said mildly. "I mentioned a plan I had, some time ago. We've got to get to Benbow."

"I've tried! I told you how I tried! He won't see anybody!"

"Desperate measures," he repeated thoughtfully. He finished his punch, put the mug on the floor, and rose. "Bring me my sword," he said.

58 The frosty blue eyes swerved as though in slots, but no other part of the old man moved, when Adam climbed through the window.

"What in Hell do *you* want?"

"Just to talk to you, sir."

"Going to kill me?"

"No, sir."

"Sure?"

But there was no glint of fear in the blue eyes.

"I'm sure," Adam replied.

"If you came from those captains, it won't do 'em any good. They're guilty. The sentence stands."

"I didn't come from the captains," Adam said. "And I wouldn't have climbed in this way except that I didn't know any other way to get here."

"You bribed one of the guards, I take it?"

"I did, yes, sir. But not the way you think. I took a look at the man who paces before the side door and underneath this window, and it struck me that he was likely to prove honest."

"Eh?"

"Some folks are, you know, sir."

"But you said you bribed him?"

"Yes, sir. I got up close to him this afternoon and whispered that I wanted very much to speak to the admiral for a few minutes and I'd be back tonight at nine. I whispered that here was a yellow boy for him, a gold guinea, provided he'd look the other way while I slipped in through the side door and upstairs."

"And he took it?"

"He wasn't going to. He was going to arrest me. But then he fell to figuring just the way I'd figured he would figure. He figured that as matters stood it would be his word against mine, and in that case, too—if he turned me in, that is—he'd have to give up the yellow boy. *But* if he could nap me when I tried to sneak up those stairs at nine o'clock, if he could catch me red-handed—d'ye see, sir?—"

"I see. Go on."

"—*then* he'd not only be able to keep his coin but he'd get credit for being vigilant and so-forth."

"Yes."

"So he did this. And I guess right now he's down there watching that side door like a chicken hawk. I couldn't have climbed up here if he hadn't been."

Adam looked out of the window, smiling a little. The guard indeed was waiting behind a bush, watching the door, his back to the vine that climbed up past this window.

"And so what do you want?" rasped Vice Admiral Benbow.

Adam crossed quietly to him, and sat at the foot of the bed.

"To talk to you, sir. I have a proposition to make."

"If it's from those captains—"

"It's *not* from those captains," Adam cried.

Benbow blinked.

"You'll mind your manners, young man. Remember—I could just raise my voice and you'd be shot."

"You could. And I would be. Yes."

They looked at one another.

"Well, are you going to do it?" asked Adam.

The tiniest of all possible smiles touched the corners of the admiral's mouth. It was as though some movement of a glacier had opened a crack through which sunlight now peered hesitantly, half afraid.

"Well, I'll hear what you have to say for yourself first anyway."

"Thank you, sir. I'm sure you'll be interested. What I propose to do is clear out that whole colony of pirates on Providence."

"You—and how many thousand men and how many ships?"

"I'm going to do it alone, sir."

Benbow sighed.

"I might have known you was mad. This whole island's packed with madmen, but I don't know why they can't leave me alone."

He reached for a bellpull.

"Please don't do that, sir!"

Benbow paused. Adam swallowed. The scene was quiet enough—the tropic night, a high-ceiled room, the little old man in bed, a smell of medicine. From the harbor came the clean sweet sound of bells striking three times—half past nine. Oh, as peaceful as all-get-out! Yet if the little old man yanked that cord the motion would end Adam Long's life. Those around Admiral Benbow adored him. Adam knew this. Why, even that whining wizened little Willis Beach, who hated and feared everything else about the Royal Navy, never had anything but praise for John Benbow. The marines, upstairs and down, guarded their master jealously. If they found a stranger in this bedroom—well, it wouldn't need a command. Adam would be bayoneted instantly.

"Give me a chance to say what I came for. After all, I do know something about Providence. I lived there for a month."

"Oho, you're a God-damn' pirate yourself, I take it?"

"I'm not a pirate, no, and I never was. I don't like pirates. They—they stink."

"Lots of men of the sea," pointed out John Benbow, "stink."

"Pirates stink in a peculiar way. Let me tell you about it, sir."

Benbow took his hand away from the bellpull.

"Oh, go ahead. Might as well listen. Can't sleep anyway."

Before Adam had a chance to start, however, there was a knock on the door. He sank to the floor on the far side of the bed.

"Come in," the admiral called.

It was the sergeant of the guard with the marine Adam had bribed. The marine told his story, though he made no mention of money. He'd got to thinking it over, he said, and he decided he ought to tell his sergeant.

"Should've done that in the first place."

"Yes, sir. But I thought I'd catch 'im in the act."

"He didn't give you any money?"

"Oh, no, sir!"

"And you say he was a very desperate-looking character?"

"Werry, sir! Scare you just to see 'im."

"Well, you did wrong. But no matter—now. So long as I've escaped. No punishment, sergeant."

"Very good, sir."

"That'll be all now. Thank you."

"Thank *you*, sir!"

A moment later Benbow said: "All right, come out again, desperate character. I want to learn how you propose to knock out a whole colony of cutthroats single-handed."

Adam nodded in a matter-of-fact way, and sat again on the foot of the bed, and told the admiral about Providence. He made no mention of Maisie, but he did describe the camp in details—its leaders, the pass, the bay, fort, beach, marketplace, warehouse.

"You really do know the place!"

"You couldn't get in there, sir. You could stand off and blast it to bits, yes, but you'd have to knock out that fort before you could put a landing party ashore anywhere near the bay, even in good weather. That would take time. And men. And gunpowder."

Benbow nodded.

"What's more," he said, "I can't spare even a fifth-rater. Need 'em for convoy duty. The merchants of this damn' place are yipping loud enough as it is—not to mention the Lords of Trade back home."

"And even if you did flatten the camp that way, and set fire to it, sir, the Providencers'd simply retreat to the other side of the island. And when you'd gone away they'd come back. They could build that camp up again inside of a week. It's nothing but old boards and tarpaulin. Loot their warehouse and that'd hurt 'em, but in the long haul it'd only make 'em all the more eager to go out and snatch cargoes."

"Aye, they'll pounce on anything that's not convoyed. And we can't keep far away from 'em on the run home, the way the winds are."

"This man van Bramm," Adam went on, "is no fool. But he's greedy. They put on a lot of talk about being brethren and all sharing alike and so-forth, but as a matter of truth it's every man for himself."

"I am not amazed to hear it."

"Van Bramm's ambitious. He wants more than his share. Naturally he's got enemies."

"Naturally."

"I reckon he's got more enemies than friends. It happens that I got acquainted with a good many of them, for the simple reason that they made me into a kind of hero there for a while, as I told you. What it came to, sir: they wanted me to lead a revolt against van Bramm."

"They ask you to do that?"

"Not in so many words. But they would have—if I'd given 'em half a chance. They're still sore, those same men. All they want is a shove, and in no time at all you'd have a civil war on Providence."

"Now see here, young man, it strikes me you're almighty glib about this. What if you do get 'em all shooting at one another—what then? Whichever side won, they'd still be on Providence. You couldn't expect to divide those pirates so evenly that they'd all kill one another off down to the last man."

"I wasn't thinking of the pirates at all, sir."

"Eh? But you just said—"

"I said I had a plan for cleaning out the colony. And I have. But I don't mean by making it too hot for the pirates. Nothing's too hot for them. They're salamanders. They can stand anything. They have to—they don't dare go back to civilization. No, it's not them I mean. It's the traders that sponge off of them."

"Uh. Go on."

"Because the camp couldn't be run without those traders, sir. You think of it like a sailing man, just as I did—at first. But if you'll think of it the way a merchant would—"

"I'll never think of anything the way a merchant does," coldly.

"Well then, think of it the way a pirate would. A pirate can't eat the stuff he steals. He's got to sell it. You can't make a supper out of silks from Samarkand. You can't slaughter a sapphire necklace and cut it up like as if it was a cow, and roast it."

"I begin to see your point, Captain."

"Take away a pirate's receivers, and what is he? And those merchants ain't going to stand around and get sabered. They don't like fighting. They'll scamper right back here."

"Where you wouldn't know 'em from any other bloody merchants!"

"That could be true, sir. But *they* don't have a price on their heads. *They*'d get out of Providence as fast as they could—and what's more, they'd stay out. And the pirates'd have to find some new source of supplies. And that wouldn't be easy to do, these days."

There was a considerable silence in the room. Poked by a vagrant breeze the curtains at the window lifted a little, then fell back, limp. A sentry could be heard pacing below.

"Let's get this matter straight, young Yankee. You say you're going to do this whole thing yourself." He leaned forward. *"How?"*

Unabashed, Adam crossed his legs; he took a knee in his hands.

"There's an ordinary called Walter's, on the waterfront over in Kingston. It's their headquarters." He looked at the admiral. "I don't know whether you knew that, sir?"

Benbow grunted.

"I didn't. Go on."

"It's a respectable place, to look at. But you can always get messages through to Providence from there. No, don't raid it! You wouldn't learn anything, and they'd only shift to another place."

"And you think you can kick up a revolt from there?"

239

"I can try, sir. I've got friends on Providence."

"You've got enemies there, too, from what you say. What about this man van Bramm? Wouldn't he be sure to hear of anything like that and nip it short before it got going good?"

Adam paused.

"Well, *wouldn't* he?"

"I reckon he would," Adam admitted. He cleared his throat, uncrossed his legs. "All right, then. What if I didn't even look in at Walter's? What if I went straight to Providence myself?"

"Alone?"

"Alone."

"I could let you have some men. Not many, but they'd be good men."

"No. That would only bring 'em together. They'd *all* turn and fight outsiders. But maybe alone I could work with my friends."

"Still sounds mad. You'd go in disguise?"

"Something like that. You could arrange to have me dropped from some vessel in convoy that's passing there at night. All I'd need is a small sloop. I could find my way in. And I know just where I'd land, without being seen."

Benbow put one hand over the other, on the coverlet. They were large coarse hands, though they were clean. He regarded Adam for a long time.

"Captain, I think you're a lunatic," he said at last.

"No, sir, I'm not."

"But I'm beginning to wish I'd had a few lunatics like you off Santa Marta."

Adam flushed.

"Why, thank you, sir!"

"And now let's get down to cases. Of course you're not offering to do all this for nothing?"

"Of course not."

"Good. And what is it you want in return?"

"Only two things. Both of them easy, for you."

"Yes?"

"First, a derelict I took last summer and brought in here. French. A brig. I'm entitled to her and I have my claim in, but the way things are done in the admiralty courts here sometimes—well—"

"Captain, when you have eliminated that pesthole on Providence by whatever means at all, the brig's yours with ribbons on it. And the other thing?"

"A word from you would straighten that all up, too. I want to see Horace Treadway's will probated and his estate settled, so that his cousin can get her just share of it and settle her debts here."

"Oho!" Now the eyes were opened very wide, and the hands on the coverlet moved a bit, and the admiral stirred under the sheets. "So now I know who you are, Captain! You're this young Yankee who set Maisie up in that house back on the Constant Spring road. Now don't stiffen! You can't even dream of calling me out. I'd only laugh at you. And I knew Maisie Treadway long before you ever met her. Tell me one thing, Captain. And stop being so uppish. After all, I've insulted better men than you—and will again, sir. Tell me: If you do your part of this bargain and I do mine, will Maisie Treadway use the money to take herself somewhere else? Could that be one of the terms?"

"Mistress Treadway," Adam said, "would be right happy to leave the colony."

"And the colony would sure be right happy to see her go. Very well. That's an agreement then, eh? Here's my hand on it."

"And mine, sir."

Two minutes later Admiral Benbow was telling an astonished sergeant of marines:

"Please escort this desperate character out. And see that he don't get hurt. I need him."

59 Not only was the sail painted black but sometimes, it seemed, so was the shore. Providence by ordinary was a light-colored island, humped with rolypoly hills but not in a proper sense mountainous, indeed little more than a glorified atoll. It had not been hard to pick up; but it was proving to be singularly hard to hold, on this night of no moon.

This was eight days after Adam had talked with the admiral, and he had been at sea virtually all of this time. John Benbow, when he made up his mind about anything, didn't dillydally. There was a real need for speed in this case anyway, he'd pointed out. The more time spent on preparations, the greater the chance that some spies from Providence would get wind of the scheme and send a fast sailing craft to warn van Bramm.

Adam had been careful. He had not even gone near Walter's saloon, the innocent-seeming pirate headquarters in Kingston. Except for the captain, nobody aboard the warship on which he sailed the very next morning after his talk with the admiral, knew who he was or where he was bound—or why.

The haste had another good feature. It shortened to a matter of minutes Adam's time for saying farewell to Maisie Treadway. He was grateful for this. It was hard for him to face Maisie now. It hurt him, inside.

"That sounds madness, Adam."

" 'Tis risky but not mad. There'll be no moon. I know the very beach where I'll land, the far side of the bay from the fort. From there it's only a short walk around to Sharpy Boardman's and you don't have to pass any other huts on the way. He's the one with the tops of his ears torn off. He'd do anything for me."

"And then what?"

"I don't know. But it shouldn't take long to find out."

"What if van Bramm hears you're coming?"

"He won't."

The skipper of the warship, too, voiced this concern: what if van Bramm had heard? Again Adam expressed assurance that van Bramm wouldn't. This was when they were swinging Adam's sloop overside, on a night of long dark rolling seas.

"They could've sailed circles around us. You know how it is in a convoy—you've got to stay back with the slowest vessel."

"He won't hear. He wouldn't believe it if he did."

"Never dreamed anybody'd be such a fool maybe," the skipper had muttered. "Well, good luck to you. Thank God all *I* have to worry about is hurricanes and the French and the Spaniards."

Adam made the last part of the outside trip as much as anything by ear, by the sound of breakers slamming against the rocks of the Point just below the fort. They'd be coming in big tonight, making a heap of noise. He couldn't see them.

Once inside the pass, however, things were quiet. No light showed. Vessels, clustered as though for protection, creaked and squealed as they rocked at anchor. Adam avoided them. His was an inconspicuous, small ratty craft. He might have been anybody from the settlement, fishing. Nevertheless he didn't care to be hailed. He had never seriously considered John Benbow's perhaps jocular suggestion that he grow a beard. Beards weren't fashionable, even on Providence, where one would stand only for slovenliness. Nor had Adam gone in for any sort of disguise. That would be sneaky, the way he looked at it.

He wore his sword, and he carried also a sheath knife. He had no other arms.

It was extremely dark, almost *malevolently* dark, with the sky showing not the smallest hint of dawn, when Adam rode the sloop ashore.

This was a desolate spot, albeit within the half-circle of the bay. The beach, shardy, was not deep. Palmetto scrub grew close to the shore, along a reaching ridge. Crabs scuttled clumsily for the sea. Each time a wave receded the little stones clicked anxiously together and the water gurgled, a throaty sound.

Adam hauled the boat in, dropped the sail, unstepped the mast. The tide was high.

He froze.

He had heard a sound above the soughing of the wind, the hiss and gurgle of water, the clack the stones made.

It was the sound of muffled laughter, a giggling, a snickering.

He looked up.

A skyline that had been all palmetto now showed jagged with men's heads. There must have been a dozen of them, rising in twos and threes, utterly black against the almost-black of the sky. They came toward Adam.

He drew.

A light showed suddenly. A man had unwrapped a lanthorn, and he held it high, and then Adam could see the fat greasy smiling face of Everard van Bramm.

"Welcome back, Captain."

The pirate ran the tip of a pink tongue lightly over his lower lip. His earrings, rubies and diamonds set in rings, swung on either side of his face.

"We have been waiting for you," he added, "for two nights and two days."

The men edged closer. He could not make out individual faces, nor indeed details of any sort, though he noted that there were muskets among them.

He touched the Book in his pocket.

"May I pray?" he asked.

"By all means pray, Captain."

Adam knelt, facing the men, the dim figures, and placed his sword on the sand before him.

He did not bring out the Book.

He prayed briefly, asking nothing for himself. He asked for Maisie, and for Deborah Selden, and Jethro Gardner, for little Lillian Bingham in London and her mother and father, the proprietors of the Hearth Cricket. He prayed, in fact, for quite a few folks. He said "Amen" aloud, and picked up his sword, and rose.

"Might we have that blade, please, Captain?"

"Why don't you come and get it?" Adam said.

PART TEN

◆

God and How to Get Water

60   This was where he was to die. He looked around. It was not much of an island—a blip, a blop, a nub of rotten rock and sere sun-scorched grass, merely a brown-and-yellow wart on the blue serene far-stretching surface of the sea.

It was his impulse, when he had waded ashore, to drop to his knees in prayer; but he resisted this, knowing that the men in the boat would take it as a sign of weakness. There was no slight trace of pity in the faces of those men, who, though they were impressed by the dignity of the occasion—for death deliberately dealt out is always dignified, even to such riffraff—remained stern. Captain Long had violated one of their few laws, so he merited their only punishment. He had gone on the account —hadn't Captain van Bramm assured them of this?—and then, immediately afterward, trusted, he had cut out the schooner, which was communal property. He had, that is, deserted. Worse, he had stolen. These men were thieves of the sea, who spent all their days stealing or seeking to steal; but perhaps for this reason they were horrified when one among them stole from the rest. They were infatuated with the notion that there is honor among outlaws.

Van Bramm had seen to it that the warmest of Adam's admirers, Sharpy Boardman and such, were at sea when Adam arrived. They had not been present at the trial, where Adam was heard in silence. Van Bramm's hold on these rascals was none too secure; but just at the moment van Bramm had been dramatically right. That Adam had killed Cark and badly wounded another man, before being brought down at long distance by realtas against which he couldn't possibly fight, told rather for than against him with the Providencers. But the fact that he had declared himself one of the Brethren of the Coast and then had cut out the schooner—this was unforgivable. He had been tried promptly, in a glinting bright dawn, and soon sentenced to be marooned. The pirates for once were efficient. Within a few hours of the time when he had so confidently stepped ashore on Providence he was being shoved aboard a barcolongo which presently put forth for this marine flyspeck of no name.

When he had asked if he couldn't at least retain his sheath knife, they told him no.

"You'd cut your wrists inside two days," they had said. "We want you to last longer than that."

They did allow him, however, to keep his Book. This was tight in a pocket of his coat when in a time of tawny sunset he waded ashore. He scorned to ask for further favors.

He did not wave and didn't even look back. Nobody shouted a good-bye.

Adam walked clear around the island, keeping to the shore. He might as well have crossed the center. It was much the same everywhere—sand and rubble, soft rock, chipped shell fragments, no trees. It was utterly dreary, bleak. The only vegetation was grass, and there was precious little of that. No birds flew overhead.

The island was roughly round and about a quarter-mile across. From almost any part of it you could see any other part. Similarly from almost any part of it, the center being only slightly higher than the shore, you could see if not immediately at least soon the sea in any direction. Nevertheless Adam determined that he would force himself to walk clear around the island like this at least four times each day, conscientiously checking the horizon.

"At least four times," he said aloud.

By the time he came back to where he had started from, the barcolongo was almost out of sight. He got down on his knees.

He prayed for a long time, and it was dark when he rose. He was already thirsty. He tried not to think about this. He made a pillow of his hat, snuggled out a soft sandy spot in which to rest his hip, closed his eyes, and after a while fell asleep.

He was astir before dawn, feeling chill, his clothes clammy. His thirst was urgent, and anything he did, any way he moved, seemed to make it worse. He walked slowly around the island. He had waited until first light in order to do this, but he seldom scanned the sea, which anyway was as bare as a baby's bottom; for the most part he regarded the rocks and sand.

These were sufficiently monotonous. The sand would make a good abrasive—but, to abrade what? The stone was soft, nothing flinty. The whole island indeed had about it a feeling of *softness,* of *chalkiness,* a feeling, too, of uncertainty, as though held above the surface by no sure shoring and likely at any moment to collapse, so that when Adam walked it he felt as more than once he'd felt in the boatyard when he walked a rickety structure of sticks, a set of scaffolding designed to endure only for a day. The very breeze, feeble though it was, seemed able to shake this key. The slow-paced wavelets, patient, unimpassioned, appeared to cause it to shiver.

He could find no stone sufficiently hard to give him any hope of using it, together with his belt buckle, to get a spark. The buckle, to be sure, was not steel but brass—it had been given to him by the Binghams of London and had been overlooked by the pirates—but it might be made to serve as steel if only a suitable flint could be found.

But the stuff underfoot might have been breadcrumbs. Cretaceous, it crumpled at a push of the thumb.

It was like this from the beginning. One of the first things he had told himself when dumped ashore—at first inwardly, later aloud—was that he would resolutely refrain from thinking of anything that would cause his heart to ache or even divert his mind from its proper channel. He had made a vow of it: *"I'll think only about God and how to get water."* Yet here he was already, striving to find not water but fire.

He retired to the middle of the island, where with steady fingernails he unwove part of his shirt, saving the threads in a small hollow box of rocks where they wouldn't blow away. He put a flat stone over this to keep out rain—if there should be any rain. He tore out some of the dry brittle juiceless grass which grew reluctantly here and there, in bunches, and put this, too, into the enclosure, weighting it with stones.

If he *did* manage to make a spark he wanted to be prepared with tinder.

After that he made another trip around the island, most of the time paddling in the shallows, stooped far over, searching for mussels or cockles or shrimps, finding none.

He scooped up some seaweed and carried this to the center of the island, where he laid it out to dry in the sun. Conceivably it, too, might be used as fuel. He wondered if he could eat it.

He prayed for a while and then tried to sleep, but he couldn't sleep.

The day was long. He was hungry, but so thirsty that he forgot his hunger. He didn't move about much. He soon came to see that the sun was going to prove perhaps his worst enemy here. He decided to try to sleep as much as possible in the daytime, prowling at night.

Since there was no scrap of shade, he was hot; and after a while, too, he was dizzy and felt sick to his stomach, which was not usual with him. He took off his clothes and waded into the water, hoping to soak some of it through his skin, at the same time cooling himself.

This gave him no relief; and indeed it made matters worse, for when the salt water dried, it left his skin itchy, so that he was forever twisting this way and that, and scratching himself.

To get his mind on something else he took to making a search for the hardest, most-nearly-flint stone available, and when he'd found one he squatted in the middle of the island, a fluffy pile of shirt threads before him, and chipped with the belt buckle.

Three times he got a small faint spick of a spark, but he could not ignite the threads. By using a page of the Book he might have been able to do this, but fire didn't mean that much to him. He wondered, truly, why he thought of fire at all. He was far from any sailing route and it could well be that the only persons who even knew of the existence of this island were the Providence pirates. *They* wouldn't rescue him unless either there was a revolution among them, in which victory went to the party headed by Adam's friends, or else Everard van Bramm, whether because of pressure or some bribe, officially called off the punishment. This latter possibility Adam considered even slighter than the former.

But there was perhaps a thousand-in-one chance of some lost sail stumbling within sight of this island, and if this should happen Adam wanted to be ready with a signal.

He worked for a long while, slowly, steadily, with vast patience, but without success. His hands became slippery with sweat.

He regarded the belt buckle. "You'd cut your wrists inside two days, we left you a knife," they had told him. But they hadn't noticed this buckle. The brass tongue, plunged into the neck at the proper place, could no doubt bring about a quick and comparatively painless death, albeit a messy one. But Adam did not consider *that,* either. He could see no profit in quitting before your time was up. And though he knew what some men said, Adam himself had always esteemed suicide a sin. God gave you your life and only God should take it away.

It was no use trying to sleep. He'd scratch. He'd twist.

If there's dew at sunup, he thought, d'ye suppose I could go around and lick it from the stones? D'ye suppose I could get some moisture that way?

"I doubt it," he answered himself aloud. "I'm not likely to be still alive by that time anyway."

His hunger, too, was a terrible thing. Once again he sloshed through the shallows, turning over stones, sticking his fingers everywhere, in search of any sort of edible matter, but found nothing. On dragging feet he returned to the middle of the island, and there he tried to eat some of the seaweed, first dry, then moistened a bit. He couldn't do it, couldn't even swallow the stuff, which caught angrily in his throat, while his mouth and nose were crammed with the sour smell of it, which clogged these like a noxious gas. He must have all but stifled himself to death, suffocated himself, in his efforts to swallow that seaweed; and at last he fell to hands and knees, shaking his head, retching—retching—while his body was racked with sobs.

"A fine way to go and meet your Creator," he told himself after a while, and he forced himself to get up and make one more trip around the island.

He was glad when the sun went down. He reckoned that this would be the last time he'd watch that happen, but he was glad all the same, for the sun had been merciless.

He went back to the center of the island, to that pathetic little well that contained the threads from his shirt, the least-soft stones, the belt buckle. He lay down.

It must be that he slept, after all; for when he was stung in the palm of an outflung hand he sat up suddenly, blinking, bewildered. It burned. But what could sting him here? What animals, what insects could there be?

He must seek them out. There might be a smitch of wetness in each. He must somehow catch them.

Then he was stung again in the same hand, and immediately afterward on his forehead, and on his chin.

The truth came: *It was raining!*

61 He sprang to his feet, flinging off his clothes. All around him beautiful luscious large wet drops of water were biffing the sand and rubble—and were instantly lost. He spread his clothes out so that no part of one article would overlap the other, and then threw himself on the ground, where he lay now on his back, now on his belly, but always, in moving, rolling to a fresh spot, so that he could squeeze the under side of his body as close as possible to whatever moisture the earth might have soaked up, while the upper side was being doused from above. He laughed and wept at the same time.

It was no more than a shower but it was a heavy one. Twice Adam wrung his clothes out above his gaping mouth; yet when the rain ceased they were blessedly soaked once more.

He rose. He felt wonderful, and was even singing.

He had been a fool for fussing with the possibilities of fire while ignoring the chance of rain. What he should have done was collect every shell and even every flat stone with any sort of concave surface, and have these ready, tilted toward Heaven, waiting. He would do this now. There still was precious water in his clothes, water that should be stored away before the sun rose.

The shower had scrubbed the sky but there was no moon, only starshine. Nevertheless Adam Long searched every square inch of that island, moving on hands and knees. He gathered more than thirty shells, a few of them little bigger than thimbles. He placed them in a series of circles around his "fireplace" in the middle of the island, where the boldest encroaching wave couldn't reach them.

By this time the sun was up, and he knew that his treasure would not keep unless it was somehow shaded. He squeezed the clothes out for the third time, catching the water, treating each pear-shaped prize with a solicitude virtually sacerdotal.

Afterward he put the damp clothes on, except his undershirt, and they felt good against his no-longer-itchy skin: they even stirred him to shiver a bit, at first.

He fetched a great deal of seaweed, which he laid out to dry. He uprooted more grass. Weaving now one of these materials and now the other, and sometimes the two together, he experimented with thatch. His undershirt was spread over the thickest of the muddle of shells-with-water, but it was by no means large enough, and anyway he sought a substitute, an alternate, for he told himself that no good mariner would set forth without at least one spare suit of sails.

His fingers soon were slippery with sweat, his back ached, and he was dizzy, swaying where he sat, sometimes missing a stroke entirely: he seemed to have lost all sense of distance. His stomach hurt, too, though surely there was nothing left in it either to bring up or to pass off.

After a while his hands began to shake, and he couldn't even see what he was working on. He put the flimsy thing down, and opened and shut his hands very hard several times. It did no good. Mumbling like a pig, sometimes sobbing a mite, he covered the filled shells. He remembered doing that. Afterward he must have collapsed: he must have toppled over like a drunkard, to lie still.

When he woke it was dark, and he was in the same place, probably in the same position, excruciatingly stiff, and even more hungry and thirsty than before.

He saw at once that his thatch mat had been blown away, exposing the shells, some of which had been tipped, while into others sand had drifted, sopping up the water. However, at least a dozen remained, and he drank the contents of two of these very slowly, carefully.

He rose, and began to go around the island again, seeking more grass and more seaweed.

". . . the night cometh, when no man can work more." What was that: John? Luke? It was one of the Gospels anyway. With Adam Long it was the other way 'round: when the *day* came, when the sun rose again, ferocious and triumphant, Adam, stunned by its heat, moved sluggishly when he moved at all. Only in the night could he work. Even then he doddered, unsure of himself, barely crawling from place to place, so that he must have looked like an old, old man, if there had been anybody to see him.

This was the time of dreams, whether day or night. There were hours on end when he was not sure whether he slept or was awake, indeed when he wasn't even sure he was not dead—and didn't care. Never morbid, yet sometimes he had thought about death, as every man should. He had pondered chiefly the *physical* aspects of it, wondering what the *sensation* would be. When you died would you instantly have a different feeling, no limbs, no skin, but be a soaring soul that could not collide with anything, couldn't bump? Would you shoot upward, making for Heaven with a speed that would have killed a living person? As you neared the Judgment Seat—horizontally? rising?—would there be a great roaring in your ears and would your face be flayed by a terrible light? Maybe it wouldn't be anything like that at all? Maybe you'd simply, quietly, without any movement, realize that you were *there*? Adam did not know. All he knew was that if death was anything like what he was now, it was a most uncomfortable state to be in; and in fact he wished fervently that if he was alive he'd die, whereas if he was dead it would change. In all solemnity he would rather take his changes in the everlasting Place of Punishment than go on this way.

Again and again he crept to the sea and submerged himself, permitting the brine to dry on his body afterward. It never gave him any relief, but still he did it.

A couple of times, when he could not contain himself, he tried to swallow sea water. Each time he brought it up, violently, and retched for a long while afterward, which weakened him even further.

He worked as much as he could, mostly at night. He made the center of the island his headquarters, and with his bare hands scooped out a sort of crater there, the walls some three feet high. This would keep his fire—if he ever got a fire—from being wuffed out in the first breeze. It gave him a little later shade in the morning, a little earlier shade in the afternoon. He also continued his efforts to weave some sort of blanket or hat or cover, but these were flimsy objects at best and not to be relied upon.

It dismayed him to learn that he could seldom read from the Book. He had counted upon the Book to be a substantial support in his last hours; and a feeling of warm delight, almost of bliss, had flooded him when the pirates conceded him this possession. But now he found that at night, even when the moon was out, he could not read without a great watering of the eyes, something that had never happened to him before, and which blurred his vision, smearing the words; whereas in the daytime the glare of the sun was so fierce that it caused his head to feel as though something was bounding and thumping around inside of it, and when he looked at the Book it seemed far, far away, held by hands that could not possibly be his, as though he was looking at it and at the hands through the wrong end of a spyglass. He had this same eerie feeling when he tried to weave grass and strands of seaweed in the daytime: he could see his hands 'way down there, and watch the fingers move clumsily, but they didn't seem to bear any relation to Adam Long himself. At another time this would have given him the creeps, this unnatural sensation. Now it only saddened him. He shook his head. He did read from the Book anyway, but it wasn't really reading, rather holding the thing there and looking down toward it with his eyes half closed, while he murmured and mumbled verse after verse that he knew by heart.

The dreams were not horrible. They didn't soothe; and indeed many seemed downright silly; but at least they didn't scare him. They were about Newport.

Before there was a tavern in that town some of the men had used to sit around out at Gibson's mill, and talk about things—talk gravely and slowly, their voices increased in volume in order to be heard over the sound of the turning stones, but not high-pitched—while, whenever he found a chance, the Duchess' brat, unnoticed in a corner, listened. Adam could hear the swish of water, the rumble-bumble of the stones, the grain's slow crunch, and through it all the voices of the serious men of Newport, seriously stating their views: he could hear these more clearly than he heard the slap of waves on the shore—even when he opened his eyes to peer once more at a wobbly horizon, he could hear the sounds and he could smell the dry clean smells and feel the coolness of Gibson's mill.

There was a place where some of the men had built a plank bridge over Pittasquawk Creek, and sometimes when he was on an errand out that way, carrying or fetching something for Mr. Sedgewick, the Long boy had used to nip under this bridge for a little while. There wasn't much room, and he'd sit with his knees scrounched up underneath his chin, not doing anything, not fishing, or even thinking, just sitting there. No matter how warm the day, it had always been cool under the Pittasquawk bridge. Sunlight slipping between the planks used to lie in strips across the satin surface of the water, which otherwise was dark—though not so dark that you couldn't see into its depths. Adam used to stare at the smooth small shiny stones down there, and at a frog which, submerged, would stare soberly back at him. The frog had such sticky-out eyes that they looked as if they might break off and go rolling away. It never moved, unless an oxcart went over the bridge, setting up a great banging of the planks and causing dust to sift down through the slits and onto the water. This always frightened the frog, which disappeared. It used to frighten the Long boy, too, but he'd stay where he was all the same; and after a while the echoes would die, the dust would be carried languidly away, the strips of sunlight on the surface of the water would straighten themselves, and the frog, reassured, would come back and would sit down again and would stare long and seriously at Adam Long, who'd stare back. It was better than fishing, any day.

This was the sort of dream he'd dream, if dreaming it was.

There was always coolness in it, often snow. For instance, when he'd seem to see again the men filing into the meeting house for town meeting, it was always in wintertime and there was snow on the ground. He could hear them scrape it from their boots over the wooden scrapers or kick it off against the end of the steps. He'd remember, too, how he used to scratch his initials and pictures into the rime of a windowpane—not so much the appearance of these scratchings as the sound his nail made and the *feel* of the writing clear up his forearm. He'd used to try to tramp out his initials, "A.L.," on the grass of a frosty morning, too. That never worked well, but it did make a delightful clinky crinkly sound under his feet. And what in this world gives more glee and satisfaction than the writing of your initials into snow with your own steaming urine at night? He didn't have any "i" to dot, as some of the kids did. Or else Adam would remember, and vividly, how on the way home from school afternoons when there was snow they would dare one another to "make an angel" by falling backward into a drift with arms outspread.

Sometimes he was asleep while things like this sauntered smoke-like through his mind, and sometimes he might have been awake. When you were dying anyway it didn't make much difference.

62 It could have been on the third night, more likely it was the fourth, that he heard the sound.

He was lying on his back, arms folded over his breast, while he studied the starry sweep of Heaven. Now and then he would close his eyes, then open them again, groggily amazed that he was still alive. He hoped that it wouldn't rain, since rain might keep him breathing for hours longer, conceivably even for another day; and he didn't want that. He was ready to die now. He truly hoped that it would be tonight, and believed it would. He didn't want to see the sun rise again. He hated the sun.

The sound changed everything. He sat up. He wouldn't have supposed a minute before that he'd be able to sit up again. His heart beat fast.

It was a scrapy sound, underlaid by a tinkle of tiny pebbles being batted together, the whole suggesting that a heavy object was being dragged in a slow and furtive manner across the beach. It was steady: it did not stop and start.

He could not see what caused it, for the sound came from one of the few stretches of beach not visible from his headquarters here in the center of the island; but it was not far away.

The sea all around was completely clear, it was blank. But he could still hear that sound.

He crept toward it. He peered over the top of a small dune—just in time to see something low but very wide and ponderous plop into the water and disappear.

The Devil? It was his first thought, of course, but he quickly discarded it. Everybody knew that the Evil One had a fondness for appearance in the guise of something that retreats, thus luring his humanly inquisitive victim toward him. Nor did Adam think himself so pure that he was impervious to the Devil. What he had done with Elnathan Evans remained on his conscience, for instance, as did indeed, though to a lesser extent, since it was different here, what he had done with Maisie. He was not prepared, the way a man ought to be, to meet his Maker. But he was as much prepared as he *could* be, now.

No, it wasn't arrogance but just the opposite quality, that of humbleness, which caused Adam to dismiss the thought that the Devil might be pursuing him. That the Duchess' brat should be at heart veritably humble was a notion many a Newporter would have larded with scorn, for in Newport they esteemed him a cocky lad. Yet it was the truth that Adam Long did not think himself of sufficient importance to attract such a personage as the Prince of Darkness to an out-of-the-way place. He knew that in the eyes of God one immortal soul is equal to another, any other; and because he was a man he had a soul, howsoever battered it might be. He knew, too, that Satan or any of Satan's more reputable minions could travel astounding distances in almost no time at all, moved of course by magic. But even then he didn't believe that he was about to be tempted. The Devil had better things to do—or, to put it another way, worse things.

A boat? He had perhaps wildly hoped this, for a split-second. But a boat doesn't slip quietly out of sight into the sea.

A log seemed most likely; and if that's what it had been he ought to get down there and be ready to catch it when it was rolled up on shore again. But it did not come back. There was no break in the water except what the little waves made. A log would—

Suddenly it flashed upon Adam what he had seen.

A turtle!

They come big in those waters, some of them a quarter of a ton, and to anybody's taste they're a delicacy. Adam had eaten green turtle many times at Providence, where it and buccan, smoked beef, were favored food. He knew nothing about how they were caught or how butchered, but he did know that there was a great deal of meat in a turtle. There would be a great deal of blood, too.

The thought of that blood must have dizzied him even beyond his ordinary state of confusion, for he squatted there staring at the place where the turtle had disappeared for many minutes before he began to ask himself why it had come out of the sea in the first place. Well, he had heard that the female turtle goes ashore only to lay her eggs, which she buries in the sand. Eggs! Slavering, shaking like a man with a fever, he crept down to the beach. But though he crawled for hours, his face close to the sand, peering, squinting, sniffing like a dog that seeks a buried bone, he could find no trace of eggs or a nest.

The moon rose, but Adam didn't rely on his eyesight. He dug with his hands. Again and again he ran sand and stones through his fingers. He divided that whole section of the beach into imaginary squares, and riffled each, and patted it. He enlarged his field. Having been over it once, he went over it again. His fingers cut, his eyes watering, he sobbed —but he continued to search. The dreams were gone now. He scrabbled.

Even when the sun came back, he did not cease to work. He didn't even go to the center of the island for his hat, a carelessness that was his undoing. He never truly quit that task. He simply became aware, after a while, that he was no longer working and was in fact lying flat. His head was a turmoil of pain. If he'd had anything to be sick with, he would have been violently sick; as it was, his innards hurt like fire. All his muscles ached, all his bones and joints. He rolled over—it took mighty near all of his strength—and learned that the sun his enemy was low.

He wanted to give up. He wanted just to close his eyes and relax, drifting into death the way they say a man does when he freezes.

He didn't. Somehow he struggled to his knees again, and somehow went back and forth over the beach, setting it to rights, filling holes he had made, smoothing the surface, straightening the sand, tidying. There wasn't any nest. That turtle somehow had been scared away. It might come back tonight. Do turtles smell? They certainly see. This one, if it returned, must note no change.

Each movement an exquisite agony, Adam dragged himself to the leeward end of this beach, where he lay on his belly, placing sharp stones under his chin in an effort to keep himself from relaxing. He watched the beach. He watched— He didn't stir, but just lay there looking along that beach, striving to keep his eyes open. He did not think of anything save those eyes. He believed that his pain was too acute to let him sleep,

254

and his one problem, as he saw it, was to face the beach and keep his eyes from closing.

Time can do curious things; and pain, too, is a trickster. Adam might have fallen asleep in the conventional sense, or he might have been brushed by a wave of unconsciousness, as he had been that morning when he suffered the sunstroke. When next he became aware of anything at all it was not of opening his eyes—as far as he could tell he had never closed them—but of the brightness of the beach. The moon was up, the breeze had fallen. And ten feet away, looking right at him, was the biggest turtle he had ever seen.

What he had thought the previous night when he'd glimpsed the monster slipping back into the sea might well have returned to him now, for there was much that was diabolical in the appearance of this turtle; but it didn't.

The head was low, about on a level with Adam's own, and flat on top though jowly beneath, made up of leathery triangles, and it was extraordinarily wide when you looked right at it, as Adam was doing: it must have been fully a foot across. Though the rest of the beast was the color of mud, the feet and even more the head were scaly, shimmering, iridescent. The tip of the snout was a black shiny pinpoint, very sharp. The mouth, all floppy with folds at the corners, was hooked back in a grin of unspeakable malice. Most compelling were the eyes, small but extremely bright, hard, feline, like the mouth unadulterated evil, in the moonlight glittering sometimes green but sometimes a bright light red.

The turtle did not move. Conceivably it was as astonished to see Adam as Adam was to see it.

Adam felt a tingling all along his body and down his legs. Would he be able to spring up? Would he be able even to *get* up?

The turtle moved one paw. Adam heaved himself to his feet. The whole world rocked like a tippy canoe and he put his arms out right and left to balance himself. The turtle turned, and started for the water. Adam somehow ran after it.

The beast was amazingly fast. At any other time its retreat would have been ludicrous; it was heavy, clumsy, yet it could cover the ground.

It was within a few feet of the water's edge when Adam stooped and caught it under the plastron, or lower shell. He heaved, all his muscles shrieking in pain.

Jaws that could nip a man's hand off clacked loudly. A flipper struck Adam's wrists: it was like being hit with a sack of wet sand. He dropped the turtle, which immediately started for the water again. Adam got to it barely in time. He caught it further forward this try, about in the middle. He lifted.

Thrashing, the turtle tipped up. Its weight forced Adam to his knees. He got a better grip. His temples were pounding, ears and eyeballs, too. He drew a deep breath. If he didn't make it this time he was dead. He rose, inch by slow inch, while blackness, roaring, swam toward him.

The turtle went over. Adam dropped to the sand.

After a while, when some of his breath was back, Adam looked sideways. The turtle, like Adam himself, was on its back, all its flippers going furiously, while the tip of its bright shiny black nose, upside-down, was no more than inches from the edge of the sea. It couldn't cover those inches: it was helpless. There was rage in its breathing, a deep tubular sound. Grotesquely, all the time it grinned. It glared at Adam, who watched it for a long while.

At last the flippers ceased to work, though the green-sometimes-red eyes were lit still with unabated fury.

"I'm sorry," Adam said in a quiet voice, meaning it. "I reckon it had to be you or me and naturally I'd rather it was you."

The turtle glared.

Adam was thinking of that blood. He sat up, and slowly took off his belt. With his thumb he felt the tolerably sharp tip of the buckle's tongue.

"It's going to be almighty hard," he said sadly to the turtle. "I hope I don't hurt you too much."

When they rescued Captain Long, some four weeks later, about the only things left of that turtle were the carapace, the upper shell, which was inverted and in the bottom of which a few gills of rain-water yet remained, while over it as protection against the sun the gummy lower shell was set. The head, the feet, all the bones, had been sucked and gnawed until there was no taste of sustenance left on them, and very little shape. The intestines had been eaten. There was no blood left, not even a stain. Everything had been licked, again and again.

They had to carry Captain Long to the boat, and later they had to carry him ashore at Providence to Sharpy Boardman's tent. But he was conscious; and they did tell him that the pardon order had been issued by Everard van Bramm himself. Because of Captain Long's condition they did not tell him what the price of that order had been. When he learned the price he wished they had left him on the island to die.

PART ELEVEN

◆

Vengeance Is Mine

63 The way they fussed about him, it was funny. Each of these ruffians had a price on his head and was an avowed outlaw; yet to see them as they clucked and puttered around Sharpy Boardman's tent—tiptoeing ponderously here and there, forefingers raised—you could think of nothing but a barnyardful of ruffled fat old hens.

Adam Long did not laugh. At first he was too weak, in mind and body alike; and on the fifth day he saw something that made him believe he would never laugh again.

From time to time he asked them about van Bramm. What did the scoundrel seek? Why had he thrown a fit of forgiveness? The whole thing hinged on whether Adam had agreed to join the Brethren of the Coast before he slipped away, and since van Bramm had already taken one side, a side so much to his advantage, and since there were no witnesses save Adam himself to gainsay him, why should he switch? He might have supposed, as most of them had, that Captain Long already was dead; but even *then* where would be the profit in fetching back the corpse of a man whose friends were his, van Bramm's, most dangerous enemies? Everard van B. was no fool. He must have been paid to do what he did. What had the price been?

They evaded the question so querulously put. They were forthright men ordinarily, blunt, and not given to delicacy of feeling; yet they waxed embarrassed and strove to change the subject whenever Adam asked who had paid, and with what, for his return. Nor could Adam persist, angry though he was. He hadn't the strength.

Once when he thought that he was dying—more definitely and immediately, indeed, than he had ever thought this while on the key—he begged them to take him to Tarpaulin Hall, so that he could look again at the place where he and his love had been happy. They side-stepped this request, turning their heads away, mumbling something. He raged, or tried to, in a voice he couldn't raise above a whisper. It was useless. They pretended that they did not understand; and after a while he fell back, sobbing.

Again, clearer, though still pitifully weak, he demanded that Mistress Treadway be notified that he was alive. They could surely get word to her through Walter's. He was very earnest about this, sitting up and staring hard at them. They nodded, averting their heads. They muttered that the lady would learn, sure.

In all other matters they were attentiveness itself, fairly fawning upon him. He was never alone. They crowded into the tent, plaguing his self-appointed nurses with requests to be allowed to speak to him, even just to look at him. He was a hero, no doubt of it. He was the man who, in a vessel of his own designing, and with one of his booms a jury at that, had given them the chanciest chase in the history of the settlement; who had killed Major Kellsen; who had lordily instructed Captain van Bramm to wait; who'd slipped away under the fire of the fort's cannon, only to return alone of his own free will; and who, finally, had survived for more than a month an ordeal that would have killed any other man inside of three days. The makings of a myth were here; and the pirates of Providence, always childishly fascinated by miracles, took up the tale with avidity.

It came out soon enough what they wanted of him. Here was his revolt, ready-made. Hatred of van Bramm had reached a new high. Those pirates who had been sent on a trumped-up mission in order that they might be absent when their friend Captain Long was tried, back now, resented this; and they and others sought somebody who would lead them against the chief. The colony indeed seethed with dissatisfaction. Its financial affairs were not going well. Booty there was, but truly useful supplies were scarce. There were fewer women, fewer merchants. The buyers and sellers were clearing up their books and on one excuse or another sailing away. *They* were the ones who caused the camp to function. The complaint of the corsairs themselves, who didn't understand matters economic, was that van Bramm, the dirty whoreson, was snatching too big a share of the spoils. This, they thought, explained everything. And the logical way to cure this was to kill van Bramm.

The man, however, would take some killing. He wasn't an ant you could step on. The disaffected, having seen him in action, were not *afraid* of their chief, but they were wary. They wished to be sure of themselves—sure, that is, that they were properly led—before they started. One misstep was all you were allowed on Providence.

Adam shook a groggy head, refusing to discuss this subject. It scarcely made sense to him, the way he was.

Here was no fever, yet it was like fever. His body was not hot, he didn't sweat, but things were blurred in his vision, having a tendency to seem very far away, or, less often, startlingly close at hand. Voices reached him as though from a great distance. He was incredibly weak. They had to feed him with a spoon.

The morning of the fifth day he woke with an uneasy conviction that somebody had just been bending over him. Men were moving about, the usual ones. They were silent, and it seemed to Adam that they were furtive, avoiding his eyes. He sat up. He could actually *smell* something! And what he smelled, he swore, was Maisie Treadway.

He sank back. Of course this was only his imagination, which had been playing strange tricks of late. It was no more than another touch, if a singularly cruel one, of the fever-that-wasn't-a-fever. It would be no use to speak to Boardman or any of the rest about what, for a little while there, he'd thought he smelled. It made no sense. Tarnation! Love ain't a toilet water! Anyway, they had all been hush-up on the subject of Maisie. Whenever he mentioned her they would turn the talk to something else.

He was stronger and clearer-headed this morning, he thought; yet that feeling of uneasiness persisted.

The camp was curiously quiet.

"Open the flap," he commanded.

Sharpy Boardman complied without a word, and he and Frenchy Foureau, his tentmate, lugged Adam's cot to the entrance.

Ordinarily, even at this hour, the lane would be crowded. Now there was nobody in sight. The sun was fully up but not yet warm—otherwise he wouldn't have ventured to loll in it like this—and the dew was disappearing, to leave dust. Not even a mongrel gave movement to the scene; yet Adam sensed that behind tarpaulins and tent flaps men were watching, waiting. For what?

Adam turned. Boardman was just behind him; Foureau on the other side, near. They, too, were expecting something. They scarcely breathed.

This tent was the unofficial headquarters of an unofficial plot, and as such it was suspect by the orthodox. Doubtless somebody watched it, night and day, though Adam could see nobody now.

No, there was somebody! Far down near the beach a person in yellow had appeared. Gay colors were commonplace on Providence, but this was a remarkable yellow even here.

A woman? Yes. He saw now that it was a woman, and that there were men behind her.

He sat up. He peered, his heart beating fast.

It was more than just a woman—*it was Maisie!*

He might have shouted something. He must have tried to rise, for he became aware that Foureau and Boardman were holding him from behind, one grasping each elbow.

Was he raving? Had he gone mad entirely? He closed his eyes. Gasping, he kept them closed for a full two minutes.

When he opened them, Maisie was only fifteen or twenty feet away, still coming toward him. She was a vision of frills and furbelows, and her glorious hair was piled higher than ever and surmounted by a rickety but magnificent *commode*. There were rings on her fingers, where diamonds sparkled, and around her neck was a triple string of pearls. Her lips were painted, and there was rouge on her cheeks, patches, too, on her chin. She was laughing.

Adam sat motionless, fascinated, a rabbit before a snake.

He had previously noticed that Maisie was not alone, but he saw now that in addition to the men who trailed her, men who carried cocked pistols, there was a man on whose arm she leaned. She was talking to this man, whose earrings glittered, whose bald head shone in the sun, this squat, toadlike Everard van Bramm.

The monster squeezed her arm tight in his, and she smiled at him.

"There's nothing you can do, it's all over now," Sharpy Boardman whispered. "It's the bargain she made."

The Honorable Maisie de Lynn Treadway-Paul saw Captain Long, and she beamed at him. Captain van Bramm bowed.

Adam just looked at them.

"There's nothing you can do— She heard about the marooning somehow, and she got in touch with us through Walter's."

"She— She set the price herself," Foureau whispered.

The men with the pistols were watching Adam. They walked slowly. Here was a prearranged event, a dramatic demonstration of who owned the English lady, as formal as a court masque and easier to understand.

"She wouldn't take off her clothes for him till she'd seen you alive. She was here last night. She— She kissed you."

Adam said nothing.

The couple passed. Van Bramm took his arm away from hers and gave her a small possessive pat on the rump. She stiffened, and her step faltered; but soon she had her smile back in place, and she took his arm again, and they walked on.

The lane was quiet once more. The sun was out in full now.

"There's nothing you can do—"

"*Stop saying there's nothing I can do!*"

He swung his legs over the side of the cot.

"I want everybody who's on our side called here right now."

"Where are we going, Captain?"

"We're going to call on Everard van Bramm."

64 They persuaded him that he couldn't possibly mix it with van Bramm right now. Why, he could scarcely stand, much less swing a sword! He nodded in glum agreement. Shaken though he was, and infuriated, he wasn't blind.

At the same time his announcement was as dramatic as the midnight ringing of a bell. In minutes it was all over camp.

That very night it was reported to Adam that the fort stood empty, the cannon untended. He did not smile.

"Tell him, 'Thank you, I'm staying.' "

The next night and the next the pass was left open, and there were many to take advantage of this; but these were traders and pimps and the like: none of the Long faction left.

The fourth morning, early, a keg of gunpowder blew Sharpy Boardman's tent to smithereens, leaving, when the dust and the clitter-clatter of pebbles had settled, a great gaping crater.

Of course it *might* have been an accident. Many of the pirates, deserters from some navy or other, were opposed to any manner of discipline, while most of the others were slipshod in their habits anyway. There were frequent fires. The wonder was that this town of boards and canvas had not long ago been wiped out.

The explosion shredded the tent beyond repair but did no harm to any person. Adam and Sharpy and the Frenchman Foureau had reckoned that van Bramm would try some such trick; and though they made Sharpy's tent their daytime headquarters they were sleeping in another part of the camp.

The camp in fact was rather two camps now. Already it was largely deserted. Not more than a hundred men remained; and no women at all —excepting, unseen, Maisie.

It had apparently been van Bramm's original intention to parade his purchase, and that daily. Was this pure vanity? Or he might have calculated that the possession of Maisie would lend him the semblance of added strength, as any item of prestige does, for after all she was not only expensive and spectacular but in her person she represented a triumph over the redoubtable Captain Long. Or it could be that he thought to shame Adam off the island with displays too hard for him to endure. Conceivably, again, all three of these thoughts might have found lodgment in van Bramm's reasoning.

Nevertheless, after that first stroll past the recumbent Captain Long, and one small additional saunter the following morning, van Bramm kept his prize indoors. Nothing whatever was heard from her, whose seclusion must have been positively Oriental. The chief's shack was scarcely more pretentious than any of the others in this shabby place, and there were no windows at which the lady might from time to time be glimpsed. None but the most trusted van Bramm followers were permitted to get anywhere near that particular shack, which was down on the beach, next to the warehouse.

It was simply not safe for van Bramm and his doxie to be abroad, even with bodyguards. His trick had backfired. It did not enhance his own importance in the eyes of the others or degrade Adam Long to laughing-stock status. It had had indeed almost the opposite effect. Many men who had vacillated before now plumped with the rebels. The sight of The Smiler paddling and pawing his purchase had been too much.

A hush that was like the hush of death descended upon the colony. The marketplace, once a hubbub, stood empty save for an occasional crablike, sideways-looking figure, who scurried. There was no life on the beach. Not many men passed along the lanes, and when they did they gave one another leery looks, their hands on the handles of their knives. The fort was deserted, the cannoneers, all van Bramm men, having been called in to guard the chief's residence and the adjoining warehouse. As it happened, no new sail appeared; and none of those men who elected to remain would even have agreed to discuss a foray out into the Bahama Channel. There was a general agreement that this matter of leadership had to be settled. No shots were fired; nor were many faces punched or slashed, not as many as usual. The men were saving their savagery, storing it.

Adam and his friends were busy all day interviewing candidates, checking weapons, making and extracting promises. They were not yet ready to move upon van Bramm's house with their detailed demands.

No word came from that building, not even a sign that might guide the followers of the chief. Van Bramm the spider, the lurker in corners, had never been one for public appearances; but formerly had been heard from, directly or otherwise, every day. Now there was only silence. Could it be that he was so entoiled in the treasure he'd acquired, so busy in a bed strewn with stolen silks, also with bought flesh, that he didn't care? At any rate he remained mum.

Strength was flowing back into Adam's body. He ate voraciously, slept hard. He was on his feet all day, moving about the camp. The only time he'd stand still was when he was studying van Bramm's house. That building, whether by chance or design, stood alone; no other was near it—excepting the warehouse. The beach was wide and straight at this point, offering no cover in the form of rocks, dunes, vegetation. To the right was the warehouse, a low, long, heavy building of timber, the solidest structure on the island. On the other two sides the camp was comparatively clear, the ground flat and hard. Not even a tent stood close to the van Bramm shack, a building that bore so marked a resemblance to Tarpaulin Hall as to bring tears to Adam's eyes.

When he watched this house, Adam tried to be in some inconspicuous place. This was not from fear of being shot at, but rather because he did not want his own men to see him in what might be thought a posture of weakness, eating his heart out for his lost love. The fight was to be theirs, truly, not his: he was no more than the agent for bringing it to a head. His grief was real, but it could be decent. He didn't seek to dramatize it.

He strove to think only of the military aspect of this matter, how to stage an attack; and not to think of Maisie at all; but of course this was impossible. There were times when the black hot thoughts that surged within him while he watched that house choked him and blurred his vision, so that he had to turn away, keeping his face averted in order that nobody should see his eyes.

When you were a leader, you were not supposed to be human. You must never show a weakness of any sort. This was lonely work.

Early on the morning of the fourteenth day after Adam had been brought back from the key, when the sky was not yet streaked with dawn, though the stars were bright, he was awakened by the sound of musketry; and when he tumbled off his cot and reached for cutlass and pistols, colliding with Sharpy in the darkness, he knew that this was the signal: the battle was about to begin.

It was easy to find the fight; nor was it worth the trouble to learn what had caused it. Nobody was dead. Two men had been hit, but not badly. There was a great deal of excitement, many bitter threats. The shooting had ceased. A barricade consisting chiefly of sandbags and rum barrels had been thrown up in a lane just below the marketplace, and from over the top of this the warehouse and van Bramm's hut stood stark in the starlight, no guards being visible. The seething fury of Adam's men and the silence and lack of action around the chief's house were ominously juxtaposed. This thing had gone too far. Something would have to break. Should they attack now, or wait until daylight?

Adam coaxed a large number of them back to the marketplace, where torches bobbed. Two cannons were there, brought down from the fort with great toil. It was true that van Bramm had the only expert gunners, true, too, that he controlled most of the gunpowder, which was stored in the warehouse. Additionally, all the balls in the fort had been rolled down the slope and into the bay, from which they could only have been salvaged with a great effort, requiring much time. Nevertheless these cannons could be made to perform, after a fashion. Gunpowder could be collected from here and there—they'd need a lot of it: was this van Bramm's purpose in abandoning the cannons?—and nails, chunks of bullet lead, and even stones, could be pressed into service for a load. Adam was opposed to the use of the cannons. He had pointed out that too obviously van Bramm *wished* them used, which in itself ought to make the men wary. The truth was he feared that Maisie would be hurt; but he did not dare to admit this aloud.

Now he harangued the pirates. He'd supposed that he had no knack for this, certainly he'd had no experience; yet they listened, their faces upturned, earrings gleaming in the red light of torches.

Not to urge the men on but rather to hold them back was Adam's purpose. Far from being a firebrand, he tried to emulate the iceberg, being cold, crushing.

An attack might be repulsed. A siege was not to be considered. Even with a disciplined force it would have been difficult, for van Bramm had access to a dozen well-stocked vessels which could only be cut out one by one at night, and undoubtedly he had made other preparations for a siege. With these excited men it was unthinkable.

Adam had an alternative. He'd been thinking about this for several days.

"Charge? Don't be fools! Can't you see that's just what Old Baldy *wants* us to do? Are you going to play his game for him?"

Somebody yelled: "He'll get away!"

"He won't get away," Adam said quickly. "He'd wanted to get away he could have done it long ago. Sneaked off at night."

"How d'ye know he hasn't?"

Here was a stumper. Adam, for the first time faced with this thought, grew cold all over. No notable vessel, no large one, had departed without careful preliminary scrutiny for the past week, before which time, however, a good many had sailed with decamping merchants. Van Bramm might have slid away in one of the smaller boats, just himself and Maisie. Or again he might have smuggled her and himself off more than a week ago—neither had been seen in that time.

Adam shook his head. He simply refused to believe it.

"Look—he ain't gone. And he ain't *going,* either! It'll be over my dead body if he does—and I mean just exactly that!"

This brought cheers; but still the men were twitchy.

Adam pointed to a paling sky.

"It'll be light soon. Now what I say is that as soon as it's light enough we hang out a white flag and demand a parley."

Boos for this, hisses. Adam raised both arms.

"Wait! I'll carry that flag myself, and what I'll insist on is that van

Bramm come out and meet me in the middle of that clear space in front his house. We'll have guns or swords or knives—or just our bare hands—I don't care. But he won't dare say no."

Now here was a proposal the pirates liked. It would be a show, sure. And it might well end in a free-for-all anyway.

There was only one dissenting voice: "What happens if *he* kills *you?*"

"That," said Adam Long, "is for you to worry about."

Word came up from the barricade that a white flag had been hung out of van Bramm's door.

"Good," cried Adam. "I'll carry ours. Here, give it to me."

To this, however, they objected. They cried that this might be a trick to get Adam to expose himself. Adam scoffed. But even he was won over when Sharpy Boardman pointed out that he couldn't carry his own challenge: it would not be regular.

"You're going to fight, you can't arrange it yourself. You got to do it like a gentleman."

Adam nodded slowly.

"*I'll* carry the bloody thing," said Boardman.

He was the oldest and after Adam, the best liked. He was less excitable than many, though he hated van Bramm with the most vehement of them. Adam looked into his seamed, rough face.

"Well, you know our terms, Sharpy. Nothing less."

"Nothing less."

They were down by the barricade now. Sharpy hoisted the flag, a square of exquisitely embroidered French linen nailed to a spar. Though certainly it could be seen from the van Bramm shack, there was no sound of acknowledgement.

"Any weapons or none. But it's to be to the death."

"To the death."

Holding the flag high above his head, Sharpy Boardman climbed a barrel to the top of the barricade.

There was a terrific burst of musketry. Sharpy spun completely around, as if he'd been hit by a club, and fell right back to the place he'd just quitted, by Adam's side. He landed on his back.

Adam looked down at him. The lower jaw was broken and hung crazily awry. Another ball had smashed the left cheekbone. The body, hit in six or seven places, was just beginning to bleed, the blood rising sluggishly, soaking the coat.

"So there's our answer," muttered Adam.

He drew.

"*Well, come on, ye beefwits! D'ye want to live forever?*"

He sprang over the barricade.

65 No lead met him. He could hear his own feet strike the hard earth as he ran. He didn't know whether anybody was following.

They'd blasted at the first man who showed himself, and now they were frantically reloading—pouring the powder, ramming the cut bullets home, stuffing in the wads, priming.

It is always good to learn that your enemy's a fool.

Adam ran on.

There was a sound like that of two boards being clapped together from his right—that is, from the warehouse—and then there was another. Something touched him on the top of his right shoulder.

He heard a shout behind him. Now they were coming! There was a good deal of that clapping sound. Adam reached the door of the shack.

This was a real door, but it was not a good one, not strong. Adam had no doubt that he could smash it, but he didn't know what to do when he *had*. They'd be in the dark, in there, while he would be framed against the drizzle of dawn.

He threw himself upon the door, and so flimsy was it that he thought for a moment that it would go slamming in, himself on top. He backed away. He kicked it twice, hard. The second kick tore the hinges out, but it also caused Adam to stagger back. He caught himself. He faced an open space now, a rectangle of blackness.

What he did then he did without thinking. He *dived* in head-first—leaving his feet, flinging himself full-length.

There was a great shattering explosion that seemed to take place right on top of his head, and then he was on the floor scrabbling among the legs of stools and tables he couldn't see. Something slished the air close to his face—a knife? a saber?—and he rolled away from that. He'd worked his own sheath knife out.

Rolling, he struck somebody's legs. He threw both arms around these, and the man fell hard, cursing. Perhaps because the breath had been knocked out of him, he didn't start to struggle; but Adam took no chances, and used his knife several times.

He got to his knees, then to his feet.

Through the doorway he could see his men coming now. They were about halfway from the barricade. That's how fast everything had happened.

Then he found himself on hands and knees again. It was curious.

266

He didn't know he'd been hit, yet it seemed unlikely that he had fainted.

He could have lost consciousness only for a second. When he looked up again, the men were bursting through the doorway.

Something fell on him.

Next thing he knew was smoke. It stung his eyes and scraped his throat. It prickled the inside of his nose. Shaking his head, weeping, he started for the doorway.

"There's another one of the rats!"

"No, no!" he cried.

"My God, it's Captain Long!"

They hauled him out, forbearing to carry him lest they lose too much time. Near the door he bumped a corpse. It was like two tenders, moored side by side, bumping in the wash of a vessel that had passed nearby. The corpse had no weapon. Its face was all blood and blackened flesh. Its pockets had been turned inside-out.

Down the beach a little, out of musketshot, they paused to survey the situation. Foureau gave Adam a few gulps of rum, which helped.

The sparks rose straight and swift, in a fixed column, to a point about twenty feet above the van Bramm shack, and there they broke ranks to swoop and swing inland with the joyous abandon of children bursting out of school. The flames crackled and spat.

Van Bramm and his followers must have taken refuge in the warehouse. This was not an unexpected move, the warehouse being a structure firmly built of real timber, the only one of its sort on the island. The surprise lay in the fact that they had not clung to the shack, if only for comfort's sake, at least for a while, keeping the warehouse as a last resort. Instead, van Bramm appeared to have left no more than a forlorn hope in the shack, thinking perhaps to enfilade the attackers from the shelter of the warehouse, if the first charge was broken, but making sure all the same that arrangements to fire the smaller building were complete.

There had only been four men in that shack, Foureau averred. They were still there.

"You're sure they're dead?"

"They're dead all right."

The transfer to the bigger, stronger building had been made at night, of course, in order that it should not be observed and taken as a sign of weakness. With the shack leveled, there would be no cover from behind which to attack the warehouse.

"Change of wind," somebody muttered, "and the big un'd go, too."

Well, that was not likely. These were the trades. The thought, however, rendered them a dab grim. The warehouse was anything but fireproof. It boasted the only non-canvas roof on Providence, but that roof was made of cedar shingles, which would go up like paper. The warehouse, too, contained the colony's magazine, which was not sheathed in metal. There were three tons of gunpowder in that magazine.

They watched the fire, not knowing what to do next. Only a little further down the beach—there wasn't room between the two buildings to work even a small battering-ram—was the door of the warehouse. This was the only door, and there were no windows.

The sparks leapt straight, and broke, and went rollicking across the island. There was a great deal of smoke. One wall of the blazing shack fell in, then another. The sparks were redoubled.

"We could make out to try to force the door and then one man slip around back and toss a torch up on the roof," Foureau said slowly, thoughtfully. "*That*'d flush 'em!"

Adam's blood ran cold at the thought; but the pirates seized the suggestion with whoops of delight. It was the sort of thing that appealed to them—bold, noisy, spectacular, superlatively stupid, and cruel. Each could picture in his imagination the van Bramm men rushing out of the warehouse—for they wouldn't dare stay there when it was afire—and one by one getting picked off. It would be a grand sight, and sport. Clamorous, they were for starting this; but Adam rose.

"Ye fools! Where would you get the timber for another building like that? It'd use up in one big poof nine-tenths of the gunpowder on this island, so how could you go adventuring again—or even put up a fight if some Navy ship comes along?"

It swayed them. They wavered.

"What's more," Adam pursued, "it would ruin most of the treasure. That's *yours*. You've all got shares in it, you've worked for it and fought for it. And maybe there's a lot more than you think? Who's been checking van Bramm's accounts all these months?"

This told. Indeed it was of the very marrow of the matter; for complaints that van Bramm was not giving a proper accounting of the loot, that he had illegally allocated large portions of it for his own personal use, were the cause of the unrest in the first place.

"Blow that building up," Adam warned them, "and you'll never find out how rich you once was!"

They mumbled and muttered in acquiescence. But Foureau moved among them, waving his arms. The big Frenchman was angry. He'd tasted power, and he didn't like to see his lovely plan punctured.

"All right, all right! But answer me this, Captain: What *are* you going to do then? They got rum and food in there enough to last a month. Are we going to just sit here on our arses?"

"Sure not," said Adam. "We'll smash in. There's that mast they ain't stepped back into the *Marty*. It'd make a first-rate ram."

"But there's no room to go to that door with it, without you go right through the fire!"

"All right then, we'll go right through the fire." Adam pointed to the blazing shack. Another wall had just fallen in. Tarry materials were burning and there was more smoke than ever. "They won't expect us. They can't see us coming." He faced the men again. "Well, what's the trouble? You're not afraid of a little fire, are you?"

66 It was like Hell. There were few high-tossing tongues of flame left, but thousands of little ones licked and leapt around their feet, darting here and there, blue, purple, bright pink. There was a great deal of smoke. As they charged through the still-burning ruins of the shack they kicked up a prodigious number of sparks, which jumped at them, or seemed to, stinging faces and exposed hands. The men had submerged themselves, clothes and all, in the waters of the bay; and when the sparks spat up they hissed as though in rage, sending forth steam. Despite this precaution, several of the men caught fire.

They burst through the shack yelling like Indians, and with no pause went right at the door of the warehouse. It might have been made of bamboo, the way it splintered. They scarcely felt the shock.

They dropped the mast and stormed inside.

Adam Long was the first. In the sudden gloom of the warehouse, after the brightness of the fire, unable for a moment to see anything at all, he dropped to one knee, ducked his head, drew his cutlass.

There was almost no musket fire. The defenders scarcely had a chance to draw their steel. Many backed away at the first onrush, and a few turned and fled—whether to get weapons, to secrete their own shares of the booty, or simply in fright, was not clear.

Adam saw a huge dark blurred figure coming at him. He rose, raising his blade. The man turned and ran deeper into the warehouse, possibly because he had seen others back of Adam. Adam ran after him, not so much in pursuit as because he believed that it would be deeper in this building that Everard van Bramm and van Bramm's prisoner would be found. He did not know what he sought—an inner office perhaps, a curtained-off sanctorum. There would be something like that.

Without windows, the warehouse got its light in part from slits and broken places in the walls and ceiling, through which sunlight slanted in thin eager bright planes, and also, now, from the violated doorway which opened upon the fire, making everything around it a jumpy red. That crimson light shone, too, on uplifted swords and upon the faces of men who cried for quarter or else cursed. Though the defenders had not had their guns ready they had apparently been about to see to this chore; or perhaps they had been preparing to assemble grenades; at any rate, the floor was scattered here with a few grains of gunpowder, there with a whole pile of it, while spillings, strips, went every-which-way. These caught fire, possibly from flaming bits of clothing, and in a moment were helter-skeltering about, running in crazy spurts, darting, stopping, swerving, swaying: they might have been so many incandescent imps whirling and cavorting in diabolical glee.

Adam, however, had turned his back upon these pyrotechnics. He was running between high-stacked sacks of sugar, twisting in and out among piles of tapestries, altar clothes, crisscrossed crucifixes, and all manner of half-seen silverware. He bumped with a knee a small brass-bound box atop a chest, and it fell to the floor, coins cascading from it. Rounding a corner, he kicked another, smaller box. Pearls—large and small, egg-shaped, pear-shaped, oblong, round; pink pearls and gray ones, brown, ivory, dead white—went clinking and clattering in all directions, so that they crunched under his feet as he ran.

Now all around him the feuds these fools had been having flared up. The invaders, braced for a bitter battle, had been monstrously triumphant almost from the beginning; and the release was heady. Few of the defenders at first stood to fight it out. Most ran, ratlike, for some unseen cover. Bellowing, remembering old grudges, Adam's men tore after them. In obscure corners there were squeals, there were scufflings, sometimes a scream, where men were being killed.

Adam tripped over something, thought it moved, wheeled upon it with raised blade. No, Seth Selden was still—and would be so forever. His head had been hacked half off: the neck was a slobber of blood, flesh, windpipe. Cynically, having no preference, Seth had elected to remain loyal to van Bramm—with this result. Adam Long had never loved the little man, but after all he did come from Newport, he was Deborah's uncle. Seth's eyes were uprolled, so that the pupils could not be seen. His lips, parted, were twisted not as though in pain but rather as though in a sneer. Likely enough he had been saying something sarcastic, something bawdy, at the instant he was killed.

The noise was deafening. Men were shouting that the building was afire, that the magazine would soon go up; and a few scampered out; but most, certainly, lingered to slake their lust for slaughter, or, a little later, when they saw it, for treasure. If they gave over the chase it was not because they were gorged with blood but rather because they were greedy. Seeing the glitter of gold, they forgot about gore; and they loaded their arms with plunder from many a forgotten ship, and staggered outside—only to return in a little while for more.

The roof caught up. It made a high crisp spitty sound; and burning bits of it began to fall, tumbling like autumn leaves, trailing smoke.

Adam ran around a pile of coats, wigs, swordbelts, and silk sashes—and collided with Everard van Bramm.

Each had been running, and it knocked the breath out of them. Van Bramm was the first to recover. Stripped to the waist, as Adam had first seen him, he showed the more naked because of his bald head, which gleamed now in the light of the flames. In his right fist he gripped a cutlass. He was of course smiling. He stank of sweat and French perfume.

What Adam had expected this man to do he couldn't have said; but certainly it was anything but what van Bramm *did* do. He turned and ran.

Adam ran after him. It wasn't far. Still another door was slammed in Adam's face, a latch was thrown; but this was a flimsy affair, the portal of a rickety thin inside partition, a small house or hut, jerry-built, within the warehouse. Adam could see it clearly now, for the fire was spreading.

Adam didn't favor this with his cutlass. Instead he seized the nearest article at hand—a large branch of candlesticks, silver, heavy. The first two blows splintered the top panels. The third shattered the bolt. The door flew open.

Van Bramm had been bending over something on a bed, not ten feet away. He had a pistol in his hand, and he was turning this toward Adam.

Here it comes, thought Adam.

Then he saw that there was smoke languidly rising from the muzzle. He saw, too, that the thing on the bed was Maisie—or had been.

There was a smell of gunpowder in the room. Van Bramm had just fired, a discharge Adam hadn't heard in the noise he himself was making on the door.

"*If I can't have her,*" van Bramm screamed, "*nobody else will!*"

He threw the smoking pistol at Adam's face. He snatched up his cutlass, and charged.

Adam had to drop the branch and seize up his own cutlass, which lay just outside the door. He retreated, doing this.

Van Bramm went right after him.

Not until they were both outside the inner partition did Adam Long make his stand. His pulses throbbed; and he felt like singing. *I'm going to kill this man,* he told himself.

The Dutchman had the arms of a gorilla, so that his reach was as long as Adam's. He sweated a lot but never seemed to breathe hard. He smiled all the while.

He held his guard high, his arm stiff, as in German *schlaeger* play; and his wrist must have been wonderfully strong. He did not move much, but his eyes were cat-keen, his stance firm.

I'm going to kill him, Adam thought again; and he went in.

He stepped back an instant later with the knowledge that something exceptional would be needed to get past that guard. Three times Adam had struck, and they were fast cuts. Three times he'd been countered; and once there was a riposte that Adam believed—though he could move it around and he felt no pain there—had laid open his left shoulder. Van Bramm did not appear to have stirred. He never made an unnecessary motion.

Adam went in next time low, only half-lunging, feinting. Van Bramm at first did not respond; but when the heavy cutlass did move it was with lightning speed, and it struck Adam's blade clangorously and high, all but slamming it out of Adam's grasp. Startled, scared, Adam retreated. Van Bramm went right after him.

Adam, whose own guard was high now, made him pay for this temerity with a slash that traveled down van Bramm's right cheek from ear to chin—a thin red line at first, and then the line thickened and bulged as blood rose, and at last a large soft wet flap of skin fell feebly outward, thereafter to flump there like a dewlap. Van Bramm paid it no mind. But he backed a bit.

Adam did not immediately pursue. The two stood staring at one another, each tense, alert, his hilt held high.

Then both jumped at once. There wasn't the bat of an eyelash difference in the time. They might have been released by the same spring.

For the rest of the fight, a matter of seconds, neither gave an inch. Neither dared to. They were strong men and they fought hard. Bits of burning shingle, trailing smoke, drifted down all around them, and the roar of flames filled the warehouse.

The end came when Adam Long, stooping even lower, caught a down-cut low, and rose with his parry, thrusting. This sent his point right at the Dutchman's face. He held his blade palm-up, as if it had been a rapier. He drove down, with all his might.

The steel entered van Bramm's slightly open mouth, and Adam could feel it cracking off the front teeth; he could feel it smash into the back of the skull. It came out the other side a little.

Van Bramm made no sound, not so much as a gurgle, though blood welled up at his mouth and ran rapidly down over his chin. He went backward, arms outspread; and he fell thumpily, jerkily, carrying the cutlass with him, wrenching it right out of Adam's hand.

It took Adam some time to work that cutlass loose. He had to step on Everard van Bramm's face in order to do this.

Maisie was motionless and might have been dead. Her eyes were closed. Her face, unrouged, was horribly pale beneath the turbulent splendor of her hair. Her lips, too, had no color.

She wore a green silk wrapper, an Oriental thing embroidered with gold thread. He lifted her carefully.

Part of the roof fell in.

Bumping looters, who cursed him, he carried her outside. He put her down on the beach.

The hole was blackened by powder around its edges, a close-up shot. He took out his knife and cut away part of the wrapper. Maisie wore nothing underneath this, and the familiar flesh of her belly stunned him like a blow, so that he almost swooned.

"I'm going to die, ain't I, Adam?"

She was looking at him. She was trying to move; perhaps she couldn't. She could not see the wound he had exposed.

Adam looked at it; then he looked down the beach; he swallowed; and "Yes" he answered.

He held her close.

"I— I'm sorry I hurt you, Adam," she whispered once.

"You couldn't help it. No more'n I could."

"I want to be buried in England. You must get me there."

He promised. She told him the place, in the country, near where she had been born, and he repeated the name several times to make sure he had it right. They were both businesslike here. Then he took her in his arms again and she shut her eyes. She did not try to talk.

The pirates, maddened, scurried in and out of the warehouse, a mass of flames now, and every time one came out he carried an armful of loot. Revenge was forgotten, and danger, too. All they could think of was to pile high the gold and silver.

When the building at last did blow up, in the middle of the morning, it carried at least twenty of these grasping, hurrying men with it, and so great was the blast that for a full thirty seconds afterward bits and scraps of wood and stone and metal were falling into the sea and onto the sand as far off as where Adam lay with his love.

Maisie died about twenty minutes after that.

PART TWELVE

He Kept His Course

67 "I asked a direct question," Adam said. "I'm entitled to a direct answer."

The Earl of Tillinghast sighed. He was tired. He was a thin man, tall, with a skin like old ivory; and tiredness, you guessed, was his accustomed condition. Unlike so many aristocrats, he looked aristocratic. If there ever had been evil in him it was long since burnt out; but on the other hand there was nothing in his appearance to hint of *positive* goodness: his lordship showed rather as one who had outlived both of those attributes, and who, willing to die, perhaps even eager to, yet went on living—and doing his duty. He looked as though he hadn't got excited in years. He showed no resentment at the way Adam had burst in upon him, and even waved back a couple of footmen who offered, though not eagerly, to throw Adam out. His hands were marvelously thin and pale, the bones shining through the skin like the ribs of a delicate fan.

"You come from the American colonies?" he asked.

"Now how in the world did you know that?" Adam cried.

Slightly smiling, his lordship looked out the window. Adam, despite himself, did the same; and the sight caught at his throat. Spring had come early to Tillinghast, and loveliness lay over the fields like a lingering snow. Each tree and stile and hedgerow, every meandering lane, homely in itself perhaps, contributed to the *serenity* of the scene, as relieving to the soul as the blended greens and yellows were soothing to the eye of Adam, a man whose life of late had been pretty much all turmoil. Less than ever, since he'd seen something of the English countryside, could Adam understand why anybody would live in London. Not that he would care to live out here either! It was a shade *too* quiet! But he couldn't think of a better place to be buried in. If they were to lay you to rest here, the world would wag its way over your head pretty much as it had always done, he reckoned; and that might be a comfort to know.

True, there was no *majesty* in the prospect, any more than there was in that breathlessly beautiful little grove where the day before yesterday, under a weeping willow tree, he had witnessed the interment of Maisie de Lynn Treadway-Paul. No, no majesty; but there was peace. These places lacked harsh corners and they were not subject to sudden shifts of light, so that they imposed no strain upon you. Even his grief at the grave had not been keen, as he'd expected, but gentle; he only wept quietly, upright; and he endured for fifteen minutes the old sexton's fret-fussing about the way Maisie's remains had been shipped, before he broke in to demand how otherwise the man expected to move a corpse five thousand miles.

Yes, it was the countryside, which brought about dreams without slumber, rubbing all roughness away. Adam who had been in the tropics had never known anything as soporific as this.

But he hadn't come all the way out here, and paid all that horse hire, to admire the scenery. He cleared his throat.

"I asked you a question. I want an answer."

Lord Tillinghast nodded gravely. Though a man who had spent much of his life abroad, engaged in the honorable business of lying for his country, when he spoke it was not in the candied accents of the diplomat. He was unexpectedly straightforward. His voice, though not raised, carried conviction.

"The answer is 'No.' I am not your father."

He rose. Not glancing at his guest, he went to the window, where he stood, bathed in what in those parts passed for sunlight.

"I hope that whatever reason you may have to suspect me, you'll do nothing about it. I hope this for your own sake, Captain. Believe me, you would only make yourself appear ridiculous.

"I am not your father. I'm not anybody's father. I can't be. It, ah, it pains me to talk about this, and I shan't go into details, but you're entitled to know, Captain, that many years ago, before I inherited the title, a serving maid accused me of paternity. I denied this, but the case came to court. *I* would have settled it quietly, but my father insisted that I fight it out. He feared that half the female servants in the house, even half the women in the village, might start bringing suits if Maybelle was successful with hers. Well, I put up an unanswerable defense. Three distinguished physicians testified that they had examined me and that for reasons which they went into at great length—right there in open court— they were sure that I could not ever father a child. Oh, I won my case! And no doubt it was all very amusing—for everybody except me. I became a byword. Doggerel was written about me, songs were sung. In every taproom for fifty miles around you were bound to hear somebody or other tell some version or other of the story of how the Earl of Tillinghast lost his manhood. It was a boyhood accident, Captain, and sufficiently gruesome. But they didn't know that—wouldn't have cared if they did. They made up fantastic stories. For all I know, they still do.

That's why I've spent so little of my time at my seat, though I dearly love this part of the country. But it doesn't really hurt any more now. When you get as old as I am, Captain, nothing hurts very much. So I've come back."

Standing there at the window, slightly stooped, his hands behind his back, his head bowed, he suggested a saint.

"Now I don't remember your mother. But I can only guess—and I mean this with all respect, Captain—I can only guess that perhaps she named me as your father for purposes of *defiance*. Maybe that was her answer to a world that had mistreated her. For you understand, Captain, that in these parts to say a child is the son or daughter of the Earl of Tillinghast is the equivalent of saying that you refuse to name the father. Or if somebody *else* says that, then it's with a sneer. In the old days when a wench got into trouble they used to giggle and say that it must have been the fairies that brought that baby. Nowadays, around here, they say that it must have been the Earl."

Adam wetted his lips.

"You mean, it's a—a sort of joke?"

"Yes, it's a—joke."

Adam rose, patting his back his cuffs, straightening his sword belt. He picked up his tricorne. He bowed.

"You have been extremely kind, sir. Permit me to avow to you that I'm obliged from the bottom of my heart. I sure am."

"Won't you stay a bit, Captain? Have a glass of wine? Or perhaps a cup of this tea they bring all the way from China?"

"Thank you, no, sir. I'm about to start for home."

"Ah? And where is your home, Captain?"

"Newport, sir. In the Colony of Rhode Island."

68 Under a rat-gray sky the seas were all chuff and spit; and it looked as if a spell of weather was making up; so Adam, though he would have admired to stage a gam, ordered full canvas kept on and no recognition of the pinkie, the fishing boat they had sighted.

The latter, however, refused to be snubbed. She yawed wildly, all but fouling *Goodwill's* rudder, and the two men aboard of her set up such a shouting and mad windmilling of their arms that Adam at last fell off. The pinkie came alongside.

"What in tarnation's the matter?" he grumped.

He knew both men, Newport men, who of course had recognized the schooner; but he had never before seen them like this, jibbering, jabbering, waving their hands. Abe Moore and Henry Pearson certainly weren't drunk; nor were they in distress—their boat was tight, their faces full. Yet they hopped about like kids who have to go to the head.

A sudden fear flooded Adam.

"Say, nothing's happened to Deborah Selden, has there?"

They stared at him. They couldn't know about that letter he had written to Deborah from London, sending it on ahead. They were not to guess that he had opened his heart, pleading for forgiveness, saying, almost in so many words, that if she'd still have him he would be proud and happy to make her his wife; nor could Henry and Abe know that Adam had been fretting inwardly, worried as he was that Deborah would decide against union with so soiled a sailor.

"What's *she* got to do with it?"

"To do with *what?*" Adam said.

They looked around. Everybody was topside—and close at hand.

"Maybe we better go below," muttered Henry.

Mr. Holyoake, recently promoted from bosun, rubbered out his lower lip and caught it between fingers and let it plop back.

"You reckon he's scared?" a hand asked.

Mr. Holyoake shook an indignant head.

"He don't scare easy, that man."

Nevertheless the new mate knew that something was wrong. For some time now the skipper had been looking not morose exactly, nor even sad, but—well, *somber.* He'd looked that way all through the run. Lately, the last few days, he had been twitchety—for him.

"Couldn't find a better cabin mate," Mr. Holyoake more than once told the hands. "Thoughtful. Tidy, too. *I* don't think he's worried about anything. I think it's just that he misses that Mr. Forbes, the man whose job I got, and maybe Bond and young Rellison, too."

An added consideration, Mr. Holyoake had pointed out, might be that hogshead lashed on the afterdeck during the pull up from the islands and unloaded with such care in London. It'd held rum all right—you could hear the gurgle—but it'd held more than that.

"A woman, from what they tell me. A beautiful red-headed woman. *He* never told me that. But he used to stand by the binnacle there, hour after hour, with his head a little to one side like as if he was listening to something."

A queer way, somebody had commented, to be moving a woman.

Whereupon Mr. Holyoake had snapped in a tone very similar to the tone Adam himself used on that scandalized sexton in the lovely little glade under the willows:

"How else you going to carry her five thousand miles, when she happens to be dead?"

Adam in fact was not depressed. The burying of Maisie had saddened him, but it was a sort of sweet sadness, a gentle melancholy. More sobering, though this, too, was in the nature of a relief from pain and strain, was the news of his birth. He had always assumed that he was a bastard but now he knew that he was only an *ordinary* bastard, and maybe this was better? No dead man's hands fastened themselves upon him now. He didn't have anything to live up to, except what he'd done for himself. He could join his fellow men on terms of equality.

True, the westward passage had been a lonely one. He had missed Resolved Forbes—John Bond and Abel Rellison, too, but most of all Forbes—more than he might have expected. He and that ascetic assistant would maybe not swap ten words a week, all through the months they had shared the tiny cabin together; yet it had been good, a sound feeling, to know that Resolved Forbes was on watch. They'd communicated to one another largely by means of grunts; but each had understood.

Adam's vanity was not pricked by the departure of these three. He didn't blame them. The China run was a long one but profitable, and they'd got themselves good berths. Resolved Forbes could look forward to the time when he might become a skipper.

"And you know I'd never be that here, sir. Not unless you was to drop dead."

Adam had grinned.

"Can't blame me, can you?"

"No, sir," Resolved Forbes had said, "I can't."

Adam had given the three of them his blessing, not to mention an extra month's pay. This was at the Hearth Cricket.

"You're all fools," Hal Bingham had cried. "Any man that goes to sea, if he don't have to, 's a fool." He had filled Adam's mug, touched Adam's shoulder. "Whyn't you stay in Lunnon, Captain? With what you know, being an agent for friends back in the colonies, and watching the lists at Lloyd's and all—why, you could make your fortune."

Adam had shaken his head.

"I've got to get home."

On the way down to the dock, after that party, he had been brushed aside by chairmen. He no longer turned to snarl at such treatment; and it was only by chance that he had looked up and seen the occupant of the chair, who, his eyes half closed, sniffed a gold-filigree pomander in order to protect his nose from the stench of the city. Sir Jervis Johnston, who did not see Adam, looked much the same, still determinedly languid. He was doubtless bound for Clark's; or was there some new place now?

No, Captain Long was not, properly speaking, depressed. It could even be said, for all his seeming thoughtfulness, that there was joy in him. He was looking forward to Newport. For the first time in his life he was eager to get back. Yet he was worried. Did they still dislike him? How would he be greeted? Reports of his doings in the islands must have reached Newport by now, and Adam did have a disreputable background. Would Deborah Selden care to take such a man? And how would she refuse him—openly, so that everybody could see, in public? Or by means of a cold curt note?

Here was not the Captain Long they'd called the Duchess' brat, that swaggerer. Here was a frightened man. His facial features, his backbone, were rigid; but he was all jelly inside.

The behavior of Henry Pearson and Abe Moore did nothing to soothe him. In the cabin he produced rum. He paused a proper moment, then asked again what in thunderation was the matter.

Abe looked at the deck. Henry looked at the bottle.

"I wouldn't go back to Newport at all, Cap'n, if I was you," Henry said at last.

"Why not, man?"

"There's a royal warrant out for you. Minute you step ashore you'll be arrested."

"Arrested? For what?"

"Piracy."

69 Adam shook his head, a patient man.
      "I was never a pirate."

"Didn't say you was," Henry mumbled.

"Royal commissioners in town," Abe Moore said. "They're after the charter. And they got a good argument to take to London—if they can hang you."

"*Hang* me?" Adam started to laugh, but stopped. "They can't do that," he said firmly. "What kind of proof could they have?"

His visitors did not know. All they knew was that Newport had been in a hubbub when they departed, four days ago. They were sure that there was a warrant, that Boston men were in town, and that the customs house was agog with activity. Somebody, they didn't guess who, had collected affidavits down in the islands and presented these to the Crown—affidavits to show that Captain Long after his escape from the pirate colony at Providence had deliberately returned to that infamous place.

Sleep with dogs, they say, and you'll get up with fleas.

"That may be true, but it don't make me a pirate. Anyway I can prove I had an arrangement with—"

He stopped. Suddenly he had remembered something it was always hard to believe—that the frosty blue eyes of John Benbow no longer would glare at anybody anywhere. Those eyes had been closed in death, indeed, while Adam was marooned.

Oh, Adam had taken the precaution to frame an agreement with the admiral; but this, too, was gone. It was in London that Adam had learned of its fate. Some years back Port Royal had been largely destroyed by an earthquake—it was because of this that Kingston had been built on safer if less comfortable land across the bay—and now what was left of the town had been wiped out by fire. Back in the days of Henry Morgan, before the scum of the Antilles had betaken themselves to Providence island, Port Royal had been *the* hell hole. Pious folks said that the 'quake and now the fire were evidence of God's wrath. Be that as it may—and Adam hadn't thought on it enough yet to form an opinion—the fire had certainly destroyed all the papers in the Navy archives at Port Royal, among them the only copy of the Benbow-Long agreement.

Still Adam shook his head. He knew now who had gone to all the trouble and expense of getting those affidavits. Since witnesses were likely to be elsewhere in the world at the time of trial, admiralty cases were conducted in large part by means of depositions. Adam knew this. He knew, too, that by the judicious expenditure of money a man in Newport, if he had the right mercantile connections in the sugar islands, could collect such affidavits in regard to Captain Long. Such a man must hate or fear Captain Long very much. He may or may not have learned that Captain Long sometimes slept with his wife; but surely he had taken fright when Captain Long like a fool had let slip a reference to his knowledge of who was Thomas Hart's agent in Newport. This man, this bleak, slabsided stander-on-one-leg, understandably alarmed, fearful for his fortune, had sold out his interest in Captain Long's vessel, which might conceivably be seized in connection with the admiralty proceedings. Sure. Sure.

Another thought came to Adam now. Was this accusation and the ordeal it would mean a punishment for his sin with Elnathan? He had many times felt uneasy about that affair. And to say the least of it, it was not pleasant to reflect that Elnathan lived directly across the street from the girl he hoped to marry.

"Guilt by association don't count," he asserted flatly.

"Maybe it does when Colonel Dudley himself picks the jury."

"They got to have at least one specific accusation. You can't hang a man because he calls certain rascals by their first name."

"All we know is what we heard before we set out fishing. There was something about a brig. French. They said you seized her and killed the crew and brought her in as a derelict."

Adam laughed, relieved. He reached across Henry Pearson and snicked open the secret panel he'd long ago built in the bulkhead. He was tolerably sure that nobody else knew of the existence of this panel and of the small compartment beyond. He had done a good job of it, afterward removing every trace of the work. It was conceivable that one of the helmsmen might have peered down through the hatch and seen him open this slide and examine the *Quatre Moulins* affidavits; but it wasn't likely. Open a thing like that too often and it shows signs of wear. Adam hadn't touched it in months.

"Comes to that, I got affidavits of my own," he said.

He sprung the slide. He reached into the compartment.

It was empty.

Adam sat down on a bunk and stared at his hand as if something had bitten it and it was bleeding.

He was remembering Mr. Macgregor's extraordinary search of the schooner. But—no. If Mr. Macgregor, told of the hiding place, had taken the affidavits there would be no warrant. Adam always trusted his own judgment of men; and he believed that Mr. Macgregor, though admittedly a customs agent, was honest.

On the other hand, if in some manner Zephary Evans had got possession of those papers—

"There's witnesses," he muttered.

But—who? Maisie was dead, Seth Selden was dead. Waters and Peterson were outlaws, whose testimony, even if obtainable, would count for nothing. John Bond and the boy Rellison and Resolved Forbes, Chinabound, might be gone two, three, even four years.

"Jeth Gardner was here then. Nobody in Newport's going to doubt the word of Jeth Gardner."

"Jury won't come from Newport. This ain't colonial, this is admiralty. Only reason Dudley wants to try you in Newport is because he wants to scare us. But he won't take any chances with the jury."

All the same, nobody from anywhere, even Boston, could question Jeth Gardner.

Henry Pearson took a drink. Abe Moore was looking at the deck.

"Adam, I hate to tell you this but Jethro Gardner suffered another stroke last week. He ain't going to testify for or against anybody. He can't write. He can't talk. He can't even recognize you when you put your face right in front of him."

"Oh— I'm sorry to hear that."

"We all were, Adam."

But there had been another one aboard of *Goodwill* at that time.

Let's see now— Aye! That runty Londoner, the one who whined, the Navy deserter he had rescued from a press gang in Kingston.

"In that case," said Adam, "I would demand that Willis Beach be summoned as a witness in my behalf."

They stared in astonishment.

"Why, man, Beach is a crown witness! Why, he's the whole crown case! He's the man who's bringing the charge of piracy against you!"

70 In the drizzle of dawn they picked up Sachuest Point, and a little later they could make out Cormorant Rock and Coggeshall's and the whole southern part of the island.

Captain Long had not changed his course by one foot as a result of the news the fishermen brought. Even if Deborah Selden hadn't existed, he would have headed straight for Newport. That was his town, for better or for worse. If the folks there disliked and distrusted him so much that they would believe what was said about him by the little Londoner Willis Beach—who obviously had been threatened with a return to the Navy and was willing to sing any song the Queen's commissioners called for—then that was just too bad. He wasn't going to try to tell himself that he didn't care. He did care. He was heartsick about it. But he kept his course.

They had been seen. *Goodwill's* rig was unmistakable. They were being watched. Horsemen rode back from the beach and over the folded hills toward town, rode along the shore, too, and the crowds on foot grew throughout the morning. Past Brenton's Reef, past Graves Point, and all along the east shore of the passage going up into the bay a mass of humanity moved evenly with the schooner.

"Going to be quite a welcome," Captain Long muttered. "Reckon I better put on my red coat."

When they came into sight of the town he used his glass to pick up the Selden house, but he couldn't see Deborah.

Now the crowd was enormous, more people than Adam had supposed to be in the whole danged colony. The town was black with them—and not just along the waterfront but up the hill past the pump, past the new tavern on the road to the tannery, all up Jew Street, too, clear as far as the cemetery.

He put away the glass.

"I'll go ashore first thing," he told Mr. Holyoake.

"Aye, aye, sir."

The gig was smart now, varnished. Adam sat in the sternsheets, his hands on his knees, his chin held high. Must have been a thousand pairs of eyes watching him, he reflected. Morbid curiosity? They wanted to witness the arrest of a man who might be hanged? Or was it more personal, so many folks having waited so long for a chance to see the Duchess' brat get his comeuppance.

He kept himself cold. He did not try to pick individuals out of the crowd, for that might suggest that he was nervous. He wouldn't give 'em the satisfaction. The faces were a blur to him.

Nor would he avoid or evade anything. He'd land at the Wharf and make directly for the customs house, as he had always done.

He stepped ashore, straightened, looked up.

The crowd burst into a cheer.

They were wild with enthusiasm. The town, the whole bay, rang with their shouts. Hats were thrown. Barrel tops were beaten. Women waved kerchiefs. There were even a few muskets fired off.

An instant after Adam had straightened himself to glower at his enemies he learned that they were in fact his friends. He was surrounded by men who thumped his shoulders, pummelled his back, sought out his hands, babbled glad greetings. He had all he could do to keep his footing and was nearly congratulated off the end of the Wharf.

The tale was quickly told. The town had never been shocked. What Captain Long did when he was down in the sugar islands was Captain Long's business, the way Newport figured it. But the invasion of Stiff Necks from Boston, the periwigs, the pomposity, were resented. And when it was learned that a warrant had actually been made out—which would mean a trial, probably an expensive one, too—folks began to bubble and boil. It was clear that the whole crown case hung on the story told by Willis Beach, a man not much liked in the first place. So men went to Willis Beach. They got there just before the crown marshals, who had decided to put Beach in jail for safe keeping. They told the little man to move away.

"You mean," cried Adam, "that more than one man did this?"

"More than one! Must've been half the town did it! The Dudley men put him in jail anyway, but he broke out. He headed west, and I don't suppose he hauled up till he hit Hartford, if then. That was three days ago and I shouldn't be surprised if he was running yet."

"All this talking makes me thirsty," somebody said.

At Blake's the rum flowed like water, with everybody waving his jack and shouting a welcome. Nor was Adam expected to pay for these drinks: they wouldn't even let him pay for his own.

The disappearance of Beach blew the case sky-high, of course. The warrant might still exist but it would never be served. The charter was safe. The Dudley forces had been routed. Even Zeph Evans, a stubborn man, had decamped—two days ago, taking his wife and all his goods with him, he had boarded a coaster for New York.

Somehow Obadiah Selden got to Adam and backed him into a corner.

"I'm proud of you, my boy! Proud of you! We all are!"

Adam swallowed.

"I, uh, I sent a letter to Miss Deborah—"

"I know."

"Maybe it's too bad I did that. She'd not be likely to want somebody that's been in a—well, a sort of disgrace like this."

Obadiah laid a hand on his arm. Close though they were, they had to shout at one another in that hubbub.

"Adam, she told me three days ago, when things were at their worst, she told me she wanted you no matter what happened."

"She did? She said that?"

"She did. I warned her it looked mighty black—as it did, right then—and I said she wouldn't want to marry a man who might be hanged right afterward. And you know what she said to that, Adam?"

"What?"

"She said, 'I'd rather be Adam Long's widow than anybody else's wife.'"

Somebody turned Obadiah around. A few of the men were asking him if he couldn't persuade Captain Long to stand up on the Adventurers' Table and make a speech.

"I'll try," he said, and turned back.

But Adam wasn't there any longer. Adam was outside, running up the hill to the Selden house.

For supper there was to be turkey and brook trout and injun-and-molasses and a pie made out of rhubarb. Obadiah Selden and his favorite skipper had flip beforehand.

"'Bout the dowry." Obadiah harrumphed seriously, dipped his nose into his mug, gazed at the mug for some time, harrumphed again. "Surprised *you* didn't bring that up."

"I guess I'm surprised myself. Never even thought of it."

"Not like you, Captain."

"No, it ain't."

"Well," and he fetched out some papers, "I won't take advantage of ye. On the other hand, we've no need to haggle. You reckon these would be fair?"

He handed Adam the remaining shares of the schooner *Goodwill to Men,* and each was made out in Adam's name.

Adam gulped his flip, he was so touched, and he all but choked on it.

284

Through an open door he saw Deborah fussing in the kitchen. He started to get up.

"See here, can't I help you?"

Obadiah Selden waved him back.

"Sit down," Obadiah said. "You're a married man now."